AUGUSTINE

EMERSON LAINE

COPYRIGHT

First edition October 2020

Cover images/Pixabay
Tolucreations (background)
sharonshupingo (S flourish), AnnaliseArt (crows)

ISBN 978-0-473-45198-1 (paperback)
ISBN 978-0-473-45200-1 (ebook)

🏵 Created with Vellum

For my husband, with deepest love and gratitude for your support, patience, confidence in me, and on-going encouragement.

PROLOGUE

October 1995

Bramos watched the child sleeping. She couldn't have been more than five or six, but even in the half light of dawn her plump features were still recognisable as the woman he once knew. She held on to a small teddy bear – a blue one with a white chest and one ear missing – and when she flung her arm above her head the bear fell and landed on the floor by his feet.

He looked down and frowned.

A moan escaped her rosebud lips as a chubby hand groped for the bear, then suddenly she opened her eyes. For a brief moment their eyes met, a spark of recognition ... then the scream.

Footsteps signalled the arrival of the child's carer moments before light spilled into the room, illuminating the multitude of dancing girls that covered the cold brick walls, and a woman – nightgown flapping loosely behind her on a trail of cigarette smoke – rushed to the girl's side. 'What's all the commotion about this time?' she said. 'I've barely been gone half an hour.'

'He was here again,' the girl sobbed. 'He was looking at me.'

'Nonsense,' the woman said, 'we've been over this a dozen times. It was just a dream.'

'No it wasn't,' the girl said. She thrust out her bottom lip and it was all he could do not to laugh.

Impatience darkened the woman's face before being quickly replaced with a well-worn smile. 'Fine,' she said, 'then let's have a look, shall we?' She sighed and reached a weathered hand to the bedside light, and with a flick of the switch the room lit up forcing the shadows to the far reaches of the room. The child's eyes slid towards him, unseeing as he skulked in the corner.

'See,' the woman said, 'no-one here but me, and Uncle Ted.' She picked up the bear and waggled it in the girl's face.

'But he was here,' the girl said, 'I saw him. He was standing right there.' She pointed to the spot where the woman stood with her shawl pulled tightly around frail shoulders.

'Now that's quite enough,' the woman said, 'you can clearly see there is no-one here.' She shoved the bear beneath the covers and began tucking the child in. 'Now close your eyes, we have a big day tomorrow.'

'Sing me a song?' the girl said.

The woman looked down; eyebrows arched over tired eyes. 'If I do, will you promise to go straight to sleep?'

The child looked up, wide eyed and doubtful, but gave the merest nod of her head.

'Very well,' the woman said, and sat on the edge of the bed. The little girl shoved a thumb in her mouth – finger curled over the tip of her nose – and looked to where Bramos now stood at the foot of the bed. He smiled to himself. She knew he was there, but she would not see him if he did not wish it, and this time, he did not.

'What would you like me to sing?' the woman said. The little girl shrugged. 'How about something my mother used to sing to my sister and me, when we were scared of the dark too?' The little girl nodded, eyelids already beginning to droop, and curled up into a ball, bear hugged tightly to her chest. 'Very well,' the woman said. Then she began ...

Hush little baby, don't say a word
Momma's gonna buy you a mockingbird
And if that mockingbird won't sing
Momma's gonna buy you a diamond ring ...

Bramos stood back and leaned against the wall – arms folded, legs crossed at the ankles – and listened patiently. She had a good voice – soft, yet gravelly – and could carry a tune well, but as the child gradually drifted off, the woman choked on the final words. She leaned over and placed a gentle kiss on the girl's forehead before turning off the lamp.

Shadows crept back across the wooden floor and Bramos moved with them, drifting to stand beside the woman as she clutched something at her chest. Her shawl – frayed at the edges, its colour long faded from the forest green it once was – reminded him of the one Augustine used to wear, though hers had been made of the finest fabric money could buy. The temptation to make himself known to her then was strong, but to reveal his presence would serve no great purpose and would only trouble the child further if she were to suddenly wake up. But still, he stepped a little closer, daring her to see as she reached up to her neck and removed the silver chain that sat there. A pendant hung from it, a crystal that glinted briefly where the hunters moon caught its amorphous surface before she slipped it neatly beneath the sleeping child's pillow. He smiled. The crystal was as much a part of his past as it was the child's future.

The woman turned to him then, eyes searching, head cocked as though listening to some far-off sound. She reminded him of someone he knew – the tilt of the head, lips full and sensual despite her aging years – but the eyes were all wrong – dove grey instead of green, and full of self-loathing and fear. She shivered, knuckles white where she gripped the shawl too tight, and with one last look around the room, she turned towards the door and walked out.

1

---

13 September 2015

Rae watched the coffin being lowered into the ground and realised she had never before felt so utterly miserable. As the priest spoke his final words of committal she looked around at the gathering of family and friends and wondered if any one of them had ever truly cared for Grace Winters. She thought not, at least not in the way that she did. Funerals were never easy, that went without saying, but some were worse than others. Granddad's funeral had been a quiet affair, something that he had insisted on, but the few mourners in attendance had at least been there out of love and respect for the wonderfully compassionate man that Winston Winters had been.

Grace's funeral, however, was a different affair entirely.

To say it was lavish would be doing it an injustice. If the coffin had been made of solid gold it would not have looked out of place amongst the obscene amount of flowers that adorned the headstone – a headstone whose cost could have fed a small family for an entire year. But that was Grace all over – rich as a queen, generous to a fault and effortlessly over the top until her dying day, and Rae could not have loved her more.

She only wished the same could be said of the mourning congregation.

Umbrellas popped up as the first drops of rain fell onto the cemetery. Most were a respectful black, but the odd blue and red, and even a polka dot yellow surfaced amongst the canopy of brollies. Rae suppressed a smile. Grace would have approved greatly, however Matilda – Tilly to those who disliked her the most – was not so easily impressed.

Watching Rae with the piercing glare of a hawk, Tilly looked stiff and uncomfortable in her tailored skirt suit and ridiculous high heels, and Rae found herself wishing, just for a moment, that the inappropriate footwear would get stuck in the mud leaving Tilly to squelch her way back in only her stocking feet.

Grace would have approved of that too.

One of the umbrellas, the yellow polka dot one, found its way over Rae's head as an arm looped through the crook of her elbow and gave a gentle tug. She didn't want to leave, not yet, she would've preferred to stay with Grace a little longer, but she allowed herself to be carried along with the flow, and away from the only person who could begin to understand what she was going through.

'You OK?' Ronnie, Rae's only friend, looked glass-eyed beneath a fringe of flaxen curls. 'Stay a little longer if you need, I don't mind waiting in the car until you're ready.' She blew her nose loudly into a tissue that smelled strongly of balsam.

Rae looked back towards the grave where solemn faced

men stood idle with their spades, keeping a respectable distance until they could fill in the last grave of the day, and shook her head. 'I'm fine,' she said. 'Let's just go.'

Ronnie's cherry red rental stuck out like a sore thumb amongst the long line of black funeral cars parked beneath an ever present stormy sky and brought a rare smile to Rae's face as she headed straight for it. 'I think Cruella would rather you travelled with the family,' Ronnie said, inclining her head to where the heat from Tilly's glare could be felt four cars back from the front of the funeral procession. Rae ignored her and climbed into the red car as Ronnie gunned it into life, just as Peter, Tilly's hulking great lump of a husband, headed their way.

Peter, younger than Tilly by five years, fit into the Winters family like a puppy in a den of wolves. Rae pitied him almost as much as she pitied their equally docile son, Angus, who now held an umbrella over Tilly's head as she watched her husband trudge through the soggy grass towards Rae.

'You wanna talk to him?' asked Ronnie, as Peter's fat fingers rapped on the glass by Rae's face. Rae fastened her seatbelt and stared straight ahead. 'Fuck em,' she said, 'let's just go.'

RAE HAD BEEN STAYING in a hotel ever since Grace had taken ill, and it was here that Ronnie was headed before embarking on the long drive back to Inverness. 'You're doing the right thing, you know.' Ronnie's voice was soft but guarded as she pulled out of the cemetery and into the afternoon traffic.

Rae didn't say anything, only stared out through the rain streaked window at the blur of pedestrians going about their daily business. She was thinking of Grace. Trying to remember her before the yellowed skin and sunken eyes took over, but every time she summoned that beautifully aged face it was cruelly snatched from her as though it had never been there at all.

'I was really proud of you today,' continued Ronnie. 'I know how hard it must have been without *you know who* there, but ... well, I just want you to know I think you were really brave.'

Brave? thought Rae, *I couldn't be more of a coward if I tried.* 'Thanks,' she said, 'it means a lot you being here.'

'Least I could do for my best bud,' Ronnie said. 'I'm only sorry I couldn't come sooner, you know, before Grace died.' She cast a glance at Rae, and Rae smiled in return, but the effort of keeping up appearances for Ronnie's sake was beginning to take its toll.

'You sure you're OK?' Ronnie said. 'You look awfully pale. I could stay another night or two if you like. I'm sure Adam won't mind.'

'I'm fine,' Rae said. 'I leave for Cranston Myre tomorrow, and as forgiving as Adam is, I doubt he'd be happy if his pregnant wife was at the opposite end of the country to him for any longer than necessary.'

'It's only a train journey away,' Ronnie said, 'and besides, it might be just what he needs. Make him appreciate me more.'

'He appreciates you just fine. You're lucky to have him.'

'I know,' Ronnie said, sighing dramatically. 'He is pretty wonderful.' She glanced at Rae, then added, casually, 'I don't suppose there's any chance that you and—'

'Don't start, Ronnie,' Rae said, 'not today.'

'I'm not. I promise. I totally respect your decision. I just thought, under the circumstances ...'

Rae shot her friend a warning glance. She knew exactly where this was headed and had no intention of letting Ronnie take it any further. It had been bad enough dreading Darryl showing up at the funeral, his absence being the only good thing to come out of this depressing day.

'Don't look at me like that, Rae. I know he did a shitty thing, but none of us are perfect. I just worry about you, that's all.'

'Well don't,' Rae said, turning back to the window, 'I'm perfectly fine.'

'Really? Because you look like crap, and Darryl said you won't answer any of his calls.'

Rae snapped her head round and glared at Ronnie. 'You spoke to him?'

'Not exactly. He texted me a few times to see if I knew where you were, and—'

'You didn't tell him, did you?' Rae suddenly had visions of Darryl showing up on her doorstep – shoulder still bandaged from their fight – and her stomach dropped several feet.

'Of course not,' Ronnie said, 'what do you take me for? But he did seem really worried, Rae. Are you sure there isn't something you're not telling me?'

Darryl's face, twisted in agony, popped into Rae's mind. 'Positive,' she said, 'now can we drop it?'

'Fine,' Ronnie said. 'But at least promise you'll get a dog. I hate the thought of you being out there all alone.'

'I hate dogs.'

'Nobody hates dogs, Rae. Now you're just being facetious.'

'Fine,' Rae said, 'if it will make you feel better, I promise to think about getting a dog. Now will you please stop worrying and just drive.'

2

The drive to Cranston Myre took longer than Rae anticipated, and was in no small way down to the tumultuous amount of rain that continued to fall. Had she been in a better frame of mind she might have postponed the journey until the next day, when blue skies and fluffy white clouds were forecast, but the need to get away was far greater than the threat of any storm.

Tilly's shrill voice down the phone the previous night, demanding to know why Rae hadn't shown up at the wake had only confirmed that leaving was the right thing to do. Not that she really needed validation. Now that Ronnie had returned to Scotland there really was nothing left in Manchester for Rae. And then of course there was Darryl. Leaving Darryl behind was the biggest incentive of all.

A sign flashed by announcing Rae's exit. She indicated, changed lanes and left the motorway. She hadn't eaten since early morning, only managing half a slice of burnt toast even then, and her stomach now grumbled its displeasure as streetlights tapered off giving way to open countryside.

Evening was slowly creeping in, enveloping the countryside with its ominous presence, and echoing the emptiness that Rae had felt since Grace's death. Rae was a loner at heart, preferring her own company to that of others, but Grace's sudden demise, together with Ronnie's departure to Scotland had hit her hard. Veronica Maine, or Ronnie if you ever wanted her to speak to you again, had been Rae's closest friend since childhood, and apart from Grace was just about the only other person in the world that Rae trusted. But Ronnie didn't know about Rae's secret. Not even Grace had known about that.

In an effort to drown out the self-pity, Rae turned on the radio. *Close to You* by The Carpenters was playing, the same song Darryl would sing when nightmares woke her in the middle of the night. She turned the radio off and continued the drive in silence.

Forty minutes later the village of Cranston Myre finally came into view.

It shone like a beacon of hope in the distance and Rae felt her spirits lift a little. She picked up speed, eager to start her new life far away from the ever watchful eyes of her hateful sister and the never ending phone calls from Darryl, and with a lighter heart she reached the edge of the village and pulled over to double check the directions.

Grace had purchased a property in Rae's name when Rae was only very young, but for reasons unknown had kept it a secret. Its existence was revealed not long after Grace's death, and Rae was now the proud owner of a cottage on the edge of Dolen Forest. Grace's intentions for purchasing the cottage remained a mystery, but Rae was grateful that she had. Money wasn't an issue, but having somewhere she could go, somewhere of her own that was quiet and isolated from her estranged family, was the only thing that had kept Rae sane during the build up to the funeral. The executor of Grace's Will, an aged solicitor that had served the Winters family for more than fifty years, had contacted Rae the day before the reading of the Will. He had given Rae an envelope that contained a map and a key. The decision was left with Rae whether to tell the family where she was going or keep the cottage a secret as Grace had done. She chose the latter. When the Will was finally read, Tilly had received the lion's share of the Winters' estate, leaving Rae with a sum modest enough to keep Tilly happy. But what Tilly didn't know was that Grace had been feeding discreet amounts of money into a savings account in Rae's name for years. It was a calculated decision by Grace, and one that gave Rae the means to escape quietly while ensuring that Tilly did not feel the need to contest the Will, something that Rae was most assuredly grateful for.

The map showed the cottage wasn't far, perched on the edge of the forest, secluded for privacy but close enough to the village that Rae wouldn't be entirely cut-off from the world. It had also been empty for close to 20 years so she wasn't expecting much, but it was enough. She slid the envelope back into her bag and pulled out onto the high street.

The Rook & Wheel pub oozed old world charm as Rae drove past it, with Georgian windows, hanging lanterns and window boxes filled with flowers that refused to wilt even with the onslaught of rain. A sandwich board on the roadside promised a warm fire and the best pies in the south, and Rae decided that as the cottage had stood alone all these years, another hour wasn't going to hurt it. She swung the car around – narrowly missing two young girls huddled beneath a shared umbrella – and pulled into the empty car park. She waved an apology as she climbed out of the car, was rewarded with a two fingered salute, and grabbed her raincoat before holding it over her head and running to the door.

Inside was a large open fire that crackled invitingly, with fairy lights hanging from its mantel – an early reminder that Christmas was not far away – and thick bodied candles glowed from inside glass cases. A large, leather couch took pride of place in front of the hearth, and tables adorned with tea lights in miniature vases dotted the space in between. The pub was mostly deserted save for a man and his two female companions on the couch by the fire, and a much older gentleman perched at the end of the bar. The soft click of a pool cue could be heard through a large alcove to the right where raised laughter caught Rae's attention. She recognised two of the occupants as being the girls from the car park, both hovering over a group of young lads more engrossed in their game than their female companions. Girl number one – a pretty blonde with too much make-up and not enough skirt – looked up as Rae approached the bar and whispered into the ear of her friend; a much stockier version of herself with a face less pretty, more bulldog. Both looked at Rae and grinned.

'Pay no attention,' the bartender said, 'they're harmless enough. What can I get you?'

Rae tried to ignore the peel of laughter that echoed from the pool room. 'Coke, please,' she said, 'and a menu if you have one.'

'We normally close the kitchen at eight during the week but given its only ten past I'm sure we can rustle something up. Would steak and ale pie do you?'

'Sounds perfect,' Rae said, feeling her stomach warm at the prospect of food.

'Sit yourself down then and I'll bring it over in a jiffy.'

'Can I get one of those too, Bob.' A woman appeared beside Rae, with closely cropped pink hair that dripped water down her young face. She wore a black leather jacket with blue denim jeans and grinned at Rae as she produced a ten-pound note that she slapped on the bar.

'You've eaten here often enough Alex to know what time the kitchen closes,' the bartender said.

'Oh, go on Bob,' she said, grinning, 'Maggie won't mind.'

Bob sighed and shook his head but took the money before heading off through a small opening at the end of the bar.

'I'm Alex,' pink hair said, turning to Rae and holding out her hand. 'I've been waiting all day for you to show up.'

Rae bristled. Anonymity was the biggest draw for moving to Cranston Myre, and within minutes of arriving it was blown out of the window. 'I'm sorry, do we know each other?'

'I hope so,' Alex said, 'otherwise I've just made a fool of myself. Alexandra Graham? Didn't Grace mention me? She sure as hell talked a lot about you. You're exactly as she described, except for the eyes, she said they were brown, but they look more—'

'They're hazel,' Rae said, a little more tersely than she intended, 'they change according to my moods. I'm sorry, Alex, but Grace never said a word. How exactly did you two know each other?'

Alex looked a little embarrassed as the bartender placed two Cokes on the bar, and Rae instantly regretted being so harsh. 'Food will be over shortly,' he said, 'if you ladies would like to go and sit down.'

'Shall we?' Alex said. She picked up the Cokes and walked off without waiting for an answer.

Rae stared after her. This was not how she had envisioned the first night of her new life going, nor did she wish to eat dinner with a total stranger. Alex chose the table nearest the window and beckoned for Rae to join her by whistling across the pub and pointing to the empty stool opposite. *Great*, thought Rae, *just what I needed*. With an air of reluctance that she didn't care to hide, she walked over, dropped her coat on the floor and pulled out the empty stool.

'Sorry to put you on the spot like that,' Alex said. 'I just assumed that Grace had told you all about me. I've been taking care of The Briar for the last few months, getting it ready for your arrival today. Grace insisted the fire be lit and the cupboards full for when you got here. I would have called to confirm a time, but Grace never gave me your number.'

Rae stared at her, as though doing so would jumble her words into something that made a modicum of sense. 'The Briar?' she said, shaking her head.

'The cottage,' Alex said, 'the place you're going to be living in? It's just a nickname but pretty much everyone around here calls it that. Sorry to hear that Grace passed by the way. I knew she was sick but it's never easy when the end finally comes. I sent flowers,' she added, when Rae didn't say anything. 'Lillys. They were her favourite, weren't they?'

Rae nodded. She didn't know what to make of this strange pink-haired girl who seemed to know more about what Rae was doing, than Rae did. 'What you said, about me arriving here today, it doesn't make any sense,' she said. 'I hadn't decided if I was coming here at all until a few days ago, so Grace couldn't have known.'

'Here you are ladies.' A rotund woman with flushed cheeks placed two plates of steaming hot pie, mashed potato, broccoli, and cauliflower on the table, then disappeared.

Alex shrugged. 'What can I say? I'm just acting on Grace's instructions. Maybe she knew you better than you thought?'

The rotund woman appeared again, this time armed with cutlery, napkins and salt & pepper. She pulled out a stool and sat down, kicking her shoes off under the table. 'Don't mind if I sit here for a minute, do you?' she said. 'My feet are killing me.'

Alex picked up a knife and fork and immediately tucked in. 'Maggie,' she said, through a mouthful of food, 'this is Raewyn, she's moving into The Briar. Got any brown sauce to go with this?'

Maggie reached over and clipped Alex behind the ear. 'Don't you dare, missy, my pie can stand on its own, thank you very much. Wish I could say the same for my poor feet though.'

'You should take a night off?' Alex said. 'Get Bob to do some of the work for a change.' She winked at Rae as Maggie chuckled and leaned back on her stool.

'Hear that, Bob,' she shouted. 'Alex says I need a night off.' Bob rolled his eyes, shook his head and turned back to wiping down the bar.

'So,' Maggie said, turning to Rae, 'The Briar eh? I hope young Alex here has told you what you're letting yourself in for?'

'No, not really,' Rae said, turning to Alex when she groaned loudly.

'Leave it out, Mags,' Alex said. 'She only arrived a few minutes ago.'

Maggie folded her arms and gave Alex a stern look. 'All the more reason to tell her then, wouldn't you say?'

'Tell me what?' Rae said. She looked between the two

women and caught the look of warning Maggie shot Alex before Alex rolled her eyes.

'Fine!' Alex said, 'Margaret thinks the place is haunted, which of course it isn't, so pay no attention.'

'Not just haunted,' Maggie said, leaning in close. 'Cursed, and not just the cottage either. Those woods are not for the faint hearted, my love. Take my advice, Raewyn, you give that place a wide berth. You'll not find a single local walking in those woods. They know better, you see. Mark my words, it's better if you stay away from that place. Get your head down here if you like, we've room enough and don't charge the earth like some places, and what's more you'll have a good hearty meal like that one in your belly each and every night. I can't say fairer than that.'

'She'll end up the size of a house if she eats your food every night,' Alex said. 'Stop trying to drum up business, woman, and fetch me my sauce, this pie is dry.' That earned Alex another clip around the ear, but she laughed it off and turned to Rae. 'It's just stories,' she said. 'Old folktales, stuff and nonsense, the cottage has sat empty for years so people just make shit up.'

'And why has it been left empty all these years?' Maggie said. 'A place like that? It should be a gold mine and yet no-one has been near it for as long as I can remember.'

'Well maybe the owner didn't want anyone near it,' Alex said, 'ever thought of that?' She shook her head at Rae, and Rae raised an eyebrow in return.

'Mock all you want,' Maggie said, 'but there's something up with that place.'

'Noted,' Alex said. 'I'll be sure to have it exorcised first thing in the morning.'

'Maybe you should,' Maggie said. 'You younguns, you

think you know everything about everything, but in my experience, you know nothing at all.'

'Says the woman who thought using olive oil and vinegar instead of sun cream was a good idea.'

'That was a long time ago,' Maggie said, 'and I wish I'd never told you.' She winced as she slipped on her shoes and lifted her hefty frame from the stool. Bob was tapping the face of his watch behind the bar. 'Look at him, the cheeky beggar,' she said. 'I swear that man thinks I'm a machine. Alex, will you ask Dee to make up some more of that foot cream for me. It did miracles for my bunions last time.'

'Only if you promise to stop bad mouthing Rae's cottage.'

'How about I promise not to put you over my knee, lady. Honestly, kids these days.'

'I'll have your cream ready tomorrow afternoon,' Alex said, 'my treat. You should probably go before Bob has an apoplexy.'

Maggie thanked Alex, winked at Rae and mumbled something about men and slave drivers before shuffling off towards the bar.

'Pay no attention,' Alex said, shovelling another forkful of food into her mouth. 'Folk round here are a bit weird. Takes a while, but you'll get used to them.'

'You were about to tell me how you met Grace.' Rae still hadn't touched her food and scooped a forkful of mashed potato into her mouth.

'We didn't meet,' Alex said. 'She found me about three months ago. I'd been helping my cousins renovate their place and fancied myself as an interior designer. I'd only just got a website up and running when Grace phoned me. Asked me to spruce up the cottage, give it a clean, lick of paint, new furniture, that sort of thing, even opened a bank account especially so I could have carte blanche over the project. Quite trusting really given we never physically met, but we talked often, and I sent her regular updates. I don't think she realised just how much of a state the place was in until I took her on a virtual tour.'

'But she must have visited at some point, surely?' Rae scooped up more mash. It really was delicious.

'Dunno,' Alex said, 'didn't seem like it. All I know is she wanted it top notch for when you arrived, and no expense was to be spared.'

Rae tasted the pie. It was every bit as tasty as the mash, but she suddenly found she had no appetite. 'It just doesn't make sense,' she said, putting down her knife and fork. 'How could Grace possibly have known I was coming here today?' Alex shrugged as though the how of it was of no concern, but to Rae it meant everything. Because if Grace had known she was sick three months ago, then why had she told Alex and no-one else? It stung that Grace had felt she couldn't confide in Rae, because Rae would have told Grace anything, even about what happened with Darryl if Grace hadn't already been in hospital. She turned to the window in an attempt to hide her hurt feelings and ran a finger down the misted glass. It was still pouring outside. She couldn't have picked a worse day to pack up her life and move away from everything she knew.

'Why Grace?' Alex said suddenly. 'You never say mum, why is that?'

The question prickled but was one Rae had been asked many times over and the answer was well practiced. 'Habit,' she said, 'Grace adopted me when I was very young, but she already had a daughter who was less than pleased by my sudden appearance. I learned to refer to Grace by name rather mum. It seemed to placate Tilly, and rather than upsetting the apple cart further, I guess it just stuck. Grace didn't seem to mind, and she was a wonderful mother in every way that mattered.'

'But not *your* mother,' Alex said with a nod. 'I get it.'

Rae opened her mouth to object, feeling that she needed to defend her reasons for having never given Grace the title she deserved, but decided against it and instead grabbed her coat. 'Thank you for the company,' she said, 'and for taking care of the cottage...'

'But you've hardly touched your food.'

'... and give my apologies to Maggie, will you.'

'Wait,' Alex said, 'I'll come with you. The turn off can be difficult to see in the dark.'

'No, thank you,' Rae said. 'You finish your dinner. I'm sure I'll manage.'

RAE DIDN'T BOTHER to cover her head as she stepped out the door, and instead let the rain sluice over her shoulders and welcomed the cold water on her face. Alex had been a surprise, and an unwanted one at that, and the only thing Rae could think of right now was slipping into a hot bath before losing herself to the sweet oblivion of sleep. She slung her coat over the back seat and slid behind the steering wheel. She checked herself in the mirror and frowned at the pallid skin and sunken eyes. She needed this break more than anything. Needed the time to be alone, to figure out who she was, *what* she was, and what the fuck she was going to say to Darryl when she finally plucked up the courage to call him. She opened the glove compartment and took out her phone. It was switched on but the volume was turned low so she wouldn't have to the listen to the constant chiming of Darryl's texts. She pressed the button and held her breath as the screen came to life. Sure enough, there they were. She counted seven messages and four missed calls, all from Darryl. With a sigh she threw the phone into her bag, put the key in the ignition, and turned. The engine kicked to life briefly but died before she could slip it into gear. She turned the key again, and then again, and then again. With a sigh of frustration Rae let her head fall back. *Of all the bastard nights*, she thought. But in truth she was amazed the car had made it this far. She should have traded it in months ago but had been too preoccupied with her failing relationship, and then Grace's illness, to do much of anything. She pulled her phone from her bag and was about to search for a taxi when there was a tap on the window.

'Car trouble?' shouted Alex, over the rain.

'It's probably just the battery,' Rae shouted back. 'I was just about to call a taxi.'

'Nonsense,' Alex said. 'I'm going your way anyway. Pop the boot and I'll help with your bags.'

THE DRIVE to the cottage took less than ten minutes, but that was perhaps more down to Alex's Lewis Hamilton impersonation than anything else, and the turn off for Foxglove Lane was near impossible to see in the dark, helped in no way by the overgrown hedge that blocked the sign from view. A lone streetlight cast an eerie glow over the entrance to the woods as Alex turned onto the long driveway, expertly navigating the muddied ground with precision and speed that both impressed and terrified Rae at the same time. 'Here we are,' she said, finally grinding the car to a halt. 'Home sweet home.'

Rae hadn't expected much, but she hadn't expected to feel so underwhelmed either. The exterior was bare except for a few vines that crept over the grey stone wall, barren of leaf or flower and giving the impression of bulging veins beneath a pair of aged hands. The thatched roof sagged in the middle and any charm the pale blue picket fence may have given was marred by the grind of the gate as it swung on its rusted hinge. It was a moonless night, the only light coming from Alex's headlights, and as the wind ripped through the woods Maggie's words of warning suddenly took on a much more sinister feel.

'Doesn't look like much does it?' Alex said. 'But it's better in daylight, you'll see. I'll get the bags while you open the door.'

Steeling herself for further disappointment, Rae stepped onto the porch, inserted the key, and held her breath. A rush of warm air greeted her as the door swung open, and perhaps it was only the imagination of a tired mind, but it seemed to Rae that the house had been holding *its* breath too, and as one they released it when Rae stepped over the threshold.

'If you like I can show you where everything is,' Alex said, squeezing past Rae to dump the bags by the kitchen table. She switched the light on then turned to Rae with hands on hips. 'So, what do you think, not too shabby after all, eh?'

Rae felt some of her anxieties slip away as she looked around. 'It's ... perfect,' she said, and meant it. Simply furnished with an understated rustic charm, it was Rae down to a tee.

'My instructions were simple,' Alex said, 'muted colours, nothing fussy and definitely no chintz. Did I hit the mark?'

Rae swallowed as a lump formed in her throat. 'Smashed it out of the park.'

'Well don't thank me yet,' Alex said. 'You still haven't seen the bathroom. To say its small would be an insult to small bathrooms. I would've liked to do a complete refurb, but I did the best I could with what little time I had.'

There it was again, reference to Rae's imminent arrival. She opened her mouth to say something but changed her mind. Fatigue crawled through her veins like concrete and the last thing she wanted was more conversation. 'I'm sure it's absolutely fine,' she said, 'but I expect you've got better things to do than show me around.'

'Oh, it's no bother,' Alex said, draping her coat over the kitchen table. 'I'll stick the kettle on, shall I?'

Rae's stomach dropped. 'Alex. I'm really grateful, but ...'

'Say no more,' Alex said, grabbing her coat again. 'I have a tendency to overstay my welcome. I also talk too much so I'll spare you a headache and get out of your hair. Before I go though, I should warn you there is no central heating. The fires already stoked and there's a tonne of wood stacked in the shed out front. You'll also find the cupboards and fridge well stocked too – plenty of wine, chocolate, more wine, and some of the not so important stuff like actual food. Oh, and before I forget, there's a rather delicious looking banana cake in the pantry, and a batch of homemade cookies courtesy of yours truly, so you might want to do a taste test with those first. Other than that, everything you need should be here.'

'I don't know what to say,' Rae said. 'I feel like I'm throwing you out.'

'Nonsense,' Alex said. 'If I were you, I'd throw me out too. Right, I'll be off then. Don't forget to holler if you need anything, I'm only a stone's throw away. Maybe I'll see you tomorrow?'

'Sure,' Rae said, 'and thanks again.'

When the door closed, Rae sagged into the nearest chair. The weight of the last few weeks bore down like a mountain of guilt, and while she'd made a promise to herself to stop wallowing in self-pity, she was finding it difficult to do without either of her best friends by her side. She grabbed the phone from her bag and pulled up Ronnie's number. She may not have Grace to talk to anymore, but Ronnie was still only a phone call away. Then she threw the phone down without pressing the green button. Ronnie had problems of her own with twins on the way, the last thing she needed was a clingy friend dropping all her shit at her front door.

Rae grabbed her overnight bag, turned off the light and headed upstairs.

3

R ae woke the next morning with a dry mouth and a duvet wrapped around her like a cocoon. She threw back the curtains to greet the first dawn of her new life, then quickly hopped back beneath the covers. It was freezing, and by the distant glow on the horizon, still very early. Wrapping the duvet back around her body, she padded down the stairs to the kitchen and flicked on the light. The fire had died a lonely death in the night and for a second she considered trying to re-light it, but the thought of faffing around with wood and matches seemed like too much effort, so she switched on the kettle instead. While the water took its own sweet time to boil Rae picked up her phone from where she'd left it on the chair and switched it on. The phone was as old and knackered as her car, but Rae was a creature of habit who loathed change, however small it might be. Moving to a new village, far from everyone and everything she knew was a huge leap, but one born of necessity rather than choice. The phone came to life as the kettle finally boiled and she poured the hot water over coffee granules while the phone pinged, and pinged ... and pinged. She drank the coffee first. If she was going to face umpteen messages from Darryl, then she needed something warm inside her belly.

One message was from Ronnie with the simple words *'home safe - speak soon'* and the rest were from Darryl, all in the same thread, and all asking her to call him. There were several more missed calls from him too, none of which she intended to return. What had happened between them was still too raw and left her feeling sick and dejected whenever she thought about it, and despite his infidelity, Darryl did not deserve what she had done to him. But it wasn't only that that troubled her though. A thought had been gnawing away at her ever since she'd laid her hands on him. A feeling really, that Darryl wasn't the first person she'd hurt, that she'd done it before, to someone else. She wrapped her hands around the coffee cup and shuddered. What if she did it again? The thought terrified her almost as much as knowing there was some part of her that had actually enjoyed it. Sure, she'd been angry when she caught Darryl with another woman – unjustified as it happened, given the two of them hadn't really been a couple for some time – but it wasn't catching him with his pants down that had set her off. Something had snapped inside, some primal rage buried deep within, hidden even from Rae until that night. Whether it was the strain of knowing Grace was dying, or the confirmation that her relationship was truly dead in the water, Rae didn't know, but she had let that rage out and Darryl had bared the terrible brunt of it, and if not for the screams of the slut he'd brought home with him that night, Rae may very well have killed him.

As it happened, Darryl was only left with second-degree burns, and whether out of guilt or fear of reprisal, he had persuaded whatserface not to call the police. His wounds had been treated and his shoulder had healed, but the acrid stench of burning flesh was something that Rae would never forget, and nor should she. It was a stark reminder of the monster that lurked within, and it was also because of this – she was *convinced* – that Grace had deteriorated so quickly. Rae had never told her what happened, but Grace knew, she was sure of it, and for that Rae would never forgive herself.

She tipped the remainder of the coffee down the sink, threw her phone back on the chair, and trudged up the stairs, trailing the duvet behind her.

UNABLE TO GET BACK to sleep, Rae had finally given up and instead decided to unpack. An hour later she was showered, dressed and feeling a little more like herself when there was a knock at the door.

'I'm taking you for breakfast,' Alex said, 'I won't take no for an answer.'

She drove them to a cafe on the main street, just down the road from The Rook & Wheel where Rae noticed with alarm, that her car was no longer there.

'My friend John towed it early this morning,' Alex said. 'He'll drop it back at yours when it's fixed.'

'That was kind of you to arrange,' Rae said, though she couldn't help but feel a little disgruntled that Alex hadn't thought to ask if it was OK with her.

'Think nothing of it,' Alex said, pulling over to the side of the road. 'I called in a favour, that's all.'

Sadie-Lou's Tea Rooms was written above a Georgian window in black curlicue letters. The door was painted the same cornflower blue as Rae's picket fence and had the same basket of autumn flowers hanging beside it as had turned up at the cottage that morning. Alex caught the look on Rae's face and grinned. 'John does them,' she said. 'I asked him to make an extra one for you. Hope you don't mind.'

Inside, the cafe was almost full, save for a table by the window that Alex had called ahead and reserved. It had a frilly gingham tablecloth to match the frilly gingham curtains, with a bottle of brown sauce, laminated menu and salt & pepper pots in the shape of double decker buses. The waitress appeared from nowhere as they took their seats.

'Can I get you two ladies a drink?'

'Tea for me,' Alex said, 'and a full English.'

'Same for me,' Rae said. She had intended only to have teacakes, but the smell coming from kitchen convinced her otherwise.

'Is Sadie around?' asked Alex.

'She's out back?' the waitress said, without looking up from her pad. 'Want me to get her?'

'Nah, but if you could ask her to pop by Dee's later. I need to have a quick word.'

The waitress stopped writing and raised an eyebrow. 'Let me guess ... Michelle?'

'Something like that, yeah,' Alex said.

'I'll pass it on, Sadie will be thrilled.' The waitress left and returned a moment later with two pots of tea, cups and saucers, and cutlery bundled into napkins. 'Food won't be long,' she said, then turned to a young couple at the next table whose toddler had just knocked orange juice all over the floor.

'So, how did you sleep last night?' Alex said, pouring the tea, 'good I hope?'

'Like the dead,' Rae lied. She'd spent most of the night tossing and turning, drifting from one bad dream to another.

'Country air will do that for you,' Alex said. 'Not that you got much of that with last night's rain, couldn't wish for a better day today though. Did you manage to get that fire going?'

Rae shook her head and winced as she took a sip from the too hot tea. 'I'm sure I'll figure it out though.'

'There's plenty of wood to see you through the winter. John chopped a load before you arrived.'

Rae raised her eyebrows. 'He sounds like a real catch, this fella of yours.'

Alex spluttered her tea. 'Oh, John's not my boyfriend. God no, he's way too old for me. We're just friends. He's a moody bastard most of the time, but I like him just fine. You will too. He's probably closer to your age anyway.'

'Oh really?' Rae said. 'And what age is that?'

'Mid-thirties?' Alex said, shrugging.

'I just turned twenty-five,' Rae said, 'but thanks for the compliment.'

Alex grinned. 'Sorry,' she said, 'I just assumed you were older from the way Grace spoke about you.'

Rae prickled at that. 'What exactly did Grace say?' she said, casually stirring her tea.

'That you were branch manager of a retail shop until she became sick. That you gave it up to spend time with her, and ... that you caught your boyfriend in bed with another woman.' She grimaced at that and added, as though by way of apology, 'she did say that he got what he deserved though.'

Rae almost choked on her tea but didn't get the chance to say anything as the waitress chose that exact moment to show up with the food. 'I think Sadie's trying to fatten you up,' she said to Alex, plonking two overloaded plates of food on the table. 'You do know she's planning to fix you up with her nephew, don't you? She's hoping you'll take him as your plus one to the party.'

Alex groaned. 'Not that again,' she said. 'I swear she has an endless supply of nephews. Tell her I'm already spoken for. Besides, Rae is coming as my plus one, aren't you Rae.' She nudged Rae's foot beneath the table and gave her a pleading look.

Rae was still reeling about what Alex had just said and answered without giving any real thought to what she was agreeing to. 'Ahh, yes,' she said, 'looking forward to it.'

The waitress narrowed her eyes and looked at Rae as though she'd only just noticed she was sitting there. 'Haven't seen you around here before,' she said. 'Just visiting?'

'Rae's a friend of mine from up north,' Alex said. 'Don't forget to tell Sadie I need to see her, will you?'

The waitress raised an eyebrow but refrained from asking any more questions before walking away.

Alex picked up a sausage and bit off the end, apparently unconcerned by her string of blatant lies. She caught Rae looking at her and shrugged. 'If you saw Sadie's nephews, you'd understand the size of the bullet I just dodged. Besides, you'll soon learn that everyone around here is in and out of each other's business like a swinging door, and Carol is about as discrete as the town crier. If you want any privacy at all, probably best not to tell Carol anything.'

Rae picked up a piece of bacon and began chewing on it. 'Thanks for the heads up. What's the party for then?'

'My cousin, Emma's throwing it,' Alex said, 'the whole village will be there. You'll love it.'

'You weren't serious?' Rae said, 'I don't know anyone.'

'Precisely why you should come,' Alex said. She stopped eating and looked up. 'You'd be doing me a massive favour. You can't leave me at the mercy of Sadie's nephew, it would be a fate worse than death. Worse even. I'd rather eat dinner with Hannibal Lector.'

Rae screwed up her nose. 'I don't know ... parties aren't really my thing.'

'If you want me to beg, I will,' Alex said. 'I've been looking forward to this for ages, if only to see the look on Emma's face when it all goes tits up. She's expecting it to be all cocktail dresses and canapés but throw free booze at this lot and you're just asking for trouble. It'll be less Fred Astaire and more *Dirty Dancing*. Please say you'll come. Pleeeease.'

'You make it sound so inviting!' Rae said. 'Besides, I have nothing to wear.'

'Wear anything,' Alex said. 'It's a garden party, no-one will care. I can guarantee half the villagers will be there in jeans and t-shirt. You have to come. If we're going to be neighbours, then I think it's a prerequisite that you attend.'

'Neighbours?' Rae said. 'Where is this party?'

'Carrion Hall,' Alex said. 'You must have seen it this morning – can't miss it from your place. Big ugly thing on top of the hill.'

'The mansion?' Rae said, 'you live there?' It had been the first thing she'd noticed when she threw back the curtains that morning – a black smudge on the horizon haloed by the rising sun.

'Close,' Alex said. 'I live in one of the cottages on the grounds, but Emma lives there, Chris too – he's my other cousin. We've spent the last two years renovating it along with half the tradesmen in the village. The party is Emma's way of saying thank you, but mainly so she can show off. It would be impolite not to introduce yourself ... oh come on,' she groaned, 'you're allowed to have a bit of fun. Plus, it's my birthday on Sunday so it'll be a double celebration. Say yes and I promise not to pester you for anything else. Cross my heart and hope to die.' She drew an X over her chest then clasped her hands together, bottom lip stuck out like a sulky child.

'Fine,' Rae said. 'I'll be your plus one, but only if you stop pulling that face.'

RAE ATE only half her breakfast, and after declaring that she would have to buy bigger clothes if all the portions in Cranston Myre were so big, she decided to go for a walk rather than accept Alex's offer of a ride home. Alex offered to go with her, but Rae declined, saying she'd done quite enough already, but in truth she wanted to be alone. Alex seemed nice enough, but her constant banter was beginning to give Rae a headache.

They parted ways on Tawny Lane outside Lotions & Potions, a natural remedies shop where Alex worked part-time in-between interior design and renovating old mansions. The village was busier than Rae had expected. It was the start of autumn, the new school year had already begun, and it was the middle of the week, yet the streets were teeming with people. Not quite the retirement village she had expected then. Eager to be away from the shops and the cacophony of tourists, she turned down a quiet cobbled street, saw a sign for the village green, and headed in that direction.

It was a warm day despite the crispness in the air, and Rae began to feel her spirits lift as she followed the road in relative peace. All her life Rae had felt a sense of displacement, as though she didn't belong anywhere – not with Darryl, not at home in Manchester, and certainly not with her estranged family – but it had taken Grace's death to give her the push she needed, to make her realise that her future never was and never had been in Manchester, even if leaving also technically meant she was running away. But now that she was here, letting the ebb and flow of village life wash gently over her she knew it was the right thing to do.

The village green was the size of a small park, filled with trees beginning their autumnal cycle, and freshly painted benches. In the centre was a stone monument, a cross dedicated to the brave men and women who lost their lives during the war, and surrounding the monument, protected by an iron fence barrier, was a display of artificial poppies befitting a king. The smell of wood smoke drifted on the breeze, reminding Rae of autumns as a child, and she breathed it in, savouring the memories it evoked. Autumn had always been her favourite season, even more so than winter and Christmas. Autumn brought bonfire night and the endless task of helping Granddad tidy the garden, getting it ready for the abundance of aunts, uncles and cousins that would descend upon the Winters' house for fireworks. It had been one of Rae's favourite things to do, trailing behind Granddad with a wheelbarrow, wellington boots on up to her knees and a cup of hot chocolate (marshmallows included) waiting for them when their shift was over. Granddad would make his own fireworks – better than anything bought in a shop – that would make even the stony faced Tilly squeal with delight as they lit up the sky, and while Granddad set them off Grace would be in the kitchen, dishing out chilli-con-carne and preparing toffee apples for bobbing. It had been a wonderful time of year, when family bickering was put on hold and the usual animosity forgotten, just for that one, wonderful night – until everything changed.

Rae shrugged her shoulders to cast off the dark thoughts before they could take purchase. She closed her eyes, tilted her face to the warm sun, and let her boots sink into the soft earth, still wet from last night's rain. She took a deep breath, drawing in the country air then let it go in a slow, calming release. A breeze caught her hair and brushed it away from her neck like the hands of a lover. It felt good, soothing in an almost intimate way, and she allowed herself the slightest wisp of a smile.

Lost in the moment Rae hadn't noticed the large dog bounding towards her until it was too late. The wind was knocked right out of her as a great lumbering St Bernard knocked her to the ground. Huge paws pinned her down while a wet, slobbering tongue trailed saliva across her cheek. 'Urrggh, get off me,' she said, pushing the beast's head away only to have the attack redirected to her ear. The dog must have weighed 200lbs and smelled like it had been rolling in pig shit.

'Bart, get off her.' The dog was dragged off Rae by its collar and quickly re-acquainted with his lead before his owner – a scruffy looking man with an unkempt beard and an unsightly stain down his mottled grey t-shirt – offered Rae a helping hand. 'Sorry about that,' he said, 'he gets excited when he sees something he likes. You OK?'

Rae waved him off with an air of disgust. 'Aren't there laws about controlling your animal?' she said, clambering to her feet and trying in vain to wipe down the muddy paw prints that covered her t-shirt. She gave up and settled for zipping up her jacket instead. 'Maybe in future you should keep it on that lead.'

'He's not usually so badly behaved. I apologise, and so does Bart, don't you Bart.' Bart gave a resounding *woof*. 'He said he promises never to do it again.'

'Better not,' Rae said, glaring at the dog while she dusted off her jeans.

'Not much of a dog lover then, eh?' Bart's owner said, grinning as he picked up Rae's bag and handed it to her.

She snatched it from him and fixed him with a cold stare. 'I like them just fine when they're not knocking the wind out of me,' she said. 'Look at the state of me. I look like I've been attacked by a bear!' The man took in her appearance and made a poor job of stifling a smile. 'Well as long you're amused,' Rae said.

'Sorry,' he said, 'I can see that you are genuinely angry—'

'Of course I'm bloody angry. I'm filthy!'

'—but, in Bart's defence, he was only saying hello, weren't you Bart.' He ruffled the dog's ears, and to Rae's utter annoyance the dog barked back.

'Is that supposed to make me feel better?'

'Obviously not. What if I offer to buy you a cup of coffee, would that help?'

Rae gave him an exasperated look. Coffee, really! She was soaking wet, filthy dirty and had a good half hour walk to get home.

'A beer then,' he said, 'I'll even throw in some washing powder.'

'Stick your beer up your arse,' she said, 'and stick your washing powder too. I'd rather swim naked with sharks whilst covered in blood.' She swung the rucksack over her shoulder and turned to leave, but Bart's owner grabbed her arm.

'Hey, look,' he said. 'I really am sorry. It was my fault; I should have been watching Bart, but I was ... distracted. Will you at least accept my apology?' Rae glared at him. There was something about him. Something familiar. 'Look,' he said, 'maybe it would help if I introduced myself. My name is—'

'Not interested,' Rae said. She yanked her arm free and marched off, not daring to look back but all too aware that Bart and his owner were watching her hasty retreat. Anger flared hot in her cheeks. She knew her reaction was irrational and embarrassingly over the top, but she just couldn't help herself. Something about him had set her on edge, his eyes or his aftershave maybe? Despite his appearance he'd actually smelled kind of nice, though all she could smell now was the stink of Bart the friendly dog. She stomped all the way to the end of the green, cheeks flushed and feeling like a fool, only glancing back when she felt it was safe to do so, and further angered to find Bart and his owner were still staring after her. Unbelievable!

She pushed into the nearest shop, so eager to escape their accusatory glare that she hadn't even noticed what shop it was until she was greeted with a thick wall of incense. A bell tinkled overhead as she opened the door and a woman appeared, smiling with the anticipation of her next sale. Rae would have walked straight back out if not for Bart and his condescending owner, so she smiled back and feigned interest in a wooden chess set by the window. The pieces were crafted into witches, wizards, and goblins and came with a hefty price tag that suggested the hand carved set had been there for some time. She moved on to the next aisle – so cramped with wind chimes and dream catchers she had to remove her rucksack to keep from knocking them over. Bejewelled dragons filled the shelves of the next aisle, along with crystal balls, elvin statues, tarot cards, goblets, penta-grams, and wands. There was even a leather-bound spell book mounted onto a wooden pedestal to satisfy the discerning wiccan, and a grimoire of dark magic and enchantments. The shop owner was discreetly watching from behind the counter, pretending to flick through a magazine, and Rae was tempted to walk out (slobbering dog and arse-hole owner be damned) but the items on display inside the glass covered counter caught her eye.

Rae had very few memories of her early years with Grace, and none at all of the time before. She had become Grace's ward at the age of five after she had been found alone and afraid, abandoned by her birth mother who was later discov-ered dead in an empty warehouse with a needle sticking out of her arm. Grace became Rae's foster mother not long after, and her adopted mother not long after that. Rae's memory up until that point was a blank canvas, one that Grace either couldn't fill, or for reasons unknown, simply wouldn't. Rae suspected it was the latter, but despite her loss of memory Rae had always known one thing; that she was different, and it wasn't necessarily a good thing.

Just after Rae's thirteenth birthday Grace had given her a gift. 'It's very special,' she had said. 'A powerful thing for such a young girl to have.' Rae had held the pendant in the palm of her hand thinking it ugly and not very powerful looking at all. She had said as much to Grace, causing Grace to laugh out loud. 'Oh, my sweet girl,' Grace had said, 'one day you will understand. Until then you must promise to keep it with you, always.' And Rae had. She had treasured the pendant, wearing it everywhere she went, even at school, tucked

beneath her shirt away from prying eyes. It was unspectacular, nothing that anyone else would want, but to Rae it meant
everything, because it had belonged to Grace and now Grace
had given it to her.

'Can I help you with anything?' The shop owner sidled up
beside Rae as she peered into the cabinet, intent on finding
something similar amongst the crystal and silver jewellery.
'Are you looking for anything in particular? Everything you
see is hand crafted and each with a tale to tell. Is there something you'd like to try on maybe?'

'No, I don't think so,' Rae said, 'but thank you.' She moved
further down the cabinet and bit the inside of her lip when
the shop owner followed.

'I have others,' the shop owner said. 'If it's a necklace
you're after, I have plenty more.'

'I'm looking for something more specific,' Rae said, 'you
have lots of lovely stones, but I had hoped to find one that
matches my own.' She had checked many jewellery stores
over the years, every crystal shop and stall she had encoun-
tered, but had yet to find someone who could identify the
crystal in her pendant.

'Really?' the shop owner said, perking up. 'That sounds
like a challenge. What stone do you have? I have all manner
of things in the back still unpacked, including many
gemstones. You never know, I may have just what you're
looking for.'

'Oh, I don't want you to go to any trouble,' Rae said, 'I'm
really just interested in what kind of crystal it is.'

'Then you came to the right place. If there's one thing I
know about, it's crystals. Do you have the necklace with you?'

Rae unzipped her jacket, giving a brief apology for the
state of her t-shirt, and pulled out the necklace from beneath.

She held the stone up to the light where it changed from a murky brown to a fiery orange.

'My my, that is a beauty. May I?' Without waiting for a reply, the shop owner reached out and carefully took the stone in her hand. 'The workmanship is exquisite,' she said. 'The way the thorns weave around the crystal, it's almost ... haunting wouldn't you say?' She looked up at Rae with grey eyes full of intrigue; a look that Rae had seen many times, in many shops just like this one.

'What about the crystal?' Rae said. 'Can you tell me what kind it is?'

'Do you mind if I take a closer look?' The shop owner looked expectantly at Rae, and while her enthusiasm was touching, Rae still hesitated. 'I'll be super careful, I promise.'

'Of course,' Rae said, feeling as always, a small twinge of guilt as she lifted the necklace from around her neck. She handed it over to the shop owner whose palm was eagerly waiting.

The shop owner then pulled out a small magnifying glass from her pocket and held it close to the pendant. 'You're not from around here, are you?' she said.

'No,' Rae said. 'I arrived yesterday.'

'Just passing through, or do you have family here?'

'Neither.' Rae said. 'I'm staying at a place in the woods. You probably know it as The Briar?'

'Yes, I know it, but I wasn't aware it had been sold.'

'It hasn't,' Rae said. 'I inherited it from my mother.' Not technically true, but easier than trying to explain that Grace had bought it for Rae and kept it a secret for twenty years.

The shop owner handed back the necklace and returned the magnifying glass to her pocket. 'Carnelian,' she said. 'Quite common but very beautiful if you like that sort of thing. You have a magnificent piece. Uncut. Pure. If you're looking to sell I'd be happy to take if off your hands.' Rae pulled the leather strap over her head and tucked the pendant back beneath her t-shirt. She must have shown it to at least thirty other vendors, and none had had a clue what it was. 'Do you mind me asking where you got it?'

'It's a family heirloom,' Rae said, zipping up her jacket. 'That's all I know.'

'Well, if you do decide to sell it, you know where I am. Is there anything else I can help you with?'

Rae was about to say no, then spotted a small silver ring in the bottom left corner of the cabinet. It was old and tarnished and probably only big enough to fit the little finger, but the belt buckle design struck Rae as unusual and she thought it would make a perfect gift. 'Actually,' she said, 'I'll take that.'

IT WAS an uphill climb all the way back to the cottage and Rae was already regretting stopping by the small supermarket on her way home. She was halfway up the hill, laden with more shopping than she could comfortably carry, when the heavens opened and this time, they brought long their big brother, Billy Wind. Rain lashed against Rae's face as she struggled to keep the thin hood of her jacket up whilst juggling three heavy bags, and after some choice words that would make a hard core sex worker blush, she finally gave up and instead concentrated her efforts on getting home as quickly as possible.

Home.

The word felt hollow on her tongue. Would anywhere ever be home again?

Ducking her head against the wind, she trudged on until she reached the lamp post that signalled the turn off for Foxglove Lane. The sign was barely visible even in daylight but brought with it a brief respite from the rain. Foxglove Lane, so named for the purple flowers that edged the road in the summer, was also lined with silver birch. Their boughs swayed dangerously in the wind but kept the worst of the rain at bay whilst Rae picked her way along the gravel path, dodging the larger puddles only to step into smaller ones mistaking them for shallow. She gritted her teeth as water sluiced into her boots, and shifted balance as the shopping bags dug painfully into her hands, but her mood lifted a little when she saw that her car was parked outside the cottage. It was to be short lived however, as the moment she drew closer she realised the lights were on in her living room, and smoke was pouring from her chimney.

Rae's first thought was that it was Alex. Alex still had a spare key from looking after the cottage for Grace – she had mentioned it at breakfast and had promised to drop it in on her way home from work – and while it was a little weird that she would let herself in, not to mention highly irritating, at least she was someone Rae knew. But there was another car parked on her driveway, a white pick-up truck that Rae didn't recognise. She stopped dead in the middle of the driveway. What if it was Darryl? What if Ronnie had caved and told him where she was staying. It wasn't his usual car, but he could've hired a rental. She stood there, rain dripping down her face, stomach tied in knots at the prospect of having to face him before she was ready. She forced herself to think rationally. If it really was Darryl making himself at home, then how did he get in?

She crept up to the picket fence, swung a leg over, and

peered through the misted glass. She could just make out the figure of a man crouched by the fire, poking at burning logs. His back was broad, arms thick and strong unlike the slim figure that Darryl usually cut, and he wore his hair short and messy, not slicked back without a strand out of place. He closed the door of the wood burner and stood up, dusted his hands on the back of his jeans and turned towards the window. Rae gasped, kicked over a potted plant as she swung her other leg over the fence, and swore under her breath as she stormed towards the porch and barged through the door.

'What the hell are you doing in my house?' she said, dumping the shopping bags on the kitchen table.

Bart gave a friendly woof and ran to greet her, but Rae ruthlessly pushed his nose away and glared at his owner, who didn't seem half as surprised to see Rae, as she was to see him.

'I brought your car back,' he said. 'Alex asked me to fix it.' He was smiling, clearly still amused by his uncanny knack for getting right on Rae's tits.

'That still doesn't explain why you're in my house,' Rae said, 'did Alex ask you to break in too?'

'No,' he said, 'but she did ask if I could drop off your spare key, and also mentioned you were having trouble with the fire, so I thought—'

'What?' Rae said. 'Thought you'd just let yourself in? Make yourself at home while your dog drools all over my rug and … is that cake he's eating?' She stared incredulously at Bart munching down on a huge slice of Alex's home-made banana cake.

'It was on the cupboard,' he said, 'I didn't think you'd mind. It's a big cake!' Rae glared. She knew it was a big cake, but it was her fucking cake. 'Do you always glower like that when someone's trying to help you?' he said, 'a simple thank you would do.'

Rae blinked, of all the ...

'Thank you for what, exactly?' she said. 'For having your dog maul me in the street? Or for breaking into my house and making yourself at home while I freeze my arse off in the rain? Or should I be thanking you for something else? Perhaps you've had a nap in my bed or taken a soak in my bath. There's wine in the fridge, why don't you help yourself to that too, I'm sure Bart would like a drink to wash his cake down with.'

John, if he even was John (he could be a mass murderer for all Rae knew) considered her for a moment, his cool eyes only stoking her already raging fire. 'You do know you're dripping water all over the floor, don't you?' he said.

She did, but she most definitely didn't need him to point that out to her. She was also letting in a cold blast of air and slammed the door shut with her foot before he had something to say about that too.

John's eyebrows shot up, but he said nothing as he grabbed a bunch of keys from the mantelpiece, walked over to Rae and held them out. 'You're welcome by the way,' he said, dropping them into her hand. 'Your car should be fine for a while, but you'll need a new battery soon and your front tyres are nearly bald. Probably shouldn't leave the key in the ignition either, never know who might be hanging around.' He leaned forward, putting his face closer to Rae's than could be considered comfortable, and for one heart stopping ridiculous moment she thought he was going to kiss her. But then he grinned, reached up and grabbed his jacket off the coat rack that was directly behind her head, and called to Bart. The dog padded obediently to his master's side as John shrugged on his jacket and opened the door. 'See you around, Rae,' he said, then winked as master and dog stepped out into the rain.

Rae looked down at the keys in her hand – a twin to her own front door key, a large brass key, and the key to her car. She opened her mouth to say something but didn't know what, so closed it again and did the only thing she could think of and slammed the door after them.

UNABLE TO CONCENTRATE on much of anything Rae spent the rest of the day stomping about the cottage, cleaning things that were spotless and muttering about men and their superior attitudes. This continued well into the evening, until finally, after lowering herself into a bath of hot bubbles, she admitted that the whole unpleasant situation had been brought about by her own tendency to overreact. It didn't make her feel any better though, quite the opposite in fact. Instead of angry, now she felt like a fool and could only imagine what John must be thinking. She exhaled slowly and slid lower into the bubbles, hoping the hot water might sooth her injured pride. It didn't, and after a few minutes of wallowing she climbed out, dried herself off and headed for bed, deciding that sleep was her only solace. Tomorrow she would seek John out and apologise for her terrible behaviour, but until then she wanted him out of her head, and she would gladly surrender herself to nightmares to do it.

4

Moonlight spilled through the open curtains, washing the bedroom in a milky glow that didn't quite reach the corners. Bramos stood in one such corner, watching as he had done the night before, and would do so for many more nights to come. Her face was turned toward him, dark hair spilled across the pillow, and features, now matured and more lovely than ever, so reminiscent of the woman he had once loved. Her lips curved up in a smile as he whispered her name, lips that he longed to kiss, and he smiled remembering her touch, the smell of her hair, the taste of her mouth. Was she dreaming of him? He hoped so.

He sat down, leaned against the wall and rested one arm on his raised knee as he watched the rise and fall of her chest. The swell of her breasts was just visible beneath the thin cover of the bed sheet and the temptation to take her was almost more than he could bear. But it was too soon. *Too soon.* Time was a fickle thing, everything to some, yet meaningless to others. It moved fast or it moved slow, came to a stop or seemed not to exist at all. But for him it was nothing more than a test of his patience and restraint. He neither trusted time nor feared it. Instead, he respected and embraced it, and in return it had given him more power than he had ever dreamed possible.

But not the power to heal. It would take more than time for that.

So, for now, all he could do was watch.

He watched for a long time, until the sun crested the horizon, and the crows greeted the new day. He rose from the floor then to look out above the tree tops where Carrion Hall stood proud atop the hill, dark and brooding as it ever was, and he marvelled at how the place had withstood the test of time.

If only flesh were as durable.

She stirred then, and he turned to see her rise from the bed, dark hair loose about her shoulders. Ah, but what a sight to behold she was, more lovely in this world than she had been in the other, and as she moved to join him by the window he stepped aside, not yet trusting himself, even in shadow. He watched as the dawning light changed the colour of her eyes from the softest chestnut brown to the colour of autumn leaves, and as she turned her face towards him he withdrew into the shadows and dissipated into the night.

5

'Hey sis, where do you need me? I'm all yours for the morning.'

Emma looked up from the menu in front of her and sighed. 'Really Chris? Now you want to help?' She gave the menu back to Georgina with a brief nod. The culmination of a month's work was finally coming together, and today's opening was going to be perfect, no thanks to Christopher.

'Use me or lose me,' he said, flashing a grin at Georgina as he stole a pastry from a wicker basket on the table.

'I suppose you could pick up my dry cleaning,' Emma said, checking the drinks order for the umpteenth time that day. 'Or perhaps assist Luke with the waiters. I hired local boys thinking it would be a good idea, but I'm beginning to re-think that decision with each passing minute. They've got about as much decorum as a band of thieves.'

Chris grabbed another pastry and shoved half into his mouth. 'Not really my thing,' he said. 'What else do you have?'

Emma slapped his hand when he reached for his third

pastry. 'Why don't you help Henry with the gazebo then?' she said. 'I'm sure he'd appreciate another pair of hands.'

'He's already got Carlos helping him. You should see the two of them, it's like the blind leading the blind.'

'Then all the more reason to help them, wouldn't you say?'

'I think my talents would be better served elsewhere.'

'Then what *do* you want to do?' Emma said, losing patience.

'I could help with the food,' he said, sneaking another pastry before Emma could stop him. 'You wouldn't mind would you Georgie?' He winked at Georgina sending her face a deep shade of pink.

'The girls have that perfectly under control, thank you,' Emma said, ushering Georgina through the door with the basket of pastries in hand. 'And I'm not sure we'd have any food left if you were in charge. We could do with a few more silver platters though. I think I saw some in the attic. Maybe you could get those for me.'

'And ruin my best suit? Em. Come on. You know me better than that.'

'Then get out of my way while I do it. Honestly, I don't know why you even bothered to show up.' She pushed past Chris and opened the door into the main hallway.

'Don't be like that, sis,' Chris called after her. 'I'll check on the drinks then, shall I? You're doing a great job, Em.'

Ignoring him, Emma hurried across the hallway and through to the drawing room. She loved her baby brother dearly, but some days it was all she could do not to brain him.

Edward Frobisher was waiting in the drawing room and greeted Emma with a huge grin as he took a step back from the fireplace to admire his work. 'Not a bad job eh, Miss Ashley.'

He was a small man, with a large ego and a pinched face that reminded Emma of a weasel. She disliked him very much, but he had come highly recommended. She smiled tightly and joined him at the fireplace, careful to keep a respectable distance lest he feel the need to rest his hand on the small of her back as he had done on numerous other occasions. 'Must I remind you once again, Mr Frobisher, that I am a *Stanford*-Ashley, Stanford for my mother, Ashley for my father.'

'Of course,' he said. 'My apologies, though perhaps you would permit me to call you Emma. Such formalities seem absurd in this day and age, don't you think?'

Emma bristled at the sound of his voice using her first name. 'On the contrary, Mr Frobisher,' she said. 'I consider a lack of formality to be a lack of respect for one's peers, a mistake that has played its part in the downturn of the youth of today, wouldn't you agree?' She felt him stiffen beside her and wondered what Chris would think of her pompous attitude. Call her out for being a stuck-up bitch no doubt, but Edward Frobisher was too cowardice for that.

'As you wish,' he conceded, bowing his head in acquiescence. 'The painting then. I trust you are happy with my work?'

Emma looked up into the face of her father, a man she recognised only from the few photo's her mother had kept and felt the same twinge of sadness that she always did. He was a good looking man, not handsome in the way that George Clooney or Clark Gable were – his features were too sharp, nose just a little too large, the chin just a little too wide – though good looking in his own right, with a kind face and a warm smile. But the real charm came from his eyes. They were the colour of glacial lakes on a clear day, a blue so soft as to be almost turquoise, with flecks of amber when the light caught them just right. They were open, friendly and trusting and though it pained Emma to see, so very much like her own. The artist had captured them perfectly and Emma could only surmise that he, or she, had known her father very well. 'I have to hand it to you, Mr Frobisher, you've done an amazing job.'

Edward Frobisher nodded in agreement beside her and folded his arms. 'I'll not lie, it was a tough one, but I'm not known to shy from a challenge. Have you had any luck discovering who the artist was?'

'None at all,' Emma said. 'I've all but given up. I'm afraid our mystery painter is to remain just that.'

'Such a shame, I would've liked to know. The workmanship is quite exceptional.'

'Yes,' Emma said, 'I see that.' She stepped closer to get a better look at where the painting had been repaired and knew by the shuffle of feet beside her that Edward Frobisher had joined her. She could feel his sour breath on her neck where he peered over her shoulder, and she gave an involuntary shudder. 'Amazing,' she said, shaking her head. 'If I hadn't seen it with my own eyes, I would never believe there had been any damage at all. I have to hand it to you, Mr Frobisher, your work is nothing short of genius.' His face was uncomfortably close to Emma's and she flinched as he leaned in closer and cleared his throat.

'Perhaps, to the untrained eye, but if you look closer you can see there are tell-tale signs.' He retrieved his glasses from the top pocket of his jacket, unfolded them and carefully balanced them on the end of his nose. 'See here,' he said, and pointed to where her father's hand rested against the fireplace – the same fireplace they were now stood in front of. 'There's a slight discolouration just there, on the ring finger where a small part of the canvas had been torn away completely, and there, just above the neckline, whoever attempted to destroy this painting had all but severed your father's head. There was some damage due to mould, but nothing we couldn't handle at Frobisher & Rotherham. All in all, I think you'll agree that the result is excellent.'

Emma smiled politely. 'Absolutely incredible,' she said, stepping back and almost bumping into him. 'It really is amazing.' They'd thought the painting irreparable upon its discovery in the attic, slashed in several places and suffering from exposure to a damp, abandoned attic, but Emma was stubborn if nothing else, and had refused to accept defeat. 'I trust your invoice will be in the mail?'

Edward Frobisher's thin lips smiled wetly at Emma as he reached into his jacket. 'I have it with me,' he said, handing over a long white envelope.

'Of course you do,' she said, recoiling when his fingers lightly brushed hers as she took the envelope from him. 'I'll arrange for it to be paid immediately. I'll show you to the door, shall I?'

'I see you're having a party,' he said. 'Is it a special occasion?'

Emma bit the inside of her mouth and forced a smile. 'I suppose you could say it is, yes. The renovations on the Hall are finally complete, today is a way of saying thank you to the locals for putting up with us for the last two years. Many of them put a lot of work into restoring the Hall to its former glory, so I think a few drinks on the lawn is the least we could do.'

'Oh, it looks like much more than that,' he said, with a glint in his eye. 'Was that a bandstand I saw earlier?'

Emma accepted defeat with a sigh. 'Would you care to stay, Mr Frobisher?'

'How wonderful of you to ask, Miss Stanford-Ashley. I would be delighted.'

'Excellent,' she said. 'I'll have Georgina show you to the terrace. It will be a while before the other guests arrive but I'm sure she can fix you a bite to eat.'

She left Edward Frobisher in the hands of Georgina, a young woman with a short fuse who was not known to suffer fools, while Emma, feeling like she suddenly needed a very hot shower, left them to it.

She made her way across the newly fitted wooden floors, back through the drawing room and into the west wing where the narrow staircase that would take her to the first floor was housed. The tang of freshly painted walls still clung to the air, but this part of the house would be closed to guests once the party started. It was here that Carrion Hall had suffered most of the damage. It was also where Emma's Aunt Evelyn had locked herself in the attic after killing her husband and setting fire to the Hall. Emma had no great fondness for this part of the house and found the atmosphere to be particularly disagreeable, but it was the only way to reach the attic and the only place where she could watch John without being seen.

The attic stairwell was set back on the first-floor landing, hidden in an alcove at the far end of the house. There were two doors, one that opened up the stairs and the other that opened into the attic itself. Both were locked at all times and Emma was the only one to carry a key.

The familiar staleness hit Emma as she stepped into the

dark attic and she was reminded as always that this was far more than just an attic. During the fire it had become her aunt's tomb, sealing her in while the rest of the house perished, and miraculously protecting her from the worst of the fire. But however it came to be that the attic was mostly untouched by flame, the same could not be said for smoke. Evelyn had died from smoke inhalation, a seemingly merciful death considering her crimes, and her face had looked remarkably peaceful, as though she had died in her sleep – quite fortunate given what came afterwards. There had been many rumours surrounding Evelyn's death and more still regarding Carrion Hall, all of which Emma chose to dismiss. To give credence to any one of them would be to fan the flames of superstition that blanketed Carrion hall, and she was not one to indulge in such lunacy.

However, the great fire of Carrion Hall had been twenty-five years ago, and although the stench of death no longer permeated the air, the musty smell of abandonment could not be stifled. Emma locked the door behind her – a habit she had become accustomed to – and began the ritual of walking the expanse of the attic, flinging open the too few windows and letting in some much-needed fresh air. The flames of the great fire may not have penetrated the stone walls of the attic, but the fireman's hose knew no such boundary. Water damage had been the biggest problem when she had taken over the restoration of Carrion Hall and although the rest of the house was all but shiny new, she had insisted that the attic remain untouched.

The sound of raised voices caught her attention as she opened the last of the windows. She recognised them both as belonging to Henry and Carlos. Henry was the assistant gardener and Carlos, his younger brother. Emma had taken pains to use local tradesmen wherever possible on the restoration of Carrion Hall, and the same could be said of the hired help today. However, judging from past experience she should have known better than to put Henry working alongside his brother. They were both grown men, and each had their own particular talents, but when put together they became nothing more than squabbling children. She sighed, once more exasperated by her brother's lack of interest in anything that didn't have large breasts and a firm arse. Carrion Hall may well have been left solely to Emma, but she had never considered it as anything but a family venture. Even Alex had been included wherever possible, and she was far from Emma's favourite cousin. If only Chris would do his part, she would happily have signed over half of the estate to him long ago. But as it was, he was irresponsible and unpredictable, choosing to spend most of his time doing God only knew what with the red-haired vixen from the village. Emma may have her differences with Alex, but even she had to admit that their cousin was far better suited to running Carrion Hall than Chris would ever be.

Another voice caught Emma's attention and her pulse quickened at the sound of it. The attic windows, though useful for letting in air, were too high up to be any good for looking out of, unless of course you happened to have a handy box nearby to stand on. But where the attic and the west wing both gave Emma the creeps, the tower gave her only a sense of calm and wellbeing. She headed up the small flight of stairs that would take her into the brightly lit space where she had found herself wiling away many an afternoon when John was working in the gardens. The room was small and round and reminded Emma of a lighthouse with its 360-degree view. It was an odd addition to the attic but one that had its uses if solitude was what you wanted. From here you could see the entire estate, including the woods, and on a good day, most of the village. It was her favourite place to be when a time-out from the chaos of renovating an old abandoned Hall was needed, and if it meant traversing the west wing and the attic for her place of serenity, then she was happy to do it.

In the centre of the room there was a wicker chair with a plush cushion, and a small table with an LED lantern on top. She had carried the chair and the table herself from the terrace, not wanting to share her secret place with anyone. The lamp she had purchased on a whim the last time she visited Harleybrock. It had been used only a handful of times but of late she had found herself in need of a midnight visit more and more often. She put it down to the stress of organising the party – she had insisted on overseeing every minute detail herself – and the unexpected feeling of emptiness at having finally finished the renovations to the Hall. Rebuilding Carrion Hall had taken the best part of two years, two years that had not only given her a sense of purpose but had also brought her the only man she had ever deemed worthy of her heart.

She ignored the comfort of the wicker chair in favour of leaning on the stone sill to look out of the window. Only one of the windows opened here, and it was this one that Emma now peered out of to watch the proceedings below. John – strong, agile and deliciously handsome – had joined the fracas and was, with some measure of success, diffusing the situation between Henry and Carlos by assisting them with the gazebo, the same way her brother could have done had he but half of John's zeal.

She watched as he directed the brothers with the grace

and authority of someone with far more responsibility than tending the gardens, though that in itself was no small task. Since John had taken over as chief gardener, the Carrion estate had blossomed into something that had become quite the talking point, reaching far beyond the boundaries of Cranston Myre. So far so, that a representative of Gardens of Interest, a highly reputable magazine, had asked if they could send one of their reporters to take pictures during today's party. John being John, had of course refused an interview, preferring his own company to that of "nosey bloody reporters" but Henry had had no such qualms and was more than happy to oblige. Emma sighed as she watched his tanned arms erect the gazebo with ease, arms that had, until twelve months ago, wrapped themselves around her when the two of them had been lovers. If only John felt as she still did, she would willingly give up the Hall just to be with him, indeed she would give up everything if it meant they could be together once more. But he had made himself very clear more than once. He and Emma were over, their brief affair and been nothing more than just that. But what they'd had was so much more than just a fling, the passion they had shared was so much more than just sex, and she wasn't going to let that go without a fight.

Promoting John to chief gardener, despite her brother's arguments to the contrary, had been a smart move on her part. As chief gardener he was entitled to one of the two cottages that had been converted from the old stables and bordered the courtyard on the west side of the Hall. The new stables, something that Chris had insisted on, were now situated closer to the grazing fields on the far side of the formal gardens, with its own private access road. It was Chris's plan to include horse treks into Dolen Forest once the hotel side of

Carrion Hall was up and running, his only offering to the running of the Hall so far. But that was some time off yet, and Chris's commitment to the project still debatable. Given John's close living quarters and dedication to his job, it meant that Emma got to see him for at least some part of every day. He was still an integral part of her life whether he knew it or not, and Emma had decided long ago that one way or another she would prove to him that she was an important part of his too.

The gazebo was finally finished, thanks mainly to John, and as if sensing her presence, he turned, looked toward the tower and waved. Emma resisted the urge to jump down and hide, so startled was she that he knew she was there. Had he known she was there on all the other occasions? She waved back and smiled. Henry and Carlos waved too before all three made their way back to the terrace where Georgina was sure to be waiting with her famous pink lemonade.

Reluctantly, Emma dragged herself away from the window and headed back down the stairs into the attic. The platters were leaning against the south wall where she had left them the last time she was up here with Alex. Indeed, the last time anyone had been up here other than herself. Chris may be disinterested in anything to do with the Hall, but Alex most certainly was not. When Emma had offered her the job of assisting with the renovations, Alex had all but bit her hand off. Her passion had been admirable in the beginning, she even managed to stir up a little bit of enthusiasm in Chris, though that had been short lived, and her desire to know every part of the house right down to the foundations had been commendable. She even preferred to work in the west wing feeling that her talents would be put to best use in the worst of the damage. But twelve months into the project, when the portrait of her father had been discovered, Emma had decided to re-delegate Alex elsewhere. Alex had not been happy, but the offer of a selection of rooms to do with as she pleased did the trick. Alex was placated and Emma was left in sole charge of the attic.

Emma had never fully understood why she had felt the need to divert Alex to the other end of the house, other than the fact that she had experienced an overwhelming desire to have the attic all to herself, as though to have anyone else up there was a desecration of the space itself. A feeling that had been enforced further when she discovered Evie's diaries. The diaries were now piled on the tower floor, waiting for Emma to continue with her reading, a task she had set herself hoping to discover what had put her shy and placid aunt onto the road of self-destruction. But the diaries were long, in no particular order, and half the entries undated, so the truth of that fateful night had so far eluded her.

She crossed the open space to the cluttered south wall and counted the platters. Five in total, none of them matching and all filthy, but with a good bit of spit and polish they'd look just the part in the hands of the hired waiters. She picked them up and shuddered as a familiar coldness slipped down the back of her dress. Resisting the urge to look towards the hole in the wall she turned, and with a quickened step exited the attic leaving the dust to swirl and gather where she had just been standing.

6

R ae decided to go for a walk in the woods before it was time to head up to Carrion Hall for the party. It was one of those perfect autumn days that promises just one more taste of summer before surrendering to the harshness of winter. Over the past few days she had taken to going for a run before breakfast, and though she found it invigorating and uplifting, Maggie's words continued to play on her mind – *you'll not find a single local in those woods, at least not in those parts anyway.* Nor tourists either, so it would seem. Of the four days that Rae had so far ventured into Dolen Forest she had not seen a single soul, not a dog being walked nor a fellow runner. There were tracks aplenty, and she had checked out many of them herself already, but if it wasn't for the fact that she hadn't ventured too far she would surely have gotten lost by now. The tracks were overgrown, unmarked and in some cases, difficult to see. If the villagers of Cranston Myre did visit this side of Dolen Forest, then they did so infrequently and cared little of its upkeep. Either way, it mattered not to Rae. She found the forest to be an enchanting place, full of the sweet smells of nature that had eluded her during her years of living in a city where exhaust fumes and coffee dominated the senses. Granddad's garden had been somewhat of a haven from the hustle and bustle of city life, with its fruit trees, honeysuckle and secret hide-aways, especially with the tree-house that Granddad had built for Rae's sixth birthday, a safe haven away from an envious big sister who would tease and torment Rae until she cried. But as much as she'd loved to walk amongst the blue-bells and admire the prize winning roses, or hide in the special place amongst the tops of an oak tree, it couldn't hope to compare to having an entire forest on your doorstep.

The solitude of the cottage, coupled with the wonder of the forest, were already beginning to work their magic. Rae was feeling better than she had in weeks. Even Darryl's relentless phone calls and text messages had lessened to a degree, though she knew that if she was ever truly going to move on then at some point she would have to face him, even if only to come to terms with what she had done.

As with every morning, Rae tried to unlock the heavy wooden door that kept her from entering the still undiscovered cottage garden. The brass key that John had given her fit the lock perfectly, but it was the wrought iron bolt that had thus far prevented her from exploring the garden. Despite various attempts to lubricate the damn thing Rae had been unable to budge it an inch and it irked her something bad that she could not gain access to the garden. She had called Alex, wondering if there was some trick to moving the latch, but Alex had been unable to offer an explanation other than it was a bugger of a thing to move, though John had always managed so perhaps she should give him a call. Why was Rae not surprised? She had thanked Alex for her help, and instead decided to try an alternative solution by way of entering the garden from the forest. There was a gate at the bottom of the garden. Rae knew this because she could see it from the upstairs window, but for some inexplicable reason she was unable to locate it from the forest. The wall that surrounded the garden was easily six-foot-tall and was guarded by a dense hedge of sweet briar. She supposed it was where the cottage got its name from, but as charming as the sweeping display of scarlet hips was, it only added to her frustration by being so thick in parts that it had proved to be a formidable obstacle. The sweet apple scent was a stark contrast to the thorny stems that served the cottage well by obscuring any possible entrance into the garden via the woods, which included, it would seem, any access to the gate. She had given up, and decided that if it came to it, she would remove the back door from its hinges and use the bloody thing as firewood, just to be spiteful.

Today, she had decided, would be that day, but first she would attempt to move the unmovable bolt one more time, but today proved to be no different than any other, and the bolt remained firmly fixed like a stubborn ox. Out of sheer frustration she hit the bolt with her fist and cried out when a splinter the size of a match pierced the fleshy part of her hand. Blood oozed up instantly and slid down to her wrist, but she ignored it to press her ear to the door. A low hum came from the other side, similar to that of fluorescent strip lighting. It vibrated through the door, and the ground beneath her feet, and when she took a step back she could still feel it, buzzing through her veins like an electrical charge. Beneath Rae's jacket something warm pressed against her chest and she lifted the leather strap of her necklace to find the crystal pendant softly glowing. It pulsated in tune to the vibration making the hairs on her arms stand on end, and when she held it its surface grew hot against her skin. She tried the latch one more time and couldn't say whether it had been a conscious decision, or whether she was simply acting on auto-pilot, but the next thing she knew the bolt was sliding across as though gliding on oil, and the door quietly clicked open. The buzzing stopped, the crystal ceased to glow, and Rae slipped it back beneath her jacket as she stepped out to grey skies and she smell of damp air.

THE GARDEN WAS NOT REALLY a garden at all, but a large, paved courtyard awash with autumn colour, and the sweet briar that guarded the wall from the outside clambered over the top like a score of misbehaving children. Someone had taken great care to look after these plants, to place them around the courtyard so that everywhere you looked there was something new to see.

Ruby red leaves scorched a path along the inside of the wall, while more subdued shades of russet and gold feathered flower boxes below. Cornflower blues, violets and sun tinged yellows burst from terracotta pots dotted around the flag stone yard, while white clematis trailed from hanging baskets by the door and windows. In the centre was a sundial, or so Rae thought, but closer inspection proved it to be something else entirely. It was made of stone, painted blue and inlaid with gold carvings. There were no numerals to indicate the time of day, or images of the sun, only etchings of the moon in its various stages of waxing and waning, and strange symbols that Rae thought resembled runes. A small mosaic table was beside it, dotted with small plant pots of poppy red and buttercup yellow, and the air was redolent with the smell of flowers. She looked back towards the door, purposely left open lest the latch slide back home and lock her out, and wondered if Alex and John had felt the same strange buzzing when they opened it. Perhaps there was a power station nearby, or pylons close to the forest, though neither of those would explain why her crystal had glowed. She made a mental note to ask Alex later and headed towards the gate.

The gate was made of wrought iron and sat beneath a bricked archway covered with more of the hardy sweet briar and resisted and groaned its displeasure as Rae pushed it open. On the other side was a path, overgrown like the many Rae had seen so far, and hidden from view by a thick band of trees that seemed to go on forever. Copious amounts of black-berry bramble grew along the edges, completely covering the path in parts and snagging Rae's leggings as she picked her way through. It was no wonder she hadn't been able to locate this part of the forest before given how dense the under-growth was and the thickness of the trees. It was all she could do just to keep her eye on the path as it grew ever narrower the further away from the cottage she got. It twisted and turned, went left then right, then right again until Rae thought she must be going around in circles. She thrust her hands deep into her pockets as the temperature dropped dramatically. A grey mist settled over her like a wet blanket and she shivered as the cold crept beneath her skin to eat into her bones.

The cottage was now nowhere in sight, the trees ever denser the further she went, and any birdsong she had heard was now muted by the deafening silence that surrounded her. She shivered, hunkered down into her jacket, and had just decided to return home when a noise from behind made her spin on her heels. It had sounded like breaking twigs, and the rustle of leaves, but the only thing she saw was an endless sea of green. 'Who's there?' she called out, stamping her feet against the cold as her breath froze in the air. A crow cawed from a branch overhead, and where the path continued into the forest it only grew darker. She looked back the way she had come, where sunrays now filtered through the overhead canopy making the dew drops sparkle like diamonds. But as foreboding as the way forward was, the promise of adventure beckoned, and besides, what harm could possibly come from a gentle stroll in the woods? Said every female to be murdered in the woods ever!

She pulled her scarf tighter, checked one last time behind her, and pushed on.

The canopy of trees grew ever denser the further in she went, the air heavier as though laden with rain and Rae thrust her hands deeper into her pockets, curiosity pushing her on even while common sense told her to turn back. A twig snapped behind her and she whizzed round, half expecting to see someone following, but there was only a thick carpet of foliage and trees as far as the eye could see, huddled so closely together Rae thought they looked like a gaggle of scheming witches. She tutted quietly to herself. Scheming witches indeed! Next, she'd be seeing werewolves!

A few minutes later she caught movement in the corner of her eye and jumped. It was only slight, a flash of black amongst the endless green, but it gave rise to the hairs on the back of her neck. She quickened her pace, relieved to see the trail start to widen, fanning out on either side as it reached the edge of the tree line, and a clearing that formed an almost perfect circle waited before her. Dead centre, with branches so large and twisted with age they looked like the gnarled old fingers of a giant, was the biggest oak tree Rae had ever seen.

Some of its branches were so big and heavy they rested amongst the littering of dead leaves, while others had rooted back into the ground only to reappear again like huge wooden tentacles further along the way. Moss grew everywhere on the tree, clinging to the trunk and creeping along the branches like a luminous green overcoat. Rae had never seen anything like it. It was both magnificent and terrifying at the same time, the sheer breadth of its canopy enough to take your breath away. The clearing smelled strongly of wet earth and fungus, but here at least the sun managed to break through and chase away some of the gloom.

The tree was just ginormous. Rae stood staring up into its canopy, mouth hanging open like a child, and thought if the trunk were hollow it would be big enough to hold at least twenty or so people. Another crow cawed overhead, and she looked up to see beady eyes watching her before the bird spread its wings and took flight.

The mist seemed to hang back from the clearing, congregating at the edges as though an invisible wall prevented it from entering, but the air was no less cold, even with the sunlight on her face. Rae wondered why Alex, with her endless stream of chatter, had never mentioned this place. A tree as spectacular as this would surely be a huge tourist attraction, and yet there was no signage, no posters or pamphlets in the village stores, and other than the narrow path that led here, nothing to suggest anyone had visited in a very long time.

A secret place then, the sort of place a person could come to to hide from the outside world. The thought warmed her bones, and she placed a hand on the tree's trunk, surprised to feel the same buzz dance across her skin as she had felt back at the cottage. It hummed through the tree, a vibration of sorts that reminded Rae of an experiment she'd once watched as a child. It was with a Van de Graaff generator, and when the scientist touched it his hair stood on end. This was what Rae imagined it had felt like, and the thought brought a smile to her face. She pressed both hands to the trunk, pleased to find the vibration became stronger, humming beneath her skin like a swarm of angry bees, and when she felt a tug on her arm, as though being pulled into the tree, her hand began to throb where the splinter had pierced it. She tried to pull away, but for some inexplicable reason found she couldn't move, that she was rooted to the spot, hands latched onto the tree as though glued there, and the humming was becoming louder, filling her head with its incessant noise. She shook her head to try and clear it, closed her eyes for just a moment as the buzzing grew, rising to a crescendo until she thought she could stand it no longer, and then all of a sudden it just … stopped.

Rae cautiously opened her eyes … and was thrown into a moment of chaos.

She was still in the forest, still stood by the tree, but the clearing was surrounded by fire. There was shouting and screaming, the sound of swords clashing, horses whinnying, and orders being barked, but she could see nothing through the haze of smoke that cloyed at the back of her throat, making her eyes water and her lungs constrict with fear. She fell forward, coughing and retching, blinded by the sting of tears, unable to comprehend what was happening. Then once again, everything suddenly stopped. She wiped her eyes and climbed to her feet. The fire had gone, as had the sounds of fighting on the other side, but the smell of burning still hung in the air, and now, walking proudly towards her, was a heavily bearded man.

He had long dark hair pulled tight into a plait, black armour on his torso but bare, tattooed arms. His pants were black leather with boots laced up to the knee and there was a shield at his back, the hilt of a sword sticking out over the top, and embedded with an orange stone that looked very much like Rae's crystal. He had a cut above his left eye that was bleeding profusely, and he was saying something to Rae that she couldn't hear. He was angry, yelling at her and pointing to the tree, and his eyes, like two rings of liquid honey – golden eyes – burned with fury.

The jolt back to reality was so sudden that Rae's stomach lurched upwards and she fell forward onto her knees and vomited into the leaves. She sat back on her heels, breathless and reeking of smoke, and wiped the sleeve of her jacket across her mouth, noting with disgust that her jacket was black with soot. On the trunk of the tree, where her hand had been pressed against it, was a bloody handprint, and as she watched, the handprint disappeared, absorbed into the tree like water on a sponge. She scrambled to her feet, steadied herself against a branch while her head stopped spinning, and froze when she realised she was not alone.

The wolf, if it even was a wolf, stood not three feet away, head bent low, hackles raised, and teeth bared to their roots. It growled – a deep guttural sound that turned Rae's already sloshed up guts to water – and took a cautious step forward. Rae took a cautious step back, then another, then another, mind racing, trying to make sense of what was going on. She slowly reached into her jacket pocket and gripped her keys, the largest of the bunch – her car key – poking out between two fingers. If the wolf attacked she would aim for the eyes, and if that didn't work then ... she turned when she heard the crunch of leaves behind her, but before she could see who it was, everything went black.

WHEN ALEX ARRIVED at the cottage Rae was still sitting on the edge of the bed. She'd woken up on the forest floor, nauseous and with a banging headache, but no lump, laceration, or mark of any kind to show that she'd been hit over the head. She'd gotten out of there as quickly as possible, but a feeling of disquiet had stayed with her.

Alex honked the horn again and Rae stood up to check herself in the mirror. She had finally settled on a navy-blue dress to wear to the party but was still unsure about the plunging neckline. It showed more cleavage than she was used to, but the girl in the shop had insisted it was perfect, and Rae, more interested in getting it over and done with, had taken her word for it. Now though, she wasn't so sure. She adjusted her décolletage for the hundredth time and threw a pale blue wrap around her shoulders.

They could just as easily have walked to Carrion Hall – the drive up the hill took all of two minutes – and Rae almost wished they had when she saw the long line of traffic slowly inching its way through the huge iron gates. It seemed the entire village had turned out to get a glimpse of the newly renovated Carrion Hall, and possibly half of the next village too. Alex joined the back of the queue, surprisingly patient as one by one the cars passed through the gates, and despite herself Rae felt a twinge of nerves.

'Will you stop fussing,' Alex said as Rae adjusted her dress again. 'You have great boobs, stop trying to hide them.'

'Easy for you to say,' Rae said, glancing at Alex's shirt buttoned all the way up to the collar.

'If I wasn't cursed with a boy's chest then I would be wearing the sluttiest dress that money can buy. I can undo a few buttons if it will make you feel any better?'

Rae shook her head and sighed. 'Sorry,' she said, 'I just get nervous at parties. I did say —'

'That parties aren't your thing,' Alex said. 'I know, but you have nothing to worry about. You look stunning, and even if you didn't, no-one would care.'

The queue was moving quickly now and Carrion Hall loomed menacingly before them. Gothic and brooding even in bright sunlight it cut an imposing figure against the backdrop of a near perfect blue sky. Rae leaned forward in her seat to get a better look at the Georgian mansion with its crimson ivy-covered walls and grimacing gargoyles watching from the steepled roof. It was as impressive as it was unnerving, built of blue-grey stone with huge windows spaced uniformly apart, and a large carving of a crow in mid-flight perched above the imposing double doors. Guests were being directed away from the main entrance and ushered to the right of the building where a large expanse of lawn had been reserved as a car park. From there, wait staff in white jackets and black bow ties handed out drinks from silver platters, whilst directing guests through a bricked archway dotted with red and white roses. Alex swerved her car to the left and headed towards the west side of the mansion where gravel gave way to cobblestones. They veered right and turned into a large courtyard flanked on one side by garage doors (Rae counted five, all closed except for one that housed a white pick-up truck) and two neat little cottages on the other, each with a bottle green door, matching lantern and basket of red and white flowers. It was outside one of these where Alex parked the car.

She climbed out and checked her hair in the side mirror – now a more sombre shade of pink than the hot pink it had previously been – and opened the door of the second cottage, threw the keys in and slammed the door shut. She was wearing a pair of skin-tight shiny black pants that reminded Rae of Sandy in *Grease,* except instead of four-inch heels Alex wore a pair of riding boots. 'How's your car?' she said, looping her arm through Rae's as they headed toward another archway surrounded by rhododendron bushes. 'Did John drop it off OK?' There was a glint in her eye that suggested she already knew the answer.

'As if you didn't already know,' Rae said. 'Should I even ask what he said about me?'

Alex laughed. 'Probably not, but I can read John like a book. I think he likes you.'

'Likes me? I highly doubt it, I was horrible to him.'

'Maybe he fancies a challenge,' Alex said. 'God knows he didn't get one with Emma. She practically fell over with her legs in the air the moment they met.'

'They're together?' Rae said. She couldn't help but feel a prick of disappointment, ridiculous as that was.

'*Were* together,' Alex said, 'though try telling Emma that.'

'Recent break-up?'

Alex shook her head. 'Twelve months ago. She's not quite at bunny boiling stage yet but give it a couple of months. John will be at the party if you want me to fix the two of you up?'

'And get slung out by the hostess for drooling over her ex. Maybe not.'

Alex lifted an eyebrow. 'Drooling?'

'You know what I mean. Can we drop it and talk about something else?'

'Please yourself,' Alex said, then nudged Rae with her elbow, 'but I hear he's wicked in bed.'

She led them round the back of the Hall where most of the guests had already congregated on the lawn. Most hung around a gazebo where a make-shift bar had been erected, but many others had wandered onto the terrace to watch an elaborate champagne fountain in the process of being poured. A bandstand stood to the left of the gazebo, where a string quartet played classical music, and beyond the bandstand, behind a low hedge of hawthorn, Rae could see a raised pool area and a tennis court. Next to that, down a small flight of steps, was a maze of rosebushes that encircled a magnificent ornate fountain.

Alex pointed to a row of poplar trees that bordered the gardens just beyond the fountain. 'The grazing fields are through there,' she said. 'If you follow them downhill, they'll take you back to your part of the woods.'

'Do you go there much?' asked Rae.

'What, the woods?' Alex said, 'sometimes, why?'

'Have you ever seen anything strange there, like a large dog, or ... a wolf maybe?'

Alex looked at Rae curiously, 'you're not worrying about what Maggie said, are you? She was just spouting off a load of hocus pocus bullshit. Honestly, you have nothing to worry about.'

'I know,' Rae said, 'but I've been doing a bit of exploring, and today I found—'

'Drinks, ladies?' They were interrupted by the arrival of a grinning young waiter with a crooked bowtie and a half empty tray of filled champagne flutes.

'Well, well, well,' Alex said, taking two glasses and

handing one to Rae. 'Damien Barnes, part of the hired help. I never thought I'd see the day.'

'Your cousin pays well,' Damien said, lifting one of the glasses and drinking its contents in one gulp. 'Plus, the booze is free.'

'I'm not sure the booze is meant for you,' Alex said, 'but I won't say anything if you don't. I want you to meet my new friend, Rae. Rae, this is Damien, the local bad boy and now waiter extraordinaire.'

He was only young, eighteen or nineteen, with dirty blonde hair and a dimple in his chin. Rae recognised him as being one of the lads playing pool at the pub the night she arrived.

'You're the girl staying at The Briar,' Damien said. 'I've seen you in the woods a few times.'

'What were *you* doing in the woods?' Alex said. She narrowed her eyes at him and Damien seemed to blanch for just a moment before quickly recovering.

'This and that,' he said, 'ask me no questions and all that.'

'Do you run?' asked Rae, shifting the position of her wrap as Damien's eyes slipped below her neck.

Alex laughed. 'If Damien is running it's because he's being chased. Don't go pissing around at Rae's place,' she said to Damien, 'that side of the woods is private property, as you well know, and if you're caught hunting—'

'I'm not hunting,' Damien said, 'no-one hunts in there anymore.'

'Just as well,' Alex said. 'You'd scare off a sabre-toothed tiger with the amount of aftershave you're wearing. I don't suppose you've seen my cousin around have you? The nice one, not his evil sister.'

Damien nodded and helped himself to another glass of

champagne. 'He was in the tent last I saw him, talking to that Bidfest guy.'

'I think you mean *gazebo* and James *Bidwell*,' Alex said. 'Maybe you should hand out the alcohol instead of drinking it, and by the way, your new employer is giving you the evils from the terrace.'

Damien glanced over his shoulder to where a blonde in a long red dress was watching with interest. 'Maybe my luck's in,' he said, turning back, 'she's been eyeing me up all morning.'

'As unlikely as that is,' Alex said. 'I can think of nothing more entertaining than watching you try to tackle her ladyship.'

'Hold that thought,' Damien said, 'danger is my middle name.' He winked at Rae, threw back another glass of champagne then headed off in the direction of the band stand, closely followed by the blonde.

'He'll be shit faced before the days out,' Alex said, looping her arm back through Rae's. 'Come on, I want you to meet Chris.'

'What did you mean about the woods being private property?' Rae said as they headed towards the gazebo.

'Just this side of it,' Alex said, 'the whole area belonged to Carrion Hall once, but half was donated to the village a long time ago. Even The Briar was part of the Carrion estate until Richard gave it away to his mistress.'

'You mean Richard Ashley?' Rae said. She'd done a little research on Carrion Hall in light of her visit today and knew that it had been owned by Richard Ashley and his wife, Evelyn before she stabbed him to death, set fire to the hall and locked herself in the attic. 'Do you know why he give it away?'

'Nope,' Alex said. 'But it's yours now.' She stopped briefly to greet a bunch of people, quickly but politely, not getting caught up in banal conversation before leading Rae towards the far side of the gazebo where two men could be heard having a heated discussion about horses.

'He's not boring you with talk of the stables again, is he?' Alex said, planting a kiss on the cheek of the shorter of the two – a man with little hair on his head and an abundance on his face. 'It's good to see you James.'

'Not half as good as it is to see you,' James said. 'Looking gorgeous as ever, Alexandra. And who is your lovely companion?'

'This is Raewyn Winters,' she said. 'Rae has just moved into The Briar. Rae, this is James, and my cousin, Chris.'

James took Rae's hand and raised it to his lips. 'Absolutely charming,' he said, 'Alexandra has the most exquisite taste in friends.'

'Which is more than I can say for you,' Alex said, 'I hear you're defending Nathan Wright next month. You can't possibly think he's innocent.'

'It doesn't matter what I think,' James said, 'only what I can prove, and that is about as much as I'm willing to say on the matter.'

'And rightly so,' Chris said, 'discussing work in front of our guest is just plain rude. Raewyn, it's lovely to finally meet you. Alex has talked about nothing else since you arrived.' He was a good head taller than James, with dark, almost black hair and eyes the colour of olives just before they ripen. He swapped Rae's empty glass for a full one and smiled warmly. He had a nice smile.

Alex shook her head and rolled her eyes. 'Don't listen to

him,' she said, 'if his lips are moving it's usually because he's lying.'

Rae laughed. 'Call me Rae, please,' she said, 'and I have a lot to thank Alex for. She's done a wonderful job with the cottage.'

'Told you I'm not just a pretty face,' Alex said, pulling tongues at Chris.

'And not even that on most days,' Chris said, dodging Alex's foot when she tried to kick. 'And how are you finding life in a small village, Rae. Alex tells me you've come here from Manchester. It must be quite a change coming from a big city?'

'A little,' Rae said, 'though honestly, it's exactly what I wanted.'

'Dead after 8pm,' muttered James, nudging Alex in the ribs.

'James is a city man too,' Chris said. 'Born and raised in London. The country air doesn't really agree with him.'

'The smell of *horse shit* doesn't really agree with me,' James said.

'You talk it often enough,' Alex said, 'I thought you'd be used to it by now.'

'Ha ha,' James said, 'you won't be saying that when I put you over my knee, young lady.'

'Your dodgy ticker couldn't take it, *old man*.'

'Maybe not,' James said, 'but I'm willing to give it a try if you are.'

Chris shook his head. 'Please excuse their juvenile behaviour, Rae. Neither one of them get out very often. Can I assume that as you like it here, you'll be staying for a while?'

Rae nodded. 'For the time being, at least.'

'Then tell me, Rae, do you ride?'

'Horses you mean?'

Chris laughed. 'Well I wasn't suggesting anything else. Alex and I are going for a ride in the woods tomorrow and I would be honoured if you would join us?'

'Yes, you should,' exclaimed Alex. 'You'd love it.'

'I haven't ridden in ages,' Rae said. 'And I was never very good at it, I'm not even sure I remember how.'

'Of course you do,' Alex said. 'It's just like riding a bike, and it would be great to get another opinion. Emma refuses to come with us, not that she'd be much fun anyway.'

Rae looked at Chris. 'Opinion on what?'

'On whether it's fun or completely boring,' Chris said. 'When Carrion Hall becomes a fully functioning hotel, we intend to offer horse treks through Dolen Forest as part of a weekend package. Alex and I will run it together, but it's aimed more towards the novice rider so your lack of experience would be perfect. What do you say?'

'I don't know,' Rae said. 'It really has been a long time.'

'Nothing too adventurous,' Chris assured her. 'It'll be an easy pace and the company will be second to none, my cousin excluded of course.'

Alex beamed at Rae. 'Say you'll come, please. You'll be doing us a favour, honestly, and what better way to see more of the forest?'

'Just an easy trek you say?'

'Scouts honour,' Chris said.

Rae bit her lip. It wasn't that she was afraid of going back into the forest. If anything, she was more curious than ever, but what if something happened while they were together? What if she had another ... episode? She wasn't sure she wanted to share something like that with anyone, let alone two virtual strangers.

'Come on,' Alex said, 'it's got to be better than moping around that cottage all day.'

'Well when you put it like that,' Rae said, 'how could I refuse?'

'You couldn't,' Alex said, smiling. 'We wouldn't let you.'

'Excellent,' Chris said. 'Then I shall leave the arrangements in Alexandra's capable hands. Now if you'll excuse me, there's someone I need to speak with.'

'Looks like someone's in for an ear bashing,' James said, as Chris headed towards the brick archway by the car park where a redhead was waiting. She wore a long a dress, a red one that looked a lot like the one the blonde on the terrace was wearing and tossed her hair seductively as Chris approached. 'What I wouldn't give to have a woman like that in my bed.'

'She'd eat you alive, and you know it,' Alex said.

'And I would enjoy every single moment of it,' James said, 'and on that note, I suppose I should go and see where my lovely wife has got to.' He nodded to Rae, kissed Alex on the cheek, then turned and headed off towards the Hall, stopping on the way to flirt with a group of girls who were young enough to be his daughters.

'Don't let him fool you,' Alex said, watching him go. 'I've never seen anyone more devoted to their wife than James is.'

'Who's the woman?' asked Rae. Chris was guiding her back towards the car park and didn't seem entirely happy to see her.

'That, is Dee,' Alex said, 'the woman I work for, and Emma will be mighty pissed if she sees her wearing that dress.'

'So, they're together, Chris and Dee?'

'Not exactly,' Alex said. 'Chris has an infatuation with her nether regions, but beyond that I think they're just friends. Dee has quite the reputation around here, and Christopher would be wise to remember that if he ever hopes to own half of this place.'

'You mean he doesn't already?'

'Nope, and he never will if he continues to bed Dee. Emma can be quite the bitch when she wants to be. I thought he would've seen sense by now, but apparently not. Shall we move on then? Barbara Dalemore is headed straight for us and unless you want to be stuck listening to anecdotes about the cake decorating business for the next hour then I suggest we get a move on.'

Rae caught a glimpse of a middle-aged woman in a white dress that looked more like a paper doily before Alex grabbed her hand and guided her through the crowd and past the bandstand, stopping only to grab refills on their way. They passed a young woman dressed demurely in a dusky pink dress and Rae had to do a double take before realising she was the girl from the Rook & Wheel, the pretty one with the short skirt who had given her the two fingered salute. She was accompanied by a much older man with piggy eyes and a ruddy complexion who grabbed her arm to pull her along as she turned back to look at Rae and Alex.

'Who was that?' asked Rae, as they stopped beneath a tree draped with twinkling fairy lights.

'Michelle,' Alex said, grimacing as the man gave Michelle a hard shove towards the Hall. 'And that fat bastard is her father.'

Rae recalled Alex talking about Michelle at the cafe. Michelle's father gave her another hard shove, almost knocking her to the ground, and Rae felt Alex tense beside her.

'And what are you two whispering about?' They both turned as one to find the woman from the gift shop standing behind them. 'Shouldn't you be mingling with the crowd instead of lurking suspiciously over here?'

'We're hiding from Barbara bloody know it all,' Alex said, 'what's your excuse?'

'Same,' the woman said, 'and trying to avoid anyone who looks like they actually want to be here. How are you?' she said to Rae. 'I'm glad to see your necklace on such fine display.'

Rae instinctively put a hand to her chest. 'I'm good,' she said. 'It's nice to see you again.'

'The two of you have met?' Alex said. 'Why am I not surprised? If a pin drops in the Myre Connie knows about it.'

'Which is why you should mind your manners,' Connie said. 'There's a tale or two I could tell about you lady.' She winked at Rae and held out her hand, 'I'm Constance, but everyone calls me Connie.'

'Raewyn,' Rae said, 'but you can call me Rae. And that reminds me.' She pulled a small box wrapped in blue paper from her bag and handed it to Alex. 'I almost forgot. Happy birthday!'

Alex beamed from ear to ear. 'You shouldn't have,' she gushed, 'but I'm glad you did.' She tore the paper off with glee and when she opened the box her eyes lit up. 'It's gorgeous,' she said, sliding the ring onto her little finger. 'Thank you, Rae. I love it.'

'You're welcome,' Rae said, 'it's the least I could do after all you've done for me.'

'So, where's the lady of the manor?' Connie said, 'I haven't felt her eyes boring holes into my skull yet.'

'I imagine she's keeping a low profile,' Alex said, admiring her ring.

'Oh yes, the dress,' Connie said. 'Seeing Dee turn up in the same bizarre outfit as Emma is the only thing that's made this farce of a party worth attending. I'm not even sure who looks the most ridiculous in it, Dee with her heaving bosom, or Emma with the chest of a boy and the hips to match. Whose idea was it for Dee to wear the same dress? I don't doubt it was intentional, but someone had to let slip what Emma was wearing.' She looked pointedly at Alex, and Rae was surprised to see a sly smile play across Alex's lips. 'Just as I thought,' Connie said. 'You'd do well to be careful, missy. Emma may have a stick up her arse but she's not stupid.'

'It was a joke,' Alex said. 'Emma will see the funny side ... eventually.'

'I expect we'll find out soon enough,' Connie said. 'Here comes that gardener of hers, which means m'lady won't be far behind.'

Rae spotted John striding across the lawn towards them, dressed in the same faded jeans as the last time she saw him, with a casual white shirt tucked half in, half out. Unshaven with tousled hair he looked every bit like he'd just woken up and remembered he was supposed to be at a party. Suddenly very aware of her exposed cleavage, Rae pulled her shawl across her chest and folded her arms.

'Wait for it,' Connie said. 'I think he's been spotted.'

Sure enough, Emma seemed to appear from nowhere. She all but ran across the lawn to catch up with John and whisper into his ear. Her hand rested on his shoulder for a moment too long and it showed in the flicker of irritation that flashed across his face.

'I swear she shoved a homing beacon up his arse when

they were shagging,' Connie said. 'She's like a bitch on heat. Honestly, it's embarrassing to watch.'

Another woman joined them with a camera bigger than Rae's handbag. Emma attempted to straighten John's hair while John tucked in his shirt, glancing every now and then at Rae and her companions with a less than impressed look on his face.

Alex laughed. 'Look how he oozes enthusiasm,' she said, 'I did warn Emma, but that woman will not listen.' She snorted as John batted Emma's hand away then laughed out loud as he grabbed the poor young photographer by the elbow and dragged her away from Emma and towards the pool.

'Shit, now she's coming this way,' Connie said. 'I'll catch you two ladies later.' She ducked behind the tree and scurried off just as Emma approached with waiter in tow.

'Was that Constance I saw?' Emma said, instructing the waiter to change Alex and Rae's glasses for full ones before sending him away.

'It was,' Alex said. 'She really wanted to stay and chat, but I believe she had urgent business with a chocolate gateau.'

'I'm sure she did,' Emma said, smiling tightly. She turned to Rae, steely blue eyes lingering on Rae's dress just long enough for it to be uncomfortable. 'Aren't you going to introduce me to your friend?'

'Of course,' Alex said. 'This is Raewyn Winters. Rae, meet my cousin, Emmaline Ashley.'

'*Stanford*-Ashley,' corrected Emma, loosely shaking Rae's hand. 'Pleased to meet you Raewyn. Have you known Alex long?'

'Less than a week, actually,' Rae said.

'Rae has moved into the cottage,' Alex said. 'I did tell you about it.'

'Of course you did,' Emma said. 'It must have slipped my mind. And do you live alone, Raewyn, or is there a Mr Winters?' It was said in a way that suggested Emma already knew fine well that Rae lived alone, and the way she looked down her nose at her without actually looking down her nose, ground Rae's gears something fierce.

'Just little ole me,' she said. 'Wouldn't have it any other way.'

'Quite,' Emma said. She smiled, but it was one of those smiles that suggest they know something you don't. 'Alex, would you mind asking Georgina if we have more canapés, we seem to be running low on the terrace.'

'Ask one of the waiters,' Alex said, 'isn't that what they're here for?'

'All the waiters are busy handing out drinks,' Emma said, 'it will only take a moment. I'll keep Raewyn company while you go.'

Alex looked at Rae and rolled her eyes. 'Fine,' she said, 'but be nice otherwise you'll have me to answer to.'

'Forgive my cousin,' Emma said, 'she has an odd sense of humour.'

Rae stifled a smile as Alex pulled faces behind Emma's back. 'You have a beautiful home, Emma. You must be enormously proud of it?'

'You've been inside then?' Emma said. 'Tell me, what did you think of the wood panelling at the entrance. It was Alex's idea, but I can't help but think its little ... distasteful.'

'Oh. I haven't actually been inside,' Rae said, 'I was referring more to the exterior, and the gardens.'

Emma nodded, giving Rae a patient smile. 'Then I must

insist that you do before you leave. It's quite something, even if I do say so myself, though my part in the renovations has been mostly supervisory. Do you know your cottage used to be part of the Carrion Estate?'

'I do,' Rae said, glad Alex had already told her, 'lucky for me your father gave it away.'

Emma's eyebrow lifted just a little. 'Yes, well, I daresay he had a lot on his mind at the time. Love can make people do the strangest things.'

'Of course,' Rae said, 'it was terrible what happened here. I'm sorry you lost your father under such tragic circumstances. It must have been very difficult for you and your family.'

'I was just a baby,' Emma said, 'but don't believe everything you read in the newspapers. They seldom tell the whole truth, if indeed any of it at all. I would be interested to learn how you came to acquire the cottage though. I hadn't realised it was for sale.'

'It wasn't,' Rae said, 'it's been mine for a long time.'

Emma's eyes narrowed slightly. 'Really? I hadn't realised.'

'Most people don't,' Rae said. Emma eyed Rae suspiciously, but she was damned if she was going to tell this woman anything.

'Yes, well, it was nice to meet you Raewyn,' Emma said. 'And if you ever need anything, don't hesitate to drop by.'

'Thank you,' Rae said, 'I won't.' But Emma had already turned her back and was sashaying across the lawn.

THE SUN WAS at its highest point as Rae wandered through the maze of rose bushes, admiring the award-winning flowers in every shade of pink she could think of, and some that she couldn't. When the pinks ended, she followed the red, then white, and finally a glorious display of yellow the soft shade of wild buttercups. She found one of the yellow roses on the ground, left there to die alone and unloved. She picked it up and smiled grimly. Comparing her life to a fallen flower was a new low even for her. She inhaled the sweet perfume, then placed it behind her ear and headed for the fountain.

The day had turned out gloriously warm, and Rae abandoned her blue wrap to the edge of the fountain where she sat on it and leaned her head back to let the cold spray cool her warm cheeks. She leaned back a little further, then a little more and wondered what Emma would think if she were to fall in. Probably have her thrown from the premises for being drunk and disorderly and smiled at the idea. She thought of John and Emma together – him being rough around the edges, and Emma, primped and preened to perfection and full of her own importance. An unlikely couple, and yet the two had dated. What would a man like John see in a woman like Emma? Same thing as any other man she supposed. Emma was attractive, rich, and single, what man wouldn't want to bed her? She sighed and turned to dangle her fingers in the water. That was probably an unfair assumption. According to Alex it was John who had dumped Emma, not the other way round, and what right did Rae have to make such an observation anyway. And more to the point, why did she even care?

Why indeed!

She trailed her fingers across the dazzling surface of the water, distorting her reflection as it looked back at her with the same question she asked herself every day – who are you, and where did you come from?

If I had the answer, I would tell you, she thought.

She straightened up and sipped her drink, eyes closed to the warmth of the sun, just enjoying a quiet moment, tucked away from a party she had no wish to be at. A loud cheer went up and Rae opened one eye to see the string quartet give way to a man in full country attire carrying an electric guitar.

'You might want to take it easy in this sun.'

A shadow fell across her face and she had to shade her eyes to see who it was. 'Oh, it's you,' she said, as John joined her on the edge of the fountain.

'Were you expecting someone else?'

'Hoping is a better word,' she said. 'A waiter would've been good, I'm almost empty.' She waggled her glass in his face and felt her pulse step up a notch as his shoulder brushed against hers.

'Looks to me like you've already had enough,' John said.

'Well that's really none of your concern, is it?' Rae said, amazed at her capacity for rudeness where this man was concerned.

'You could be a bit nicer to me,' John said. 'I did fix your car.'

'And broke into my house.'

'Technically, I let myself in.'

'So that makes it OK?'

'I was trying to do you a favour.'

'Then please don't.'

John narrowed his eyes and Rae glared back. 'You're glowering at me again,' he said.

'I have good reason to,' Rae said. She imagined him falling into the fountain. It would only take a slight push, catch him off guard and then ... splash!

'OK,' John said, holding his hands up. 'You win. I apologise for letting myself into your house, and I'm sorry my dog attacked you. Can we maybe start again, perhaps on the right foot this time?'

Rae eyed him coolly. She wasn't sure why he wanted to bother. She wasn't even sure why she was still being horrible to him.

'Come on,' he said, nudging her elbow. 'Everyone deserves a second chance, don't they?'

Not always, thought Rae. 'Alright,' she said, 'just as long as you promise to keep your dog under control.'

'Agreed, as long as you agree to keep your temper under control.'

'I don't have a temper.'

'You do a little.'

Rae opened her mouth to say something to the contrary, then changed her mind and closed it again. She sighed. 'You're right,' she said, 'I overreacted. But you shouldn't have let yourself in to my house. I mean, who does that?'

'Was that an apology?'

'No.'

'Then I accept.' John smiled and leaned forward to rest his elbows on his knees. 'You know, most women would love to come home to a handsome young man in their living room,' he said.

Rae looked over at the makeshift dance floor where Damien Barnes was doing a drunken version of a line dance. 'You're not that young,' she said.

'But I *am* good looking?' He turned to look at her with one eyebrow raised.

Rae shrugged. 'If you like that sort of thing.' Boy oh boy, was she flirting with him now? She really was drunk.

Another cheer went up from the crowd and both Rae and John looked towards the band stand as Alex, accompanied by

James and two other people Rae didn't know, began what Rae could only describe as a dance-off. 'Have you and Alex been friends long?' she said.

'A while,' John said, 'we met in Edinburgh when I was living there. It was through Alex that I got the job here.'

'I've never been to Scotland,' Rae said, 'my best friend lives there now, just outside Inverness.'

'You lived in Manchester but never visited Scotland?' John said. 'Really?'

Rae shook her head. Grace had spoken of Scotland often, but it had never occurred to Rae to visit, not even when Ronnie moved there.

'You should go,' John said, sitting up straight, 'it's a lovely place.'

'I will, one day,' Rae said.

They both turned back to the commotion on the dance floor, John seemingly lost in his thoughts, Rae sneaking sly glances at him now and then. It was nice, the silence between them. Rather than feeling awkward, it felt ... familiar. She thought of their meeting on the village green, the feeling that they'd met before when he touched her arm. That same feeling washed over her now as she discreetly observed him from the corner of her eye, like slipping into a warm bath. It wasn't just the way his eyes crinkled when he smiled, or the rich, earthy smell of him that reminded her of leather. It wasn't even the way he looked at her, as though they had known each other forever that set her pulse racing. It was more than that, and all those things combined. She knew him, really *knew* him, she just ... didn't remember him.

She watched him closely while his attention was on the dancing (James Bidwell, jacket and tie discarded, shirt sleeves rolled up, attempting a Cossack dance-off with a wiry man in too tight jeans and a dodgy moustache) until he suddenly turned to face her. He smiled and Rae's cheeks burned hot. John didn't say anything, but Rae did the same thing she always did in moments of discomfort and reached for her pendant. The movement drew his eyes to her chest and his expression suddenly changed from one of mild amusement to one of shocked surprise.

At first Rae thought he was staring at her cleavage and didn't know whether to feel complimented or insulted, but then she realised he was staring at her pendant and for some reason that made her even more uncomfortable.

'There you are, I've been looking all over for you.' Emma suddenly appeared in front of them wearing a smile that fell well short of her eyes.

'What do you want, Em?' John said. His tone was clipped, almost hostile as his expression turned to one of impatience.

'I haven't interrupted anything, have I?' Emma said. 'Only the reporter is desperate to get another photo of you John. I tried to put her off, but you know how these people are.'

'Actually,' Rae said, 'I was just leaving,' She stood up, but the moment she did the ground tilted sideways and she sat back down with a thump. John put a hand on her arm, but Rae waved him off. 'I'm fine,' she said, 'just a little too much champagne, like you said.'

'Champagne isn't for everyone,' Emma said. 'Perhaps you should go home and sleep it off. I'll see if one of the staff can drive you.'

'Half your staff are pissed,' John said. 'I'll take Rae home myself.'

'I'm sure that's not necessary—'

'I'm fine, honestly,' Rae said. 'I just need something to eat, that's all.' She stood again, a little steadier this time, and held up a hand when John moved to assist her. 'I can manage,' she said, taking a cautious step forward. The ground remained blessedly still but the sun was unbearably hot. She needed shade, she needed water, and she needed out from under Emma's supercilious glare.

'I'll walk you up to the house,' John said, 'there's water on the terrace.'

'John,' Emma said, 'the photographer—'

'Can wait,' John snapped. 'You can see Rae isn't feeling well.'

Rae felt Emma's stare like a blast of ice-cold wind. 'For goodness sake,' she said, 'I'm not a child. I'll be fine on my own. Go get your picture taken.'

John looked a little hurt by her outburst, and rightly so. If awards were being given out for callous bitches, then she'd be right up there on the tallest podium. But he nodded and released her arm graciously. Rae imagined the self-satisfied smile on Emma's red lips as she walked away but didn't have the guts to turn back and see it.

ONCE AT THE terrace Rae discovered she had no appetite for the smoked salmon pâté nor the poached quail's eggs. Not even the avocado bruschetta that everyone seemed to be enjoying. Instead, she headed through a set of French doors that led directly into the foyer of Carrion Hall. The scent of lavender hit Rae like a perfumed wall but the hallway was blessedly cool and devoid of guests. She sat on the bottom step of a grand staircase that swept up to a wide landing giving access to the east and west side of the Hall. The wood panelling that Emma so disliked covered all four walls on the ground floor, but Rae found she didn't mind it all and hoped that Alex had installed it with the sole intention of displeasing her cousin.

A door swung open to Rae's left and a waitress appeared carrying a platter of pastries in one hand and a tray of drinks in the other. She spotted Rae and offered her both. The food she declined, but the wine she accepted. Alone at last she wandered through the double doors to her right. A brass plate on the door said it was the drawing room and the strong smell of furniture polish suggested it was more a show piece than a room where someone actually lived. It was nice enough as drawing rooms go – extravagantly decorated with overstuffed chairs, antique cabinets and vases that looked like they cost more than your average person earned in a year – but the place gave Rae the chills. A fireplace big enough to step into glowed with slow burning logs, but the room felt eerily chill. A portrait hung above the fire, of a man dressed in jodhpurs and a white shirt open at the neck. He had warm eyes and a kind smile and was leaning against the very fireplace he now hung above. Painting had once been a hobby of Rae's. Grace had suggested it as a way of expressing her emotions when they became too much, and it had given her peace for a while, but when her nightmares began manifesting on the canvas Rae had given it up. She had been average at best, preferring water colours to oil, and felt a twinge of jealousy at the artist's obvious talent. He, or she, had captured something quite remarkable. A moment that felt unselfconscious and spontaneous in a way that Rae could never hope to achieve. It made her feel as though she had just walked in on a very personal moment and was in no doubt that the subject of the painting had known the artist well, perhaps even intimately. She studied his face, his hands, and the piercing blue of his eyes, like glacial waters on a summer's day.

'I see you've found Richard.'

Startled, Rae turned to find Chris stood behind her, an amused expression on his handsome face. 'There's a family resemblance, don't you think?'

Rae nodded and turned back to the painting. He was a handsome man for sure, but not in an obvious way, more charismatic than straight up good looks.

'I'm kidding of course,' Chris said, coming to stand beside Rae. 'Miss Winters, are you drunk?'

'Of course not,' Rae said, 'well, maybe a little, but don't tell your sister, she's already tried to send me home once.'

Chris's eyebrows shot up at that. 'Then what will she say when I tell her you were perving at her father?'

'I was not *perving*,' Rae said. 'I was admiring the painting.'

'If you say so,' Chris said. 'I hear he was a charming and likeable man in life, if not in death.'

'What on earth do you mean by that?'

'If you ever have the misfortune to spend a night or two in the west wing, Miss Winters, then I'm sure you'd soon find out. Richard Ashley is said to roam these halls in search of his lost love. Have you heard about the fire that destroyed most of the Hall?'

'I've read about it,' Rae said, nodding.

'Then you'll know that dear old Aunt Evelyn was a very jealous woman, and when she discovered that her husband was having an affair, she not only stabbed him to death, but set fire to the Hall and locked herself in the attic, thus sealing her own fate.'

'So I believe,' Rae said. She thought of the look on

Emma's face when John had touched Rae's arm. Maybe it ran in the family. 'But isn't he your father too?'

'Same mum, different dads,' Chris said. 'Uncle Richard had more than one affair. Quite the family scandal. Mum didn't know she was pregnant until some time after the fire, but by then she'd already inherited Carrion Hall from Aunt Evie's Will. It seemed only fitting that it should fall to Emma eventually.'

'It can't be easy for you,' Rae said, 'knowing your sister owns all of this.' Tilly had inherited most of Grace's estate, but she knew that if the shoe had been on the other foot, Tilly would have fought tooth and nail to take it from Rae.

'Not at all,' Chris said. 'Emma is welcome to it. There are greater things in life, Miss Winters, than money or bricks and mortar. And now that I have divulged the gruesome truth of the Stanford-Ashley name, it's your turn. Are there any ghosts in your closet that I should know of?'

'None that I'm aware of,' Rae said, which was only half a lie. If any ghosts lurked in her closet, she had yet to discover them for herself. 'And if there were, I'm sure they wouldn't be wandering the halls at night.'

Chris smiled. 'You don't believe in ghosts, do you Miss Winters?'

'I wouldn't say that exactly, but then I haven't ever seen one myself. Have you, *Mr Ashley*?'

'No. But I'm willing to stake one out if you are. We could share a room in the west wing, and maybe a bottle of wine or two?'

Rae laughed. 'I let you persuade me to go riding tomorrow, but I think ghost hunting is pushing it too far.'

'Forget the ghosts then. Just the wine?'

'As tempting as your offer is, the answer's no. In fact, I

think I've had quite enough already. It's high time I took your sister's advice and made my way home.'

'Then let me drop you off,' Chris said. 'My car is right outside, and no offense, but you don't look in any fit state to drive.'

'Well, *no offense*, Mr Ashley, but I believe you've had a drink or two yourself. Besides, I intend to walk home. I think the fresh air will do me good, and if I stay here much longer, I can't promise I won't throw up on your sister's rug, and then where would we be?'

7

Emma kicked off her heels as the last of the guests finally said their goodbyes. The day had gone on far longer than she had planned, and she was absolutely exhausted. Leaving Georgina to oversee the clearing up, she headed upstairs for a much-needed bubble bath and de-stress. The party had gone smoothly enough, with only the odd altercation to deal with and one or two mishaps in the kitchen, both of which could've been easily avoided if only the waiting staff could refrain from drinking the alcoholic beverages. But for now, it was all over and done with. Most of the staff had gone back to their homes, and Georgina once more had the kitchen to herself, which meant that Emma could finally relax.

As she made her way up to the first-floor landing, and across to the east wing bedrooms, Emma thought about John and the way he had looked at Raewyn Winters. Indeed, she had thought about little else all day. Was Raewyn about to become a problem? Maybe. Maybe not. But she was certainly one to watch.

While the bathtub slowly filled Emma unzipped her dress and let it fall to the floor. Tomorrow she would have Henry burn it with the leaves. The dress had cost a pretty penny and had been carefully selected with John in mind. Emma knew his tastes well and silk had always been a favourite. But now the dress was tainted, ruined by the appearance of the harlot and the stir she had caused, no doubt deliberate to cause a scene on Emma's big day. If her intention had been to embarrass Emma, then she had wasted her time and that of the seamstress who had undoubtedly had to alter the dress to accommodate that mountainous chest. But she *had* succeeded in making Emma look foolish, and that was something she could not forgive.

Emma sank into the bubbles, savouring the exotic aromas as the soothing waters slipped over her breasts and up to her shoulders. She closed her eyes and sighed. It would take more than bath oils to ease away the day's tension, but it was a start at least. A smile played across her lips as thoughts of John flitted through her mind. She had invited him without any hope of him actually turning up. It was only fitting, of course, that he should be there to show off his marvellous creations, but it had never crossed her mind that he would take her up on the invite. Gatherings weren't his thing, too many people asking too many questions. He wasn't much of a talker at the best of times, though in the early days that hadn't proved to be much of a problem. The physical side had always more than made up for their lack of conversation. But relationships based on sex seldom lasted, and theirs had proved to be no exception.

She lifted a foot out of the water, admiring her freshly painted toes, then dropped it back in causing a ripple effect so that the water sloshed up to her chin. Seeing John talking with Raewyn at the fountain had grated on Emma like finger-nails down a blackboard. The girl was unexceptional – mousey brown hair poorly styled, and little make-up – not his usual type at all. So, what had he been doing with her? Maybe they had been talking about the roses, or perhaps they had been discussing the weather. Whatever it was it had given cause for John to look at her in a way he had never looked at Emma, and that just wouldn't do.

She reached for the glass of La Grande Dame that waited patiently beside the bath. She had refrained from drinking anything but water throughout the day, preferring instead to observe her guests at their finest and reserve the expensive wine for when she was alone, though in truth, she had secretly hoped that John might join her. Wishful thinking on her part, but all was not lost.

She took a long, slow drink of the fine wine and set the glass back down on the floor. The arrival of the Briar girl had put a spanner in the works for sure. Emma was as certain as she could be that John had not been with anyone else since he ended their relationship. Indeed, the only woman he seemed to spend any time with was Alex, and Emma knew without a shadow of a doubt that Alex posed no threat. Emma had suspected for some time that men weren't really Alex's thing. The girl was pretty enough and had had her fair share of suitors over the years, but none ever stayed longer than a week. Emma smiled as a thought suddenly struck her. Raewyn had been Alex's plus one. Perhaps there was more to their friendship than just friendship. Alex did seem rather smitten with the girl. In fact, the more Emma thought about it the more it made perfect sense.

Didn't it?

She sighed again and snatched back the glass of wine.

She was clutching at straws, she knew. Perhaps it was time to move things along with John. She had waited long enough after all, and neither of them was getting any younger. Maybe she just had to be a little more forthright, take the bull by horns, show him that she wasn't going anywhere and that her feelings for him were stronger than ever. Maybe she should do it tonight, strike while the iron was hot.

She reached for the wine and refilled her glass. There was plenty of time to finish the bottle first. Too many people still milled about the grounds, too many tongues to go wagging back to the village, and Emma had no intention of giving them any more gossip than they had already gleaned from the day. She sank further down into the bubbles and closed her eyes. Night would come soon enough, and she was a patient woman if nothing else. She had proved that much at least over the last twelve months. What did a few more hours matter?

8

Dee stretched out on the bed, satisfied and content. Sex with Chris always left her feeling this way and it was all she could do not to purr. She saw him watching her and trailed a finger seductively along the dark lines of her tattoo. The tattoo was a firm favourite with Chris and never failed to turn him on. He especially liked how the dragon's head reached down into the depths of her belly to breathe its deadly fire into the pits of her womanhood.

'Light one up for me too, will you?' she said, seeing Chris take his cigarettes from the bedside table. She rolled onto her side and lightly stroked his inner thigh. She loved his legs – long, lean and permanently tanned – tennis player's legs, with the stamina to match.

'You don't smoke,' he said, placing a cigarette between his lips.

'First time for everything, or haven't you figured that out yet?'

Chris gave her an impassive look before obligingly lighting another cigarette and passing it to Dee. He leaned back against the headboard and took a long, exaggerated drag of his own before blowing the smoke back out into the cramped space that was Dee's bedroom. Dee sat up, cross legged, and faced Chris. She put the cigarette between her lips and drew deeply, pulling the nicotine deep into her lungs. Chris seemed mildly amused as she blew the smoke back out and smiled triumphantly.

'There's a lot you don't know about me, Christopher Ashley.'

'So it would seem,' he said, casually pulling the bed sheet up over his exposed manhood and knocking Dee's enquiring hand out of the way. Dee tried to push the sheet back down again, but Chris slapped her hand away and gave her a warning look. She pouted but settled for playing with the hairs on his leg instead.

He was frowning again. Deep creases furrowed his brow as he stared at an invisible spot on the bedclothes. 'You're moody tonight,' she said. 'What's wrong?'

Chris ignored her and took another long drag of his cigarette. He exhaled sharply when Dee nudged him in the ribs. 'Leave it out, Dee,' he said. Then with an irritated sigh threw back the cover and climbed off the bed.

Dee watched, mildly amused as he threw open the door letting much needed cool air filter through to the muggy room. She shivered as the cold breeze caressed her naked flesh and flopped onto her back, enjoying how her nipples grew hard to the night's kiss. Chris seemed not to notice. He stood leaning against the door frame looking out into the purple shadows, glorious in all his nakedness and softly lit by the hue of a half moon.

'It's a good job I don't have neighbours,' Dee said, admiring the perfect curve of his arse and the soft, downy fuzz that grew there. She stubbed out the cigarette, wrapped a thin sheet around her body, and moved to join him at the open doorway.

Chris' face was obscured from view, but she knew he'd still be frowning. Something was troubling him tonight and she'd bet anything it had to do with his sister. Maybe turning up at the party had been a step too far. Chris had warned Dee to stay away, even though she'd gone to so much trouble to purchase the exact same dress that miss high and mighty was wearing. But Chris hadn't seen the funny side and had been less than impressed when Dee went against his wishes and turned up anyway. Oh, to see Emma's face would have been a treat indeed, and one that Dee had looked forward to for days, but in the end the humiliation of Chris's sister had played second fiddle to someone else.

Dee had her own reasons for being troubled tonight, though hers were not for sharing. A feeling she had thought never to know again stirred inside her gut like the flutter of tiny wings. She hadn't seen the girl at the party – didn't get the chance to with Chris's swift intervention – but Dee knew she was there as surely as she knew it was more than fate that had brought her back.

'Come back to bed,' she said, rubbing her nose lightly over Chris's shoulder. 'It's getting cold.'

'I'm smoking,' he said, without looking round.

'So, put it out. I'll make it worth your while.'

When he didn't answer Dee opened the bed sheet wide and pressed herself against his back. She pulled the sheet back together in front of him, so they were both locked together, skin to skin, front to back. Holding the sheet closed with one hand she softly glided her other across his chest, caressing the tight muscles there while crushing her body closer to his. Her heavy breasts pressed against the wide arch of his back as she rested her head against his shoulder. She smiled, he always smelled the same, a light mixture of brandy and tobacco, now with the overlaying muskiness from their recent lovemaking. She loved his smell; it was familiar, and she liked that.

Chris was fun. He was handsome, sexy as hell and a much welcome change from the men Dee usually took to her bed. They had been together for more than a year, ever since Chris made himself a permanent fixture at the renovation of Carrion Hall. A renovation that Dee was still coming to terms with. She had known the Hall all her life, had spent a brief part of her youth there before it was burned to the ground, but even now, after all these years, she still struggled to come to terms with what had happened there.

She shrugged off the memory like an old coat and clung tighter to Chris, feeling the breath leave his body as he expelled the last of his cigarette. He flicked the butt out into the night but made no effort to move, instead choosing to stand motionless, staring into the fading light as though there was something to see other than an overgrown garden. Dee wished she could read his mind, but telepathy was not one of her strengths. If it was, then she would not be standing here today. She had learned the hard way to be content with what she had, and while she had no choice but to leave his mind wandering the ether, his body was a different matter entirely. Moving her hand lower she began gently caressing his belly button, twirling her finger round and round the pitted circle, and when he didn't object she moved lower still to entwine her fingers in the damp, curly hairs beneath it.

'I can't stay tonight,' he said.

'Why not?' she whispered, tracing kisses across his back.

'I have somewhere to be in the morning.'

'So. Cancel it.'

'I can't, it's important. I made a promise.'

'More important than me?' When Chris didn't answer she added, half joking, 'better not be another woman.'

'And if it were?'

Dee hesitated for only a second, but it was enough to make Chris's back stiffen. She ignored it and resumed her exploration of the forest between his legs. Their relationship was not exclusive – an unspoken agreement that worked in both their favours – but it wasn't like Chris to be so blatant about seeing other women. Discretion was hardly his strong point, and neither was it Dee's, but they each made a point of never speaking of other lovers and never, ever, rubbing it in each other's faces. Dee's conquests had become less and less since meeting Chris, but she still preferred, when the mood struck, to seek her pleasures out of town. Chris, however, preferred to keep it local, and if the rumours were true then he had bedded half the available women in the Myre, and plenty that weren't. She didn't like it, but neither would she do anything about it. Chris was a good many years her junior and although her potions kept her body firm and akin to that of a woman far younger than her years, as with anything, it wouldn't last forever.

'It's Alex,' Chris said after a moment's silence. 'I promised I'd give her a hand with something tomorrow.'

Young Alexandra Graham, a lady of many talents and friend to all (even Dee, and she could count all her friends on one hand with three fingers missing). 'Then at least come back to bed for a little while,' she said, rubbing herself suggestively against him.

'Jesus Dee,' he sighed. 'You're insatiable.'

'Only with you, my love.' She slid beneath his arm, coming round so that she was facing in front of him. Chris, a good two foot taller than Dee and considerably heavier, looked down at her as she smiled seductively up at him. 'One for the road?'

His brows arched as his eyes slowly roamed over her breasts. He took one idly in his hand and brushed his thumb back and forth across the erect nipple. Dee moaned and let her head fall back, and grinned when he pressed his hardness against her belly.

Without warning, Chris suddenly lifted Dee in one strong, fluid movement and pushed her against the wall. She wrapped her legs tightly around his waist as he buried his head between her breasts, and cried out when he entered her, quick and hard and strong. When it was over, and they were both hot and breathless, he carried her back to the bed and laid her gently down on the covers, and she watched in silence as he dressed, wordlessly kissed her on the forehead and let himself out, leaving Dee to an empty bed and the whispers of the night.

She lay there until the cool air became too much, then grabbed her robe from the floor, stepped into her slippers and padded towards the open door. She stopped short of closing it when she caught movement by the garden wall. The moon was only in its first quarter but still cast enough light on the overgrown lawn to show the animal as it stepped out of the shadows. It crept from the safety of the tall grass and moved cautiously towards Dee, stopping only when it reached the pool of light that spilled from the open doorway. Dee held her breath. Grymlocks were rare creatures, and more often than not, portents of doom. She had never seen one personally but had witnessed the damage a single bite could do. It nudged closer, yellow eyes fixed on hers, and dropped something on the ground from its mouth. Dee gave an involuntary shudder as the teddy bear rolled over into the light. It was old, dirty and scorched, and had one ear missing. The Grymlock backed away and disappeared into the night, leaving Dee to stare at the old bear, its fur still wet from the creature's poisonous saliva. She shivered and closed the door.

The message was clear.

Deliver the girl.

Or die.

9

E mma had been clockwatching for the best part of an hour, waiting until a suitable time when she could slip out unseen and go to John. But despite the alcohol, nerves were beginning to get the better of her. Taking her glass and the bottle of wine with her, Emma quietly left the bedroom and headed towards the west wing, and the only place that gave her any peace. Traversing the length of the attic floor was never pleasant. It was dusty and cold and filled with brooding shadows, but it was a necessary evil to reach her happy place. As was her habit, she locked the door when she entered, feeling as always, the need to protect the space from prying eyes, and began the grim walk to the other side.

The tower was her special place, her haven where she could see all and be disturbed by no-one, and the one place she felt her aunt's diaries would be safe. She sat on the wicker chair, turned on the lamp and wrapped herself in the thick, woollen blanket she always kept there. Then she filled her glass, picked up one of Evie's diaries, and began to read.

Mum and Dad insisted I go to the Ashley Christmas party this year. I tried desperately to get out of it but the whole family was going, and they refused to listen to my excuses. Cady interfered as usual, insisting I wear the green dress that Aunt Charlotte gave me for my eighteenth birthday. It was tight and uncomfortable, but I agreed to wear it just to keep her happy. Cady looked effortlessly gorgeous as ever. I sometimes wonder if we really are sisters.

Carrion Hall looked amazing. Fairy lights hung from everywhere, and a huge Christmas tree had been placed in the middle of the driveway taking up a bunch of parking spaces that made Dad complain more than usual. It reminded me of a picture I'd seen of Times Square in New York. Cady wasn't impressed, but I loved it.

Mum and Dad mingled right away, leaving Cady and I to do our own thing. Cady was in her element, flirting with everything that moved, while I did what I always do, and spoke to no-one. I slipped away unnoticed and went to explore Carrion Hall and its hundreds of rooms, most of which were locked, and somehow managed to get lost. I was beginning to panic when I stumbled upon an open room filled with moonlight and nothing else. It was very peaceful inside that room, and the view from the window took my breath away, so much so that I hadn't noticed I wasn't alone until a man spoke up.

'Breath-taking, isn't it?' he said.

I nodded in agreement. His face was hidden by shadow, but I was quite sure I knew who it was.

'You're Noel's daughter, Evelyn?' he said.

'Everyone calls me Evie,' I replied, 'apart from my Aunt

Charlotte who insists that a person's full name should always be used.'

He chuckled. 'I believe I've met your Aunt Charlotte. A formidable woman.'

'That's putting it mildly,' I said.

He stepped forward into the moonlight then and introduced himself as Richard. But I already knew. We'd met before, three years ago when I was eighteen.

'Would you like a drink, Evie?' He was holding a bottle of wine and offered me his glass, but I refused and said it was probably time I was getting back.

'Don't,' Richard said. 'Stay a while, please.'

Something in his tone made me stay. He sounded sad, lonely, and after all, the quiet of the empty room was far more appealing than the raucous behaviour that was going on downstairs. Richard joined me by the window, and I discovered that he had been up there most of the night, reluctant to endure yet another Christmas party that had been thrust upon him by an aging family member. 'It's tradition,' he said. 'I must uphold the Ashley reputation even though it is all but dead in the water. There are no heirs you see. Once my uncle dies there will be only me and the empty rooms of this godforsaken house.'

I suggested it was perhaps time he broke tradition, and did something simply to make himself happy, upon which he put down his glass, stood and held out his hand. 'Then dance with me, Evie,' he said, 'that would make me happy.'

It wasn't my first dance by any means, but it was the first one that I didn't want to end. Richard had a way about him. He made me feel at ease instead of pressing on me that I was saying the wrong thing, or doing the wrong thing, or thinking the wrong thing. He was kind, and I liked that.

We danced in silence, and when the song finished and another began, we danced again, and again, and again, and again – wordlessly and effortlessly as though we had danced this way a hundred times before.

When the dancing was over, we sat beneath the window while Richard told me about his family – almost all of them dead and he, an only child. And I told him about mine – all alive and stiflingly close. The time passed so quickly and yet also seemed to stand still. It wasn't until Cady came looking for me that we realised how late it really was.

I made my excuses to leave, but as we stood, Richard took my hand. 'Can I see you again, Evie? Tomorrow perhaps?'

I laughed and said tomorrow was Christmas day. 'Then the day after that,' he said. 'I'll take you riding in the snow.'

Cady smiled and answered for me. But even if she hadn't, I would've gladly accepted.

Richard called for me early this morning. Mum and dad weren't too happy. Richard is quite a bit older than me, but they always said I have an old soul and besides, there was nothing they could do about it.

Richard took me riding as promised and even managed to deliver on the snow. We rode all over the Carrion estate, which is so much bigger than I thought, and then continued into Dolen Forest. We stopped at an empty cottage where Richard had arranged for someone to light the fire ready for our arrival. There was a blanket on the ground, a picnic hamper filled with food and a bottle of wine with two glasses. We ate, and drank, and talked, and laughed, and just when I thought the day couldn't be any more perfect, Richard surprised me with a kiss. It was only brief, a peck on the cheek, but I think it was perhaps the most perfect kiss in the world.

Tomorrow we are going riding again, and this time I am

invited to stay for dinner.

Today was even better than yesterday. We went to the cottage again, only this time it didn't end with a kiss. We made love in front of the fire. It was my first time, and I was nervous, but Richard was gentle and considerate and took things slow. I want to tell Cady, but I don't think she'd understand. She'd say we were moving too fast, but I can't wait to see him again.

Today Richard took me shopping. He's having a dinner party on New Year's Eve, just a few friends this time, with me as the guest of honour. He bought me a very expensive dress, long and black and much more daring than I would normally wear, but he said I looked beautiful in it so I will wear it just for him. Mum and Dad think things are moving too fast. We argued, I told them to mind their own business and now I feel bad. I wish they would just be happy for me.

Today is New Year's Eve and I'm nervous as hell. This will be the first time I have had a date for the new year, and I'm worried I will embarrass Richard. What if his friends don't like me? What if I can't hold down a decent conversation? It wouldn't be the first time. Will they think I'm stupid? Will they laugh? Maybe I should cancel!

I'm so embarrassed. Last night was awful. Richard's friends were perfectly nice, but I was so nervous I ended up drinking too much. The last thing I remember was throwing up in the downstairs toilet. I woke up this morning in a guest room wearing one of Richard's shirts. Mrs Carter, Richard's housekeeper, brought me breakfast. It was very kind of her, but I couldn't look her in the eye and she must have thought I was terribly rude. She informed me that Richard had gone for a ride and would be back shortly, but I was too ashamed to wait. I rang Dad to come get me, but it was Cady that picked me up in Dad's car. I guess he just couldn't face me. What am I going to do?

I'm so happy. I feel like the luckiest girl in the world. Richard is so amazing, and I am completely head over heels in love with him. I needn't have worried about yesterday. Richard was only cross that I didn't wait for him to return from his ride. He really is the most wonderful, gentle, caring man in the whole world.

Hello dear diary. I've been far too busy having a wonderful life to write to you lately but thought I should stop by to tell you how happy I am. Cady said I'm like a whole different person since I started dating Richard, and I feel like one too. Even mum and dad have finally accepted that we're together. Life is truly wonderful.

Dearest Diary, I think I may be pregnant. What will Richard say? What will my parents say!

The doctor has confirmed it, I'm ten weeks pregnant. How am I going to tell Richard? He'll think me such a fool. I don't even know if he wants children. This is such a mess.

Guess what my dearest little diary. I'M ENGAGED! Me. Evelyn Stanford. Engaged! I can hardly believe it. I don't know what I was so worried about because Richard was over the moon about the baby. We're going to be married as soon as possible and Cady will be my maid of honour. Mum and Dad were shocked, and maybe a little angry, but they'll come around. I know they will.

A noise down in the attic dragged Emma out of Evie's story. Probably just a mouse, but strange noises were not uncommon in this part of the house and she reluctantly put Evie's diary back on the pile and gathered her empty wine bottle and glass. The founding stages of young love would just have to wait, though it had warmed her heart to read how Evie had felt upon meeting Richard. It was how Emma had felt with John to a degree, though she also knew her love for

John now bordered on obsession. Something she could neither help, nor wished to.

She climbed down the winding staircase of the tower and crossed the attic floor swiftly, not wishing to linger. She could navigate the floor with her eyes closed if she so wished, but it was creepy enough without the adding to the drama. The prickling sensation of being watched was ever present and had become almost commonplace, yet it still managed to quicken Emma's pulse as she walked past the hole in the wall where Evie's diaries and her father's portrait had been discovered. The hole had since been covered up with a tapestry of Cranston Myre. It had been a gift from a local lady who made patchwork quilts and embroidered cushions, but Emma had thought it ugly and decided the best place for it was up here where no one would have to look at it. It served a purpose by hiding the gloomy hole where Evie, in her madness, had hidden the two most precious things she owned, but even covered up, the hole still managed to draw Emma's eye like a magnet.

It was quite by accident that the hole had been discovered. When she had been cleaning out the attic with Alex, a rather old and ugly grandfather clock had been knocked over and fell against the wall. The bricks, hastily placed to hide the painting and diaries, had given way easily and the atmosphere in the attic had never been the same since.

But as always, Emma reached the other side of the attic without incident and locked the main door as she left. She padded quietly down the few steps to the second door, the one that would take her out onto the first floor landing, but stopped with key in hand when there was a dull thud on the door behind her.

The west wing was well known amongst the staff for

unusual noises. Some even claimed to have seen her father walk the corridors while others complained of hearing a baby cry, but Emma frequented the west wing more than most and had never heard so much as a whisper except for when she was inside the attic. Up there, where Evelyn had died, she sometimes thought she heard voices – her name spoken mostly, but once or twice she'd caught the name of another drifting from behind the tapestry. She reminded herself of this as she climbed back up the stairs and took a deep breath before turning the key.

The air inside the attic was eerily still, more so than usual, but it was otherwise just as she had left it. She scanned the room slowly, refusing to give in to the jitters, but could see nothing out of the ordinary. She even made herself look to the tapestry behind which the darkest shadows lingered, but even that offered no sign of a disturbance. She shook her head and tutted – annoyed with herself for letting the attic get under her skin. She turned to leave but stopped when something behind the door caught her eye.

For one heart stopping moment she thought someone was there, but shadows have a way of playing with the mind, and when Emma realised that it was nothing more than a dead bird behind the door, she heaved a sigh of relief. The crow lay still and lifeless, its black wings spread wide as though it had died mid-flight, and Emma nudged it with her foot, half expecting it to move. She frowned and looked to the windows on the other side of the attic. All were closed and there was no other way for the bird to get in. It must have flown in earlier that day, when she had been up here looking for platters. Even so, she couldn't help but think of how Evie had been found and shuddered as she quickly locked the door behind her and hurried down the stairs.

Safely back in her room, Emma sat down heavily on the bed. It was only a bird she reminded herself, and only one. Crows were not uncommon at the Hall, it was named Carrion Hall for a reason after all, but it wasn't just the sight of a dead bird that had gotten under her skin. When Evie's body had been discovered in the attic, the official report was that she had died from smoke inhalation. That wasn't entirely true. Where smoke damage had been considerable inside the attic, the same could not be said of Evie's lungs, at least, what was left of them. An autopsy had showed that Evie had died long before the smoke had reached her, but what it didn't show, what the so called experts had been unable to conclude, was what *had* killed Evie, because when her body was finally discovered, a mass of Carrion Crows were still feeding on her carcass. Somehow, between them, the Ashleys and the Stanfords had covered most of the story up, so the *official* report was smoke inhalation, but the rumour that followed was that Evie had not yet been dead when the crows began their feast.

JOHN'S COTTAGE was the first of two that bordered the west side courtyard. The second belonged to Alex. Both were dark and devoid of life as Emma approached, confident given the lateness of the hour that she would not be seen, but not so confident as to wait for John to open the door. She wore only a trench coat and knee length boots and shivered as she inserted her master key into the lock. She was unsettled, the dead bird in the attic had unnerved her more than she cared to admit, and was in need of comfort more than ever, so taking a deep breath of midnight courage, she opened the door.

Somehow, inside the cottage felt colder than outside as

Emma carefully closed the door behind her. It was deathly quiet inside and so sparsely furnished that it wouldn't be much of a stretch to believe no-one lived here at all. Even the curtains, carefully chosen and hung personally by Emma, didn't look as though they had ever ventured from their silver tiebacks as moonlight poured through the exposed window. John was a man of simple means, Emma had always known that, even loved him for it, but sometimes she wondered if he would be happier living in a tent.

She passed quietly through to the kitchen, careful not to let her boots echo on the wooden floor and headed straight for the staircase that led directly to John's bedroom. Emma had visited the cottage only a handful of times, and none of them by John's invitation, but she had tread the floorboards a thousand times inside her head and knew the way by heart. She tiptoed up the stairs, wincing at every creak and thankful that she had at least insisted that John's dog be relegated to the kennels of an evening. The odds of John welcoming her into his arms were not in her favour. He was as likely to throw her out as to invite her to his bed, but she wasn't going to let a small thing like rejection get in her way now. John's mood had turned sour following the departure of Raewyn Winters, and he had spent the remainder of the afternoon taking his frustrations out on a bottle of whiskey. Emma had been wise enough to leave him in peace – she had witnessed his black moods before and knew better than to pursue him during such moments – but while she knew nothing good would come from her persistent enquiries, it never stopped her wanting to ask what it was that troubled him so.

At the top of the stairs she stopped. Moonlight may be allowed to spill through the downstairs windows, but up here, where privacy was needed, it was cloaked in darkness.

She held her breath as her eyes slowly adjusted to the dark and listened for any sign of movement. When there was none, she quietly removed her boots and dropped her coat to the floor.

Flush with the thrill of what was about to happen, Emma shrugged off the cold like an unwanted jacket. John hadn't touched her in more than a year, but just the thought of his hands on her body sent gooseflesh rippling over her skin. The carpet beneath her feet was cold as she tiptoed across the room, and she was just able to make out the outline of John's bed. She whispered his name, half expecting an angry grunt in reply, but when none came, she moved closer, pulled back the duvet, and climbed between the cold, cotton sheets.

It took a moment for it to register that the bed was empty, and when it did Emma yelled her frustration. She jumped up and threw back the curtains letting moonlight spill into the room. The sight of a perfectly made bed only confirmed what Emma already knew – that John had not been home that night. Indeed, the only wrinkle in the sterile room was the imprint where Emma had just lay. She took a deep breath and blew it out slowly in an attempt to curb her anger. It was past midnight, where the hell could he be? As if answering her call a fox cried out in the distance and Emma turned her gaze towards Dolen Forest. Out there, just beyond the borders of the Carrion estate, was The Briar, and if Emma was foolish enough to bet her life on anything, then she would bet it on John being there.

She closed the curtains and retrieved her coat and boots, cheeks flushed with foolish pride and heart aching with jealousy. Clearly, she had underestimated the exchange by the fountain.

A mistake she would not make again.

10

R ae was drowning in a lagoon of the most perfect shade of blue. Suspended just below the surface she was unable to rise or fall, breath held tightly in her chest as she watched the glorious display of a great black Thunderbird. It swooped towards the water's edge, each time turning just before breaking the surface to spread its mighty wings and glide gracefully by. Rae had watched the display over and over again, unable to tear her eyes away from the bird as it soared high into the sky, only to turn and dive once more. She tried to reach out to it but found her hands were tied behind her back, and when she tried to kick herself above the surface, she found that her feet too, were bound tightly. As she finally ran out of air and her lungs burned with the desperate need to draw breath, the Thunderbird swooped again, its radiant eyes locked on hers, enormous clawed feet reaching down towards her, and then ...

Rae woke with a start, throat like the Gobi Desert and a tongue as rough as sandpaper. A dull pain throbbed at the base of her skull as she swung her legs over the side of the bed and ran her hands over her face. Why oh why had she insisted on drinking so much last night? The champagne was bad enough, but the half bottle of wine she cheerily downed when she got home didn't seem like such a great idea now. She rubbed the back of her neck and rolled her head from side to side, trying to dislodge the alcohol induced brain fog. Not much hope of that. Still half pissed and shivering in her underwear, she grabbed her dressing gown and headed for the bathroom.

Thoughts turned to John as she emptied her bladder and she rubbed the tips of her fingers over her temples, berating herself for letting him get into her head again. He was just a guy who looked vaguely familiar and had managed to get under her skin – nothing more than that, and certainly no-one to get hung up about. She washed her hands, drank from the tap, and headed back to the bedroom.

On the floor by the bed lay her crumpled dress where it had been discarded the night before. On top of the dress lay her necklace. She picked it up and tied the leather strap around her neck. She hated not wearing it. The weight of the crystal against her chest always made her feel safe, less alone … somehow. She shivered, pulled her dressing gown tighter and climbed back into bed. The clock on the bedside table read 3.15am. Less than four hours until she had to get up. She plumped her pillow, snuggled into it, and pulled the covers high … and that's when she heard a whisper, coming from the corner of the room.

'Augustine.'

Rae bolted upright in bed and switched on the bedside lamp, but even as her eyes scanned the room her brain told her there was no-one there. She had imagined it, a trick of the mind as it settled in for the night. But the tiny hairs on the back of her neck disagreed.

The baseball bat she had accepted at Ronnie's insistence was propped up beside the bed. She had laughed it off when Ronnie gave it to her, 'for protection' she had said, but as Rae slid from beneath the bedclothes it was the first thing she reached for.

Shadows lurked in every corner of the room like great hulking monsters, not moving, just watching – all except for one. Something moved between the wardrobe and the wall. It was only a slight shift, barely anything at all, but enough to draw Rae's eye and send a shiver down her spine. *Monsters don't exist*, she told herself, isn't that what parents tell their children when they put them to bed at night? When they close the wardrobe door and check beneath the bed. It's what Grace would tell Rae when she awoke screaming in the night, terrified of the dark. But people could be monsters too. Hadn't Rae done something monstrous to Darryl? So when her eyes settled on that particular corner of the room, and the shadow began to grow, rising upwards just like the figure of a man rising from a crouched position, Rae's stomach clenched like a closed fist and a cold sensation crept like icy fingers down her back.

The shadow grew bigger and bigger, then drifted over to hover by the window – not a man, but a swirling black mass shaped like a man. Rae held the bat steady in front of her as she took a step backwards, but the black mass moved with her, gliding through the bed as though it wasn't even there. She turned heels and bolted for the door, caught the handle and pulled only to have it wrenched from her hand and slammed shut in her face.

Then the lights went out.

Panic swelled like an inflated balloon as Rae threw her back up against the wall. *Get a grip*, she thought, *it's just a dream, just another dream*. She felt for the overhead light switch, found it, and turned it on.

Nothing happened.

Shit!

Her breath came in short, sharp gasps and was the only sound in the too quiet room, but she didn't need to hear him to know he was still there. *Him?* She thought. Was it a him? Or was *it* simply an it? Whatever it was, it was watching her ... *observing* her, and the thought made her heart beat so hard she thought it might break a rib.

With the wall firmly at her back, Rae edged around towards the bedside table where she knew she'd left her phone. She reached the corner, edged a little further, reached the table and fumbled with the lamp switch, but the lamp was just as dead as the overhead light. She grabbed her phone and pressed the button, then remembered she'd switched it off when she came to bed last night (why the fuck did she do that?) A sliver of light suddenly appeared through a break in the curtains, then disappeared again as though someone had briefly brushed past them. Rae held down the on button just as a cold breeze lifted the hairs on the back of her neck. She jumped, swung the bat around but hit nothing. Blood pounded in her ears as she put the phone down and gripped the bat with both hands while she waited for the ancient piece of crap to come to life. The room was so still it was as though the air had been sucked right out of it, then something that felt very much like a cold finger brushed across her cheek and she screamed. She swung the bat again, hit the lamp and sent it careering across the bed together with the baseball bat that was suddenly yanked from her hands. She grabbed for the phone, knocked it on the floor, fell to her knees scrambling in the dark (it had to be there somewhere, fuck fuck fuck), found it and picked it up just as the screen came to life. A burst of artificial light illuminated the short distance between the bed and the floor, and when Rae looked up, she saw the face of a man looking down at her.

THE SMELL of burning brought Rae to her senses. The broken lamp was on the bed, along with the baseball bat whose handle was still smoking from the scorch marks left by her hands. She snapped to attention, jumped to her feet and threw the bat into the bathtub.

She doused the smoking bat with cold water whilst trying to make some kind of sense of what just happened. She was still drunk, had to be, or dreaming. Could be an episode of night terrors though? God knew she'd had enough of those as a child, waking Grace up in the night, screaming that there was a man in her room. But that didn't explain the bat, how it had been torn from her hands, or how the handle was scorched black.

She turned off the tap and returned to the bedroom where the overhead light now worked perfectly fine. It had come on the second she saw *him* sat there, looking down at her with those strange eyes of his – golden eyes. She shuddered at the thought, took the lamp off the bed and placed it on the floor. As much as she would've liked to come up with a reasonable explanation, no amount of night terrors was going to explain what had happened here tonight. It was her childhood all over again. The nightmares, hallucinations, the impossible truth that she had burned something with only her bare hands, and now there was golden eyes, a man she felt she knew (just another one to add to her arsenal of strange men that were inexplicably familiar to her). But golden eyes was different (aside from the fact that he wasn't actually real), because when he'd reached down to Rae, palm faced upwards as though wanting to take her hand, she'd seen a mark there, burned into his skin. The very same mark that sat just above her navel.

She closed the bedroom door behind her and let herself into the spare room. She locked it behind her, climbed into bed (light on) and tucked the phone beneath her pillow.

Maybe tomorrow she'd see about getting a dog after all.

11

———

The next morning Rae decided to walk up to Carrion Hall in the hope that the fresh air might clear her head. She followed the fence that bordered the forest until she found a stile right where Alex had said it would be, climbed over it and walked through the grazing fields, head bent to thoughts of last night. All her life she'd suffered from nightmares, night terrors, sleepwalking, waking in the night sweating and screaming, terrified of her own shadow, and it wasn't until Grace gave her the pendant that things had begun to calm down. Over time the night terrors had eventually stopped, the sleepwalking ended, and the dreams had lost much of their potency, but not once did she ever recall anything quite so vivid as last night.

Augustine. That was the name she'd heard whispered. It was also a name she recalled coming from Grace's lips once or twice, but Augustine who? A quick google search had turned up nothing that made any kind of sense, but the name gently tugged at the back of her mind like déjà vu.

All thoughts of ghosts had evaporated with the rising of

the sun. Rae no more believed golden eyes was a ghost than she believed The Briar was haunted, but short of accepting she was completely losing her mind, she was at a loss for any other explanation. But insane or not, the scorched bat could not be so easily ignored, and it clung stubbornly to the fore-front of her mind like barnacles to a rock.

The necklace hung around her neck like a talisman and bumped reassuringly against her breasts as she quickly made her way towards the poplar trees. The trees had already turned a glorious autumn yellow and swayed gently on the morning breeze but did little to lift Rae's spirits. Neither did the unmistakable whiff of horse manure or the sound of raised voices as she drew closer to the stables. Her phone buzzed in her pocket and she reluctantly pulled it out expecting to see another of Darryl's messages, but it was from Alex ...

'feeling rough?'

Then another ...

'turn around.'

Rae turned to see Alex only a few steps behind, decked out in jodhpurs, tailored tweed jacket and riding boots. She grinned broadly and lifted her chin towards the yelling at the end of the tree line.

'I was hoping those two might have run out of air before you got here,' she said.

Rae could see Chris and Emma going at it hammer and tongue, but they were still too far away to hear what was being said, and when Emma spotted them walking towards her, she bristled, spun on her heels and stormed off towards the Hall.

'Has something happened?' Rae said.

'Emma's probably pissy about you coming riding today. I told you she was the jealous type.'

Rae frowned and kicked a stone out of her path. 'Maybe Emma should learn to mind her own business then.'

Alex raised an eyebrow. 'You're a grumpy guts this morning. Late night was it?'

Rae thought of the bat, still soaking in the tub. 'Later than I would have liked,' she said.

'Alone? Or ... perhaps you had a little ... company?'

'Meaning what?'

'Meaning John,' Alex said, 'I want to know every disgusting detail about what happened between the two of you.'

Rae shrugged. 'I don't know where you're getting your information from, but we barely spoke.'

'That's not what I heard,' Alex said, 'a little birdie told me the two of you were very cosy at the fountain.'

'That little birdie wouldn't happen to be Emma, would it?'

Alex pulled a face.

Great, thought Rae. As if she didn't have enough to worry about without some psycho ex-girlfriend on her case. 'John and I spoke briefly and that was it,' she said. 'I went home alone. Ask Chris if you don't believe me.'

'What are you two gossiping about?' Chris said. He was waiting by the end of the tree line, looking dashing in the same rig-out as Alex and making Rae feel rather underdressed in her faded jeans and red hoody. He signalled to a young man stood waiting on the other side of the courtyard and handed Rae a riding helmet. 'Good to see you've sobered up, Winters.'

'Rae was just saying how much she enjoyed the party,' Alex said, 'weren't you Rae.' She winked mischievously before skipping over to the young man who was now approaching with two horses in tow – one chestnut, one dappled grey.

'Glad to hear it,' Chris said. 'Though if you'd hung around a little longer, I might have given you the grand tour.'

'Trust me, I saved us both a world of embarrassment by going home,' Rae said. 'I don't normally drink like that. Two wines are usually my limit.'

'Then that's something we'll have to remedy,' Chris said. 'This is Michael, our stable hand, and this lovely young lady is Daphne.' He stroked the nose of the dappled grey mare, whilst Michael fetched a mounting block. 'I chose her especially for you,' he said. 'She's a gentle sweetheart and happy to take it slow. Perfect for a hangover.'

'That's very thoughtful of you,' Rae said, climbing into the saddle. 'My stomach is eternally grateful.' Chris fixed the stirrup length, and Rae could've sworn she saw him smirk when he reached beneath her thigh.

'Right then,' he said, 'ready for an adventure, Miss Winters?'

'Ready as I'll ever be,' Rae said, 'as long as Daphne remembers this is not the grand national.

'Daphne will follow the other horses, so you've nothing to worry about,' Chris said, 'and there are sick bags in the saddle, just in case.'

'Ha ha,' Rae said. 'Can we just get moving before I change my mind?'

DESPITE HER LACK OF EXPERIENCE, Rae soon relaxed into the gentle rhythm of Daphne's gait as Chris led the way on a magnificent black stallion called Jericho. Alex fell back to walk beside Rae on the chestnut mare as they crossed the grazing fields towards the forest.

'So, what *were* you and John talking about at the fountain then?' she said.

'Nothing?' Rae said, already tired of being interrogated. 'I imagine he was glad to see the back of me.'

'Not the impression I got,' Alex said. 'I think he has quite the thing for you.'

'You'd both do well to steer clear of him,' Chris said.

He pulled Jericho back to walk alongside Alex, as Alex mouthed the word 'jealous' to Rae. 'And why is that?' she said, 'what words of wisdom do you wish to impart on us today, Master Ashley?'

'The guy is bad news,' Chris said, 'he has no respect for women, or anyone else for that matter.'

Alex laughed out loud. 'Pot and kettle springs to mind. You probably don't even know the names of half the women you've slept with.'

'Half the women I've *dated* haven't been to prison.'

'That you know of,' she scoffed. 'Go on then, I'll bite. What did John do that's got your knickers so twisted?'

'Grievous bodily harm, amongst other things,' Chris said. 'His real name isn't even John, it's James, James Harvey Baxter, born to Frank and Miriam Baxter who both live on the east coast in Northumberland. He had a brother, Ben, who disappeared when John was only eighteen. Attended Edinburgh School of Horticulture when he was nineteen, got expelled when he had an affair with his tutor and broke the nose of another. Moved from place to place after that, held down one dead-end job after another until he finally met Emma.'

'I didn't ask for a biography,' Alex said. 'Last time I checked bumming around wasn't a crime.'

'No, but attacking a policeman is,' Chris said. 'When he was twenty-four John got into a bar fight with two men. He broke the arm of one, bit a chunk of ear from the other, and head butted the arresting officer. He spent eight months in Durham Prison before moving back to Edinburgh, after which he pretty much fell off the radar, until now.'

'And your point is?' Alex said.

'My point, dear, sweet, naive little cousin, is that John is a loose cannon. Unpredictable at best and not deserving of your affection.'

'And you know all this how exactly?'

'I have my ways,' Chris said. 'You don't think I'm going to let my sister date some random cowboy without knowing something about him, do you? Besides, Emma had just become a very wealthy woman. He could've been any old arsehole out to make a quick buck. As it turns out, I was right … he is an arsehole'

'I can't decide whether that's creepy or you're just an over-protective brother?' Alex said.

'Neither,' Chris said. 'I would do exactly the same for either of you two.'

'Oh. Please don't,' Alex said. 'And if you recall, it was John that ended the relationship, not Emma, so that puts paid to your gold-digging theory.'

'And look at him now,' Chris said, 'a well-paid job, free accommodation. He hardly suffered from his dalliance with my sister, did he?'

Alex laughed out loud. 'Dalliance? Did we just step back in time by a few hundred years?'

'You may mock,' Chris said, 'but mark my words, John is trouble.'

WHEN THEY REACHED the fence where the grazing fields ended and Dolen Forest began, Chris dismounted, opened the gate and led everyone through. 'It's pretty much plain sailing from here on in,' he said, climbing back onto Jericho and pulling the horse level with Rae. 'But the path gets narrower as we go so it'll have to be single file once we reach Old Man's Grave.'

'Old Man's Grave?' Rae said, 'that sounds ominous.'

Chris smiled wickedly. 'It's the hollow trunk of a wych elm where a body was found some years ago. The initial theory was that it was an old man, but later investigations suggested he was in fact quite young and the cause of death could not be determined. It was as though the life had been sucked right out him.'

'Which is completely untrue,' Alex said, falling in beside Rae.

'Not so,' Chris said. 'There were plenty of witnesses when he was discovered. His chest was laid open wide and most of his organs removed. Some say a wild animal had eaten them, but others say they were used for dark magic.'

'Don't listen to him,' Alex said. 'It was later proved to be a large dog, you know ... one of those big grey ones.'

'A dog?' Rae said. 'How do you confuse a dog with a person?'

'My thoughts exactly,' Chris said.

'You don't,' Alex said. 'But when did the truth ever get in the way of a good story?'

'And there are many more just like it,' Chris said. 'This

forest is riddled with gruesome tales of murder and black magic.'

'All of which we won't be telling the guests, when and if we ever have any,' Alex said. 'Not unless we want to scare them off, isn't that right, Christopher?'

'Probably not,' he said, grinning, 'though in my experience, the more macabre the better.'

Alex fell back as the path began to narrow, leaving Chris to ride alongside Rae. 'So, Miss Winters,' he said, 'what brings a sophisticated woman like you to dreary old Cranston Myre?'

'Sophisticated?' Rae said. 'Why Mr Ashley, I do believe you have mistaken me for someone else. There isn't a sophisticated bone in my body.'

'You discredit yourself, Miss Winters,' he said. 'You have more charisma in your little finger than most of the inhabitants of the Myre put together. You're a little shy admittedly, but charmingly so, and I suspect beneath the coy demeanour is a woman of great passion. Tell me if I'm wrong.'

'You are most definitely very wrong.'

'Modest too,' Chris said, 'I like it. But I think perhaps I glimpsed the real Miss Winters yesterday. I very much enjoyed the company of the drunken woman drooling over my sister's late father.'

'I'm afraid she's been locked back in her box,' Rae said. 'Drinks far too much and has been known to act foolishly, especially under the influence of alcohol.'

'Is that so?' Chris said. 'Then might I suggest you drink a little too much more often.'

'Don't mind me back here,' called out Alex. 'You two go right ahead with your flirting, I'm fine on my own.'

Chris smiled broadly, winked at Rae then kicked Jericho

on so that he was once again in the lead leaving room for Alex to pull up from the rear. 'Is that better?' he called over his shoulder.

'Much, thank you,' Alex said. 'If I can protect just one innocent female from your bullshit then my job here is done.' She turned to Rae and shook her head. 'Honestly, if he put as much effort into the stables as he does chatting up women we'd have the business up and running by now.'

'I can hear you,' Chris said.

'You were meant to,' Alex said.

DESPITE HERSELF RAE began to relax as the horses ambled through the forest at a hypnotic rhythm, the ground soft beneath their feet and the air redolent with the sweet smells of autumn. She lifted her face to the sky, eyes closed to the dappled sunlight, lungs full of crisp country air. It was a moment of absolute tranquillity that the others must have felt too as conversation ceased to be necessary and silence became their new companion. The horses plodded on unawares, their hooves silently moving through the fallen leaves as a sense of calm came over Rae. She watched the treetops sway on the breeze and allowed them to lull her into a state of equilibrium like nothing she had felt before. Trusting in Daphne to lead the way, she let her mind wander and her soul reach out to the forest and was vaguely aware that Alex had moved up front to begin a discussion with Chris. They were talking about shrubs and different varieties of fern, but the sound of their voices was oddly distant, as though Rae were listening to them from down a very long tunnel. At the same time the drilling of a nearby woodpecker became thunderously clear, as did the scurrying feet of a squirrel as it scampered up a tree. Rae felt at one with the forest, a feeling so visceral as to be almost ineffable. Even Daphne seemed to sense it as her swagger slowed to the gentle sway of the trees.

Without intent or desire Rae had reached a place within herself that she never knew existed, a place where spirit and nature harmonised, and the complications of the physical life ceased to be of relevance or concern. A thought came to her unbidden then, that her life needn't be the convoluted mess that dominated her every waking thought, and that the future need not be marred by her past mistakes, as terrible and formidable as they were. There was balance to be had, a way to purge herself of the guilt and feeling of dread that followed her around like a skulking shadow, and a way to restore the equanimity that had eluded her since the death of Grace. The balance was out there. All she had to do was find it.

Then just as suddenly, everything changed.

A shift in the atmosphere, almost imperceptible in its subtleness, that gave rise to the hairs on Rae's neck. Daphne stopped and seemed to stiffen as Rae looked about, holding her breath as all around her the forest seemed to do the same.

Then there it was ... the soft, muted thud of another's heartbeat.

If Alex or Chris noticed it too they gave no indication as their conversation continued up ahead, and if not for the curl of Daphne's lip and the irritated flick of her tail Rae might have thought it only her imagination.

But it wasn't. It most definitely wasn't.

The sound was unmistakable, though the improbability of it was not lost on Rae. There was no-one else around other than their own little party and unless someone had wandered close by holding a foetal monitor then the chances of Rae hearing a heartbeat was unlikely to say the least. But there it was, clear as a bell, and if she was not mistaken, picking up speed.

She looked to Chris and Alex, but they were each caught in a heated discussion that Rae could no longer hear. Then suddenly she saw something, just beyond a hedge of hawthorn. The deer looked at Rae with only casual interest before returning its head to the leafy bush from which it was feeding, but it was one of the most beautiful things she had ever seen. Its thick white coat provided little camouflage against the varying greens and browns of the forest, yet the deer seemed not to care as it happily grazed, ignoring Rae now that it had perceived her as little or no threat. Rae watched on, mesmerised by its beauty, awed by its grace and grateful for the never-ending delights that the forest had to offer. Then, without warning, the deer suddenly lifted its head, sniffed the air, and was gone. A huge smile broke over Rae's face as the subtle sounds of forest life gradually returned and Rae found herself once more within earshot of Alex's raised voice. She was telling Chris he knew nothing about the medicinal qualities of horse chestnut and would be best off letting her do all the talking on their future treks. Rae smiled and clicked her tongue to move Daphne along. The path was already narrowing down to single file with the undergrowth becoming ever denser and making the path less obvious to follow. Chris and Alex were getting further and further away, seemingly oblivious to Rae having fallen so far back, but Daphne refused to move.

The horse raised her head and flicked her ears as she snorted her displeasure. 'What is it girl?' Rae said, stroking Daphne's neck and trying to soothe the agitated horse.

Daphne shook her head and stamped the ground as something moved amongst the carpet of ferns. Rae just caught a glimpse of black fur before Daphne suddenly reared up. The horse bolted into the trees, and it was all Rae could do just to hold on as Daphne veered left and right, gaining momentum where nature allowed, jumping over logs and whizzing past branches. Rae clung on for dear life, head bent to the horse's neck, tugging on the reins when she could, praying she wouldn't die when she couldn't, but Daphne just kept right on running, heedless of the rider glued to her back. Tree after tree flew by, and Rae thought about throwing herself from the horse's back, but the trees were too dense, the horse too fast, so she clung desperately on, fearing for her life until suddenly, out of the blue, the trees parted and Daphne came to a skidding halt. Rae was catapulted into the air and landed heavily on the ground like a discarded sack of spuds.

She lay amongst a mulch of dead leaves, gasping for air as her diaphragm violently contracted. *Gentle sweetheart my arse!* she thought, and sat up to tell the horse exactly what she thought of it only to find that Daphne had taken off.

Wonderful!

She turned her attention to the underside of her arm where it was bleeding profusely, probably needed stitches, and with any luck, soon to be infected given the state she was in. The rest of her seemed basically OK other than a few scratches and bruises, but when she tried to stand up a spike of white-hot pain shot through her ankle.

Fantastic!

By some weird coincidence, Daphne had dumped Rae at the clearing, and the giant branches of the oak tree seemed to reach out to her as though welcoming her back. The thought sent a shiver down her spine, but visions of hot bearded men was infinitely preferable to being dumped in a pile of dead leaves with God only knew what crawling amongst them, and with that in mind she quickly scrambled onto her left foot and hopped towards the tree.

A cold wind blew through the clearing, closely followed by a distant roll of thunder as Rae lifted herself onto a branch. Overhead fat bellied clouds inched slowly across the sky, and as Rae reached for her phone – realised that not only was the phone missing, but so too was the pocket it had been in – the first drops of rain fell.

Perfect!

She scanned the area for a piece of wood large enough to act as a make-shift crutch. The cottage couldn't be more than a fifteen-minute walk from here, more if she was hobbling, but definitely doable and better than hanging around waiting to be rescued, but there was nothing obvious that she could use. She carefully lowered her foot to test it, but the second her boot touched solid ground she was rewarded with another shot of pain.

Then it began to rain.

Sheets of ice fell from the sky, and if that wasn't bad enough, Rae had to inch right up to the trunk to have any hope of shelter. But whilst the tree vibrated softly beneath her, it seemed there were to be no visions today, and thankfully, no sign of the wolf either, though she would've gladly taken either of those things over the freezing cold that was slowly eating its way into her bones.

She consoled herself with the knowledge that Chris and Alex couldn't be far away, and all she had to do was hunker down and wait. But minute after minute passed by and each time Rae thought she heard someone coming it turned out to be just the wind. She hugged herself tightly, shivering beneath the thin fabric of her jumper, and waited.

And waited.

And waited.

It began to dawn on Rae there was a very real possibility that she would have to rescue herself, crutch or not. Crawling was out of the question, which left hopping as her only other viable option. It wasn't ideal, and she wasn't even sure she'd make it, but anything was better than waiting for hypothermia to set in. She readied herself for the inevitable shot of pain as she dropped off the branch but stopped when she heard something over the roar of the rain. She had to strain her ears to hear it, but there it was again, a dog was barking.

She yelled out and was flooded with relief when her name was called back. 'I'm over here,' she shouted, 'in the clearing, by the tree.' She expected Chris to come bounding over, awash with relief at having found her alive, and couldn't decide whether she was pleased or disappointed when it was not Chris but John who stepped from the trees looking less relieved, and more annoyed. Bart was by his side, dripping wet but full of slobbering kisses as he bounded over to greet Rae.

'What the hell were you thinking?' shouted John, as Bart shoved his wet nose into Rae's hand. She shoved it away, but Bart persisted, trying to lick the blood that had crusted on her arm. 'We've got people out looking for you everywhere.'

He had a face like thunder and glared at Rae as though she'd deliberately set out to ruin his day. Whatever she had been expecting of her rescuer it certainly wasn't this. 'I didn't do it on purpose,' she yelled back. 'The horse bolted.'

'And where is the damn horse?'

'How should I know?' Rae said. She wanted to tell him to stick his crappy rescue up his arse, but the thought of staying out here any longer was even less appealing than John's bedside manner.

'Are you hurt?' he said, 'is anything broken?'

'I don't know,' Rae said, 'I can't put any weight on my ankle.'

John removed his coat. 'Put this on,' he said.

'You keep it,' Rae said, 'I'll be fine.'

'Just put it on, Rae,' he said, then crouched down to look at her feet. 'Which one is it?'

'Which one is what?'

'Which ankle is hurting?'

'This one.' She raised her right leg, wishing it had been Chris who had come to rescue her after all. She threw John's coat around her shoulders and winced as he tried to move her foot.

'I need to remove the boot,' he said, placing one hand behind her knee and the other over the zip.

'What? No. Leave the boot where it is. I'll be fine if I can just—'

'Broken or sprained, the ankle will be swollen. We need to get the boot off and see what we're dealing with. Hold steady and I'll be as careful as I can.'

Before Rae could object John had unzipped the boot and began to pull. It hurt. It hurt a lot, and she was uncomfortably aware that she had grabbed John's shoulder and was gripping the hard muscle there like a clamp. He seemed not to notice as he carefully removed the boot and examined her ankle.

'Can you move it?' he said.

Rae managed a small, circular movement before crying out in pain.

'It may just be a sprain,' he said, 'but either way we need to ice it before the swelling gets any worse. Ready?' He stood up and held out the boot, and as Rae took it from him he slipped his arm around her waist and hooked his other beneath her knees.

'What are you doing?' Rae said, throwing her arm round his neck for balance as John lifted her from the branch.

'What does it look like?'

'You can't carry me all the way back to the cottage,' she said. 'Put me down, all I need is your arm to lean on and—'

'I can throw you over my shoulder if you prefer,' John said. 'Or I can dump you on your arse and leave you here, your choice.' He stood there waiting, rain sluicing down both their faces.

'Fine,' Rae said, 'but be careful, it looks really muddy.' John gave her a sore look but was mindful of anything that might knock Rae's foot as he carried her into the trees, for which she was most assuredly grateful, even if she was having a hard time showing it. 'How did you even find me?' she said. 'I didn't think anyone else knew about this place.'

'I didn't,' he said breathlessly. 'Bart found you.'

'Is Alex out looking for me?'

'Amongst others.'

'And Chris?'

'Are you going to ask questions all the way back or do you think you might give me a chance to breathe, you're not exactly a lightweight!'

Rae scowled. It was on the tip of her tongue to tell him to put her down so she could walk, all she needed was a bit of support and she'd manage just fine, but his threat of dropping her in the mud still lingered between them and given his current state of mind she had no doubt he would do just that.

He carried her all the way home, through the back door that she'd forgotten to lock, and placed her carefully down on the couch. Then he disappeared, returning a moment later with a blanket, paper towels, antiseptic cream and a bandage. Rae thought to comment on how well he knew his way around her house but thought better of it.

'You're soaked through,' John said, 'get undressed while I fetch some ice, then we'll look at that arm.'

Bart stood guard while Rae slipped out of her clothes beneath the blanket. 'And what are you looking at?' she said, pulling tongues as the dog cocked his head to one side. He padded over to sniff her discarded boots and she shooed him away with her good foot just as John returned.

'Drink this,' he said, handing her a cup of something hot and steamy. 'It's chamomile, might help with the swelling.'

He propped her ankle on top of three cushions then placed a bag of frozen blueberries on top. Rae gasped from the cold but made no word of complaint as John turned his attention to her arm. The silence stretched between them as he cleaned up the blood, smeared cream over the wound, and wrapped the bandage like a pro. Then he turned to Bart. The dog had already shaken himself off when they entered the cottage, but now John used one of Rae's best towels to dry him down. She bit the inside of her mouth as he dropped the filthy towel on the floor, wet and full of dog hair. 'Thank you,' she said, trying, and failing, not to sound sarcastic.

John moved to the fire and began stacking kindling. The weather seemed to be getting worse outside and Rae could only imagine the sorry state she'd have been in if John hadn't shown up. 'There's a dryer in the kitchen if you want to throw your clothes in it,' she said, helpfully. John didn't answer, only threw paper on the fire before lighting a match. The fire went up with a roar and he threw on a couple more logs before closing the door and turning to Rae. His face was grim as he stripped off his t-shirt and laid it on the rug by the fire.

'You said there were others looking for me,' Rae said. He was toned, and strong, and had a large scar down the centre of his chest. 'Maybe we should let them know I'm home?'

'They know,' John said, 'Alex will be here shortly to take over.'

'I hardly think I need babysitting,' Rae said. Did that sound ungrateful? Judging by the look on John's face, yes it did. She bit her lip as he turned back to the fire. Why was he so angry? She didn't ask to be rescued! 'Look, if you want to go, I'm sure I'll be fine—'

'Stop talking for a minute, would you?' he said. He bent down on one knee and prodded at the burning logs as though they too personally had offended him.

Rae opened her mouth and was about to tell him to sod right off, and where did he get off speaking to her like that, when he suddenly stood up and came to sit beside her on the couch. She shifted uncomfortably beneath the blanket when his hip brushed her thigh before he leaned forward to scratch behind Bart's ears.

'You were lucky today,' he said. 'It could've ended much worse for you.'

'I realise that,' Rae said. 'But you make it sound as though it was my fault.'

'Horses don't just bolt,' he said. 'Something must have spooked her.'

'Something did,' Rae said, 'a wolf, a bloody great big one.'

'There are no wolves in Dolen Forest, Rae.'

'Are you calling me a liar?'

John sighed. 'You saw it yourself?'

'I saw a glimpse of it,' Rae said, 'and it's not the first time I've seen it.' She immediately regretted her words and shoved her face into the chamomile tea. She didn't want anyone else to know what had happened at the tree, not yet.

John narrowed those blue-grey eyes of his, then turned back to Bart. 'Like I said,' he said, 'there are no wolves in Dolen Forest.'

'And I know what I saw,' Rae said.

'*Think* you saw.'

'So, you *are* calling me a liar?'

'I'm saying you must be mistaken,' John said. 'It was probably a dog.'

It was on the tip of Rae's tongue to say it was no fucking dog that she saw, but John spoke first. 'The forest is a dangerous place, Rae. You'd do well to remember that.'

Rae groaned loudly and put her cup on the floor. 'If one more person tells me that I think I might actually scream.'

'Then maybe it's time you started listening.'

'And maybe you should mind your own business.'

'If I had, then you'd still be sat in that tree.'

They glowered at each other until Rae finally relented and looked away. 'I *am* grateful to you for finding me,' she said, 'even if it doesn't seem that way.'

'You're right,' he said, 'it doesn't,' and turned back to Bart's ears.

Rae glared at him. 'I didn't set out this morning with the intention of getting stranded in the forest you know, and if you're that offended then why don't you just bloody well leave?'

He stiffened, but when he next spoke his voice was a little softer. 'What if I tell you there's more to the forest than you know,' he said, 'and maybe I'm concerned for your safety?'

Rae gave him an incredulous look. 'Surely you don't buy into all this bullshit about black magic and dead bodies?'

'People have been going missing in these woods for years,' he said, 'what makes you think it's any different now you've turned up?'

'In that case why aren't people shouting from the roof tops to stay away if it's so damn dangerous?'

'Because if people really knew what went on here there'd be no tourists.' He pulled a soggy piece of paper from his jeans pocket and handed it to Rae.

'What is it?' she said.

'A list,' John said, 'of people that have gone missing in the area over the last twenty odd years. Thirty-three in total, and that's just the ones I know about.'

'I don't understand,' Rae said. 'Why would you have this?' She handed the paper back to John without looking at it.

'I had an older brother once,' he said. 'He was an architect, a good one too, but he decided to take some time out, travel the country, visit old buildings that interested him. Cranston Myre was as far as he got. He met a girl here, decided to stay on a little longer, and that was the last we ever heard from him.'

'Maybe he moved on and just never told you.'

John shook his head. 'That was fourteen years ago. He never left the Myre. His disappearance was investigated by the police and the last person to see him alive was the girl he met. She said he'd been acting strange the last few days they were together and had taken to going for long walks in the forest. That's where he was headed when he never came back.'

Rae didn't know what to say. She knew how hard it was to lose someone you loved. 'Were you close?' she said.

John nodded. 'I was eighteen when he went missing, and I had to watch Ben's disappearance eat away at my parents day after day. It almost killed them. He was smart, well educated, focused – it didn't make any sense for him to just ... disappear.'

'Did the police ever find anything?'

'Nothing,' John said, 'that's my point.' He turned to Rae and leaned his arm against the back of the couch so they were close, too close. 'Every single person on that list travelled through Cranston Myre at one time or another, and every single one of them was reported missing some time later, and the police never turned up a damn thing. I came here because I swore that one day, I would find out what happened to Ben, but when I started digging all these other people crawled out of the woodwork. It's why I came here, Rae, to find out what's going on in these woods.'

'I thought you moved here at Alex's invitation,' Rae said.

'She told me about the job at the Hall,' he said, nodding. 'But only because I was already coming to the Myre. You can see why I want you to stay out of the woods, Rae. It's not safe for you, not until I find out what's going on.'

Why do you even care? she thought. 'Alright,' she said, 'say you find some evidence that the police missed, some vital clue that leads you to what happened to Ben. Then what? It was fourteen years ago. If someone killed him, they're long gone by now.'

'That's where you're wrong,' John said, 'those other people, some of them went missing only a couple of years ago, one of them just last year. Whatever was going on in the forest when Ben disappeared is still going on today.'

'So, what would you have me do?' Rae said. 'I live on the edge of the forest, it's pretty hard to avoid it.'

'Move out,' John said, 'sell this place if you have to, but stay out of the woods.'

'And where would I go? This is my home, John, I'm not going to run away because of a hunch.'

'Then stay with me,' he said, 'at least until I figure this out. I'll take the couch and you can have the bedroom.'

'I'm sure your ex would love that,' Rae said. 'She didn't even like me talking to you yesterday.'

'Pay no attention to Emma, she's ... difficult.'

'Difficult or not, I don't think staying with you would be a good idea. I'm truly sorry about your brother, but it doesn't change anything. I live here, and I'm not leaving because of something that may never happen.'

John frowned. 'You're being unreasonable.'

'Am I?' Rae said. 'I barely know you and you're asking me to move in with you. Don't you think that's unreasonable?'

'God damn it, Rae, are you always this stubborn?'

'Are *you* always so pushy!'

John pushed himself off the couch and went to stand in front of the fire, back to Rae as he ran a frustrated hand through his air. 'There's something else,' he said, 'something I want to show you.' He sat back down next to Rae and showed her the inside of his wrist. There was a scar there, faint, silvery lines that would have gone unnoticed had John not pointed them out.

Rae looked closer and her throat constricted. 'What is it?' she asked casually, though her heart was beating like a jungle drum.

'Don't you know?' John said.

He was watching her intently, studying her reaction and Rae felt herself wilting beneath his gaze. She swallowed. 'Should I?'

His eyes flicked to the blanket where her hand gripped the pendant tightly. 'Maybe not,' he said, 'I just thought ...' he stood up, 'I don't know what I thought. Maybe I should go.' He paused by the fire, tanned skin glowing softly by the flickering light, then turned back to Rae. 'If I ask you a question will you answer me honestly?'

'I'll do my best,' Rae said, pulling the blanket a little tighter.

'It's none of my business, but ... is there anything going on between you and Chris?'

Rae blinked. She hadn't expected that. 'You're right,' she said, 'it isn't any of your business. But the answer is no. I only just met the guy yesterday, what sort of girl do you think I am?' *The sort who tells bare faced lies when she meets someone who might actually know what the fuck is going on,* she thought. *And why? Because she's a goddamn coward.*

'It's not what I think of you,' John said, 'it's him. He's trouble, you should stay away from him.'

'That's funny, because he says the same thing about you.'

'I'm just trying to help,' John said, 'Chris isn't the man you think he is.'

'You have no idea what I think,' Rae said, 'unless you can read minds now, too?'

'I get it,' John said, 'he's charming, handsome—'

'Sounds more like you're the one that should stay away.'

'I'm serious.'

'So am I.'

John gave a frustrated sigh. 'I can see I'm wasting my time.' He picked up his t-shirt and stopped short of pulling it over his head. 'I'm not trying to offend you, Rae, just—'

'You couldn't be more offensive if you tried you arrogant arse,' she said. 'I think you're right. You should leave.'

'Finally, we agree on something.'

Bart suddenly jumped up and ran to the door. A second later the door flew open and Alex swept in on a tide of wind and rain. 'Oh, thank God,' she gushed, 'we've been looking for you everywhere. We found Daphne alone and thought the worst. Are you OK?' She pulled off her boots and removed her drenched jacket before running over to give Rae a hug.

'I'm fine,' Rae said. 'Just a sprained ankle. You on the other hand look worse than me.' Her pink hair was plastered to her head and mascara ran in streaks down her face.

'Not my best look, I'll admit,' Alex said, 'and maybe some mild hyperthermia, but nothing a hot chocky wouldn't cure.' She moved to stand in front of the fire beside John, who had thankfully pulled on his t-shirt and was standing stiffly, with arms folded and still glaring at Rae. Alex looked between them and nudged John lightly with her hip. 'Hey hero, what's with the long face?'

John didn't answer, and Rae breathed a sigh of relief when the door opened again, and Chris walked in. Chris had changed into a long raincoat and looked only mildly flustered as he gave her a peck on the cheek.

'Glad to see you're OK, Winters,' he said, 'Daphne sends her regards.'

'I'll bet she does,' Rae said, 'but I'm glad you found her. She took off right after she dumped me by the tree.'

'Tree?' Chris said, unbuttoning his raincoat.

'The big oak tree? The one in the clearing?' Someone had to know about it other than Rae and John, and if Chris and Alex were doing horse treks through the forest, then surely they knew it inside out?

'Ah, that old thing,' he said, 'I hope you weren't too badly hurt?'

Rae caught a glance between Chris and Alex, but John was too busy making a fuss of Bart to notice. 'Nothing serious,' she said, 'just a sprained ankle.'

John suddenly grabbed his wet jacket that had been slung over the armchair and turned to Alex. 'Make sure she sees a doctor if that ankle gets any worse,' he said, 'and keep an eye on the swelling. You can call me if there's any problems.' He called Bart to his side, but Alex grabbed his arm.

'Wait for just a minute,' she said, 'Chris, before you take your coat off, would you mind popping out to the shed and fetching some more wood for the fire.' Chris glanced at the wood basket that was brimming over with wood, but nodded graciously, pulled up his hood, and walked out the door. 'You shouldn't let him wind you up so easily,' Alex said when Chris was gone. 'You know what he's like.'

'As do you, Alex. The man is trouble.'

'Well as coincidence would have it, that's exactly what he says about you, so it seems like I'm stuck between a rock and hard place.' She sighed at the black look that crossed his face. 'Come on, lighten up,' she said. 'Apart from Rae's hobbled foot no one really got hurt, did they? And anyway, you make such a dashing hero, all wet like that. You've got muscles bulging everywhere. I've a good mind to get lost in the woods myself.'

'Just make sure she stays off that ankle,' John said. 'And keep it iced.'

'I can take care of myself,' Rae said. 'Please stop treating me like a child.'

'Then stop acting like one,' John glared at Rae and she scowled right back.

'Right then.' Alex looked from one to the other. 'Don't worry your pretty little head about Rae. I'll make sure she behaves herself.'

'Call me if there's a problem,' he said, 'I'll be at home all night.'

'I've got your number on speed dial,' Alex said, ushering him to the door. 'I'll let you know if she so much as moves a pinkie.' She all but shoved him out into the rain, then turned to Rae. 'Well that wasn't even remotely awkward,' she said. 'I knew he had the hots for you, but my God, the air when I walked in was positively steamy.'

'That's not what that was,' Rae said. 'We were just—'

'None of my business,' Alex said. 'Now then, what does a girl have to do to get a warm drink around here? Christopher,' she shouted. 'Would you hurry up with that wood. We're dying of thirst in here.'

12

R ae woke to the sound of someone hammering on her door. She groaned, climbed out of bed and opened the bedroom window. 'Who is it?' she shouted, leaning over the windowsill. 'Alex, is that you?'

Chris took a step back armed with a bunch of flowers and a huge grin. 'Not unless she's had a sex change recently. Get up sleepy head, I'm treating you to lunch.'

Rae glanced at her watch. 'Lunch? What time is it?'

'Almost eleven. Are you going to let me in, or should I climb up the trellis?'

'As much as I'd love to see you try,' Rae said, 'I think we'd better stick with the door. Just give me one minute.'

She pulled the window closed, grabbed her robe and ran to the bathroom mirror. Eleven o'clock? How the hell had she slept in so late? Alex had insisted on cooking Rae dinner last night, before hanging around to watch a movie, all on the pretence of a girlie night in, but Rae knew she still felt guilty about the accident, regardless of how many times Rae had reassured her that it was no-one's fault. But guilty or not, by

8pm Rae had kicked Alex out in favour of a hot bath and an early bed. She'd been snoring before her head hit the pillow, which was exactly where she'd still be if Chris hadn't hammered on her front door loud enough to wake the dead.

She sighed at her reflection in the mirror – red, puffy eyes and hair that looked like something even a caveman would be ashamed of. It would take a lot more than a minute to make any improvements on that. She settled for brushing her teeth and a quick attempt at taming the bird's nest on her head. Chris was already knocking again by the time she reached the door.

'Good morning, gorgeous,' he said. 'Going for the natural look today, I see.' He handed Rae the flowers as she stepped aside to let him in. 'By way of apology,' he said, 'for screwing up your day yesterday.'

'You didn't have to do that,' Rae said, 'but thank you, they're lovely.'

'Beautiful flowers for a beautiful lady, and one more gift.' He produced a small white box from behind his back and handed it to Rae. 'I took the liberty of putting my number in, Alex's too.'

Rae opened the box and shook her head. 'Chris, this is too much. It must have cost a fortune.'

'No amount is too much for your safety, Miss Winters. The chance of finding your phone in the woods is slim to say the least, so please accept the phone, if only to make me feel less guilty.'

'You have nothing to feel guilty about,' Rae said. 'It wasn't your fault the horse bolted.'

'I agree,' he said. 'But I did invite you on the ride, and if I hadn't, you'd still have your phone and a healthy ankle, which, by the way, looks remarkably better.'

'Oh. It is,' Rae said, waggling her ankle to prove it. 'I can hardly believe the difference.' Even her arm had healed, leaving not so much as a blemish.

'That's unfortunate,' Chris said. 'I had hoped you might need some assistance in the shower. I even brought my own soap.'

'Very funny,' Rae said, though she wasn't entirely sure he wasn't serious.

'Right then,' Chris said. 'Are you going to get dressed or do I have to take you to lunch looking like that. Bed hair I don't mind, but I absolutely refuse to take you anywhere in your jim jams, charming as they may be. You have fifteen minutes and counting.'

LAST NIGHT's storm had paved the way for another beautiful autumn day, and Rae wound down the window of Chris's car to breathe in the fresh air while he navigated the winding country road. 'Where are you taking me?' she asked, as they sped past open fields fringed by sycamore trees in shades of russet and gold.

'Harleybrock.'

'It's not posh, is it?' she said, 'I'm not really dressed for posh.' She looked down at her black canvas jeans and white long sleeve tee and wondered if she should go back and change.

'Not even remotely,' Chris said, 'Harleybrock is a *village*, not a restaurant. There's a charming little place on the river where I thought we could eat, then if you're feeling up to it, we could visit the carnival if it's still there.'

'Sounds great,' Rae said. She wound down the window and breathed in the sweet smell of burning leaves. She always loved autumn – chilly nights, balmy days and spectacular colours. Granddad had loved it too, though in all fairness there wasn't much that Winston Winters didn't love, especially bonfire night, at least until …

'Penny for your thoughts,' Chris said. 'You're not still sulking over that phone, are you? I can scuff it up if it will make you feel any better.'

Rae blinked and wound up the window. 'I was thinking about my granddad, actually. He always loved this time of year.'

'And what about your parents? Are they still around?'

'Ah, well. It's a bit more complicated than that,' Rae said. 'I don't remember my real parents. I was kind of adopted when I was five.'

'*Kind* of adopted. Is that a legal term?'

Rae laughed. 'Maybe, in some circles, I guess.'

'Have you ever tried to find your real parents? We could be related for all you know! I'm into many things, Miss Winters, but incest is not one of them.'

'I highly doubt it,' Rae said, 'but you never know.' Chris gave her an enquiring glance. 'I was abandoned when I was five,' she said, 'and to cut a long story short, my adopted mother, Grace, took me in and the rest is history. My real parents were never found. I don't even know my birth name.'

'Then how do you know you weren't conceived by aliens,' Chris said. 'You're not hiding scales beneath that shirt, are you?'

Rae laughed. 'What if I were? Would that bother you?'

'I'd think it quite kinky, actually. It seems we have a lot in common. My father decided family life was just too hard and took an extended leave of absence when I was only four. Emma was only six at the time, then five years later our mother, Cadence, passed away from heart disease, leaving Emma and I to be raised by a great aunt with a heaving bosom and an upper lip that would make Thomas Magnum envious.'

Rae laughed. 'Well from one orphan to another, I think we turned out just fine.'

'Agreed, and now that the conversation has taken a decidedly morbid direction, I think it's time to lighten the mood. We're here, and you, Miss Winters, are in for a treat.'

THEY PARKED on the roadside and walked the short distance along the wharf to where The Harleybrock Barge was moored. The deck was littered with fairy lights, and a gang plank with railings draped in burgundy silk welcomed them aboard. Chris took Rae's hand and led her below decks where booth seating ran along the port side and an elongated bar filled the starboard side. Seafaring trinkets hung from the low-slung ceiling and various versions of the ship's wheel stole every available inch of wall space that wasn't already taken with photos of customers at different stages of inebriation.

Chris had reserved them a table at the far end, tucked into a cute little hideaway that fit neatly into the bow and offered plenty of privacy and an excellent view of the murky waters of the River Dyne. Rae squeezed behind the triangular table to sit on a bench seat covered lavishly in purple velour. 'I can honestly say I wasn't expecting this,' she said, running a hand across the black tablecloth embroidered with miniature skulls and crossbones. 'It's like the Jolly Roger meets Zoltar. Have you eaten here before?'

'Many times,' Chris said, 'though never with such exquisite company.'

'Are you going to pay me compliments all day?' Rae said, 'because I still have to get my head through that narrow door.'

'Maybe,' Chris said, 'does it bother you?'

'No.'

'Then stop complaining and let's order.'

The menu was a simple offering of award-winning pies, sausages, cajun chicken and lasagne. Rae had half expected Chris to take her to some fancy French restaurant that served delicacies she'd never heard of, or nouvelle cuisine with portions that wouldn't fill a child. She ordered sausage and mash, whilst Chris opted for the beef lasagne and ordered them both a glass of house wine.

'So, Miss Winters,' he said, settling back into his seat as their waiter took his leave. 'Tell me a little bit about yourself. Why aren't you married with babies yet?'

'Hmmm.' Rae frowned. 'Since you put it like that, I really don't know. Getting married and having babies is, of course, every girl's dream.'

'But not yours?'

'Not really.'

'Then what *do you* aspire to?' He leaned forward, olive eyes like pools of liquid as they stared into hers. 'Surely you don't intend to sit in that little cabin of yours for the rest of your life?'

Rae smirked and sipped her wine. 'I happen to like my little cabin, and yes, for the time being, that's exactly what I intend to do, at least until something interesting comes along.'

'And by interesting, you mean ...'

Rae shrugged. 'I guess I'll know when I know.'

'And the boyfriend,' Chris said, 'what happened to him?'

'Who said there was one?'

'There's *always* a boyfriend.'

'OK, Mr Smarty Pants. If you must know we broke up before I moved here, for reasons I'd rather not go into now.'

'Your decision, or his?'

'Mutual. And what about you, *Mr Ashley*, why isn't there a Mrs Ashley with little baby Ashleys running around?'

'Who said there isn't?'

Rae smiled. 'I suppose she could be the mysterious redhead I saw you with the other day.'

Chris laughed. 'Dee? Most definitely not. Dee is ... she's ... a friend.'

'Just a friend?'

'When it suits.'

'Ah,' Rae said, 'friends with benefits, say no more, though I have to admit I didn't think they actually existed.'

Chris leaned forward and whispered discreetly. 'I wouldn't quite describe Dee like that,' he said, 'at least not to her face anyway.'

Rae smiled. 'Noted, though I hear your sister disapproves.'

Chris sat up and threw his arm over the back of his seat. 'My sister would disapprove if Beyoncé herself begged me to marry her. She's woefully critical of anyone who tries to win her baby brother's heart, so be warned, Miss Winters.'

'You have nothing to fear from me,' Rae said, 'I haven't been single since I was seventeen and intend to enjoy it for as long as I can.'

'Couldn't have put it better myself,' Chris said. He held up his glass and clinked it against Rae's. 'To being single, and long may it last.'

THE DISTANT SOUND of bagpipes brought a smile to Rae's face as she walked down the wharf alongside Chris. Lunch had been delicious; the wine crisp and sweet and the company scintillating. Even Chris's outrageous flirting had become less uncomfortable and more commonplace as the conversation flowed effortlessly. They reached the car but instead of opening the door, Chris looped Rae's arm through his and kept on walking until they reached a green footbridge that crossed over the river. Chris led her across it where they followed a brick pathway that led up and over a hill. At the top of the hill they stopped. Below them was the village green, a much larger version of the one at Cranston Myre, and filled with the kind of childish delights Rae hadn't seen in a long time. Bouncy castles, lucky-dip stalls and dodgems. Trampolines, water games, fair rides and pony rides. There was something for everyone, and if amusements weren't your thing then there was always the beer tent, or cake tasting, or a pie eating contest. There was even a tug-of-war between peopled in fancy dress, and despite it being the middle of the week the place buzzed with laughter and conversation and shouts of joy. It was the carnival, and Rae hadn't been to a carnival since forever.

Rae had a go at the hoopla stall and managed to land two out of three rings on the bowling pins before giving up. Chris tried his hand at Tin Can Alley – shoot down five cans and win a prize. He did it on his first attempt and presented Rae with a stuffed dragon which she then named Elliot after her favourite children's movie, and not, as Chris suggested, after the boy in *E.T.*

There was an inflatable bungee run which Chris insisted they try. Rae refused politely. Two minutes later she was strapped in and running down the runway trying desperately to place her tag further down the line than Chris.

Chris won that too.

Then he suggested they try inflatable sumo wrestling.

'No way,' Rae said. 'I am not getting into one of those suits.'

'Come on,' Chris said. 'It'll be fun. You know you want to.'

The rubber suit was hot, and Rae tried not to think about how many people had been sweating in it beforehand. But Chris was right, it was incredible fun. He won that one too, if you could call it winning. They were both laughing so hard it was impossible to tell. Rae spent most of the time lying on her back like a bloated starfish, while Chris bounced around like a pro.

Hot, exhausted, and thoroughly parched they finally stumbled into the beer tent. 'I don't think I've ever laughed so much,' Rae said, pressing an ice-cold glass of Coke to her hot face. 'My cheeks hurt so much I don't think I'll be able to smile again for a month.'

'I'm glad you enjoyed it,' Chris said, 'but the day is still young. If I've not tired you out, I believe there's bungee jumping down at the wharf.'

'Oh no.' Rae shook her head determinedly. 'Sumo wrestling was one thing, but there is no way you are getting me to do a bungee jump.'

'Not even if I promise a hot tub and a very expensive bottle of champagne afterwards?'

'Not even if you promise to paint my toenails and braid

my hair. How on earth are they doing a bungee jump over the wharf anyway? I didn't see anything when we were down there earlier.'

'They're not.' Chris smiled slyly. 'I was hoping you might agree to skip the jump and go straight to the tub.'

Rae shook her head. 'Do you *ever* give up?'

'Not when I see something I like,' he said. His eyes glistened with mischief and Rae felt a warning flare at the back of her head.

'Single, remember,' she said, 'we toasted to it earlier?'

'That was before I saw you in a sumo outfit.'

Rae laughed, but it was cut short when someone bumped her from behind, knocking the Coke over her chest and rendering her white top practically see-through.

'Don't worry, I'm sure there's something behind the bar to clean it up,' Chris said. 'Don't go anywhere.'

He disappeared before Rae could object. She put the glass down beside Elliot, and whipped out a tissue from her bag, but it was clear there was no salvaging the state of her top and she gave up before she'd even started.

'I see the ankle's better.'

Rae spun round to find John standing behind her looking uncharacteristically smart in a fitted black shirt and designer jeans. His hair, usually unkempt, was neatly brushed back, and even his beard had had a trim. The sight of him stirred up feelings that took her quite by surprise and caught off guard, she found she could only stammer. 'Oh,' she said, 'I ... err ... hi ... yeah ... the ankle,' she looked down and waggled it in front of him, 'the magic of blueberries, eh. Who knew?'

John, still with the same stern look on his face from yesterday, only frowned. 'What about the arm?'

'That's all better too,' Rae said, 'maybe it was your

chamomile tea that did the trick?' She felt bad by the way things had ended yesterday, and thought a little light hearted-ness might break the ice that seemed to have formed between them, but by the look on John's face it would take more than a couple of lame quips. A lot more.

'Good,' he said, 'I just came over to make sure you're OK, and now that I know you are ...'

'John, wait.' Rae grabbed his arm. 'About yesterday ...'

'Forget it,' he said, 'you were right, it's none of my busi-ness what you get up to.'

'What I get up to? What the hell is that supposed to mean?' She immediately bit her lip when his nostrils flared. Why was she always on the defensive with this guy?

'It doesn't mean anything, Rae' he said. 'Look, I didn't come over here for another argument, and besides, I think your date is waiting.' He looked over to the bar where Chris hung back, pretending not to watch their exchange.

'He's not my date. We were just—'

'None of my business,' John said, 'see you around, Rae.'

Rae watched him walk off feeling rattled and oddly dejected. He re-joined a group of friends who were all laughing at something one of them had just said, and Rae tried not to think they were laughing at her, or the brown stain down the front of her top. One of the group – a blonde woman, more mature than Rae, but tall and pretty – rested her hand on John's shoulder. It was a possessive move, almost intimate, and when she discreetly glanced back to see if Rae was looking Rae felt her skin tighten just a little. *Don't be so ridiculous*, she scolded herself, *now you're behaving just like Emma.*

'What was all that about?' Chris handed Rae a bar towel with an apologetic smile. 'Sorry, it was all they had.'

'Nothing,' Rae said, 'actually, Chris, do you mind if we just go? I don't think there's any salvaging this top.'

IT WAS late afternoon when they finally pulled up outside the cottage and the sun was already on its slow descent. The heat of the day was dissipating fast and the hint at an overnight frost hung in the air as shadows stretched lazily across the driveway. The journey home had been a quiet one. While Rae was still thinking about John, Chris seemed to be lost in his own thoughts, his previous cheery mood now replaced by something more sombre. He brightened a little when she invited him in for coffee.

'Would you mind starting the fire while I quickly change and make the drinks?' she said, casting off her leather jacket and heading upstairs without waiting for an answer. John had gotten under her skin more than she liked to admit and she needed a moment to herself. She quickly changed into an oversized black jumper and headed back downstairs, head still full of the pretty girl with her hand on John's shoulder. She slammed two mugs on the kitchen cupboard and switched on the kettle. 'Instant OK?' she called out, yanking the milk out of the fridge and dropping it next to the mugs.

'Perfect,' Chris called back, 'three sugars.'

She smiled and took a teaspoon from the drawer. A man after her own taste then. Certainly more suited to her than someone who had no business telling her what to do. She glanced into the living room where Chris was still busy with the fire. He was taller than John, leaner too, but what he lacked in muscle he more than made up for in charm and wit. Both were handsome men, but where Chris was clean cut and fresh, John was rugged, rough around the edges and more often than not, abrasive. The two couldn't be more different and yet both had so much in common. Their fondness for Alex for one. Then there was Emma, sister to one, ex-lover to the other, and, it seemed, the reason for the animosity between the two men. And now here was Rae, a friend to Chris certainly, but what of John? She grabbed a steaming mug with each hand and padded into the living room, handed one to Chris then curled up on the couch. She expected Chris to take the armchair, but instead he took the seat next to her and kicked off his shoes.

'Do you mind if I ask you a question?' Rae said.

'In my defence the socks were a gift from Emma,' Chris said, 'and she has terrible taste in footwear.'

Rae laughed. 'It's not about the socks, and you can tell me to mind my own business if you like, but ... I wanted to ask you about John.'

'Ah, him again,' Chris said.

Rae put down her coffee and twisted round to face Chris. 'I don't mean to pry,' she said. 'It's just that whenever the two of you are in the same room storm clouds seem to hover. I know that he dumped your sister, but ... I just wondered if there was more to it than that?'

'Is there something going on between the two of you?'

'God, no,' Rae said, sounding less than genuine, even to herself. 'I'm just curious, that's all.'

Chris sighed and put down his own cup before turning back to Rae. 'Have you asked him about it?'

'Ha,' Rae said. 'He's more likely to tell me mind my own business than you are.'

Chris smiled. 'Beautiful *and* smart. Seriously though, can we change the subject? I'd much prefer to talk about you.'

More like you're avoiding the question, thought Rae. 'That might prove to be a very boring conversation,' she said.

'I doubt it,' Chris said. 'Someone as captivating as you couldn't have a boring bone in her body.' He took Rae's hand in his and very lightly brushed his lips across her knuckles.

Rae gently pulled her hand back. 'My head is in danger of exploding if it gets any bigger.'

'It's not flattery to tell the truth.'

He moved a little closer, and just because she was feeling out of sorts with herself, Rae let him take her chin in his hand and tilt her face to his. His eyes glowed softly by the light of the fire and he smelled of expensive aftershave, mixed with a light sprinkling of perspiration. It had been a long time since Rae had felt desirable, and against her better judgement she allowed him to kiss her. His lips were warm and soft as they gently brushed hers, lingering for a moment before parting and tasting her as though she were a delicacy to be savoured. He was a good kisser.

He slid his hand round to the back of her head and curled his fingers into her hair, pulling her closer as his tongue slipped into her mouth. She gasped, and the next thing she knew she was lay down with Chris on top of her.

His breath came hot and heavy as his hand slipped beneath her jumper looking for the clasp on her bra. Rae grabbed it and gently pushed him away. 'I'm sorry, Chris. I can't do this.'

'Sure you can,' he murmured, tracing soft kisses across her face, 'would you be more comfortable if we moved it upstairs?'

'No,' she said. 'I really am sorry, but you have to stop.'

Chris sat back looking mildly confused and ran a hand

through his dark hair. 'What is it?' he said, 'was I moving too fast?'

'No,' Rae said. 'It's nothing like that.'

'Was it something I did?' Then he smiled devilishly, 'or was it something I didn't do?'

'No,' Rae said. 'You've been great, and I've had a brilliant time today, it's just ... I don't think I'm ready for anything more than friendship right now. It's my fault, I shouldn't have let things go so far.'

'Don't apologise,' he said. 'It was me who came on to you, remember.'

'I know, but ...'

'Don't beat yourself up about it, Winters,' he said gently. 'You really didn't stand a chance.'

Rae laughed nervously. 'Well as long as you're modest about it.'

'Modesty is for amateurs.' He stood up, slipped on his shoes and reached for his jacket.

'Well now I feel like I'm throwing you out,' Rae said. 'I can fix us another coffee if you want to stay?'

Chris smiled. 'No offence, Winters, but your coffee is shit, and if I don't leave now I am likely to drag you upstairs and have my wicked way with you, whether you like it or not.' He leaned over and kissed her on the forehead. 'I would like to see you again though, for dinner maybe?'

Rae hesitated. It was probably a bad idea.

'Just as friends,' he said, 'scout's honour.'

'Somehow, I don't see you as a boy scout.'

'You may find there are many things about me that will surprise you, Miss Winters. Tomorrow then?'

Rae bit her lip. She really shouldn't. 'OK,' she said, 'but make it Thursday, I have things to do tomorrow.'

13

D ee stepped aside as Chris burst through the door. She was used to his moods by now (and it really didn't take much to put him in a bad one) but something told her this one was different. 'Who's pissed you off this time?' she said, following him into the kitchen.

'No-one,' he said, pouring himself a whiskey, 'just a shitty day.'

Dee suppressed a smile and moved to stand in front of him. 'Where were you? I tried calling you.'

He swilled the whiskey round his glass, threw it down his neck and poured himself another. 'Out.'

'Well, yes,' Dee said. 'I gathered that much. But out where?'

'None of your business.' He drained his glass again, poured a third shot then pushed past Dee to drop down on the couch. Dee leaned on the breakfast bar, chin resting in her hand, and watched with amusement as Chris put his feet up on the coffee table. He was goading her, trying to start a fight.

'I saw your sister today,' she said casually. 'She came into my shop.'

'Well maybe she was shopping for face cream,' he said.

'She was looking for Alex, actually. Wanted to know if she'd seen John. Apparently, he wasn't at work today.' Chris' jaw tensed and Dee allowed herself a small, satisfied smile. 'Alex didn't say as much but I got the impression she thought he was with a woman. She seems to think he has a thing for this new girl, the one that's recently moved into The Briar. Have you met her yet?'

Chris ignored her teasing, as she knew he would. She also knew she would pay for it later, but that was the nature of their relationship. She turned away, reached into the highest cupboard, and took down a glass from the top shelf. It was a special glass, engraved with the same dragon that hugged her left hip. It was a gift from Ivan, one of her previous lovers and someone who had proved to be more useful than he could ever have imagined, and as a mark of respect she tipped the glass towards the end of the garden where his unmarked grave lay.

She glanced quickly over her shoulder to be sure Chris wasn't watching then reached into the pocket of her robe and removed the small glass vial she'd placed there earlier. To the untrained nose the vial contained nothing more than herbal water, but the herbs were only a disguise to hide the real nature of what lay within. She shook its contents so the clear liquid became murky, like watered down milk, then poured it into her glass. She topped it up with a double shot of whiskey and dropped the empty vial into the bin.

She sauntered into the living room and sat on the coffee table opposite Chris, legs crossed, making sure the hem of her robe rose high enough to expose plenty of thigh. 'Alex told me about your riding trip,' she said, absently gliding her big toe up and down Chris's leg. 'I hear it didn't go too well?'

Chris idly swilled the drink around his glass and sighed. 'And your point is?'

'My point is that you were with someone today. I can smell her all over you.'

'Leave it out, Dee. I'm not in the mood.'

Dee narrowed her eyes and smiled. *No*, she thought, *but you soon will be.* Holding the glass to her lips she threw her head back and swallowed. Then she placed the empty glass on the coffee table and reached up to release her mass of red hair from its clip. The locks tumbled around her shoulders, down her back and over her chest, covering her breasts where the robe had already begun to fall open. 'Problem is,' she said, loosening the robe further to let the floral silk slip down to the waist. 'I suspect that someone else has an eye for the newcomer.' She shivered luxuriously as her skin tingled from the effects of the tonic, and opened the robe further to reveal just a hint of the dragon below.

Chris watched as she slowly trailed a finger down her cleavage. He smirked, drained his glass and placed it on the coffee table beside Dee's as Dee got up from the table to sit in his lap. She straddled his legs, pulled her knees up tight around his hips, and whispered into his ear. 'Tell me about her,' she said, slowly undoing the buttons on his shirt. 'What is she like?'

Chris grabbed one of her breasts and ignored the question. Not one to be discouraged, Dee took hold of his face and teased her tongue wetly over his lips before flicking it into his mouth and kissing him deeply. Chris responded half-heartedly, but as the contents of the vial passed from Dee to Chris he reciprocated with much more fervour. The smell of whiskey was strong as their tongues mingled, the kiss becoming hotter as the tonic took hold. Dee pulled back and asked him again. 'Tell me who were you with today, Christopher.'

'Don't call me that,' he said, groping for her other breast.

Dee expertly redirected his hands to her hips then continued to unbutton his shirt. 'Tell me what you know,' she said, lowering her head to suckle on his nipple. She smiled as he moaned and felt his excitement press between her legs.

'Stop teasing, Dee,' he said.

'Oh, I'm not teasing,' she said, moving her lips to brush past his ear. 'You'll get everything you want, *Christopher*, but not until you tell me what I want to know.' A low moan came from deep in his throat as she began to undo his pants and she smiled to herself at how easy it was to manipulate the so-called stronger sex. A firm pair of tits, a tight arse and a willing tongue was all it took to make them do exactly what you wanted, and what she wanted right now, was information. 'Now tell me,' she said again. 'Tell me who she is.'

DEE THREW a blanket over Chris's sleeping body, knowing he'd be lucky to wake by morning, and left him there, snoring on the couch where their lovemaking had been almost violent in its urgency. She headed for the bedroom where her much needed elixir was hidden, pausing only to grab the bottle of whiskey on her way through. Any chance of being disturbed by Chris had been eradicated the moment her aphrodisiac had touched his lips, but she locked the bedroom door anyway before lifting the loose floorboard beneath her bed and removing the strongbox from its hiding place. The iron box was as old as the hills – an ancient artefact of her youth that had once belonged to her mother – and was an ugly looking thing but impenetrable without its key. It was the perfect place to keep that which was most precious to her.

She placed the heavy box carefully on the bed, reached behind the headboard where the key was safely taped, and inserted it into the keyhole. Inside were her most treasured possessions, handed down from her mother when Dee was too young to know what they were for. A mortar and pestle made of human bone, turned brown with age and cracked down one side, an uncut chunk of black tourmaline, and her sister's personal obsidian scrying mirror. It was the mirror, shaped and polished into a smooth, flat oval that Dee took from the box, together with two black candles and a small, blue glass jar.

She set the obsidian and candles aside and opened the jar, letting its contents spill out onto the bed; two syringes, each containing a highly concentrated version of her very own elixir. The Lix – as she liked to call it – was much more complicated than the tonic she had used with Chris, its ingredients far less accessible and much less palatable than the sacrifice of mere stoats and weasels. But it was a means to an end and a drug of necessity rather than choice.

She poured a small drop of whiskey over the smooth surface of her thigh, then, taking a syringe in one hand and stretching a patch of skin with the other, Dee removed the hypodermic cap with her teeth and plunged the needle deep into her muscle. The effect was instantaneous, the pain sharp but fleeting. A shockwave passed through her system akin to a jolt of electricity, and more enjoyable than any sex she had ever had. Tiny electrodes sparked to life beneath her skin, lighting her up from within and giving life back to her aging body. But how long would it be before she needed another hit? How long before she was forced to make another kill?

Returning both syringes to the glass jar, she dropped it back into the strongbox and turned to the mirror. There was a time when a single concentrated shot would last six months at least, but the period between doses was getting shorter and shorter. The last hit had been only two weeks ago, the one previous to that, just a month and the means to make another almost depleted.

She dropped her robe to the floor to admire her tight curves; she still had the body of a twenty-year-old, but without more elixir it wouldn't last long. She sighed and pulled the robe back on. The problem was, taking human life was becoming increasingly dangerous. The sins of the past had yet to catch up with Dee, but if someone were to mysteriously disappear again then suspicions would surely rise. Ivan had been easy – with no close family and years of travelling behind him he'd fallen off the radar long before Dee had gotten hold of him, but people like Ivan were hard to come by.

She picked up the obsidian and candles and carried them to her dresser. Then she lit both candles and placed one on either side of the scrying mirror, turned off the lights, and sat on the edge of the bed. Scrying had never come easy to Dee. That particular talent had been her sister's and one that Dee had never really cared for. Extispicy was Dee's preferred method for the extraction of information, but tonight the entrails of a small animal were not readily to hand. But Chris had provided her with the base information, now maybe the scrying mirror would fill in the rest.

She closed her eyes and tried to relax. Relaxing wasn't something that came easy to Dee – her mind was like the M25 during rush hour at the best of times – but she had learned to be patient if nothing else. Sat cross legged on the bed, she stared into the black glass until her heart slowed and her mind stilled, until the room around her faded at the edges and her reflection in the mirror was all she could see. It took concentration, and a lot of self-control not to look away, but she had to know everything if she had any chance of being prepared in time for the lunar eclipse.

She stayed like that for a long time, looking beyond her reflection into the depths of the glass, until finally she felt her mind begin to drift. It felt a lot like falling asleep as her mind separated from her physical self so her conscious self could float weightlessly somewhere in between. This was the part she struggled with. The whole separation thing made her feel nauseous, but when it worked – which was only half the time – it worked well.

She could see herself now – perched on the edge of the bed, legs folded beneath her, arms useless by her side – but while her body was confined by gravity, her mind was free to roam. She left the room and floated to the next where Chris snored peacefully on the couch. Beneath the coffee table, hidden in a box that had been shoved hastily out of sight when Chris was banging on the door, was a bunch of old photographs. She made a mental note to retrieve them before Chris woke up. She floated into the hallway and saw the rug that hid the door to her secret cellar. In her in-between state, Dee could see beyond the floorboards and past the stone cellar floor where energy flowed like a raging river. Unharnessed energy. Dangerous energy in the wrong hands. The ley line had been there since the dawn of time, and there were many more like it in the area, but they all converged at one place, a special place that Dee knew well. At the clearing beneath the sacred oak.

She was thinking of the sacred oak when she felt her conscious self being drawn back to her physical self. She floated downwards, feeling the pull of gravity grow stronger as her mind and body were reunited. She opened her eyes. The obsidian mirror was still on her dresser, but it was now a pool of still water instead of a hard lump of black rock. Dee reached out and lightly touched the tip of her finger to the surface, sending ripples to the outer edges that bounced back and returned to the centre. The surface became still again, and a face appeared, though it was not her own reflection looking back this time.

She recognised the girl at once – hazel eyes bright with intelligence, nose slightly upturned, and hair straight as a pin, just like her mother's. She'd somewhat aged since the last time Dee had seen her, but the stubborn expression was just the same. It made Dee smile, but then the face began to change. Not the features, they stayed the same, but the eyes narrowed into something cold and calculating, and the mouth twisted into a cruel and vengeful smile. It sent shivers racing down Dee's spine and guilt tugged at her heart. Then the face faded, and in its place was a village. Dee had seen this village before. Her mother had drawn pictures of it for Dee and her sister when they were only children. But the village was on fire, and though no sound came from the scrying mirror, Dee felt the screams of the villagers. She knew the story well, every living Draiocht worth their salt did. It was drummed into them as a child so that they would not forget the horrors that the Arnach sisters had brought upon them. For all the good it did. Dark magic had become the backbone of Draiocht existence since the sisters' death and there were few that wouldn't welcome the return of the twins. But the stories had worked their magic on Dee and her sister, for a time at least. As children they had hugged each other in the night, knowing they were safe, that the Arnach sisters were long dead, but also knowing that the prophecy of their return was whispered on every Draiocht's lips far and wide. And just like the sisters in the story, unified in their power, Dee and Louisa had been unified in their fear.

The image changed again then, and this time Dee saw herself, her younger self with lank, dishwater hair, and a cleft lip. The image made her cringe but remembering who she was and how her transformation had come to be was an important part of who she was today. She just didn't understand why the scrying mirror was showing it to her now. Perhaps because her time as Deandra James was almost at an end, or perhaps because it was important to remember where her roots lay. Either way it didn't matter. The mirror hadn't shown her anything she didn't already know. She blew out the candles, replaced everything back in her lockbox, and climbed into bed, but a dull throb behind her eyes confirmed that sleep would not come for a while yet.

Plagued by thoughts of the upcoming eclipse, Dee tossed and turned as she played every possible scenario over and over in her head. She knew why Raewyn was here, had strong suspicions as to Chris's infatuation with her, and was almost certain the girl remained clueless as to who she was. But what she didn't understand, and what the mirror had failed to tell her, was why The Order had not yet come banging down her door. Three weeks from now the moon would turn to blood – the fourth lunar eclipse of the holy tetrad, and a super moon to boot – a powerful night when the veil between worlds would be at its weakest, and when a monster would seek to rise. Which meant that in three weeks' time Dee needed to not only have finished her serum, but she had to kidnap Raewyn Winters, perform a ritual sacrifice, and prepare herself for the worst night of her life.

She was going to need more help.

14

Rae stood in the centre of a large room, a room she perceived to be at Carrion Hall though the reasoning of it was not clear to her. The fireplace she recognised at once, she had stood before it many times and yet she could not recollect a single moment. It was the same with the portrait that hung above it. The man in the picture was known to her; the deep groove of laughter lines that touched the eyes, the contour of his lips, her mouth even remembered the taste of him, but her mind could not put a name to the face, nor could she remember how she knew him. The familiarity with her surroundings was disconcerting. Every sense, every fibre of her being felt connected to this room and to the man in the picture, and yet her mind refused to acknowledge what she knew to be true, and it withdrew like a hand snatched from a fire.

She closed her eyes, counted to ten, and when she opened them again was disappointed to see she was still in the same room, still in front of the painting looking up at a man whose name eluded her, and still none-the-wiser as to why she was here. But now there was something different too. She looked down, and there, cradled in the crook of her elbow, was a baby. A sleeping child wrapped in a white blanket and snuggled deep into her as though it had been there all along. She smiled down at the sweet little face and trailed a finger over the delicate button nose. She did not know this baby, and yet again the sense of familiarity was so strong she could almost taste it.

She held the baby close, drinking in that soft, unmistakable infant smell and looked up at the man in the painting. The child belonged to him. The sudden knowledge came to her unbidden and the taste of it was like acid in her mouth. She looked back at the sleeping child, but her arms were now empty and only the charred remains of the blanket remained, black and bloody and covered with tiny thorns, blackberry thorns. She recognised them from the thickets that grew around the cottage and threw the blanket to the floor, sickened and horrified. Then she began to cry, but instead of tears, blood spilled from her eyes, stinging and blinding until she wiped them clear with the hem of her nightgown. When she could see again, the room was still the same, but also different. Now there was a blue chaise longue placed in front of the fire. Rae knelt before it, running her fingers across the lush velvet surface, remembering how luxurious it had felt against her bare skin as she made love to the man in the picture.

Richard.

The name came to her like an autumn leaf floating on the wind and she said it out loud, letting the fullness of it linger on her lips. She turned back to the painting, but it was no longer Richard who looked down at her, but the face of Christopher Ashley, so filled with wanton lust that it sickened

Rae to the stomach. His mouth twisted in a lascivious smile and Rae turned away in disgust, but when she looked again it was no longer Chris, but John's face she saw. He wore a frown of disapproval, something which Rae found oddly comforting, but his eyes were not their usual blue-grey. Instead, they glowed like liquid amber and as Rae watched in horror, his face began to melt. His nose became a blob of blistering paint and the cheeks sagged like moulded clay, but Rae could neither scream nor look away. The painting began to smoulder and blacken, and somewhere in the distance a baby began to cry. Rae wanted to run, to get away from the abomination before her, but she was paralysed, frozen in place, unable to do anything but watch as John's liquefied mouth slowly opened and began to scream.

RAE SAT bolt upright in bed, flung back the covers and ran for the bathroom. She just made it as the contents of her stomach lurched violently upwards. The dream had been one of her most vivid yet and the smell of burning paint still clung to the back of her throat. She spat into the toilet, rinsed her face with cold water and leaned heavily on the sink. Red, puffy eyes stared back with the raw look of someone who has not slept in weeks. *If only that were true*, she thought. Sleeping wasn't the issue, it was what came with it that was the problem. She brushed her teeth, swilled with mouthwash then closed the bathroom door and switched on the shower. As the water heated she stripped and examined herself in the mirror. Her birthmark had been bothering her lately, ever since arriving in Cranston Myre it had begun to itch and burn. She ran a finger lightly over the raised markings, angry and red as though infected. It had never troubled her before, had never been more than a faint scar just like the one on John's wrist until now, and she had never queried its existence beyond asking Grace what it was. Grace had waved the question away. 'It's exactly what it looks like,' she had said, 'a birthmark, nothing more.' But now, Rae was beginning to wonder.

She stepped into the bath where the shower hung over the small tub. The room was already full of steam, but instead of cooling the water down, Rae turned it up. She needed to cleanse herself, to rid herself of the dream that still clung to her skin. And the water felt good, so good she turned it up further. She closed her eyes as it thrummed against her skin and tried to empty her head of all thoughts of John, but no matter what she did she couldn't un-see his face. He was everywhere – in the village, at the party, the forest and Harleybrock, and now even in her dreams. She turned the tap again, this time all the way round to the little red dot, and put her head into the stream, but still it wasn't enough. The hotter the water got, the better Rae felt, but there wasn't enough heat in the world to purge her of thoughts of John.

The room was now so steamy that Rae could barely see, but she didn't mind, in fact she liked it. The scalding water made her feel alive, and the steam gave her a sense of isolation. It stirred as the bathroom door suddenly opened and Rae held her breath as it was quietly closed again. She could see him stood there with his back against the wall. She'd been expecting him and was only surprised by how long he had waited. She felt a flutter of excitement as he began to undress. He had a good body, muscular and strong, and she could see by his erection that he was just as aroused as she was. He silently climbed into the bath, eyes slowly raking over her body, lingering only a moment on the spot above her belly button before rising to look into her eyes with an intensity that tugged deep inside her belly. Rae opened her mouth to speak but was silenced with a kiss that stole her breath away. She gasped when his fingers touched the raised edges of her birthmark and moaned when they brushed over the exposed area between her legs. He smiled. He was arrogant, sure of himself, sure of *her* and she liked that, she liked it a lot.

'You came,' she whispered, as his hand moved round to cup the curve of her arse. 'I wasn't sure that you would.'

His dark hair was loose and matted around his shoulders, the scar on his forehead pink against his olive skin, and his eyes, those beautiful golden eyes, were like liquid honey as he pulled Rae into him, skin to skin, heartbeat to heartbeat. 'How could I not,' he said, 'when you make it impossible to stay away.'

His breath was hot on her face, his mouth deliciously sweet as it devoured hers, but Rae pushed him away. 'I want to hear you say it,' she said.

He nodded, chin slightly tilted upwards as he eyes roamed over her body, down to her toes and ever so slowly, back to her face. 'I want you,' he said, his voice thick with desire, 'and I *will* have you. But not yet, my sweet Augustine, first you need to wake up.'

Rae woke with a start, heart hammering in her chest and skin still tingling from a touch she had never known. She'd had vivid dreams before, but never anything quite like *that*.

It was 8.30 in the morning and Rae had spent the last couple of days milling around the cottage, googling everything from raised body temperatures to spontaneous combustion, looking up unusual birth marks and studying reincarnation. She'd gone for several walks in the forest, ran into the village a couple of times and binge watched the entire box set of The Walking Dead, all in an attempt to keep herself busy so she wouldn't do anything stupid, and by stupid she meant visiting the oak tree alone.

But that was before the dream.

She quickly showered and dressed then headed out the back door with the new phone from Chris in one pocket, a paring knife in the other, and the scorched baseball bat in her hand.

The forest was quiet, and the air, thick with foreboding, but it only added to her heightened sense of excitement as she pushed through the soggy undergrowth. She wore leggings, thick olive-green ones that sat low on her hips so as not to irritate her birth mark, which was now redder and angrier than ever, and long boots to keep her legs dry. It was cold in the forest, damp and rich with the smell of earth, but alive too. She could almost feel the oak tree out there, humming with life, waiting to show her its secrets, and when she finally stepped into the clearing, her stomach knotted with anticipation.

The tree seemed bigger than ever, looming over her like an aged aunt, beckoning her closer, wanting to whisper in her ear, and a crow landed on the branch nearest her head, eyeing Rae with its beady black eyes. It was joined by another, then another, each cawing in unison until Rae swung the bat at them. 'Go on, get outta here,' she cried. They scattered, black wings disturbing the mist that seemed to be ever present of late, and re-grouped two branches higher.

The sun was finally out after two days of cloud, but you would never know it by the damp and bitter air that shrouded the forest. Rae zipped her jacket higher and looked about, ears strained for any sign that a large predator may be lurking nearby. She'd thought of the wolf often since their impromptu meeting, and whilst she had been certain at the time that it was a wolf, now she wondered if John was right, and it had been nothing more than a stray dog after all. Even so, she did a quick perimeter check before returning to the trunk and placing a hand against the cold bark.

The ground vibrated beneath Rae's feet – its gentle hum travelling up her legs to pump blood to her heart – and she even imagined she could hear the cries of battle seeping from the tree's roots, but there was no connection, no drawing from her arm, and more importantly, no vision. She propped the bat against the tree and took the kitchen knife from her pocket. When the tree had shown her a vision last time, she had been bleeding from a large splinter in her hand, and when she'd woken up, her hand had been numb and the wound significantly bigger. She pressed the tip of the knife against the fleshiest part of her palm and hissed through her teeth as the cold steel bit into her skin. Blood oozed up immediately, crimson against the white of her hand, and before she could change her mind, she pressed her bloody palm up against the tree.

The draw on her arm was instant, and she closed her eyes, braced for the inevitable wave of nausea. But the transition from one reality to another was much smoother this time, and when Rae opened her eyes it was as though she had never left.

Golden eyes was there with her and her skin warmed at the sight of him. He was dressed for battle, black armour moulded to his body, muscular arms bare and bloody. The gash on his forehead bled, as did his left shoulder where the snapped off end of an arrow poked through the armour. He was angry, yelling at a woman to Rae's left, a woman dressed for battle just like him, only her armour was white with a black bird on the chest, wings splayed wide. Her white hair was long and braided with wisps plastered to her sweaty, blood splattered face. She looked at Rae, eyes pale and fierce, lashes white as snow and her skin, so light as to be almost translucent. Her lips were pulled back in a snarl, baring teeth that were stained with blood. Rae couldn't hear what they were saying – their voices were muffled, as though talking through a wall of water – but they were battle angry, butting heads over something in the woman's hand. She held up a dagger – a fancy thing with carvings in the blade and gold filigree on the hilt – and pointed it at Rae. She said something that turned golden eyes' face to thunder. He turned to Rae, eyes blazing, just as another man approached.

This man wore the same armour as golden eyes, but the top half of his face was covered with a black helmet, the bottom shielded with a beard the colour of brick dust. He held a spear in one hand and a shield in the other and bowed to golden eyes before removing his helmet. They spoke briefly and Rae felt the white-haired woman slip something small and solid into her hand. She was whispering into Rae's ear – Rae felt her breath, hot and wet against her cheek, could smell the sweet, metallic scent of fresh blood – but her words were soundless, their meaning lost in the underwater fug that filled Rae's head. Then golden eyes looked to Rae as the soldier turned towards her, his spear tipped and ready. Rae gasped. He had a mark on the inside of his wrist, pale and silver like a faded scar. The white woman stepped between them, shielding Rae with her body, dagger at the ready, but the vision was beginning to fade, blurring at the edges, and just as the dagger came swinging down, everything went black.

RAE AWOKE to a wet tongue licking her face and roughly pushed Bart away. 'What are you doing here?' she said, standing up and dusting herself off. Her hand throbbed and her head felt like it had been split it two, but the memory of the vision stayed with her, especially the man with the spear. Bart looked up at her, tail wagging and tongue hanging awkwardly out of his mouth. If Bart was here, that meant John wouldn't be far behind. She scratched behind the dog's ears and looked up as Alex stepped from the trees.

'There you are,' she said, 'I was beginning to worry. Do you always go out and leave your door wide open?' She held up two cups of coffee and held one out for Rae. 'I come bearing gifts,' she said. 'Emma is on John's case about finishing the flower beds after he played hooky the other day, so he needed someone to walk Bart, and guess who drew the short straw.'

'Is she his keeper as well as his boss?' Rae said tightly. She took a sip of coffee then pulled a face. 'Urgh, it's cold, how long were you looking for me?'

'A while,' Alex said. 'What were you doing out here anyway?'

Rae glanced back over her shoulder. The baseball bat had fallen over and was partially obscured by leaves. Explaining a walk in the woods was easy enough, but coming up with a reason for carrying a baseball bat with two scorched handprints on it would be a tad more difficult. 'Just out for a morning stroll,' she said.

'You always carry a knife when you go for a walk?'

Rae shoved the paring knife back in her pocket and hoped that Alex hadn't spotted the blood on the blade. 'For carving,' she said, 'I was going to carve my name into the tree but changed my mind. Stupid idea really. Cruel to trees.'

Alex smiled and called to Bart. 'Can't have him getting lost,' she said, clipping on his lead, 'daft bugger couldn't sniff his way out of a paper bag.'

'Then how did you find me?' Rae had assumed Bart had led Alex straight to her, the same way he had with John.

Alex shrugged. 'Blind luck,' she said, 'and now you owe me hot coffee. Throw in a piece of toast and I promise not to tell the forestry commission what you were about to do to their tree.'

ALEX STAYED at Rae's for a half hour then made her excuses and left. Rae gave it another hour then jumped into her car and drove up the hill. The gates to the Hall were open when she got there, but instead of pulling up at the main door she followed the drive round to the courtyard and the two cottages where John and Alex lived. Alex's car wasn't there, but John's truck was. She parked alongside it, climbed out and headed towards the fountain.

John was hard at work digging up new flower beds, just like Alex said he would be. His assistant, Henry, was working only a few feet away on a separate flower bed and waved hello as Rae approached. He was a good-looking lad, twenty at most with blonde, almost white hair that stuck up in tufts, and as Rae waved back John gave him a cold look that clearly said, 'Back to work'.

'I wasn't expecting to see you.' John dropped his spade and grabbed a bottle of water. He was sweaty, brow creased with concentration, or maybe he was just pissed at seeing Rae. Either way her heart kicked at the sight of him.

'That makes two of us,' she said, noticing how his eyes changed from blue-grey to startling blue when the sun caught them in just the right way. 'I was hoping we could talk?'

'About what?' He used his t-shirt to wipe his face and Rae caught another glimpse of the scar on his chest.

'About the other day,' she said, cutting a glance at Henry. 'When you found me in the forest.'

'You made it perfectly clear that I should mind my own business. What's changed?'

Rae shoved her hands deep into her pockets and shrugged. 'I wasn't sure if I could trust you then.'

'And now you can?' His brows arched but there was no amusement in those changeable eyes of his.

'I don't know,' Rae said, 'can I?' It was a fair question, and one Rae wasn't sure either of them could answer. *Did* she trust him? Or was she only here because curiosity was getting the better of her? John didn't answer, only picked up his spade and began to dig. 'I came here because we have something in common,' she said.

'Don't tell me, you finally realised Chris is a dick?'

Henry sniggered, but wisely didn't look up. 'Very funny,' Rae said, 'but no.'

'Then either spit it out, Rae, or let me get on. You can see I'm busy.'

Henry gave Rae an awkward smile then discreetly moved a couple of flower beds over, giving them a little privacy. Rae bit the inside of her cheek. There was no going back once she'd told John about her birthmark, certainly not if she told him about the vision. John thrust the spade into the ground so hard Rae wondered what the pile of dirt had ever done to him. She opened her mouth to say as much but suspected her feeble attempt at humour would be most unwelcome, so instead turned her back to Henry, unzipped her jacket and lifted her top.

John didn't even look up. 'If you're trying to seduce me, you're wasting your time. I've got more important things to worry about than your ego.'

'My ego is just fine,' Rae said, 'which is more than I can say for yours. Will you just bloody well look up for one second?' He glanced up at her, then looked again and froze. 'I was born with it,' Rae said, 'and I know I should probably have told you before, but—'

'Jesus, Rae.' John stepped forward and tugged down her top. 'Not here. We can talk at my place.' He threw down his gloves, told Henry to take lunch, then grabbed Rae's arm and dragged her across the lawn towards the cottages.

John practically shoved Rae inside and locked the door behind them before heading straight for the kitchen and grabbing himself a beer. 'Drink?' he said, holding one out for Rae. She declined, and remained in the doorway, arms folded while John went to stand by the window. It seemed an eternity before he finally spoke, and when he did his voice was tight. 'Why now?' he said, staring out the window at a large bush of purple flowers.

Rae felt her blood rise in response, but bit down on her lip and took a slow, calming breath. 'I wasn't about to expose my mid-riff to someone I'd only just met,' she said, 'besides, you weren't exactly forthcoming when I asked you what it was.'

'That's because I don't know,' John said.

'Did you know about me though? I mean, it seems odd

that you would show your scar to me unless you suspected I either had one, or knew what it was.'

John slowly nodded. 'I suspected,' he said, 'but I wasn't sure.'

'How?' Rae said.

John only shrugged. 'A feeling.' Rae couldn't argue with that. It was only because of a feeling that she was even stood here. 'You said you didn't know if you could trust me,' he said, 'but how do I know if I can trust you?'

'You don't,' Rae said, 'but you came to me first, remember?'

John turned and looked at her, eyes still full of suspicion, but nodded and pulled out a chair. 'Alright then, if we're going to do this we'd better sit down.' Rae joined him, heart pounding, nails digging into the palms of her hands while she waited patiently for him to tear his damn eyes from the label on his beer bottle. 'Remember the first time we met?' he finally said.

'How could I forget?' Rae said. 'I still have the bruises to show for it.'

John smiled and looked up. 'They say dogs have a sixth sense. Bart seems to be quite taken with you.'

'I wish I could say the feeling was mutual. But what does your crazy mutt have to do with anything?'

'Because,' John said, 'instead of watching Bart that day, I was gawking at you like a damn fool, and the reason I was doing that, was because I recognised you the moment you stepped foot on that green.'

Rae felt a prickle at the back of her throat. She got up and turned on the tap. 'Recognised me from where?' she said, holding a glass under the running water. She could feel John's eyes on her back.

'From my dreams,' he said. Rae turned back to the table and could've sworn his face had turned two shades darker. 'Every night for two years I dreamt of you,' he said, 'or at least someone who looks exactly like you. Her hair was longer though, darker, and she had a tattoo just here.' He pointed to the space between his left ear and his eye. 'Tribal, I think. The eyes were the same colour, but fiercer, maybe. Her whole face was fiercer now I come to think of it.'

Rae sat down and drank from the glass. 'So, what you're saying is … I'm the girl of your dreams?' It was a lame attempt at humour, but right now she would do anything to diffuse the awkwardness building between them.

John frowned and slouched back in his chair. 'I'm trying to be serious.'

'I know,' Rae said, 'Sorry. OK, so we both have identical markings but on different parts of our bodies, and you claim to have been dreaming about me for the last two years.' It was difficult not to smile, but the stern look on John's face suggested that if she wished to continue this conversation, then she'd better not. 'Are you still having these dreams?'

He frowned as Rae bit down on her lip. 'No,' he said, 'the moment you showed up the dreams stopped, and this thing …' he held out his arm so Rae could see the marking on his wrist '… started to itch.'

He managed to make it sound like an accusation, and Rae wondered if perhaps there was more to this dream girl of his than he was letting on. She lightly touched her stomach where her own mark was still raised and sore. 'What were the dreams about?' she asked.

'Let's just say we were close and leave it at that.' This time it was Rae's turn to blush, and she was grateful that John tactfully got up from the table to fetch himself another beer. 'You were wearing that, too,' he said, casually pointing to Rae's necklace as he sat back down. The pendant had worked itself loose and was sitting on top of her t-shirt.

'You mean *she* was wearing it,' Rae said.

John shrugged. 'Same thing.'

Rae twirled the crystal thoughtfully between thumb and finger. 'I've seen something too,' she said, 'a man with a mark on his wrist, same as you.'

John froze with the bottle halfway to his lips. 'Describe him.'

'Reddish-brown hair, long beard, your build I suppose.'

John leaned forward, brow creased. 'Describe his eyes,' he said, 'what colour were they?'

'Blue,' Rae said, 'but not your blue. Lighter, more like ...' she groped for the right word, the right shade to describe those striking eyes, but couldn't think with John staring at her like that.

'Topaz?' John offered.

'Yes,' she said, 'that's exactly it. But ... how did you know?'

'Where did you see him?'

Rae itched the palm of her hand where she'd cut it with the knife only that morning. 'I'm not sure you'd believe me.'

'Try me,' John said.

She thought about the tree, what she'd done to see its secrets, how she'd put herself in danger just to get another glimpse of the man with the golden eyes. 'I had a vision,' she said, feeling stupid even as the words left her mouth, 'but I think it was from a long time ago. Nothing recent. I'm not sure why I think that, it's just ...' she shrugged, 'a feeling?'

'Remember I told you I came out here because of my brother?' John was suddenly animated, as though Rae had told him exactly what he wanted to hear. Rae nodded. 'Well that wasn't the only reason,' he said. He held out his wrist again and Rae saw the silver outlines of his mark and the red scratches where he'd been itching. 'This thing appeared six years ago. I woke up to it burned into my wrist as though someone had branded me with it. Some years later I see a newspaper article about the upcoming renovation of Carrion Hall. They showed a picture of the Hall before the fire, and then years later.' He got up, rummaged in a draw, and pulled out a series of articles. He handed one to Rae, pointing to a picture after the fire. 'See anything strange?'

Rae looked over the photo. The Hall had been in a worse state than she imagined. Almost the entire west wing was a blackened shell, with the east wing not faring much better, but the top floor, by the attic and the tower, seemed reasonably intact. Years of neglect had also taken its toll with the overgrown gardens working their way in to the building. But she saw nothing out of the ordinary. 'What am I missing?' she said.

John pointed to the area between the Hall and the cottages where a man could be seen walking across the cobbles. Rae looked closer and felt gooseflesh raise on her arms. 'That's him,' she said, pointing to the photo. 'The guy I saw, it's him, I'm sure of it.' The beard was shorter, but the hair was just the same, long and tied at the neck. It looked like he'd spotted the photographer just as the photo was taken, and those piercing eyes stood out like chips of blue ice.

John sat back heavily in his chair. 'That's Ben,' he said, 'that's my brother.'

Rae's jaw went slack. She checked the date of the photo – July 2008. 'You said Ben went missing fourteen years ago,' she said, 'but this is dated only seven years ago.'

'I know,' John said, 'which proves Ben was still here seven years ago, and not missing as we all thought.'

'So, what are you saying? You think Ben is still in Cranston Myre.'

John shook his head. 'But I do think he stayed here for something more than a woman.' He got up again and rummaged in the draw, pulled out a small notepad and handed it to Rae. 'Have you ever heard of the word Draiocht?'

Rae shook her head. 'What does it mean?'

'Different things to different people, but in a nutshell, it means witchcraft, and look at this.' He pulled a piece of paper out of the notebook and opened it up. It was a photocopied page from a book called *Demons in Disguise* written by Nigel Hughes. A small paragraph had been highlighted in green and John asked Rae to read it out loud.

'Another form of demon to live amongst us was once referred to as the Draiocht,' she read. *'The Draiocht are similar to the druids in that very little is known about them. There are no written words, no records, no scrolls or drawings to confirm the Draiocht ever existed (or still exist in today's modern society), other than a handful of random carvings that can be found on ancient buildings throughout the United Kingdom and sporadically throughout the world. Some believe these are sites where regular meetings were held, maybe even still held today. The only records we do have are few and far between and are the crazed recollections of people who claim to have witnessed a Draiocht ritual during the last century or two. If the words of the few are to be believed, then the Draiocht are a society of men and women engaged in such matters as human sacrifice, Extispicy, cannibalism and dark magic. They hide in plain sight, blend into society as healers, apothecaries, herbalists, and homeopaths. They promise to heal, to give life where there is only death, to fill a barren woman's belly with a*

desperately wanted child, give youth to an aged face and strength to the weak, but make no mistake, to be party to a Draiocht ritual is not for the faint hearted. Sacrifice, blood offerings, necromancy, witchcraft, sorcery – all these things have been associated with the Draiocht at one time or another, but ask anyone today if they are real and you will be met with a resounding no. They are urban legend, whispers on the wind, shadows in the night. They do not exist, nor have they ever existed. But dig deep enough and you might just be surprised.'

Rae looked at John. 'I don't understand,' she said. 'What does this mean?'

'Open the notebook,' he said, 'first page.'

Rae did. It contained a list of places throughout England, Scotland and Wales, Cranston Myre amongst them. More than half the places had the name of a building attached to it – churches, castles, stone monuments – whilst others listed forests, beaches and caves. Cranston Myre had Dolen Forest written beneath it, with the number five and a tick.

'See numbers one to four?' John said, 'they're the places Ben visited before coming here. He called home from each and every one of them, even sent pictures of him stood outside the buildings he was supposed to be visiting.'

'But you don't believe he was visiting those buildings?'

John shook his head. 'I think it was a smoke screen. Cranston Myre was the last place he visited, and the only one with a tick beside it. Now look at the back, on the inside cover.'

Rae flicked through. In the top left-hand corner, scraped into the cover was the word Draiocht.

'I still don't understand,' she said, 'are you saying Ben was into witchcraft?'

'I'm saying Ben lied about his purpose for travelling

around the country, and that whatever he was looking for I believe he found it here, in Cranston Myre.'

Rae looked at the notepad again and ran a finger over the word that had been scraped into the inside cover. *Draiocht*. The word meant nothing to her and yet something at the back of her mind was bothering her, like an itch that she couldn't reach. She flipped back to the first page and one of the places that Ben hadn't visited yet. It was marked as number eight on his list. An island off the coast of Scotland called Jura that Rae recalled Grace mentioning once. 'Why are you telling me all this?' she said. 'What does any of this have to do with you and me?'

John leaned forward, elbows on the table. 'How did the vision happen? You said you saw Ben in a vision, but *how* did it happen? Did it come from nowhere, were you in the bath, walking down the street? It might be important.'

Rae bit the inside of her lip, anticipating a telling off for going into the forest alone. 'It was at the tree,' she said, 'the oak tree where you found me. There's something ... strange about it. The first time, it happened by accident, but the second time, when I saw your brother, I ... I did it on purpose.'

John didn't flinch. Didn't rant or rage, only pressed further. 'How did you do it?'

'I just touched it,' Rae said. 'There's some kind of energy beneath it, flowing through it, or ... something. I laid my hand flat against the surface and the next thing I knew I was thrown into another time. There was fire, and screaming and shouting, and a man wearing armour with a cut above his eye.'

'Ben?'

'No,' Rae said. 'Someone else.'

'You recognised him?'

Yes, he was in my bedroom, and in the shower too. 'No,' she said, 'never seem him before.' She glanced down at her hands, heart racing, and picked up the glass of water.

'Tell me what happened when you saw Ben,' John said.

He was going to spear me, she wanted to say, but the desperate look in John's eyes touched her heart and she couldn't bring herself to tell him. 'Nothing happened,' she said, 'he was talking to the other guy and a woman, but I couldn't hear what either of them were saying. They all wore armour and looked like they'd been fighting.' She shrugged. 'Like I said, I got the feeling it was from a long time ago, an echo of the past maybe?' John blew out through his cheeks and ran a hand through his hair. 'So, what does it all mean?' Rae said, 'you must have a theory?'

John got up and wandered back to the window. 'I've been stuck in Cranston Myre for too long,' he said. 'I need to re-trace Ben's steps, see if I missed anything.'

'That doesn't answer my question,' Rae said, 'tell me honestly, do you think that you and I are one of these … Draiocht?'

John drew long and hard from his beer then dropped the empty bottle in the bin. 'The only thing I'm certain of, is that Ben was caught up in something sinister, and I mean to find out what that was. In the meantime, you should stay away from the forest. You can move into here while I'm gone—'

'Hang on a minute,' Rae said, 'nothing's changed, John. I'm not leaving my home.'

'Fine, then come with me.'

Rae shook her head. 'No. Whatever's happening, it's happening here. We should stay in Cranston Myre.'

'And do what, Rae? I've been here for two years and found

nothing until you showed up, and even now all we've got are dreams and visions. I need something solid. I need to know that Ben is OK.'

'Then go,' she said, not meaning it, not really. John was the closest thing she had to an explanation, but she'd be damned if she was going to beg him to stay. 'Do what you have to do, but I'm staying put.'

John stared at her for a moment, nostrils flaring, but she stared right back. There was no way she was going to budge. 'Have it your way,' he said, 'but at least promise me you'll stay out of the forest until I get back.'

'Of course,' Rae said, crossing her fingers beneath the table. 'I won't step foot in the place.'

15

E mma watched from the tower as John dragged Raewyn off to the cottage. She'd been watching him for the better part of an hour so caught the show as Raewyn flashed him right before John decided he could no longer keep his hands off her. Unsettled after reading another of Evie's diaries, Emma had only come up to the attic to replace it with another when she had spotted John across the lawn. Had it been another day, had Emma not found John's bed empty the week before, then she might have thought Raewyn's sudden appearance a coincidence, her attempt to seduce him misguided, or even John's apparent inability to keep his eyes off her for more than a nano-second simply down to curiosity. But as it was Emma was feeling neither foolish nor naive.

It occurred to her as she watched the two of them rush off to fornicate, that she was not so different from her Aunt Evie after all. Evie may have had the fairy tale beginning, but even after three years of blissful happiness she too had found herself stood by this very window, silently watching while another woman stole the affections of the only man she had ever loved, just as Emma now watched John make a fool of himself with the newcomer, a girl who had appeared from nowhere and seemed to have embedded herself in every corner of Emma's life. Alexandra was clearly enamoured with the woman, as was Chris if his sudden fascination with the woods was anything to go by, and even Georgina, not given to expressing her opinion one way or another, had stated, quite out of the blue, that it was about time some young blood was injected into The Briar – whatever that meant – and now John.

And now John.

How many hours had Evie stood by this window, watching helplessly while another woman stepped into her shoes? How many more would Emma do the same?

Evie had locked herself away and poured her grief into the pages of a diary that no-one would ever read, and while she enveloped herself with sadness her husband drowned his sorrows between the legs of another woman. How long had Evie allowed the affair to go on before it all became too much? Before she decided enough was enough and tried to destroy that which she could no longer have?

Only Evie could answer that question.

Emma dropped the Diary back onto the pile and took up another. Maybe the answer was here, written between the pages of misery that had been Evie's only comfort during her months of self-reproach. Evie had miscarried three times before Richard sought refuge elsewhere, and three times over she blamed herself for failing to give him the family he so desperately wanted. If not her fault, then who's? Certainly not Richard's. He was as healthy as a horse, and, if the wagging tongues were to be believed, virile as ever. But not Evie. She was weak and sickly and plagued by her own failings as a woman, it stood to reason that it was she who was to blame, and because of that she allowed Richard his indiscretions with a woman nearly half his age.

The toxic mixture of grief and guilt engulfed Evie so completely that she didn't see what was happening to Richard until it was too late. He had become obsessed with the girl called Louisa, consumed by her beauty, enchanted with her guileless ways, until he saw nothing but her and felt nothing but his desire to have her. He no longer sought to comfort Evie, no longer tried to calm her fears, to reassure her that all was not lost, that they would find a way back, together, somehow. Instead he became content to leave her locked away with her books and her tears while he drowned his new love in affection and showered her with gifts. He was bewitched, blinded by passion, inflamed by desire and while his temptress inveigled herself deeper into his life, Evie became an empty shell, trapped by the notion of her own inadequacies.

But people saw, and people talked, and eventually help was sent in the form of Daegan Gilhooly.

It was Mrs Carter, Richard's housekeeper, who introduced Evie to Daegan. Concerned over Evie's health and her refusal to see any more doctors, Mrs Carter had called on Daegan's skills as a healer. Daegan's methods were frowned upon by many but Mrs Carter was an open-minded woman and saw Daegan for what she truly was; a gifted young woman with a desire to heal. Evie had refused to see her at first, but Mrs Carter could be persuasive when necessary and Daegan, being close to Evie's own age and plagued by her own insecurities, seemed harmless enough. Evie relented and it wasn't long before Daegan became a permanent fixture at Carrion Hall.

As the two girls became friends Evie began to regain a little of her spirit. She opened up to Daegan and in return Daegan confessed her own secret, that not only was she Louisa's sister, a fact that often brought her great discomfort, but that Louisa was already carrying Richard's unborn child. The news had hit Evie hard and in a fit of rage she had sent Daegan away, only to call her back the very next day when Mrs Carter confessed that Louisa was to take up residence in the little cottage in the woods, the same cottage that had been Evie and Richard's special place.

Evie and Daegan struck up a new friendship, one borne of a common desire to end Louisa's reign over Richard's heart and to give Evie the child she had thus far been unable to carry. It was a bond that would bring Evie back from the brink of madness, if only for a moment, before she once more fell prey to the demons that ate away at her heart.

With the final diary tucked neatly beneath her arm Emma made her way across the attic floor as the beginnings of a headache throbbed behind her eyes. Evie had been a weak and vacuous woman, but even she had found the strength of will to save the man she loved from his own foolish temptations. Her methods had been a little cabalistic for Emma's taste, but at this point she was willing to try anything.

ALEX WAS busy with a customer when Emma walked through the doors of Lotions and Potions. She smiled and raised an eyebrow before turning back to a balding middle-aged man with an overflowing basket and an unpleasant sheen of sweat on his pasty forehead. Dee's shop was the last place Emma wanted to be, and had it not been for the turn of events in the gardens that afternoon she would have quite happily driven the forty or so miles into Harleybrock to purchase her goods. But she had wasted enough time waiting for John to realise his mistake in ending their relationship, and if John's face when he looked at Raewyn was anything to go by, then she had precious little time left.

She found what she was looking for with relative ease. Dee's shop was well stocked with every outlandish herb, root, powder, and oil you could think of, and immaculately presented. It was the *only* positive thing that Emma could attribute to the woman, yet still she loathed to admit it. Even so, there was one more ingredient to find and no amount of searching had turned it up. Armed with candles, a glass bottle, strainer, dried jasmine, rose petals, pine pollen extract and Mucuna powder, Emma made her way towards the counter with an excuse ready on hand should anyone begin asking awkward questions, but in her haste to be done hadn't noticed Alex sneaking up beside her until a ridiculous shock of flamingo hair caught her unawares.

'What you got there, Cuz?' Alex said, nosing in Emma's basket. 'Pine pollen and *Mucuna*? You do know what they're used for, right? Are you planning to lure some poor unsuspecting fella back to your place for a bit of slap and tickle?'

'Don't be facetious,' Emma said, 'of course I know what they're for. They're also full of anti-oxidants and have immeasurable health benefits.' She sighed irritably and straightened her dress as an excuse to dry her clammy hands. 'If you really must know, Georgina and I are experimenting with various herbal tonics, lotions, and smoothies for when the hotel opens. If we can put something half decent together then maybe we can add them as a complimentary ...' she waved her hand in the air, grasping for the right word. 'Oh, I don't know. It's just an idea and something to do.'

'You know Dee can make just about anything you need?' Alex said. 'She's really good, knows her shit if you know what I mean.'

'I'm sure she does,' Emma said dryly. 'But it would be a nice touch for the guests to know that the product was made in-house by the patrons of the hotel.'

Alex nodded. 'It's a good idea, Cuz. I'm free tomorrow if you need any help?'

'Only with locating the last ingredient,' Emma said. 'Ashwagandha. Do you have it?'

'Capsule or powder?' Dee stepped from the next aisle, red hair hanging loosely about her shoulders and an inscrutable smile on her face. 'Is it for personal use, or—'

'Powder is fine,' Emma said.

Dee glanced casually at Emma's basket before reaching behind her and plucking a small packet of fine powder from the shelf. 'We stock it in larger quantities if you think—'

'Small will be just fine,' Emma said. She took the packet from Dee and turned to Alex. 'Would you till this up for me please, Alex.'

'Actually,' Dee said. 'Alex, would you mind bringing through some boxes of elderberry syrup while I see to Miss Ashley.' She took the basket before Emma could object and walked behind the counter. Alex shrugged apologetically then followed Dee before disappearing behind a black velvet curtain.

'Have you done this sort of thing before?' Dee asked, scanning each item before placing it into a paper bag.

'Exactly what sort of thing are you referring to?' Emma said.

'Making tonics and lotions,' Dee said. 'It's not as simple as people think. Too much of the wrong ingredient and you could end up with a nasty rash.'

'Really,' Emma said. 'Because from what I've read it really doesn't seem that hard.'

Dee raised an eyebrow but never faltered for a second. 'Do you mind if I ask where you got your recipes from?'

'As a matter of fact, I do,' Emma said. 'What's the matter, Dee? Worried about a little competition?'

Dee smiled and dropped the last item into the bag. 'Just be careful how you mix them, we wouldn't want to make your man too randy, would we? That will be sixty-eight pounds and forty-three pence.'

Emma handed over the money. 'Have you seen Christopher today?' she said casually. 'I can't seem to keep track of him these days. He seems to be spending a lot of time with the new girl that's moved into The Briar. I believe they've hit it off quite well.'

'Really?' Dee said, 'Alex also speaks highly of her, John too from what I hear.'

It was on the tip of Emma's tongue to hit back with another childish retort when the black curtain was pushed aside and Alex stepped out armed with two cardboard boxes, one balancing on top of the other. 'I'll be done here shortly,' she said. 'Fancy some lunch? My treat?'

'It's a bit late for lunch,' Emma said, though in truth she hadn't eaten all day.

'Oh, go on,' Alex said, 'I could do with the company. Meet me at the Rook in fifteen minutes?'

Emma's immediate reaction was to say no. She had never been overly fond of Alex, not in the way that Chris was. She tolerated her because she was family and because Chris thought the world of her, but she couldn't deny that she *was* hungry, and Alex did like to talk, so given her friendship with both Raewyn and John perhaps it was an opportunity not to be missed. 'OK then,' she said. 'Fifteen minutes, and don't be late.'

THE PUB WAS MOSTLY empty when Emma walked in, but it could have been full and she would have spotted John right away. He was stood at the bar talking with the landlord and was wearing a clean white shirt that set off his tanned arms. Having no compunction whatsoever about interrupting his conversation, Emma took the stool next to John and dropped her bag on the floor. 'Fancy seeing you here,' she said. 'I thought you were working.'

John and the landlord exchanged glances before the landlord made his excuses and left. 'Emma,' John said. 'I didn't think you liked pubs.'

'I can always make an exception,' she said. 'Don't worry, I'm not checking up on you. I only wanted to ask how your new designs are coming along. You promised me a spectacular winter garden in time for Christmas.'

John took a long drink from his pint. 'Henry and I made a start on the new beds today.'

'Oh?' Emma said, feigning surprise. 'That's wonderful, only ... it's just that ... well, I've had a few ideas of my own. Nothing too drastic, but I thought we might discuss them over dinner. Tonight maybe?'

'Can't it wait until tomorrow?'

'Why? Do you have plans?'

'Would it make any difference if I did?'

Emma smiled and laid a hand on his arm. 'It doesn't

matter if you're too busy. I just thought ... whilst it's fresh in my mind ... and before you get too far along ...'

'What time, Em?'

Emma smiled to herself. She liked it when he called her Em. 'How about seven?' she said, as the doors flew open and Alex walked in, 'I'll have Georgina rustle up something special.'

'Hey, you two.' Alex kissed John on the cheek and narrowed her eyes at Emma. 'Did I miss anything?'

'Not a thing,' Emma said, 'shall we grab a table then?'

EMMA CHOSE a table with an excellent view of the bar and could feel Alex's disapproving eyes boring into her skull as she read the menu.

'Please tell me that you are not still interested in John,' Alex said.

'Why on earth would you say that?' Emma said. 'You and I both know that ship sailed a long time ago.'

'Is that right,' Alex said, 'because you couldn't be more obvious if you tried. You were one step away from licking his face when I walked in.'

'I was doing no such thing,' Emma said. 'My only interest in John is those green fingers of his.'

'Liar,' Alex said.

'Excuse me?'

'I'm not blind, Emma, and neither is anyone else. It's painfully obvious that you're still in love with him, and if it's obvious to me you can be damn sure it's obvious to John.'

Let's hope so, thought Emma. She sighed and put the menu down. 'I think you're seeing something that isn't there,' she said. 'Can we drop this ridiculous line of conversation and order some food?'

'No, we can't,' Alex said. 'You can act as innocent as you like, but I know you. You're up to something.'

'Well then I don't think you know me very well at all,' Emma said. 'And I'm sure you have much better things to do than worry about me.'

'Why did you invite John to dinner?'

Emma risked a small glance towards the bar. 'To discuss work,' she said. 'He *is* my gardener, or haven't you noticed?'

Alex glared across the table. 'Please tell me you didn't buy a basket full of aphrodisiacs for John.'

'Now you're just being absurd,' Emma said. 'I told you what those purchases were for. I have no romantic interest in John, or anyone else for that matter. Now can we please drop this ridiculous line of questioning, or would you prefer to dine alone?'

Alex sat back in her chair. 'Fine,' she said, 'I'll drop it, but only if you promise not to interfere between John and Rae.'

Emma felt her stomach drop. 'What on earth are you talking about?'

'I saw the way you looked at Dee when she mentioned them. If looks could kill we'd be visiting Dee in the morgue right now.'

'Well you might be visiting her, I certainly wouldn't.'

'You know what I mean. Promise me you won't hassle Rae.'

'Alexandra, I have never *hassled* anyone in my life. If that girl chooses to hang around John like a lovesick teenager then it is of no interest to me.'

'So, you've noticed them together then?'

'That's not what I said. Don't try to put words in my

mouth. Now do you think it's possible we could change the subject. If I'd known I was coming here for an interrogation I really wouldn't have bothered.'

Alex narrowed her eyes. 'OK then,' she said. 'Consider it dropped for now. But I still don't believe you.'

'Hallelujah,' Emma said, 'I'll try not to lose any sleep over it.'

16

Georgina finally answered the door after the fourth ring of the bell. She casually informed Dee that Emma was busy but would be down shortly if she cared to wait in the drawing room. The decision to visit Emma had been the result of much contemplation and a certain amount of soul searching on Dee's part. But in the end Dee owed it to herself, and to Evie to get Emma as far away from here as possible.

Knowing something and seeing it for yourself are two very different things, as Dee had discovered that morning when she saw Raewyn at the Briar. She'd gone deep into the forest on a whim, hoping that a visit to the sacred oak might bring her some clarity, but instead she had found Raewyn there, hand pressed to the tree and eyes like frosted glass. Then Alex had showed up and Dee had retreated into the trees, but not before waiting to see what Alex would do. The fact that Alex was even there was a surprise – few seldom made it through to the sacred oak – but more surprising than that was that Alex had not appeared shocked or upset to find Raewyn in such a state, and had only watched from a distance until Rae finally snapped out of her trance. Dee had quietly slipped away but had decided to keep a close eye on Alex from now on.

The shock of seeing the child returned, however, had been somewhat numbed by the fact that Dee had emotionally prepared herself for it. But the shock of seeing Richard's painting was not so easily absorbed. She knew, of course, that the painting had been restored. Chris had complained constantly about how much Emma was spending on the damn thing, but what she didn't know was the level of emotion it would evoke when she saw it again. They had done a good job of patching him up. The slash across his face was unnoticeable from this distance, but the fact that it could no longer be seen made no difference to Dee. The memories of that night were still so raw that the desecration of Richard's portrait could have been only yesterday, and the knowledge of her failure so overwhelming that even now it rose like a stone to her throat. She dropped a hand to the pocket of her skirt where her knife rested reassuringly against her thigh, the same knife that had destroyed the only kind man she had ever known.

'What do *you* want?'

Dee turned to find Emma stood in the doorway, hands on hips wearing a red silk robe and matching towel wrapped around her head. The subtle sweetness of rose petals and jasmine drifted into the room and Dee allowed herself the merest hint of a smile. 'I have a proposition for you,' Dee said, 'something that will be mutually beneficial.'

'What could I possibly want from you?' Emma said, oozing the same old charm that Dee had come to expect from her.

'If we can go somewhere more private then you'll find out,' Dee said. 'I think you'll find it worth your while.'

'I'm busy,' Emma said. 'Whatever it is it'll have to wait.' She turned to leave, but Dee wasn't giving up that easy.

'It's about John Baxter,' she called out, 'and the ingredients you bought from me today.'

Emma halted, bristled, and turned back. 'That's none of your business,' she said icily. 'And I'll thank you not to assume what my purchases were for.'

'I know what you're trying to do,' Dee said, 'but it won't work, at least not the way you want it to. I'm here to offer an alternative.'

'An alternative to what, exactly. As I told Alex, those ingredients are for—'

'Smoothies and lotions,' Dee said, 'I know. I also know you're lying, because I've made that same recipe myself many times, so unless a one-night stand with John is all you're after, I suggest you hear me out.'

Emma's face turned redder than the towel on her head. 'I think it's time for you to leave.'

'And I will,' Dee said. 'But not until we've had a little chat, or would you prefer I discuss it with John instead? Look, all I'm asking for is ten minutes of your time. What harm could it do. You may even like what I have to say.'

Emma pressed her lips tightly together. Maybe threatening to go to John wasn't the best idea, but short of tying the woman up how else was Dee going to get her to listen?

'Ten minutes?' Emma said, 'then you'll leave?'

'Cross my heart and hope to die,' Dee said.

'One can only hope,' Emma said. 'Very well, follow me.'

Emma turned and headed back out into the hallway and Dee had to hurry just to keep up. There was a door behind the staircase that opened out into a wide corridor, and Emma led them through it, striding ahead like a woman on a mission. She stopped outside a set of double doors, opened one of them and indicated with an impatient swish of the hand that Dee should hurry up. 'Spit it out then,' she said with an impatient look on her face. 'I haven't got all day.'

Dee guessed they were inside the library, or the beginnings of one anyway. A large open fireplace stood idle in the corner, its hearth shiny and new, and a burgundy Chesterfield was placed haphazardly in front of it as though left there temporarily. A coffee table designed to look like a pile of enormous encyclopaedias sat beside it, and a lamp, still in its plastic wrapper, sat on top. Empty bookshelves lined the walls with stacks of books propped up on the floor, waiting to be put away. The whole place gave off an air of abandonment, and Dee wondered what Emma spent all day doing locked away in this monster of a house. 'This place could do with a bit of a clean,' she said, running her fingers over the dusty jacket of a book and wondering if Emma had read a single one of them. She didn't seem the type somehow.

'I'll be sure to pass your concerns on to the staff,' Emma said. 'Now if you wouldn't mind.' She gestured toward the Chesterfield, but instead of sitting down Dee opened her bag and took out a brown, plastic bottle.

'Ashwagandha liquid extract,' she said. 'The powder you bought today doesn't absorb into alcohol so well. This is much better. Consider it a gift.'

'How very generous,' Emma said, 'and it isn't even my birthday. You have eight minutes remaining.'

Dee placed the plastic bottle on the table and shrugged. 'It's there if you want it, but if you want John back in your bed permanently, then I have a much better solution.'

Emma didn't say anything, only looked at Dee as though she was something the cat had dragged in.

'The tonic you're attempting to make,' Dee said, 'the one you're going to slip into John's drink tonight when he isn't looking. It won't work. It was designed for instant gratification, an easy fix for a one night stand and 99% of the time it works just fine. John will become aroused only moments after drinking it and will most likely go all night long, but one night isn't what you're after, is it? The good news is I have something that will make John love and adore you for the rest of your life, or until you tire of him, but something tells me that's not likely to happen.' She pulled a small glass vial out of her bag and held it up for Emma to see. 'No more Raewyn to worry about, no more cold empty bed, and no more tonics.'

Emma didn't move, didn't even look at the vial in Dee's hand. 'So, is that it then?' she said. 'You're trying to sell me a love potion? That's what you came over here for? You're even crazier than I thought, now please leave before I have someone escort you out.'

Phase two then, thought Dee. 'No,' she said, slipping the vial into her pocket. 'Not until you've heard everything I have to say.'

'There's more!' Emma gave a scornful laugh. 'You're only one step away from being tied to a stake and thrown on a bonfire as it is—'

'Daegan Gilhoolly,' Dee said. 'I assume you know the name?'

Emma's eyes narrowed. 'What do *you* know of Daegan Gilhoolly?'

'A lot more than you might think,' Dee said. 'You've been reading Evie's diaries, yes?'

Emma paled. 'I have no idea what you're talking about.'

'Yes, you do,' Dee said. 'I also know that's where you got the idea for the tonic, because Evie used it too.'

'That's quite enough,' Emma said, 'I want you out of here, now.'

She opened the library door, but Dee was quick on her feet and was over to Emma in a flash and slammed the door shut. 'Just sit down and listen to what I have say,' she said.

'I'll do no such thing,' Emma said, 'get out of my way, or I'll–'

Dee took out her knife and held it in Emma's face. 'I didn't come here to hurt you, Emma, but if you don't sit down and let me speak, I will.'

Emma turned paler than the marble hilt of Dee's knife, but her eyes lost none of their steeliness. 'You're crazy if you think you'll get away with this.'

'I'm not trying to get away with anything,' Dee said. 'I only want you to pay attention to what I'm about to say. Now go park your bony arse on that settee before I lose my temper.'

Emma eyed the knife. She might be a bitch, but she wasn't a stupid one. She backed away from Dee, then turned and casually walked over to the Chesterfield. Dee took a deep breath. She hadn't intended to use the knife, not for this anyway, but Miss High and Mighty had given her no choice. She reached behind her and locked the library door, then popped the key in her pocket next to the vial. Her next words would have to be chosen carefully. Too much and Emma would be scared off, but too little and she'd think Dee a fraud. Dee had always known about Evie's diaries. She'd seen her writing in them often enough but had long suspected they had burned along with half of Carrion Hall. But the fact that Emma was attempting to make a tonic that Dee herself had created was at least promising, it meant that Emma was either open to possibility, or she was desperate enough to try anything. Dee hoped it was a little of both.

Emma sat patiently on the couch watching Dee with calculating eyes. 'You're almost out of time,' she said. 'You've wasted eight minutes on this ridiculous charade. Two more and I'll be walking out that door whether you try to stop me or not. Might I suggest you get on with whatever it is you feel merits threatening me with a knife.'

Dee smiled. Emma was tougher than she'd given her credit for. 'Then I'll get right to the point,' she said. She walked over to the Chesterfield and stood in front of Emma. 'You want Raewyn Winters out of the picture and John all to yourself, yes or no?'

Emma lifted her chin slightly. 'You seem awfully vested in this. What's Raewyn got to do with you?'

'That part is none of your concern.'

'It is if you're intending to commit a crime,' Emma said. 'Is the girl in any danger?'

'I don't intend to 'off' her if that's what you mean,' Dee said. 'Let's just say that Raewyn is complicated and leave it at that. You've been reading Evie's diaries, yes? And I assume that because you have the recipe to make the tonic that you have also read *why* Evie was prepared to go to such extremes. You know about Daegan's sister, Louisa, I presume?'

A flare of intrigue lit up Emma's eyes. *Finally*, thought Dee. 'Go on,' Emma said. 'I'm listening.'

'Louisa was talented,' Dee said, 'beautiful too, but it takes more than just good looks to turn a man's head the way she turned Richard's.'

'He was bewitched,' Emma said. 'Evie said as much.'

Dee smiled. 'Bewitched, enchanted, spellbound ... call it what you will, but it all boils down the same thing. Louisa drugged Richard, forced him into loving her, and, depending on how much you want John, I'm proposing to do the same for you.'

Emma raised her eyebrows. 'You want to *drug* him? Are you insane?'

'It's only what you were going to do tonight. This is just a more ... long-term solution.'

Emma opened her mouth and closed it again, and Dee took that to be a positive. She wasn't out and out saying no at least.

'How do you know about the diaries?' Emma said. 'I was alone when I found them, and I've told no-one.'

'I have my ways,' Dee said.

'You'll have to be more specific than that,' Emma said. 'If you're going to hold a knife to my throat then I'd at least like to know the reason why. You wanted me to listen, now I'm listening. How did you know about the diaries?'

Dee felt a cold draft on the back of her neck. 'It isn't important.'

'It is if you want to stay out of prison,' Emma said. 'What makes you think I won't call the police the second you leave here?'

'Because I know that look in your eyes. You'll stop at nothing to save the man you love from making a huge mistake, and John being with Raewyn *is* a mistake. I'm offering you the solution. You're a smart woman, take it.'

Emma laughed, but it was nervous laughter and Dee could see that despite her misgivings that she was mulling it over. 'For argument's sake, let's just say you're right,' Emma said. 'How do I know you can deliver?'

'I guess you'll just have to trust me.'

Emma snorted. 'That's a tall order coming from you.'

'Perhaps, but it's the best offer you're going to get.'

'You say you know Evie's diaries,' Emma said, 'but Evie never resorted to such extremes.'

'Evie's situation was different,' Dee said. 'Richard already loved her, he just needed reminding of that fact.'

Emma scowled, but they both knew Dee was right. 'You keep referring to Evie as though you knew her,' Emma said. 'Why is that?'

'Again,' Dee said, 'not important. Let's focus on the real issue here.'

Emma shook her head. 'Not good enough.'

'Look,' Dee said, 'we can go on like this all day, or I can just show you what I can do.' She reached into her bag and removed another vial – a larger one that contained a brown, oily substance. She handed the vial to Emma and told her to remove the cap.

'What is it?' Emma said, screwing her nose up at the strong smell of aniseed.

'I'll show you,' Dee said. 'Give me the towel off your head.'

Emma raised an eyebrow but did as she was asked. Dee placed the towel over the table, held her hand above it, then quickly sliced the knife across the palm of her hand. She inhaled sharply as cold steel bit into flesh, but it was a pain born of necessity and one she had endured many times over. It passed quickly and Dee closed her hand around the wound letting blood drip onto the towel. Emma, however, was not used to such things and stared at Dee as though she was stark raving mad.

'What on earth are you doing?' she said, 'have you completely lost your mind?'

'It's only a scratch,' Dee said. 'When I open my hand, I want you to pour the contents of that vial along the cut, got it?' Emma gave Dee a dubious look, but to her credit she nodded and moved a little closer. Dee slowly opened her hand. The cut was deeper than she would have liked, but a superficial wound would not have been as impressive. 'Do it,' she said, readying herself for the pain. Demonstrations were all well and good, but this part hurt like a bitch.

Emma kept a sceptical eye on Dee as she leaned over and poured the brown liquid into the cut. The oil mingled with Dee's blood and began to hiss and fizz like water thrown on hot coals. The smell always reminded Dee of roasted pork, so not exactly unpleasant, but the white froth that poured from the wound was like something from a rabid animal's mouth.

Emma watched in astonishment. This part was always the most impressive. As the oil soaked into Dee's skin, the wound began closing up from the inside out, knitting rapidly together like a slash wound in reverse. 'Impossible,' Emma said, shaking her head. 'I've never seen anything like it. What was in that vial?'

'Something rather more complex than a love potion.' Dee wiped her hand on the towel and flexed her fingers as the unavoidable pins and needles took hold. 'That was just a small example of what can be done with the right ingredients,' she said. 'Unfortunately, blood is usually a factor in making them work, but with your tonic only a drop will be needed, a pin prick at most.'

Emma sat back against the couch, eyes wide with incredulity. 'Who are you?' she said, '*what* are you?'

'A friend, believe it or not.' Dee pulled the first vial from her pocket and held it out for Emma. 'This one is for you. It's only a sample – a try before you buy if you like – a drop of your blood will activate it, then John is all yours.'

Emma blinked and looked down at the vial. She took it

from Dee and held it up to the light. 'Did you use this on my brother?'

Dee laughed. 'The last thing your brother needs is any help in that department.'

Emma made a face. 'Alright,' she said, 'let's just say I'm gullible enough to fall for this, what do you want in return? I'm sure you're not doing this out of the goodness of your heart, if you even have one.'

Dee pulled a document from her bag and dropped it in Emma's lap.

'What's this?' Then Emma's eyes widened. 'This is a joke, right? You expect me to *sell* Carrion Hall to you?'

'I'll pay you twice what it's worth,' Dee said. 'You won't get a better offer anywhere else.'

'Why?' Emma said, 'what does someone like you want with a place like this?'

'What do you care?' Dee said. 'You'd be set for life with the man of your dreams by your side. Isn't that what you wanted?'

Emma looked at the vial then handed it back to Dee. 'No deal,' she said, 'and your time is up.'

Dee shrugged and put the vial back in her bag. Rome wasn't built in a day after all. 'You have a week to think on it.' She wiped the knife on Emma's towel, sheathed it and put it back in her pocket. 'If you change your mind you know where to find me. In the meantime, whisper a word of this to anyone and it'll be Raewyn's blood that I slip into that vial, not yours.'

'You said she's bad for John.' Emma got up from the couch, pulled her robe a little tighter. 'In your words "John being with Raewyn is a mistake". Why is that? Is she like you? Is she a witch?'

Dee sighed and took the door key out of her pocket. Why did people always think that? 'I'm not a witch, Emma, and neither is Raewyn. But you're right, she is like me, so don't fuck with her.' She unlocked the door, paused, and turned back. 'What I'm offering you is only the tip of a very large iceberg that gets us both what we want. But make no mistake, Emma, I want the Hall, but I don't need it. Take the offer or don't, either way my life will continue to tick along nicely, but what you have to ask yourself is this: can you spend the rest of your life without John knowing that you could've done something about it? I've left the liquid root extract for you, just in case you decide to go ahead with the whole seduction plan tonight. Call it a gesture of good will.' She winked and walked out of the room, leaving Emma still holding the document.

Dee smiled to herself as she walked out Carrion Hall. The meeting had gone better than she'd hoped. Emma was her mother's daughter alright – stubborn and sceptical right until the end – but what Evie had lacked in confidence Emma had in abundance. She'd take the offer. Dee was sure of it.

She had to. For her sake, and for Dee's.

17

E xhausted from thinking about things that made no sense, Rae took a long bath, stuck a frozen lasagne in the oven and retired to the couch in her PJ's with a book, but after twenty minutes of re-reading the same paragraph several times over, she threw the book down. John would not get out of her damn head, and not only that, she'd also begun to court the idea that Grace's motivations for purchasing the cottage were not entirely innocent.

The idea that Grace could be involved in something as heinous as the Draiocht was ridiculous, preposterous, and yet the little that Rae knew pointed to exactly that. Grace had given Rae the crystal, Grace had purchased the cottage in Rae's name and made sure Rae received the key upon her death, and Grace had talked about the island of Jura, one of Ben's suspected meeting places of the Draiocht. Of course, it was possible it was all just coincidence, but as much as Rae wanted to believe that, she knew in her heart it wasn't true.

She lay back on the couch and closed her eyes, remembering her waking dreams as a child. Hallucinations Grace had called them, though Rae wasn't entirely sure that was true, when Rae had seen fishes swimming around the room, a disembodied hand dragging itself across the floor, or beetles crawling over her bed. Terrifying for Rae, worrying for Grace, but it had been the hallucination of a shadowed man standing beside her bed that had made Grace hesitate before entering Rae's bedroom at night.

Rae rolled her crystal back and forth across her chest and thought of the night golden eyes was in her bedroom. He'd been a shadow to begin with too. Could they be one and the same? The hallucinations had stopped the day Grace gave Rae the pendant, and Rae had thought nothing of it at the time, glad to be rid of them, but now ...

She held the crystal up to her face – unspectacular in every way if not for the web of silver thorns that encompassed it. It was little more than a month past her thirteenth birthday when Granddad had lit the final firework of the evening, but it had failed to go off. Not long after that everyone had gone home. Tilly had gone to stay at a friend's house, and Grace and Granddad were in the kitchen cleaning up. Rae had remained outside, wanting to watch the neighbours' fireworks and to look at the stars, despite the fact it was beginning to rain. She remembered looking towards the bottom of the garden and seeing someone stood there, and for reasons she couldn't fathom, even to this day, she had walked towards him. If she saw his face, she didn't remember, only that he held out the dead firework, and she took it from him.

The next thing she remembered was waking up in bed with no memory of how she got there. Grace was beside her, face pale and drawn, and Rae could tell she'd been crying. She told her Granddad had died, that he'd had a heart attack, but Rae later discovered that he'd tried to reach her before the firework went off. The shock of seeing a firework explode in his granddaughter's hand had caused Winston Winters' heart to fail and he was dead before he hit the ground. Rae hadn't had a scratch on her. It was right after that that Grace gave Rae the pendant.

She got up and walked to the window. It was full dark outside but what was to stop her visiting the tree now? Maybe it would show her something more useful this time? Like who the heck golden eyes was for starters, and the woman – the albino who had tried to protect Rae in her last vision – who was she? But then a set of headlights came into view and all thoughts of the tree were forgotten as Chris climbed out of his car, suit jacket pulled tight against the wind. Rae hadn't heard from him since dinner last night, where he'd been only a shadow of his usual flirtatious self. In fact, he'd shown more interest in his phone than any conversation with Rae, which was why she was so surprised when he suddenly showed up at her door.

'Hello stranger,' she said, opening the door to a cold blast of wind. 'I wasn't expecting you tonight.'

'You gonna let me in, Winters? It's freezing out here?'

Rae caught a strong whiff of alcohol as he brushed past and headed straight for the fire. Suddenly conscious that she wasn't wearing a bra, she reached behind the door and took down a long woollen cardigan.

Chris held his back to the wood burner, warming his hands. 'Got anything to drink?'

'Tea or coffee?' Rae tied the belt on her cardi, wishing she hadn't chosen to wear these particular pyjamas with matching bunny slippers.

'I was thinking something a bit stronger,' Chris said. 'Got any whiskey?'

'I have wine?' Then she remembered the Cognac that Alex had donated. Still overcome with guilt after the horse-riding debacle, she had insisted that a decent bottle of booze was the least she could do

'Perfect,' Chris said, 'you pour the drinks and I'll crank up the fire.'

Rae fetched two cut glass tumblers down from the kitchen cupboard and poured them each a shot. Chris, having thrown another log on the fire, removed his jacket and joined Rae at the table. 'Cheers,' he said, then threw back his head and smiled with approval. 'That's good stuff, Winters. You have great taste.'

'*Alex* has great taste,' Rae corrected, 'I wouldn't know a good brandy from a bad one.'

'Be a shame to keep it all to yourself then, and is that food I can smell?'

Rae smiled. 'You're welcome to share my frozen lasagne if you wish, but I can't promise it'll taste any good.'

'Well when you put it like that how could I resist? I will accept your heart felt invitation to dinner, but only if I can assist with my world-famous salad.'

'Wow,' Rae said, '*world* famous, I'm impressed. I would never have pegged you as a cook.'

'Since when did throwing a bit of lettuce around have anything to do with cooking? Go put your feet up and I'll take over from here.'

Rae gave him a dubious look, but Chris had already donned her fuchsia pinny and was rolling up his sleeves.

. . .

THE LASAGNE WASN'T TOO bad as frozen packet foods go, and Chris kept true to his word by producing a very passable salad, though perhaps not quite so delicious as he had boasted. His presence had proved to be a welcome distraction as he told stories of being raised by an aunt who believed children should be seen and not heard. By all accounts his sister, Emma, had been the one always in trouble, and Chris, the sweet little angel, something that Rae had difficulty believing. They didn't touch on his mood at their previous meeting though, and while Chris entertained Rae with anecdotes about previous girlfriends, she couldn't help but wonder why.

'Maybe I should invite you round more often,' she said, clearing away the dishes. 'This would've been a very dull evening of burnt lasagne and a not-so-scary book if you hadn't turned up.'

'As I recall, I wasn't invited,' Chris said, 'but you are welcome nonetheless.'

He stood to help Rae clear the dishes, but she refused. 'You've done enough,' she said. 'Go sit.'

'I quite like the bossy Winters,' Chris said, 'it makes your eyes go all smouldery.'

'My eyes do not smoulder,' Rae said. 'You've just had too much to drink.'

'Well bloodshot didn't have quite the same ring to it,' Chris said, and laughed when Rae threw a piece of lettuce at him.

Dishes done, they both retired to the living room. Rae took the chair by the fire, still mindful of the last time they were alone together, while Chris dropped down onto the couch. 'I don't bite, Winters,' he said, loosening his shirt collar and kicking off his shoes. 'Come join me over here.'

He'd brought the now half empty bottle of brandy with him and placed it on the floor by his feet.

'I would, but I'm concerned you may be flammable,' Rae said. 'There's more alcohol in your blood than there is in that bottle.'

Chris paused with the glass halfway to his lips and grinned. 'Then let's be flammable together.' He picked up the bottle and moved to sit on the floor by Rae's feet. Rae lifted her legs and tucked them beneath her, covering her glass as Chris attempted to top it up.

'Don't be dull, Winters,' he said, 'it's not as if either of us have work tomorrow.'

'Maybe not,' Rae said. 'But you still have to get home, and I have an early start tomorrow.' It was a lie, but the look in his eyes was starting to make her nervous.

'I could always stay?' he said, running a finger suggestively over Rae's leg.

'I don't think that would be a good idea,' she said, 'for either of us.'

Chris smiled and put down his glass, but Rae caught the shift in his mood, the slight stiffness in his shoulders. 'Can I give you a piece of advice?' he said.

'If it's about my cooking skills, then I don't think you're qualified,' Rae said, 'I didn't want to say anything earlier, but your salad wasn't all it was cracked up to be.'

'I'm trying to be serious, Winters.'

'So am I.' She didn't like where this was headed. Not one little bit.

'Just listen to me for a minute, will you? It's not often I have something important to say.' Chris took hold of Rae's hand and looked earnestly into her eyes. 'Don't waste your time on John,' he said, 'he doesn't deserve you and he never will. You should be with someone who sees you for the amazing woman you are.'

'Someone like you, you mean?'

Chris released her hand and picked up his glass. 'Why not me?' he said. 'I'd take good care of you if you'd let me.'

Rae bit the inside of her mouth. This wasn't how she'd pictured her evening going. 'What makes you think I'm interested in John?'

'I've seen the way you look at him. I saw the same look in Emma's eyes not so long ago and look where that got her.' He threw back his head, downed his drink in one and stood up. 'Look,' he said, 'the guy is a miserable fucker who will rip out your heart and stamp all over it. You can do a lot better. Mind if I use your bathroom?'

'Top of the stairs, can't miss it,' Rae said. She watched him go and rubbed the back of her neck. Awkward situations always made her nervous, and the night had definitely taken an awkward turn. She blew out her cheeks and collected the brandy from the floor. She'd call Chris a taxi, he was in no state to drive and the weather was awful. But then a brisk walk up the hill and some fresh hair might sober him up. She heard the chain flush and gathered the glasses from by the fire. As soon as he came down, she'd ask him to leave, politely but firmly, make sure he knew where they stood. But no sooner had she put the glasses in the sink than music drifted in from the living room and Chris appeared by her side.

'Dance with me, Winters,' he said, green eyes flashing in the warm light as he guided her back towards the fire.

'I think maybe it's time you went home,' Rae said. "These Eyes" was playing on the radio by The Guess Who, which seemed rather apt given the way he was looking at her.

'Do you trust me, Winters?' he said.

'Of course,' Rae said, only half lying. 'Why wouldn't I?'

He turned her hand over to where the arterial vein glowed blue beneath her skin. 'If you were mine,' he said, kissing the spot where her pulse hammered fiercely, 'I would treat you like a queen, make you laugh every day, and make love to you every night.'

'Chris,' Rae said, 'It's getting late ...' He pushed up the sleeve of her cardigan and trailed kisses along the inside of her arm, and when he reached the crook of her elbow he softly tickled the delicate skin there with his whiskers until Rae yelped and pulled her arm away. 'Well the laughing part is certainly true,' she said, pulling down her sleeve. 'Though most of the time it's at you, not with you.'

'I can make the sexy part true as well, if you'll let me,' he grinned. He grabbed the belt of her cardigan and pulled her to him.

'Go home,' she said, placing a hand on his chest, 'it's getting late, and I want an early night.'

'Sounds perfect,' he said. 'I'll join you.'

'I mean it,' Rae said. 'Go home. I have plans in the morning. I need to sleep.'

Chris rolled his eyes, eyes that were now filmy from a half bottle of brandy. 'OK,' he said, 'I'll go, but only if you allow me one dance before you throw me out in the cold.'

Rae shook her head.

'Come on, Winters,' he said. 'One dance then I'll go. Cross my heart and hope to die.' He crossed his fingers and held them over his chest.

Rae sighed. 'Fine,' she said, 'one dance, then you, my friend, are gone. Deal?'

'Deal.' He grinned broadly, put his hands behind her waist and pulled her into him.

Rae slid her hands over his shoulders, and against her better judgement, allowed herself to relax as Chris sang softly into her hair. He had a good voice, deep and soothing, hypnotic almost as she rested her head against his chest, listening to the soft thud of his heart. The room was warm and cozy while outside a howling gale blew making the fire hiss and spark, and when the song ended and another began, Rae barely noticed. It was as though a warm blanket had descended on the room, covering them with melodious comfort, and Rae lost herself for a moment in the cocoon of tranquillity, so much so that it felt perfectly natural when Chris lowered his head and touched his lips to hers, and to her shame she kissed him back. She couldn't help it. His lips tasted like honey and nutmeg, and it had been such a long time since Darryl had shown her even the faintest interest. And boy oh boy, was he a good kisser.

Her cardigan slid to the floor as Chris released the belt, and when his tongue mingled with hers her body responded in a way that felt disturbingly treacherous. It felt good to be touched like this, to be wanted, desired even, but while her body was in heaven her mind was setting off alarm bells all over the place. She didn't want this. Not really. Hadn't wanted it from the very beginning, so why was she allowing it to happen now? 'I'm sorry, Chris,' she said, 'this is a mistake.'

'You're thinking too much,' Chris said. 'Just relax and let it happen.' He began edging her towards the couch, one step at a time while his lips nuzzled her neck, and when he pushed her back onto the soft cushions and swiftly removed his shirt, Rae felt the first flutter of panic.

'Chris,' she said. 'I don't want this. You have to stop.'

His skin was flushed, stomach rigid, and when she tried to get up, he pushed her back down and lowered himself on top of her. His eyes had taken on a glazed look and his breath, now hot and heavy, reeked of brandy. He buried his face in the crook of her neck, lips kissing, sucking, nuzzling.

'Stop,' Rae said. She lifted his face as it moved down towards her cleavage. 'I think you should go.'

But Chris was no longer listening. Nimble fingers fiddled with the buttons of her pyjama top, but Rae slapped his hand away. 'I mean it,' she said. 'You're going too far.'

Chris looked up with a devilish glint in his eye. 'Stop fighting me, Rae, and you never know, you might even enjoy it.'

That earned him a slap across the face. 'Get the fuck off me, NOW,' she said, and pushed against his chest. Chris pushed back, pinning her to the couch and grinning as though this was all some big, stupid game. So she hit him again, and again until a dark look came over his face, and just when she thought she'd gotten through to him, his fist slammed into her cheek.

Shock, pain, panic – all these things crashed into Rae as blood filled her mouth, then a sweaty palm clamped down over her lips and Chris's knees forced her legs apart. She screamed inside her head, bucked and heaved beneath his crushing weight, twisted and pushed, but her efforts only seemed to heighten Chris' pleasure. His face was red with excitement, eyes glazed with lust, and nothing she did seemed to make a blind bit of difference. Fear gripped her like iron fist, and as his hand began tugging at her underwear, she realised she had to do something, *anything* to make him stop.

The very real possibility that she was about to be raped injected fire into Rae's veins and she grabbed Chris's wrist with both hands and twisted as hard as she could. He was strong, stronger than she thought possible, but the effort moved his hand just enough so that she could sink her teeth into the fleshy part of his palm. She bit down hard, drawing blood, and when Chris yelled out, she used the temporary distraction to get a foot beneath his hip. She pushed with everything she had and sent him sprawling onto the floor, giving her the upper hand for a fraction of a second that she used to her full advantage. She pounced on top of him, madness raging through her veins. She hated him, hated his face, his leering eyes, his slick, disgusting tongue. She hated everything about him. He was a vile, repulsive thing, not worthy of her mercy, not worthy to breathe the air she breathed. She grabbed his hair with both hands, lifted his head and slammed it into the floor, again and again and again. She wanted him to hurt, wanted him to suffer as he would have made her suffer, but once more Chris surprised her with his strength.

His lips pulled back in a snarl as his hand shot up, grabbed Rae's throat, and squeezed. Then his other hand joined in and both worked together, trying to choke the life from out of her. Blood thundered in Rae's ears as she tried to prize the fingers from her neck. She couldn't breathe, couldn't move, and she clawed desperately at her throat before catching her reflection in the window on the other side of the room. Her hair had been pulled half out of its tie, face red and puffy, eyes bulging wide. She was pathetic. Weak and naive. It made her sick to her stomach to feel so helpless.

But she wasn't helpless. Far from it.

She released Chris's fingers and instead concentrated her efforts on his face. With one hand she grabbed his cheek, fingers clamped tightly around his jaw, thumb pressed firmly into the opposite cheek. There was a fluttering along her spine, like butterflies with their wings on fire, that spread into her stomach, growing like a swirling mass of hate. It filled her like a great pulsating thing, building in momentum as the heat grew, moving into her chest, spreading through her arms, demanding to be released. Chris' eyes were wild, so different from the man who had taken her to dinner, to the carnival and made her laugh. This was not a man beneath her, but an evil thing that had to be stopped, at any cost. *Let's see how many girls want you after this, you fuck,* she thought, and with one last surge of heat she released her vengeance, and let it explode into his face.

18

Emma was dressed in her most provocative outfit. It was a little over the top for the occasion, but the turquoise silk clung in all the right places and draped suggestively where needed – perfect for an evening of seduction. She had bathed in rose water, dabbed splashes on all her erogenous zones, and had prepared the tonic according to Evie's diary. A small glass bottle was now hidden inside her bra. Leaving nothing to chance, Emma had also placed scented candles on the dining room table and splashed rosewater all over the room. It smelled thickly of vanilla and flowers, but not unpleasantly so and she put another dab in her cleavage, just for good measure.

Georgina had prepared a delicious dinner of roast lamb and minted potatoes, and a bottle of Merlot was sitting corked and ready between the two place settings. The lights were dimmed, the fire was lit, and soft music was playing in the background. All that was needed now, was John.

A man of his word and ever punctual, John turned up at exactly 7pm.

'Thanks for coming,' Emma said, noting the rolled-up drawings tucked neatly beneath his arm. 'I thought we could eat in the dining room. It so seldom gets used with only Chris and I living here.' She showed him through to the formal area, just beyond the drawing room where her father's painting sat above the fireplace. 'Terrible weather again tonight,' she said, 'I hope another storm isn't moving in.'

John removed his jacket, placed it casually over a chair and began unravelling the drawings. 'The first stage should be complete in a few days,' he said, 'but that all depends on what changes you have in mind.'

'Actually, I thought we might eat first,' Emma said. 'It would be a shame to let Georgina's meal ruin. You know how she can be where food is concerned.' She took the drawings from him, rolled them back up and placed them on the floor beneath the table, out of sight, out of mind.

John frowned but pulled out a chair and sat down. 'I didn't realise it was going to be so formal,' he said.

'Oh, it's not,' Emma said. 'But as I rarely go out these days, I thought it would be nice to make the most of tonight. You don't mind, do you?'

'Knock yourself out,' he said. 'Where is the lovely Georgie then?'

Emma cringed at the familiar use of Georgina's name. A ridiculous reaction but one she couldn't help. Georgina was closer to Emma's age than John's, and rather unfortunate in the looks department, but a more loyal friend you couldn't wish for. 'She's been in a terrible mood all day,' Emma said, 'In fact, why don't you pop your head in the kitchen and let her know we're ready. I know she has a soft spot for you. I'll pour the wine while you're gone.'

As soon as John was out of the room Emma removed the

vial from her bra and tipped half the contents into his glass. Then as an afterthought, tipped in the remainder too. She gave the glass a swirl, had a sip just to be sure there was no odour or taste, then dropped the empty vial into a vase of flowers just as John returned.

'She'll be out in a second,' he said, accepting the glass from Emma.

'Then let's drink while we wait.' She raised her own glass to her lips and watched closely as John did the same. A swarm of moths did a merry dance inside her stomach while she waited for any sign of a reaction. Evie's diary had said the tonic would work quickly but hadn't been specific as to whether that meant seconds, minutes, or even an hour.

Georgina appeared then, carrying two plates of food which she placed carefully on the table in front of them. 'I've put a little extra seasoning on yours,' she said to John, 'I remember that's how you like it.'

'Thanks, Georgie,' he said, 'I'm looking forward to this.' He gave her a friendly wink then picked up his knife and fork and dived straight in.

Flushed with pride, Georgina patted him lightly on the shoulder then left without a word to Emma.

'I can't think what her problem is today,' Emma said. 'She's been off with me ever since I returned from the village.'

'Everyone has a bad day Emma, even the hired help.'

Emma flinched. They both knew that Georgina was much more than just the hired help. Georgina's family had worked at Carrion Hall since the day it was raised from the ground. As far as Emma knew, the Hall had never been without a Carter in service, even during the long period where the place was uninhabitable after Evie's moment of madness. Georgina's father, husband to the one and only Mrs Carter who had brought Evie and Daegan together, had remained here, looking after the place and keeping it free from vandals and squatters until Emma took up residence. Georgina was probably more a part of Carrion Hall than Emma ever could be, and John knew that all too well.

They ate their meal in companionable silence, John wolfing his down and Emma only picking at the lamb. In truth she found it difficult to swallow. Whenever John raised his glass to his lips, her heart would almost stop. But so far there had been no visible sign that the tonic was having any effect whatsoever.

'How's your mother?' she asked, when the silence became uncomfortable. She didn't much care for the answer but hadn't anticipated the awkwardness between them while she waited for the tonic to do its work.

'Good,' John said. 'Why do you ask?'

'Just making conversation,' Emma said. 'And your father? Is he still working? Or ...'

'Retired,' John said. He put down his knife and fork and took another drink of wine.

Emma held her breath. 'And how's the new apprentice working out. I haven't seen him around for a few days.'

'He's been sick,' John said. 'But Henry and I are managing fine without him.' He stopped with the fork halfway to his mouth when he caught Emma watching him. 'Is that a problem?'

'No, no problem,' she said. 'Just wondering, that's all. More wine?' She refilled her own glass and topped up John's without waiting for a reply. 'You know, at this rate I may have to open another bottle,' she said. 'Maybe I should fetch one from the cellar, just in case. Or would you prefer something different? A Rioja perhaps?'

'Stop fussing, Emma. This is fine.'

'Sorry,' she said. 'You know how I get sometimes. Got to have everything just perfect.'

She sat back and took a long, slow drink, watching John closely for a sign, *anything* that would suggest he felt even the tiniest bit interested in something other than the food he was shovelling into his mouth – a mouth she dearly wanted to kiss. Was it her imagination or had the room suddenly gotten warmer? She gulped down more wine and held the glass to her cheek as a bead of perspiration slid down the small of her back.

'Maybe you should slow down with that,' John said, pushing his empty plate away.

'Maybe I'm not drinking enough,' she said. 'Red wine is good for you, full of antioxidants.'

'Not the way you're drinking it.' He took out his cigarettes, placed one between his lips, then as an afterthought, lifted an enquiring brow.

Emma shook her head – he could smoke a whole bloody pack if it meant he'd stay the night – but the longer the evening went on, the more she suspected Evie's tonic wasn't working. She looked down at her pile of untouched food and pushed the plate away. Perhaps Dee had been right, she should have used the liquid extract instead of the powder, but she'd been so inflamed by the woman's audacity that she had tipped the liquid extract down the sink the moment she had left.

'I never did like this room,' John said, 'doesn't look like you've done much with it.'

'I haven't really done anything at all.' Emma joined him by the fire, taking the bat-winged chair and crossing her legs so the hem of her dress rode higher than was entirely necessary. 'Apart from a little freshening up it's almost exactly the same as Richard had it. This was one of the few rooms relatively untouched by the fire, and as I understand it, one of his favourites. I thought it would be nice to leave it as it is.'

John nodded. He was leaning against the mantelpiece, his full attention on the flames as the fire hissed and crackled. His brow was slightly furrowed, his back rigid, and Emma decided she would take it as a sign that the tincture was finally working, and it was his inner turmoil that made him seem so tense. She watched him carefully, the curve of muscle beneath his shirt, the firm set of jaw beneath his permanent stubble, the crease of his brow as he stared quietly into the fire ... too quietly.

'What's this all about, Emma?' he said suddenly.

'What do you mean?' She ran a hand over her dress, discreetly lowering the hem to a more respectable level.

'All this,' he said, waving his hand around. 'The dress, the candlelit dinner. What's going on?'

'Nothing's going on,' she said, 'just two friends having dinner. I can blow out the candles and go change if you prefer.' She smiled amiably, but her skin tightened with doubt. She was no expert on potions, magical or otherwise, but was pretty sure that this one wasn't working.

John flicked the remainder of his cigarette into the fire and turned to face Emma with that all too familiar frown on his handsome face, and she wished with all her heart that he would come back to her. That whatever had gone wrong between them could be forgotten or forgiven, because she loved him, loved him with all her heart and for the chance of just one more night together there wasn't anything she wouldn't do, including, it seemed, plying him with drugs and alcohol.

'You didn't ask me here to talk about landscaping, did you?'

Emma's resolve faltered for an instant, and she looked away, allowing herself a brief moment of shame. The levels to which she would stoop to have John back surprised even her. If he knew what she was doing, what she was trying to do, and even worse, that she was now considering Dee's offer, she would surely lose him forever. She asked herself was it worth it, using trickery and manipulation to win him back when the price of failure was so high? But then an image formed in her head, of John with Raewyn that afternoon, bodies entangled in a lover's embrace, and all her reservations evaporated. 'Of course I did,' she said. 'I'll call Georgina for desert and then we can look over the plans if you like.' She stood, but John stopped her with a touch on her arm.

'Sit down, Emma,' he said. 'We need to talk.'

'It's your favourite,' she said, 'Georgina would be disappointed if we didn't eat it.' Why had she ever thought that Evie's tonic could help her? She must have been out of her mind. Rose water indeed!

John pulled up a footstool and sat down. 'I know things haven't been easy since we broke up,' he said, 'but all this tonight.' He sighed and leaned forward, elbows resting on his knees. 'Emma, it's got to stop, you need to move on ... we both do.'

'You're reading too much into it,' she said. 'I told you, tonight is just a business meeting, nothing more.'

'And the candles?'

'A little over the top, I grant you, but there is nothing sinister behind it. Can't a girl get dressed up for dinner anymore?'

He eyed her suspiciously then sighed. 'OK, I'll buy it. But

you need to know that I'm leaving for a few weeks, maybe longer.'

Emma's grasp tightened on her glass. 'What do you mean? Where are you going?'

'There are things I need to do,' he said, 'things I can't do here. I understand this puts you in a difficult situation with the garden, so consider this my weeks' notice.'

His words hit her like a slap in the face. 'But you can't,' she said. 'I need you here. The gardens need you.'

'There are plenty of other gardeners far better than me.'

'No, there aren't,' she said. 'The winter garden, you can't just leave it half finished.'

'You have the plans,' he said. 'Henry is more than capable, especially now he has Jackson to help. It's not the end of the world, Em.'

'Yes, it is,' she cried. 'You don't understand.' Her eyes welled up as she grabbed his hand and clung to it like a desperate fool. 'You can't leave. I won't let you.'

John reached out to brush a fallen tear from her cheek. 'You can't stop me, Em. You can't move on while I'm living on your doorstep, and I can't stay. It's for the best.'

Emma clutched his hand to her chest. Whatever was left of her heart was breaking all over again. 'How can I make you stay?' she pleaded. 'Is it money? I'll double your wages, triple it ... and you can stay here in the Hall, you can have an entire wing if that's what you want.'

'It's got nothing to do with money,' John said. 'This is about me, and what I have to do.'

'But you can't go,' she sobbed. 'I won't let you leave me.'

'I'm not leaving *you,* Emma. Get it through your head, we are not together and never will be. This game you're playing has to end.' He pulled his hand free and stood up, then looked down at her with softer eyes. 'I'm sorry,' he said, 'it's my fault. I should never have taken this job in the first place. It wasn't fair to you.'

'This is about her, isn't it?' Emma said. 'Tell me this hasn't got anything to do with that girl.'

'What girl?' John said.

'You know damn well who I mean.' Anger welled up inside Emma like an angry geyser, and as much as she wanted to clamp her mouth shut before something truly awful came out, she simply couldn't.

'If you're talking about Raewyn, then no, not exactly.'

'Are you sure? She's been sniffing around you ever since she arrived here. I'm not the only one to notice.'

'Is that what tonight's been about?' he said, 'You think that Rae and I are together?'

'Aren't you?'

He shook his head and turned away.

'Don't you dare walk away from this,' she said. 'You knew exactly why I invited you here tonight, and yet you still came.'

'We both know that's not true,' John said.

'Isn't it?' she stood up, fists clenched tightly at her side. 'Why did you take the job here, John? There are a hundred other places you could work at, and yet you chose to stay here, with me. Why do you think that is?'

'OK, now I'm leaving,' he said. He walked to the table, grabbed his jacket and headed for the door.

'Are you fucking her?' The words were out before she could stop them, and this time Emma knew she'd gone too far.

John stopped and turned, anger flaring in his oh so beautiful eyes. 'That's enough,' he said, 'You've had your say, now drop it.'

But she couldn't. She couldn't drop it any more than she could stop the aching in her heart. 'You didn't answer my question.'

'And I'm not going to.'

'Then you are fucking her?' She stood before him, head held high, yet all too aware that she was digging herself into a hole she'd never climb out of.

'Don't push it,' he said, angrily.

Emma felt her legs giving way. This wasn't how tonight was supposed to go. 'Don't go,' she said. 'I'm sorry. I didn't mean what I said. I don't know what came over me.'

'The same thing that always comes over you, Em,' he said. 'Look, I have to go—'

'Not like this,' she pleaded. 'Please don't leave like this. At least stay for dessert. We'll discuss the gardens and nothing else, I promise.' She reached for his hand, but John snatched it away as his phone began to ring.

'I have to go,' he said, shrugging on his jacket. 'I'll move my things out of the cottage tomorrow.'

19

C hris lay on the floor, clutching his cheek and moaning loudly as Rae pulled on her cardigan and fastened the belt with trembling hands. Her heart rate was gradually slowing to something resembling a normal rhythm, but the surge of energy that she had just discharged into his face still reverberated through her body like a battery running down to empty. She walked into the kitchen, turned on the cold tap and washed her hands under the icy flow. Blood and flesh mingled with the soapy water and slid down the plug hole.

Chris's blood!

Chris's flesh!

She flinched as he called out again, then leaned over the sink and vomited.

'What the fuck have you done to me?' Chris cried.

Rae wiped her mouth, soaked a tea towel and pressed it to her face.

'You fucking bitch. What have you done?' He'd managed to get to his feet and was looking at his reflection in the front room window, horror etched on what was left of his hand-some face.

Rae wet the towel again and took it over to Chris, for the all the good it would do. 'I'll ring you a taxi,' she said, 'you should probably get that seen to by a doctor.' Chris snatched the towel from her, staggered, and grabbed the back of the armchair to steady himself. 'You might want to zip up your pants too,' she said, handing him his jacket. 'It's chilly outside.'

Chris glared at her, his face disturbingly pale. 'You just sealed your own fate you dumb bitch,' he said. 'This isn't over by a long shot.'

'As have you,' Rae said, 'you tried to rape me, or have you forgotten already?'

Chris gave a mirthless laugh and the left side of his face pulled up in a grotesque smile. 'You should be so lucky,' he said, 'if I really wanted you, I'd have had you already.'

Rae felt her blood run cold. What the fuck did that mean? 'I can always even things up for you,' she said, 'do the other side of your face before you go.' The thought made her want to vomit all over again but seeing Chris pale even further made it worth it.

He pressed the tea towel to his face and snatched his jacket from Rae's hand. 'See you soon, Winters,' he said.

'Not too soon, I hope.'

Chris stumbled toward the door but stopped with his hand on the doorknob. *Go*, thought Rae, *please just go*. For one awful moment she thought he was going to come at her again and backed up towards the fire where the poker was propped up beside it. She grabbed it and squeezed, ready to do what-ever it took to get this monster out of her house, but then he pulled open the door and walked out without a backwards glance.

Rae quickly closed and locked it after him. She listened for the sound of his car disappearing down the driveway then slid to the floor in a heap of shaking limbs as the full weight of her situation came crashing down. She buried her face in her hands. *What had she done?* It was Darryl all over again. The anger, the *hatred* that had poured out of her was frightening. Darryl had only been unfaithful, but even then her disgust and loathing of him had been overwhelming. Whatever it was, whatever this ... thing inside her was, it wasn't her, not really, and it terrified her almost as much as knowing that if she wanted to, she could've done a whole lot more than just ruin Chris' pretty face.

20

John was already at the end of the driveway by the time Emma jumped into her MG and gunned it into life. She hit the accelerator hard and sped after him. She couldn't be sure it had been Raewyn on the other end of the phone, but from the little she was able to hear she was certain it was a woman.

Her suspicions were confirmed when he pulled into Foxglove Lane and Emma smashed her fist into the steering wheel with frustration. She pulled the car to a screeching stop, then reversed and parked just far back enough that she would not be obvious if John were to suddenly about turn and drive out onto the road. She turned off the engine and tapped her foot lightly, wondering what to do next. She was afraid of what she might find if she walked down that driveway, but not knowing was even worse. *You're being ridiculous,* she thought. *Pull yourself together and go home. He'll never forgive you if you follow him down that lane.*

But common sense was on the losing side tonight, and she opened the car door, and climbed out.

Emma quickly made her way down the long driveway towards Raewyn's home, shivering when the icy wind snatched her breath away, and cursing the black strappy heels she'd chosen to wear for her evening of seduction. Had she been in a more sensible frame of mind she might have paused to grab the boots and jacket that were always by the front door, but whilst hindsight may be a beautiful thing, it wasn't going to keep her warm as the wind sliced through the delicate fabric of her dress. More than once she tripped and fell, swore profusely, got up and dusted herself off before hurrying along, keeping close to the tree line until the cottage finally came in to view.

The lights were on downstairs, and by hiding behind John's truck she could safely peer through the kitchen window where John and Raewyn were sat. A lump formed in her chest when she saw that John's arm was around Raewyn, and she hugged herself tightly, more to keep from shaking with rage than from the wind that tore through her hair. John was hers, had always been hers, and now he was in the arms of another woman. It wasn't right, wasn't fair, wasn't what she'd worked her arse off for over the last twelve months, doing everything she could just to keep him close, keep him interested, for the all the good it had done her. And now here he was, looking at The Briar girl as if she was the only girl in the world. It made her want to vomit. Made her want to kick down the door and drag Raewyn out by the hair, but neither of those things was going to win him back. There was only way now that Emma could get John to come back to her, one way to make sure something like this would never happen again. Only question was, did she have the stomach to go through it?

21

Rae had called John out of sheer desperation. She needed someone to talk to, and John was the only person she knew who could even begin to understand. But as soon as he arrived, she realised her error. Confessing her birthmark was one thing, but telling him what she'd done to Chris was another thing entirely. She steeled herself ready to face him, to tell him it was a false alarm, that she thought there was a prowler outside. But as soon as she opened the door, he took one look at her face and pulled her into his arms.

He was strong, and solid, and smelled of soap and freshly laundered clothes. He felt good, he felt safe, and despite making a promise to herself that she would keep her shit together, she broke down and cried. John made hushing noises into her hair while Rae sobbed into his chest. She could feel the beat of his heart through his shirt, the reassuring warmth of his arms around her body, but nothing he did could erase what she'd done to Chris, or what he'd tried to do to her.

She was still crying when John guided her to the table and sat her down. He fetched them both a glass of water, handed Rae a box of tissues and waited until the sobs subsided. Rae blew her nose noisily and glanced at the kitchen bin where her cardigan and been quickly dumped when she saw John's car on the driveway. There was blood down the front of it, all over the belt where she had tied it after massacring Chris' face, and more smudged down the sleeve. The sleeve was now poking out from beneath the bin lid.

'Thanks for coming,' she said. 'I hope I didn't drag you away from anything?'

'Nothing important.' John's face was etched with concern, but his eyes were wary. As if he could possibly have any notion of what she was about to say.

Rae made a half-hearted attempt at a smile. 'I must look awful.' She wiped her pyjama sleeve across her face and glanced again at the bin.

'You've looked better,' John said. 'Want to tell me what all this about?'

Rae nodded as more tears slid down her face. 'I should have listened to you,' she said. 'I've been such an idiot.'

'Listened to me about what? Don't tell me I got something right for a change?'

She bit down on her lip and looked away. The guilt of what she'd done lay heavy on her chest, but it was nothing compared to her fear of what John would think once he knew the truth. Once he knew what horrors she was capable of.

'Rae, I can't help if you don't tell me what's wrong,' John said. 'Has someone hurt you?'

'No,' she said, but the lie tasted like acid on her tongue. John took her hand in his and she felt that tug of familiarity once again. She lightly touched the edges of his scar with the tip of her finger, and just to know they had this one thing between them, this one thing that meant she was not alone, offered some small amount of comfort.

'Rae,' John said, gently. 'Tell me what happened. Maybe it's not as bad as you think?'

'No,' she said hoarsely. 'It's worse, much worse.' She pulled her hands away and tucked them into her sleeves. They were normal, everyday hands, with blue veins and broken nails. No burn scars, no puckered flesh or blistered skin. Not so much as a pink glow to show what she had done. No-one could ever prove it. No-one would ever believe Chris if he was brave enough to admit it, and she doubted very much that he was. But *she* knew what she'd done, and it cut her like a knife. 'You were right about Chris,' she said. 'He's not the person I thought he was.'

John tensed. 'Go on,' he said.

Rae swallowed. Her throat was suddenly unbearably dry. She knew how this was going to look. The time she'd spent with Chris, inviting him to stay for dinner, the drinking, the dance ... the kiss. Had she encouraged him in some way? Is that what John would think? 'He came round tonight,' she said, 'just turned up out of the blue. He'd been drinking. I could smell it on him, but we opened a bottle of brandy anyway and he stayed for dinner. We had a few drinks and when I thought he'd had enough, I asked him to leave.'

'And did he?' John's face was carefully guarded, but Rae could feel the anger rippling off him in waves.

'No,' Rae said, 'not right away.' She looked down at her knees, embarrassed by how stupid she'd been. 'He promised to leave if I gave him one dance, so ... I agreed ... then he kissed me.' She looked up, waiting for the inevitable *I told you so*, but John didn't say a word. He didn't need to. 'I kissed him back,' she said, hating herself even as the words tumbled from her mouth. 'But only for a second, then I asked him to stop. I didn't want anything to happen between us, John. I made that very clear. It's important that you know that.'

'Did he hurt you?' John said.

A fresh wave of shame washed over her already drowning body, and she shook her head. 'No,' she said. 'I stopped him before he could.'

'Then who gave you that bruise on your face?'

Rae reached up and gingerly touched her cheek. She'd all but forgotten that Chris had hit her. John's eyes grew dark as Rae tried to explain. 'I stopped him, John, before it could go any further—'

'Where is he now?'

'I don't know. He left—'

'Damn it, Rae. I warned you about him.' His fist slammed down on the table making Rae jump.

'I know you did,' she said. 'And you were right, but—where are you going?'

'To find him?' John was already heading for the door when Rae jumped to her feet.

'No,' she said, grabbing his arm. 'You can't go. There's more. You have to hear all of it.' She stood in front of him, hand pressed against his chest, eyes pleading. 'Please John, there's no-one else I can trust.'

John looked down at her, nostrils flared, face flushed with anger. He wanted to hurt Chris, hurt him bad, and Rae couldn't blame him. But that part had already been taken care of. What she needed now was someone to talk to, someone who would listen, and by some miracle, maybe even understand. 'I know what you want to do,' she said. 'But believe me, he's hurting more than you can know. Please John. Stay and let me finish.'

John paused with the door half open.

'*Please*,' Rae said. 'I *need* you to stay.'

He looked down at her upturned face and touched her bruised cheek with such tenderness it brought tears to her eyes all over again. 'OK,' he said, 'I'm sorry. Of course I'll stay.'

Rae knew it took every ounce of strength for him to sit back down, and she was grateful for it, but she also knew it was going to take every ounce of strength for her to tell him what came next. 'Thank you,' she said, taking her place back at the table. 'There's so much more I need to tell you, and I'm scared that if I don't ...' Her voice cracked. This was so much harder than she thought it would be. 'You have to hear all of it, and then if you still want to leave, I won't stop you.'

John was breathing heavily through his nose, but his eyes were gentle as he nodded for her to continue.

'I hurt Chris in a way you can't imagine,' she said, looking down at her hands. 'When he ... when Chris ...' she clenched her fists and took a deep breath, '... when he attacked me tonight, I tried to fight him off, but he was too strong. I was afraid of what he was going to do, and I was angry, *so* angry. I saw red, and I know it's no excuse, but I didn't know what I was doing until it was over.' She risked a glance at John's face and saw only confusion. She got up and walked over to the sink, poured herself another glass of water and stayed there. It felt easier this way, with her back to him so she didn't have to see the look of horror when she told him what she'd done. 'I burned him, John,' she whispered, 'melted half his face off. Could've killed him if I'd wanted to.' Tears stung her eyes, but she wiped them away angrily, tired of her self-pity. 'I get this feeling,' she said, 'it's like ... rage, only stronger. It takes over me, builds and builds until I have to let it out.' John was silent behind her. Probably too disgusted to speak. 'I know how it sounds,' she said, turning around. 'I'm either lying or crazy, right? But it happened, and it's not the first time either.'

'Have you spoken of this to anyone else?'

Rae felt a bubble of hysterical laughter rise in her throat. 'Tell who?' she said, 'Grace was the only person who might have had a clue what was going on, and she's dead. I burned a man with my bare hands John. *Twice*! Who the hell am I going to tell that to?'

'You told me.'

'You're different,' she said. 'You're somehow part of this ... whatever it is.'

John didn't disagree. 'And you've done this before?'

'Yes, but I'd rather not talk about it.'

'It might be important.'

Rae shook her head. Even after all this, she still wasn't ready to talk about Darryl, not yet.

'At least tell me if you were wearing *that* both times.'

He pointed to Rae's pendant and she grabbed it, nodding. 'You think it's connected?'

John blew out through his nose and stood up. 'I don't know,' he said. 'But I need to think.' He grabbed his jacket and shrugged it on.

'Wait,' Rae said, 'you're not leaving? What if Chris comes back?'

'If what you say is true, then I doubt he'll come within a mile of you. But just in case, lock the door and if he does come back, call me.'

'*If* what I said is true? Do you honestly think I could make this shit up? A man tried to *rape* me tonight John, and you need to go away and *think* about it?'

John didn't answer but stopped short of walking out the door. He turned and looked at her with different eyes, as though he was seeing her for the very first time, and that more than anything cut her deep. 'We'll speak tomorrow,' he said. 'Make sure you lock the door when I'm gone.'

Rae watched him walk to the car, waited for him to turn and say he was sorry, what was he thinking? It must have been the shock making him act like a complete and utter prick. But he didn't say any of that, he just climbed in his truck, turned on the engine, and without even looking up to see if she was still stood there, reversed the truck and drove off.

22

Emma hid shivering behind a tree until John's car was out of sight and remained there until the downstairs lights went out. She was frozen and heart sore, but not entirely defeated.

She had watched through the kitchen window while John and Raewyn talked, ducked out of sight when he opened the door, and almost cried when he touched Raewyn's face in a way he had never touched hers. Then the door had closed again, and Emma had to clamp a hand over her mouth just to keep from screaming.

The wind had torn through the forest with a force that threatened to uproot trees, but Emma had stayed where she was, trying not to think of John's hands on Raewyn's body and his lips on her mouth, but it was the *only* thing she could think of as she sank further and further into despair. Her life wasn't supposed to turn out this way, *she* wasn't supposed to turn out this way, and if it wasn't for The Briar girl, then things could have been very different. The injustice of it all was enough to make her sick.

But then the door had opened again, and this time the air between John and Raewyn was colder than the air outside. Emma had watched, mesmerised as John walked over to his truck and climbed in, and even allowed herself a brief smile at the look of shock on Raewyn's face when he drove away. Maybe all hope was not lost after all then. But did their fight mean John would stay, or was he still planning to leave Cranston Myre? The thought of him leaving filled Emma with dread and she again thought about Dee's offer – one shot of tonic and John would be hers forever. And did she really care who owned Carrion Hall? But then the thought of that crazy witch's poison inside John's body was enough to make her shudder. She hugged herself tightly as a cold blast of wind sliced through her dress. A light came on in the upstairs window of the cottage and Raewyn's face appeared at the window, pressed against the glass like a ghostly figure. Emma waited until the curtains were drawn before stepping out from behind the tree. She'd go home, think it over, try and come up with a plan that didn't involve poisoning the man she loved, but as she left the cover of the sycamore tree something sharp pricked at the back of her neck. She reached around, thinking a sharp twig had struck her in the wind, but her arm felt heavy, and as she tried to take another step forward the ground suddenly rushed up to meet her, and then everything faded to black.

23

Dee was down in the cellar when something solid hit her front door followed by a barrage of frantic knocking. With a sigh of irritation, she quickly washed her hands, climbed the stone steps and lowered the heavy trap door back into place. Whoever it was had better have a damn good excuse for banging down her door at this time of night.

'About fucking time,' Chris said as she opened the door.

His face was ashen, blistered and red along the jaw line, and charred black around a gaping, oozing hole of burnt flesh on his left cheek. He looked like something straight out of a horror movie as he stumbled through the door, with Dee just managing to get beneath his shoulder as his legs gave way. He moaned, head lolling to one side while Dee half walked, half dragged him to the bedroom where he dropped onto her mattress like a dead weight. She swung his legs onto the cotton duvet and slid a pillow beneath his head.

'What have you done this time?' she said, throwing a blanket over his shivering body. His face was a mess, and she knew of only one person capable of causing a burn like that.

'Can you fix it?' Chris' voice was gravelly and thin, the sound of man in a great deal of pain.

He gritted his teeth as Dee moved his head to the side to get a closer look at the damage. 'Maybe,' she said. Apart from a very distinctive thumb print, the right side of his face was miraculously unharmed. 'How did it happen?'

'Does it matter? Can you fix it or not?'

Dee blew out slowly. 'It's bad,' she said. 'I can keep it clean and ease the pain, but you should probably see a doctor.'

'No doctors,' Chris said. 'You must have something in the cellar. I don't care what you have to do but do something.'

Dee frowned. 'What do *you* know of my cellar?'

'I know you're not doing cross stitch down there. Can you help me or not?'

Dee considered it for a moment. Chris was new to the ways of the Draiocht and had expressed his desire to be tutored more than once, but he didn't know about the darker side of what Dee did, nor had she ever told him about her cellar. 'OK,' she said, 'I'll try to fix it, but I'm making no promises, and I have questions that I expect you to answer.'

'Fine,' Chris said. 'Just hurry up. I'm in a lot of fucking pain here.'

Dee left the room, lifted the trapdoor in the hallway and ducked down into the cellar. She returned a moment later with a large tub of willow bark paste, and a drink that resembled stagnant pond water, both in taste and smell. 'Drink this,' she said, holding the glass to Chris' lips. 'It'll help with the shock.' It also contained a strong sedative, but Chris didn't need to know that.

He took one mouthful, pulled a face, and drank the rest at Dee's insistence. Then she hooked a large blob of brown goo on the end of her finger and began smoothing the paste over the part of his face where the burn had gone through to the hypodermis. 'Who did this to you?' she asked. She knew fine well of course, but wanted to hear him say it.

'Raewyn,' he said, and sighed as another dollop was applied to the delicate area just above his cheekbone.

'You're damn lucky she didn't touch your eye,' Dee said, 'an inch higher and you'd have lost it.'

'You don't seem surprised,' Chris said as another dollop was applied to his lower face. The paste was fast acting, almost instant pain relief, and would kill even the most resilient of germs. But what it would not do was repair the damage. It would take a shot of elixir to do that, and Dee wasn't sure she wanted Chris to know it even existed.

She glanced at him before scooping more paste onto his face. 'Tell me how she did it.'

'You know fine well how she did it,' Chris said. 'Just as you know fine well what she is.'

Dee smiled. 'You're right,' she said, 'I do. But the bigger question, Christopher, is how do *you* know?'

Chris looked away as Dee smeared the rest of the goo over his chin. 'I had no choice,' he said. 'You weren't giving me anything.'

'I was protecting you,' Dee said, 'and that isn't an answer. Who gave the order?'

He hesitated, then ... 'It was Connie. And I didn't go to her if that's what you're thinking. She came to me. She wanted me to push Rae, see what it would take to set her off, what she would do and how she did it.'

Dee wiped her hand on a towel and replaced the lid on the tub of paste. 'And what *did* it take?'

Chris looked away and Dee nodded. Knowing Chris, she

could only guess. 'I see,' she said. 'And if she hadn't stopped you?'

'Then I'd have stopped myself. I'm not an idiot Dee. I know my limits.'

Dee wasn't convinced. She climbed off the bed and placed the tub on the dresser. 'Doesn't it bother you that Connie put you in a position where you could have been killed? Raewyn doesn't yet know what she is, or what she's capable of. None of us do.'

'I had to prove myself somehow,' he said. 'Connie said she'd introduce me to The Order if I did as she asked, which is more than you've done in a year.'

'For good reason,' Dee said. 'You're not ready, though I don't suppose that's an issue any longer. Did she tell you *why* she wanted to know what Raewyn would do?'

Chris shrugged. 'She wants to be prepared. She doesn't trust you, she thinks you're going to back out, like ...' he stopped when Dee raised her eyebrows.

'Like I did last time?' she offered. 'So, Connie's told you everything then?' Chris didn't reply, but then he didn't need to. 'How very trusting of her,' Dee said, 'and does she know you've already done the dirty deed?'

Chris slowly shook his head. The sedative was starting to work. 'I came straight here,' he said, eyelids drooping. But Dee wasn't finished with him yet. She pulled out a roll of gauze and began wrapping it around his head, pressing down a little firmer than was entirely necessary. Chris snapped wide awake. 'I want you to do something for me,' she said. 'When Connie asks you how tonight went, I want you to lie. I want you to tell her that you couldn't go through with it. That you tried to make Rae angry but she wasn't having a bar of it so you gave up. Can you do that for me?'

'Why would I do that?' Chris mumbled, 'I want to be part of The Or—'

'Don't worry about The Order,' Dee said, 'I'll make sure you're accepted. I'll even give you a personal recommendation, but you have to promise me that you'll lie.'

Chris slowly nodded and Dee smiled. Chris was hot headed and unpredictable – an exciting combination in bed, but not so much when it came to the use of sorcery, and Connie should have known that. Teaching Chris how to use sorcery was like giving a three-year-old a box of matches to play with, and she had no intention of introducing him to anyone, let alone The Order. But she didn't believe Connie did either. She'd used him. But to what end?

Dee retrieved her lockbox and removed the key from the back of the headboard. What Chris had done tonight could've jeopardised everything they'd been working towards for the last twenty-five years. The fact that she'd tested her gift once was bad enough, and that arsehole Darryl had probably deserved it, but if Raewyn continued to discover what she could do then all their lives could be in jeopardy. It was a fine line that Dee was treading. On the one hand she needed Rae to be able to protect herself when the time came, but on the other, she also needed her to be compliant and not burn their faces off before Saoirse was free. So why did Connie want Rae to test her strength a second time? The only reasoning Dee could think of was that Connie wanted to be certain where Raewyn's limits lay. If Connie planned to use an inhibitor, and that inhibitor could be applied to Raewyn's hands, then Raewyn would be rendered useless and easy prey for the likes of Saoirse. Perfect for Connie, not so much for Dee.

She opened the lockbox and took out the blue jar. Only

one syringe remained of her personal elixir, and she would need most of it to heal Chris, if indeed it would heal him at all, and after what he'd done tonight Dee wasn't sure that he even deserved it. But as volatile as Chris was, she would likely need him over the coming days. She had an assistant coming in by train tomorrow, someone eager for a place by Connie's side. He was coming at Connie's invitation, but the last thing Dee needed was a spy in her camp. Chris could prove the antidote to that little problem, and if not ... well, there was always another plot at the bottom of the garden.

She jabbed the needle into his thigh, injected half the elixir and waited for any immediate reaction. When there was none, she returned the rest of the elixir to the jar and replaced the box back beneath the floorboard.

MR MITTS, so named by Dee for his cotton soft paws, lay prepped and sedated inside a cage. Dee had taken the cat when she caught it roaming in her garden. It was a stray, a wild cat that had become accustomed to being fed, but the bite on her hand proved that his trust in Dee was limited. She felt a small twinge of guilt as she took him from the cage and laid him on the table. Chopping up small animals wasn't her favourite thing to do, but out of all the animals Dee had used over the years, cats were by far the more productive when it came to divination.

Dee had limited talents, and none of them came naturally. Most were learned from a mother dedicated to giving her daughters the best life she could, some from a sister who took pity on her useless sibling, and the rest from years of hard work, study and dedication. But one thing Louisa had not been able to teach her baby sister, and something their mother had disapproved of, was the form of divination known as Extispicy.

Dee ran a hand over Mr Mitts' sleeping body. He was breathing softly, his heartbeat nice and regular. The cat would never feel a thing, but that did little to ease Dee's conscience as she injected him with a concentration of Oleander and waited for his heart to still. Giving quick thanks for his sacrifice, she then lit a candle and opened the cellar grate so that Mr Mitts' soul could go peacefully. It was a ritual she followed for her own peace of mind, preferring to believe that every soul was destined for another place, whether it be heaven, hell, or somewhere in between. It was the only way she could do the things she did. Then she set to work.

With quick and efficient fingers, the cat's liver and spleen were carefully put aside. The heart, kidneys and lungs were put into separate jars of embalming fluid, and the blood allowed to drain into several grooves carved purposely into the table and left to drip over the edge into a large, green bucket. Dee worked with a purposeful rhythm. She had performed this task a hundred times over, almost always seeking the same reassurances, and this time was no different. She swiftly removed the cat's intestines and laid them out on the table, next to the liver and spleen, then she began dissecting.

A few minutes later, she had the answers she was looking for.

Saoirse would return on the night of the eclipse, and Raewyn would make it possible. This, Dee already knew. The Order would be there, Connie chief amongst them, as would Dee and Chris. But this time the intestines showed there were others too. Shadows cast over the resurrection, faces she couldn't see. This could be either good news or bad, but Mr Mitts wouldn't yield an answer either way, and as she looked closer another anomaly presented itself. Raewyn's birth had been predicted many hundreds of years ago. A child born of one world, destined to save another – a child who bears the mark of Servia, with fire in their heart, The Eye of Eilidh at their back and the Sword of Neskylia by their side. The Sword of Neskylia had remained in Aster when the portals were sealed, but the fire and The Eye, Raewyn had. She also had the mark of Servia, burned into her stomach just above her navel, but according to Mr Mitts, so did another.

Dee bagged up the cat's remains, threw them into a freezer and washed her hands. Maybe she'd read it wrong. Extispicy wasn't a perfect science after all. Or maybe Mr Mitts had been infected with a parasite. She climbed the stairs, dropped the trap door and pulled the rug over it. Raewyn was the reincarnation of Augustine, there was no doubt about that, and what she'd done to Chris tonight only proved it further. But knowing there was someone else with the same mark only added to the tension.

She quickly checked on Chris – sleeping like a baby - and went to the living room where her box of photos was still tucked beneath the coffee table. Inside were the pictures of friends long dead, people who had given themselves secretly to the cause, knowing that what they did now could save millions of lives in the future. Dee owed them everything, and no matter what it took, she would not let them down.

24

Sunlight filtered through the half open curtains and Emma used her hand to shade her eyes from the unwelcome glare. It was still early morning and the temptation to remain in bed was strong, but so was the need to have a shower. She sat up, pressed the heels of her hands against her throbbing temples, and looked down at her bruised and bloodied legs. She was still wearing the silk dress from the night before, but it was torn in places, and filthy dirty. Memories flitted back like shards of flying glass – walking barefoot in the forest, John holding Raewyn in his arms, a devouring sense of loneliness, and then ... nothing. She climbed off the bed, winced when her wounded feet touched the ground, and headed for the bathroom.

The reflection in the bathroom mirror greeted her with a disdainful look. Glass eyed and pale, she looked like she should be in a hospital bed, not getting ready for a day's work. What had she hoped to achieve by following John last night? Did she think he would change his mind and fall into her arms once she confronted him about Raewyn? Then she remembered the way he'd took off, angry and resentful, and the look of rejection on Raewyn's face when he left her. That at least should give her reason to smile, so why then did she feel sick to her stomach?

She carefully removed her dress and switched on the shower. She had a nauseating feeling that there was more to last night that she could recall. The jagged marks on her neck said as much, as did the bruise beneath her eye and the tiny cuts all over her legs and feet, but she couldn't remember anything beyond watching John drive away from the cottage. She stuck a hand in the shower to test the water and stepped in. The water stung but Emma welcomed the pain. At least it meant she felt something other than fatigue and an aching sense of loss. She closed her eyes and let water stream over her face before looking down to watch the blood and dirt swirl around her feet. It reminded her of the wine she had shared with John, and the tonic she had slipped into his drink. Dee had said it would work, if only for instant physical gratification, and she had made her peace with that, but the tonic had had no effect on John whatsoever. She also remembered he was leaving in less than a week and closed her eyes as another wave of despair washed over her.

Shower finished, Emma walked back into the bedroom filled with a deep sense of foreboding that she could not place. She gingerly touched the scratches on her neck. Someone had been with her in the forest. She recalled a hint of perfume, something familiar, something earth – cedar maybe – but when she tried to focus the memory fell away. Maybe she'd imagined that part. The cuts and bruises were most likely the result of wandering barefoot through the forest. It was a wonder she didn't have pneumonia!

Georgina was busy kneading dough when Emma entered the kitchen, preparing the freshly baked bread that Emma always insisted on. She glanced in Emma's direction then quickly did a double take. 'What in the world happened to you?' she said, wiping floury hands on her apron and coming round to get a better look. 'You look like you fought with a grizzly and lost.'

Emma smiled and dismissed Georgina's worried look with a wave of the hand. 'It's nothing. I got a little drunk last night and fell into the rose bushes. Is there anything for breakfast?'

Georgina raised an eyebrow and stood with hands on hips, regarding her employer with a suspicious look. 'A *little* drunk? And what about those things on your neck, are they from the rose bushes too?'

Emma reached up to her neck where the scarf had slipped out of place. 'Oh that,' she said. 'It's just a scratch, nothing to worry about.'

'And what, may I ask, were you doing in the gardens at night?'

'Going for a walk.'

'And did you punch yourself in the face too?' Georgina pointed to the bruise on Emma's cheek and regarded her with a sceptical look.

Emma touched the swollen skin just below her right eye and felt herself blush under Georgina's stare. 'Enough of the questions, have you seen my brother this morning?'

Georgina narrowed her eyes, then shrugged and returned to the bread. 'I haven't seen your brother in days,' she said. 'Probably with his fancy woman again. I warned him nothing good will come of that relationship, but he wouldn't listen, just as you never do. Honestly, it's like having ...'

Emma didn't hear the rest. She walked out of the kitchen, grabbed a jacket and left the house.

25

D ee had been up since first light and was looking through her box of photographs again when there was a knock at the door. She wiped her eyes, shoved the box out of sight and after quickly looking in on Chris (still fast asleep) opened the door.

Connie blustered past. 'You missed the meeting last night,' she said, walking straight into the living room. 'I'm tired of making excuses for you, Dee.'

'Keep your voice down,' Dee said, 'I have a guest in the next room.'

Connie arched an eyebrow but otherwise appeared not to care. 'The Order are worried. They're losing confidence in a leader that never shows up.'

'Let them worry,' Dee said. 'I have no time for those people. You know that.'

'Those *people* are our future,' Connie said, 'yours *and* mine. Without them our way of life would be dead.'

'Would that be so bad?' Dee flopped down into a chair and stared at Connie.

Connie gave a humourless laugh. 'Maybe not for you,' she said. 'But for the rest of us, yes. We *need* Saoirse to return. Need her strength, and her leadership. So do you, unless you want to go on injecting yourself for the rest of your life. Remember what happened last time you failed her?'

Dee most assuredly did and had no intention of repeating it. 'Don't get your knickers in a twist,' she said, 'everything is under control.' She walked into the kitchen where a large bottle of orange cordial sat beside the fridge. She handed it to Connie. 'Have them drink this an hour before the eclipse, and if anyone refuses to take it, you know what to do.'

Connie nodded. 'What's in it?'

'Something to keep them happy until Saoirse makes an appearance. It's got to be perfect this time, otherwise ...'

'Otherwise we're all dead,' Connie said dryly. 'No thanks to you.'

Dee gave her a black look, but the woman wasn't wrong. The last time Saoirse had attempted to escape, Dee had been there, and her sister too, but Saoirse had been displeased when neither of them had turned up with Raewyn, and Louisa had suffered the brunt of Saoirse's anger. Dee, on the other hand, had been looked upon favourably and offered a second chance. She had escaped with her life, but the left side of her body had been badly burned. Years of perfecting her elixir had fixed most of that, and her dragon tattoo had covered the scars that remained, but the knowledge of what she'd done would stay with her a lifetime.

'And Raewyn,' Connie said. 'She's still oblivious?'

'After Chris' little stunt last night, I highly doubt it.'

Connie's mouth curved up with a smugness that set Dee's teeth on edge. 'How did she react?'

'You had no right to put him in that position,' Dee said, 'if Raewyn had taken the bait, Chris could have been killed.'

'I had every right,' Connie boomed, 'you've dangled the carrot in front of him for long enough. Did you think he'd wait forever? There are too few men amongst us as it is. He'll prove useful when the time comes, if only for brute strength.'

Dee scowled but didn't object. 'Even so,' she said. 'It wasn't your decision to make.'

'But one that needed to be made nonetheless,' Connie said. 'I take no pleasure in going behind your back, Dee, but your support has been somewhat lacking of late. I'll feel much better once Raewyn has been picked up.'

'You know we can't take her yet,' Dee said. 'We can't risk exposure.'

'I'm well aware of that,' Connie said tightly. 'Just as I hope you are well aware that she has to die. There will be no saving her this time, not unless you want an entire race of people on your back.'

'Of course not,' Dee said, 'I was young and naive last time. Now I know what the stakes are there will be no problems from me.'

'Let's hope so,' Connie said, 'for all our sakes. What about the dagger?'

'Let me worry about that,' Dee said, 'you just concentrate on keeping The Order in line and everything should go smoothly.'

'It better,' Connie said. 'You have much to atone for, *Daegan Gilhooly*.'

'Don't call me that,' hissed Dee. 'That was a long time ago.'

'Not so long that I've forgotten who you really are,' Connie said. 'The red hair and big tits don't fool me. You may have modelled yourself on your sister, but you're still the same flat chested coward you always were. If Louisa were here today, she'd wipe that priggish look right off your face.'

'Well she isn't,' Dee said, 'and as long as I'm the only gate-keeper here, the priggish look remains.'

Connie gave her a contemptuous look, but just then Chris walked into the room. 'What's a gatekeeper?' he said. He was wearing only boxers and looked remarkably good for a man who'd almost died.

'Well aren't you a sight for sore eyes,' Connie said, smiling like the cat that got the cream, 'How did last night go?'

Chris looked guiltily to Dee and shrugged. 'It went exactly as you said it would,' he said, 'but you could have warned me what she would do.'

'If I had, would you have done your job properly?'

'I'd have been prepared at least.'

'And then what?' Connie said, 'what's done is done, no point arguing about it. You should be congratulating yourself on a job well done. Now we know what to expect we can take precautions. Dee, I'm sure with your talents you can rustle something up by tomorrow?'

Dee nodded, though somewhat reluctantly. It was all she could do not punch Connie in her arrogant fat face. 'I can make something to keep her in check during the ritual, but it won't last forever,' she said.

'It doesn't need to,' Connie said, 'just until she's no longer a problem. You're sure you can have it ready in time?'

'I wouldn't be much good at my job if I couldn't,' Dee said.

'Good,' Connie said. 'I don't want to leave anything to chance. Not this time around.'

Dee bristled but said nothing. It wasn't worth getting into a slanging match with the wretched woman.

'So, what happens now?' Chris said.

'Now, Connie is going to leave while I examine you,' Dee said, 'aren't you Connie?'

Connie sneered and threw her bag over her shoulder. 'Don't worry, I'm going,' she said, 'but remember what I said, Dee. No third chances. You mess up this time. We all die.'

Dee scowled at her back as Connie left and locked the door behind her. 'Thanks for the back-up,' she said to Chris, as he plonked himself down on the couch.

He shrugged. 'She was never going to believe me if I told her anything but the truth. What was all that about everyone dying?'

'Nothing,' Dee said, 'just a bitter old woman with a grudge.' She sat down next to him and ran her fingers over his newly healed cheek. 'No scarring,' she said. 'Even your stubble has grown back.'

'That's because I have a bad ass nurse to take care of me,' he said, grabbing her boob and squeezing.

Dee pushed his hand away. The thought of Chris touching her after what he'd done made her feel nauseous. 'Tell me how you're feeling,' she said. 'Any headaches, nausea, pain anywhere?'

'I feel great,' Chris said, 'better than great.'

'That's good,' Dee said, 'but take it easy for the next few days, and above all, stay away from Raewyn.'

'What difference does it make if Connie knows?' he said. 'Rae's as good as dead tomorrow anyway.'

Dee thought about it for a second. Chris wanted in with The Order, and didn't much care how he did it, so it was in her best interests to keep him sweet. 'We don't know that for sure,' she said, 'once Saoirse's free it'll be up to her what happens to Rae. I'm just worried that Connie will push

Raewyn too far and something will go wrong. Connie is greedy and careless, and if she wants to continue to push my buttons that's all well and good, but what she had you do was stupid and reckless.'

Chris nodded. 'Lucky for me I have you watching my back, then.'

'Lucky indeed,' Dee said, smiling, 'because if I didn't, no-one else would.'

Rae woke up miserable and cold with her crystal clutched tightly in her hand. The wind had howled through the cottage all night long, whistling down the chimney and rattling the windows like a wailing ghost, but despite feeling like the night would never end she had eventually fallen into a troubled sleep.

She'd dreamt of golden eyes again, but this time they were getting married. They were in a castle with grey stone walls that shone with flecks of silver, and a floor as smooth as marble. High arching windows looked out onto an ocean of intense aquamarine blue, stretching out as far as the eye could see where a sun, twice its normal size, glowed orange against a pale blue sky. Her dress was the colour of creamy butter, her veil edged with white silk, and beside her, dressed in white armour and looking more handsome than ever, was golden eyes. He wore a cloak of black feathers that trailed behind him, his hair neatly tied at the nape of his neck, and he was smiling, eyes bright and full of laughter.

But then suddenly it was night-time, and they were riding

on horseback, tearing through the countryside with Ben close at their backs. Rae's dress flapped in the wind, her veil torn from her head, dark hair spilling out behind her. It began to rain, heavy sheets of ice that drenched them in seconds, but they rode on, harder and faster, heading for the forest where the shadows loomed deep and the darkest terrors hid. Rae was afraid, but the reason why was lost on her as the horses slowed and a light appeared up ahead. Fire the cold blue of winter, rose high and bright, engulfing the forest and filling the night sky with its black, acrid smoke. The horses pulled up short and golden eyes turned to Rae, but then it was no longer him, and instead the white-haired woman from her vision was beside her, pale eyes glistening bright by the light of the fire. 'It's time,' she said, but Rae shook her head. Then she woke up.

Rae cradled her knees to her chest. The dreams always felt real enough at the time, but when she woke up she accepted them for what they were – an overactive imagination playing havoc with her sleep. But the visions were different. They *were* real, she was sure of it. She uncurled and reached across the bed for her phone. No missed calls, no texts, nothing. Not even a call from Alex and they were meant to be going to the movies that night. She dialled Alex's number and hung up when it went to voicemail. She'd probably spoken to Chris. Maybe even seen his face and was right now giving a statement to the police. Rae covered her face with the pillow and screamed. How had things gone from bad to worse so fast? She crawled out of bed and headed downstairs, eyes avoiding the couch where the wet tea towel still lay, and went straight to her bag where it hung on the back of the door. Inside was a small notebook where she kept Ronnie's address (thank God she didn't rely on her phone for everything), then she opened the browser on her phone, punched in Harleybrock train station, and switched on the kettle.

An hour later she was bathed, had packed a suitcase and was dragging it downstairs when there was a thump overhead. Sunlight poured through the upstairs windows and there wasn't a shadow in sight, but her stomach still twisted in knots as she left the suitcase where it was and crept back towards the bedroom. She stopped at the top of the stairs when there was another thud. It was coming from higher up, somewhere in the roof space. There was a hatch outside the bedroom door that led into the attic. Rae had noticed it on her first night here when it had been left askew by whoever had been up there last. It wasn't askew now, but another thump from above confirmed that was where the noise was coming from.

A moment later she returned with a step ladder, torch and kitchen knife. The knife she placed between her teeth as she climbed the ladder. If so much as a spider jumped out at her right now then it was not going to end well for either of them. But she lifted the hatch without incident and shone the torch through the small gap. Tins of paint, that was what she saw, lots of them stacked one on top of each other, and three had fallen over – that, and a whole lot of cobwebs. She left the knife by the hatch and hoisted herself up into the cramped space. Ignoring the paint, she edged over to examine something else she'd spotted, stacked against the far wall, dusty and forgotten, but from a casual look, very well done.

The paintings reminded Rae of the portrait hanging over the fireplace at Carrion Hall, and the first one she picked up was in fact of the Hall, minus the blaze of crimson ivy and blossoming flowers. It was painted in varying shades of grey that mimicked a rundown old castle, and, coincidentally, echoed Rae's own feelings about the place. She'd had an ill feeling about the Hall since she'd first spotted it, sitting on top of the hill like a preacher overseeing its flock and couldn't imagine for one minute why anyone would want to stay there for fun.

She set it aside and lifted the next two, standing them side by side. These two were portraits of young women, possibly sisters by the shape of their eyes, though both very different in their own way. The first was bleak to say the least. Grey eyes looked out from beneath a pasty brow, and long, lacklustre hair clung limply to her face. She was unremarkable in every way and yet there was an air of melancholy that Rae found almost heart breaking. The second girl appeared a little older but with the same nose – slightly large and rounded at the tip – and the same sharp cheekbones. Ruby red hair billowed around her shoulders as though floating on a gust of wind and eyes the colour of freshly cut grass smiled confidently from the canvas. Her lips were red as fresh berries and her cheeks glowed with the freshness of youth. She was enchanting where the other was brooding, endearing where the other was sorrowful, and yet ... for all her beauty it was the first painting that drew Rae's eye.

She quickly sifted through the other paintings, mostly landscapes and still life, though all by the same artist it seemed. Then she found one at the back. It was smaller than the rest, thick with dust and unfinished. Rae blew on it, wafted away choking particles then shone the torch on the canvas. Another young woman, this one with brown curly hair and soft chestnut eyes that gazed down to where her hand rested on the swollen curve of her belly. She wore a wedding ring, a silver one with ruby clusters, and a gold *Cartier* watch, but it was what hung around her neck that made Rae gasp. A silver chain, long enough that what hung from it was mostly hidden beneath the open collar of her dress, but where the buttons bulged against her heaving bosom Rae could just make out the tip of a murky, orange crystal.

27

Dee was almost out the door when a green MG pulled up outside. An ashen faced Emma climbed out, large black bag slung over her shoulder, and an ugly grey scarf at her throat. 'Emma, to what do I owe the pleasure?' Dee said, though she could already guess the answer by the sour look on her face.

'Will Chris be coming back?' Emma said. 'I don't want him to see me here.'

She fiddled with her scarf and Dee could just make out the beginnings of a bruise on her cheek. 'Not until later. Why?'

'Can we go inside?' She glanced over her shoulder as though the trees themselves were straining to listen to their conversation.

Dee stepped aside. 'Be my guest.' She closed the door and followed Emma into the living room where Emma stood in the centre, looking nervously around. 'Can I get you a drink,' Dee said, 'you look like you could use one.'

'I didn't come here to swap pleasantries,' Emma said, 'I'd

just as soon get this over with.' She reached into her bag, withdrew a large brown envelope, and handed it to Dee.

Dee raised an eyebrow. 'The agreement? You signed it?'

Emma nodded. 'But I added a clause. If I'm not happy with your ... product, or the money isn't transferred within 48 hours, then the agreement is null and void.'

Dee didn't need to ask why. 'Give me a moment, will you?' she said. A smile crept over her face as she headed down into the cellar. If she could get Emma to leave Cranston Myre, then she would have done at least one thing right. She left the agreement in the cellar and carried back a green glass bottle. It looked very much like a fancy bottle of perfume, rounded with a diamond shaped stopper and gold filigree wound around the slender bottle neck. She handed it to Emma as she returned to the living room. 'A single drop of blood will activate it,' she said, 'and you can mix it with just about anything, but once done make sure John drinks all of it. This is a larger does than the one I offered you before, so the effects will last much longer – a lifetime if that's what you want, and if you change your mind it can easily be reversed.'

Emma held the bottle like it was going to explode. 'And you're sure he won't be harmed?'

'It's perfectly safe,' Dee said. 'Look. I have a cabin about two hours' drive south from here. Nothing fancy, but it's by the beach with no neighbours for miles around. I keep it well stocked and there's a great fireplace to keep you warm. Why don't I transfer half the money right now as a goodwill gesture, then you can go home, give John his medicine, and whisk him away for a couple of nights. The Hall will still be here when you get back, and if you're happy we can conclude our agreement then.'

Emma eyed Dee suspiciously and Dee worried for a

moment that she'd gone too far, seemed too eager to send Emma away. Emma glanced at the threadbare carpet and tired looking furniture. 'You're sure you have the money?'

'Looks can be deceiving,' Dee said, 'do we have a deal?'

Emma fiddled with her scarf and seemed embarrassed when she caught Dee looking. 'It's the weather,' she said, 'I think I may be getting a chill.'

'I didn't ask,' Dee said, 'do you want the cabin, or not?'

Emma looked like she might throw up. 'Not a word to Christopher,' she said, as beads of sweat popped up on her forehead. 'He wouldn't understand.'

'He won't hear anything from me,' Dee said. 'Are you sure you don't want something to drink?'

'No. Why would I?'

'You just ... don't seem yourself,' Dee said.

'Yes, well, it's not every day you plan to drug someone,' Emma said tightly. She popped the bottle into her bag, and as she did so Dee caught a glimpse of the scratches beneath her scarf. 'Half the money by 5pm,' she said, 'the account number is on the purchase agreement. You can text me the address of your cabin.'

'I can do better than that.' Dee went to the front door where a bunch of keys hung from a hook on the wall. She took one down attached to a plastic keyring with a picture of the ocean on it. 'Address is on the back.'

Emma took the key and nodded briefly – probably the closest she would ever come to thanking Dee – then walked out the door.

THE BRIAR WAS on the other side of Dolen Forest to Dee's house – a twenty minute drive if using the main road, quicker by foot if you knew where you were going, and Dee knew the forest very well indeed. Many years ago Richard had gifted the cottage to Louisa, thinking he'd done it out of love, of his own free will, but Dee knew that Louisa had slipped him the same tonic that Dee had just given to Emma. She also knew why Louisa wanted the cottage so badly.

The Briar sat on a ley line, a separate line to the one that ran beneath Dee's house, but the same one that ran beneath Carrion Hall. All converged at the oak tree, but this one in particular was strong, and Dee knew Louisa had drawn heavily on it during her time at the cottage. It was also where Dee had chosen to hide the secret to obtaining the Servian Dagger.

Dee had been known as Daegan the last time she held the Servian Dagger in her hand, the same night that she had betrayed her sister by hiding away two baby girls. If she'd gone ahead with Louisa's plan, and done as she was supposed to by delivering one of the girls to Saoirse, then maybe Louisa would still be alive today. But witnessing the birth of the prophesised child, and seeing her twin sister born only seconds later, had made Dee realise just how riddled with madness her sister really was. So she'd hidden the babies away, returned to Louisa empty handed, and lived with the consequences ever since.

Dee sensed the forbidding as she drew closer. It was a shield, a dome of protection for the ancient tree that had stood in this forest since long before Dee's ancestors came to earth. Anyone could enter the forbidding if they knew what to do, but few seldom did. The forbidding rendered the clearing invisible, making it seem from the outside that the forest went on and on in much the same way it had by playing tricks on the mind, scrambling the brain so you may think you're walking in a straight line, but really you're turning left or right, avoiding the clearing altogether. The trick to get past it was simple, you only had to close your eyes and step through, but unless you already knew it was there, there was no reason to walk around with your eyes shut. Louisa had expanded the forbidding so it reached from Dee's house as far back as the cottage, but access from the cottage would only be granted to those of Draiocht descent. For anyone else the moment you stepped from the back door into the garden confusion would ensue, nausea would overtake and a dash to the bathroom would become imminent. A drop of blood was the key. An unnecessary display of power by Louisa, but one that Dee was now grateful for as she travelled through the forest unseen.

The iron gate groaned as Dee stepped through it and she was unsurprised to find the garden had changed considerably since Louisa had owned it. Back then it had been wall to wall herbs, but now it was nothing more than a pretty courtyard used for taking tea or drinking lemonade in the sun. She was pleased to see the moon dial remained though, as did the sweet briar that climbed over the wall, and remembered well the fresh smells of bergamot, lemongrass and rosemary as she made her way towards the cottage.

On the left side of the cottage, below the window and three inches from the ground, was a stone no bigger than a tennis ball. There was a small carving in the middle, invisible unless you were looking for it, in the shape of a crescent moon. Dee removed a tin of grey powder from her bag, dipped in a small paint brush then carefully brushed round the outer edges of the stone. The powder burned through the mortar like fire through paper, so that Dee was able to free it from the wall without resistance. The stone had been hollowed out at the back and she was relieved to find the leather pouch still inside. She replaced the stone carefully, put the pouch in her pocket, and left the garden the same way she had entered.

The grazing fields were still wet with morning dew and soaked Dee's pants to the knee as she ran up the hill towards the Hall. Chris was at the stables as Dee knew he would be, so she avoided them by ducking through the treeline to take refuge in the maze of rosebushes. Henry – an insipid young man if ever she saw one – was digging by the fountain and didn't seem to notice as Dee hurried past. John was nowhere to be seen.

Alex's cottage was one of two, and backed onto a row of purple rhododendrons, perfect when you needed cover from prying eyes. Alex had texted Dee the day before, asking for a few days' leave so she could visit with a sick friend in London, and while Dee still harboured suspicions about her wily assistant, she had been only too glad to give it, especially now, as she crouched low behind the purple flowers, checking that the coast was clear.

John's cottage was right next door, and Dee could hear yelling coming from inside as she slipped the key into Alex's lock. Evie had given Dee a key when they were friends, with the promise that Dee could use the cottage whenever she wanted. She just hoped that in all these years the locks hadn't been changed. But the door opened with ease and Dee breathed a sigh of relief as she closed it softly behind her. She crept through the kitchen to the front room, almost jumping out of her skin when something solid hit the wall to her left. She heard raised voices again, a man and a woman, then all went silent. She only hoped it wasn't Emma, trying and failing to give John the potion.

Dee headed for the corner of the room, to just below the window where a small TV sat on a wooden cabinet. She pulled the cabinet out, tore up the carpet and removed a small crowbar from her bag. The floorboard offered little by way of resistance and she pried it loose with ease, almost crying with relief when her hand found what it was looking for. The box was a foot long and six inches wide and was made from the wood of an alder tree. It was engraved with markings of protection – the three symbols of Aster, namely the Triquetra – a knot of three overlapping, interconnected arcs representing the mind, body and soul. The ankh – a cross with an oval loop in place of the upper bar, representing life, immortality and eternal life, and the Triple Moon – the waxing, full, and waning moons close together and representing past, present and future. All three symbols had been used on Earth for centuries, but all three originated from Aster.

The box had been sealed with a thin layer of skin similar in appearance to plastic, but stronger and unbreakable without a neutraliser. Dee now had the neutraliser, retrieved from the stone in the wall at The Briar – a powder she called her DC powder, made from the dried sap of a Dracaena Cinnabari, or dragon blood tree – but judging by the smudge of red over the pale wood, someone had gotten there first.

She cursed loudly, yanked the lid open and threw the box back beneath the floorboards when she saw it was empty. Connie. It had to be. But how the hell had she known how to break the seal? She tried Connie's number, got voicemail and tried it again. This time the line started to ring at the same time that a phone next door began ringing, and both went quiet when Connie answered.

'Yes? What do you want?'

Dee looked to the empty box sticking out of the hole in the floor. 'Just calling to let you know the inhibitor for Raewyn's hands will be ready by morning,' she said. She could almost feel Connie's impatience leeching through the phone as she sighed heavily down the receiver.

'Was that it?'

At the front of the cottage, parked right beside John's white truck, was a little red Suzuki Swift, the same car that Connie drove. 'I thought I might pop by to discuss the finer details,' Dee said. 'Are you at the shop?'

A pause on the line. 'Now is not a good time,' Connie said, 'I have a headache. I'm about to close up shop and go for a lie down?'

'In that case I'll see you tomorrow,' Dee said. She hung up, switched the phone to silent and crept out the back door.

John's window was open a crack, and sure enough Dee could see Connie stood in the kitchen. She was holding out a photo for him to look at, and John – someone Dee had never cared to get to know – was holding a dagger he had no business touching.

The Servian Dagger was as old as the hills and had been in Dee's family for hundreds of years, passed down from generation to generation, and carefully guarded as though their very lives had depended on its protection. The blade was engraved with symbols from a long-forgotten language, and the hilt, carved from ancient bone, was stained black and polished to a high gloss. More symbols were engraved into the bone forming a centre line that matched up with those on the blade, and at the top of the hilt, surrounded by gold and silver filigree, was a small depression where the Eye of Eilidh used to sit. The dagger was a key, a way to open the portals of old, and John shoved it into the back of his jeans as though it were nothing more than a kitchen knife.

'You're wasting your time,' she heard him say, 'it doesn't prove anything.'

'Doesn't it?' Connie said. 'Look again.' She shoved the photo in John's face and flinched when he snatched it from her hand.

He slipped the photo into the back pocket of his jeans and opened the fridge door. 'I'll think on it,' he said. 'That's the best I can do.' Connie's nostrils flared but she held her tongue as John grabbed a beer then turned to her as though surprised she was still standing there. 'Something else I can do for you, Connie?' he said.

Connie grunted and pulled a bunch of photos from her bag and threw them on the table. 'If you have a conscience, then you'll do the right thing,' she said. 'Do it for Ben or do it for yourself, but your people need you. I'll come back later when I hope you'll have made the right decision. In the meantime, try to keep the dagger safe, it took your brother a long time to find it.'

Dee slid to the ground and waited until she heard Connie's car drive away and a door slam upstairs. Then she let herself in, listened at the bottom of the stairs, figured John was in the bathroom, and picked up a handful of the photos. There was one of Ivan the backpacker, and David – good natured David with the sweetest smile and dimpled chin – one of Alice and Jory, and Carl and Anthea. They were all there, even the pictures of Raewyn as a little girl, pigtails touching her shoulders and haunted eyes staring into the camera. These were Dee's photos, her personal collection so she would never forget. So, what was Connie doing with them?

'Find what you're looking for?'

Dee spun round to find John standing in the doorway, mouth tight and eyes hard, and looking so much like his brother it was unsettling. She pointed to the photos. 'Why did Connie give you these?'

John pulled a beer from the fridge, popped off the lid and took a long, slow drink. 'Why don't you tell me?' he said, then threw the photo of his brother into the mix. 'And while you're at it, tell me about him too.'

The photo was an old one, from before Raewyn was born, of Ben and Louisa together. They were both smiling in the picture, Ben young and tanned, Louisa, just as beautiful as Dee remembered. Louisa had been obsessed with Ben, calling him her muse, even flaunting him in front of Richard, though Richard had been too out of his mind on her poison to care. Dee hadn't liked Ben. That much she remembered. There had been an air about him, something not quite right about his interest in her sister, but after the night Louisa was killed Dee had never seen him again.

'I never knew him,' she said. 'Not really. We met once or twice, but he was Louisa's pet project and she didn't want me anywhere near him.'

'Louisa was your sister?' John said. He pulled up a chair and sat down so his body was blocking the door.

'May I?' Dee said. John nodded and she sat opposite, ready to choose her words carefully. 'Yes, we were sisters, but we hadn't been close since we were children. What did Connie tell you, John? Why did she have my photos?'

'Tell me about Ben,' he said, 'how did he seem to you?'

Dee thought back to the few times she met with Ben, the cold eyes that made her skin crawl from her head right down to her toes. 'Nothing to tell,' she said, 'Ben and Louisa were inseparable for a time, but the night she died I never saw him again. Connie knew him better than I did. Why don't you ask her?'

'I did,' John said, 'and she seems to think you killed him.'

Dee tensed and lightly touched the knife in her pocket. 'Do you believe her?'

'Why say it if it isn't true?'

'Because she's a manipulative, lying bitch,' Dee said. 'What else did she tell you?'

John eyed her carefully. 'A great many things,' he said, 'who are the other people in the pictures?'

'Friends,' Dee said, 'friends who are now dead.'

'Did you kill them too?'

Dee blew out a long breath. What was Connie up to? She casually slipped her hand into her pocket and wrapped her fingers around the hilt of the knife. 'I've never killed anyone in my life,' she said. 'Whatever Connie said, she's lying'

John leaned forward and placed the Servian Dagger on the table between them. 'The truth, Dee.'

Dee looked at the dagger, then at John and saw the raw look in his eyes. He didn't believe Connie, not really, but he was still deciding whether he could believe Dee. Dee had seldom found honesty to be the best policy in her line of work, but given her current situation was willing to give anything a try. 'They were already dying,' she said. 'They came to me, looking for help. I did everything I could for them, but no doctor in the world could have saved them.' John raised the bottle to his lips and the morning sun caught something on his wrist. 'I gave them purpose,' she said, 'a way to make their life truly mean something. They took their own life, John. I've never killed anyone, which is more than I can say for Connie.'

John didn't look surprised, neither did he take his eyes off Dee as he picked up the dagger. 'You know what this is?' he said.

'Of course,' Dee said, 'but you already know that.'

John unsheathed the dagger and held it up so the sun glinted off the blade. 'Ben found this, hidden beneath a floorboard next door. Any idea how it got there?'

'I put it there,' Dee said, 'the night Louisa died.'

John nodded as though satisfied with the answer, then touched the sharp tip of the blade to the pad of his thumb. A tiny prick of blood appeared and he smeared it over the edge of the knife and Dee felt a sudden shift in the atmosphere, as though a huge door that had been sealed for hundreds of years suddenly opened up a crack. She stared at John, open mouthed. 'You?' she said, 'you're a gatekeeper?' Gatekeepers were rare, so rare Dee knew of only two others besides herself. Suddenly Connie's motivations for visiting John became crystal clear. 'She wants you to open the portal for her,' she said. 'She's trying to shut me out.'

John leaned over the table and pointed the knife at Dee. 'I don't know what she's up to,' he said, 'but it makes no difference. Neither of you are getting your hands on this knife.'

Dee felt the first fissure of panic open up in her chest. 'John, you don't understand ...'

'I understand enough,' he said. 'You. Connie. Rae. Fuck! Even Ben for all I know. You're all into some weird shit that I want no part of, and this,' he held the knife up before returning it to its sheath, 'stays with me.'

'John, listen to me—'

'No, you listen to me, Dee, or Daeagan, or whatever the fuck your name is. The only reason I'm not going to the police right now is out of respect for my parents. If they found out about this ... about Ben ...' He shook his head and lifted the beer to his lips, cheeks flushed with anger.

'John,' Dee said, 'you have to listen to me. Connie, she's dangerous, you can't trust her. I don't know what lies she's been filling your head with, but—'

'Go,' he said, waving his hand towards the door, 'before I do something I'll regret.'

Dee swallowed. 'You know I can't leave without that dagger,' she said. 'It doesn't belong to you.'

'You're welcome to try and take it,' he said, 'but I can guarantee the only way it's leaving this room is if it's buried in your chest.'

He looked at Dee matter-of-factly, and she had no doubts whatsoever that he meant what he said. 'OK,' she said, 'I'll go. But just hear me out before I leave. Connie will tell you anything to get what she wants, and what she wants is for you to open a portal and release a nightmare like this world has never known. I want to stop her John. I *can* stop her, but I need that dagger to do it. That mark on your wrist ... do you know what it means?' John didn't answer, but his nostrils flared just a little. 'I don't know about your brother,' she said, 'but you're wrong about Raewyn. She's innocent, and if you care anything for her you'll hand over that knife right now. Think about it, John. Why else would Connie give it to you if she didn't want something in return?'

'Same reason you're here begging for it now,' he said, 'now leave before I throw you out.'

'John ... please.'

'GO,' he shouted, making Dee jump.

The door had barely closed behind her before a bottle smashed against it. She stood with her back to the wall, trying to think straight while her heart pounded in her chest.

She had to have that dagger. Without it she was no use to anyone, and if Connie didn't need her then ... she swallowed and checked her watch, ten-thirty am. She had to be at the train station for eleven. She looked back through the kitchen window just as John pulled down the blind. She had to have that dagger. *Had* to. She pulled the knife from her pocket and the DC powder from the other. She could force him to give it to her. John was a strong man, but Dee was quick and had years of experience at her back. She sighed and threw both the knife and the powder into her bag. Whatever his reasons for holding on to the dagger, Dee could no more kill him for it than she could've killed all those others. He was the anomaly, the stranger Mr Mitts had predicted, and one way or another he would be at that clearing tomorrow night, and so would the dagger.

She ground her teeth, hoisted her bag over her shoulder, and ran.

28

B y the time Rae arrived at Lotions & Potions the sky was beginning to dim, and the air had thickened to a damp, grey mist. The closed sign was still hanging in the door and she cupped her hands around her face to peer through the glass. The shop was devoid of life, and neither the off licence next door nor the barber's shop across the road had seen anyone coming or going all day.

She tried Alex's phone again, but when it went straight to voicemail she hung up.

She had spent the better part of the day walking by the river in Harleybrock, then locked away in the library pouring over books, trawling through the internet and searching anything in a desperate bid to understand her condition. Because that was how she'd come to think of it – a debilitating condition in need of a cure. But if anything had ever been written in the history of the world about freaks with burning hands, strange birthmarks, or men with golden eyes, then the Harleybrock library had no record of it. The closest she'd come to anything remotely similar was the mention of

Pyrokinesis, the ability to create and control fire with the mind. But even that didn't explain what Rae had done. Her mind had little to do with it. What she did came from the gut – a feeling rather than conscious thought that she had little or no control over once it began. Pyrokinesis, however, turned out to be a word coined by Stephen King for one of his books, so it wasn't even a real thing anyway, which meant she was either going crazy, or John was right, and she was the unwitting party of some ominous cult, and couldn't decide which was worse – that she was the accomplice of demonic creatures, or that she herself was the demon.

She had returned from Harleybrock with a train ticket to Inverness, due to leave at 3.20pm the next day, and with no particular return date in mind had wanted to say goodbye to Alex and ask her to keep an eye on the cottage. But now, as she stood on the threshold of her home, key poised in hand and pendant warm against her chest, she was beginning to reconsider. Cranston Myre was where the answers were. Not in Scotland, or Manchester, or anywhere else. She was running away again, just like she had run from Darryl. Taking the coward's way out when the going got tough. But if the past couple of weeks had taught her anything, it was that running away didn't solve anything.

The cottage was just as she'd left it that morning – red suitcase propped beside the breakfast bar, ready and waiting for the trip to Scotland, coffee cup on the kitchen bench, contents black as treacle and undisturbed, and her coat flung over the back of the couch, abandoned in favour of a thick jumper and scarf. Everything in its place, nothing moved, and yet somehow the cottage felt alive, as though the room had emptied the moment she turned the key in the lock.

She let her eyes roam over every corner, every nook, every

cranny, lingering on shadowy corners, searching for something out of place, something that would explain the unpleasant sensation that crawled down her back. Her boots echoed loudly on the hard wood floor as she made her way slowly through to the back of the cottage, switching on every light as she went. She stopped when she saw the white footprints by the back door. There was a footprint on each stair, starting from the tin of colonial white paint that dripped from the top step, and led out through the back door and into the garden. Rae touched a finger to one of the prints – still wet, so recently done, which meant the intruder couldn't be far, if indeed they were gone at all.

She opened the back door and peered out into the garden. The rusty gate was wide open with the ghostly footprints leading right up to it, and beyond that, the forest beckoned. She closed the door, locked it with the key and slid the latch home. It was almost full dark, and as strong as the temptation was to investigate further, she'd yelled at the TV screen too many times to go running out into the night with the vain notion that, should she happen upon her unwanted visitor, she could apprehend them without being subjected to some serious bodily harm herself. So instead she picked up the tin of paint, replaced its lid and stood it against the wall, together with the torn canvas of one of the paintings from the attic. It was the one of the dowdy young woman, and the frame had been broken with the backing paper ripped off. Whatever the intruder had been looking for, it seemed they knew exactly where to find it.

A quick check of the attic space confirmed nothing else had been touched, so Rae replaced the hatch, double checked all doors and windows, and dialled Alex's number. Anyone could have broken into the cottage, but the back door had been locked when she left that morning, and the key was still hanging from its hook in the kitchen. It was one of the first things Rae had checked. The door wasn't damaged, which meant either the lock had been picked or the intruder had a spare key. But Alex didn't answer her phone, and after the third attempt Rae gave up.

Next morning Rae awoke to the sound of rain, but still no word from Alex. She quickly showered, grabbed her coat and headed out the back door.

The painted footprints ended just outside the gate leaving no clue as to which way the intruder had gone, so she headed for the oak tree instead and quickened her pace when the clearing came into view.

Rae's bones hummed to the tune of the tree as she stepped into open ground, that strange vibration that made her skin tingle and the hairs on her arms stand on end, singing in her veins. A crow cawed from high in the tree and when she looked up many eyes looked back, black and unblinking.

The draw of the tree was stronger than ever today, and the paring knife, absently slipped into her pocket before leaving the cottage, found its way into her hand. One more vision before she left for Scotland. One more peek before she turned tail and ran from her problems, just like she always did. She sighed and a great white plume of breath filled the air around her. What right did she have to dump her troubles at Ronnie's door? The woman was almost ready to give birth for God's sake. What right did she have to dump her troubles at anyone's door for that matter? *You're all alone in this girl*, she thought, *better get used to it*. She lifted her face to the steady stream of rain, hoping the cold water would wake her from the permanent fug she seemed to be in of late, but the glacial waters of the New Zealand alps couldn't snap her out of the mess she'd made for herself this time. She took the knife from her pocket, realised she hadn't even cleaned the blood off from last time, and held it out to the rain, rubbing at the steel tip with the edge of her sleeve. Then something to her left caught her eye. Something poking out of the ground, partially covered by leaves.

She moved closer to get a better look. Was it a tree root? It didn't look like a root – too white, too ... awkward. She nudged it with her boot then clamped a hand over her mouth.

Not a root, but bone.

Human bone.

And judging by the flesh still attached to it, reasonably fresh.

JOHN'S DOOR was partially open when Rae pulled up in her car, but she sat there for a moment longer, trying to untangle the jumble of thoughts that were racing through her head. A body had been buried at the tree in a grave shallow enough that an animal had dug it up. Two fingers had been missing from the hand, another gnawed down to the bone, and a fourth – only half eaten – was bent awkwardly to one side. The little finger remained untouched though, and the belt buckle ring that Rae had bought for Alex was clearly visible. She gripped the steering wheel tightly and stared at John's front door. She didn't even know why she was here, but John had been the only person she could think of as she had run from the forest and jumped in her car.

The door suddenly opened, and Connie stepped out, holding an umbrella over her head with a phone to her ear. She ended the call the moment she saw Rae. 'My God,' she said, opening the car door. 'What on earth happened to you?'

Rae couldn't speak. All she could see was Alex's hand, sticking up out of the cold, wet earth.

'Inside,' Connie said. She took Rae's arm and ushered her through the front door, removed her wet jacket and sent her into the kitchen. Rae was still shaking when Connie followed her in and threw a blanket around her shoulders. 'Sit down while I make a brew, then you can tell me what's happened.'

Rae was numb to the bone, sick to the stomach, and reeling from her gruesome discovery, yet all she could think about was what the police would say when they saw Chris' face. Because they *would* see his face now, there was no getting away from it. An investigation would be made, the forest would be cordoned off ... people would be questioned.

'What's she doing here?' John stepped into the kitchen, hair still wet from his recent shower, and smelling of soap, but Rae could still smell the whiskey on him even from across the room.

'I've made you a black coffee,' Connie said, placing a mug in front of him, 'you'd do well to drink it.'

John took the seat opposite Rae, tried the coffee, winced, got up and replaced it with a beer. Connie tutted, handed Rae a bright yellow mug filled with hot tea, and sat down next to her.

'So, what's had you out in the rain then?' she said, 'you looked like you'd seen the devil himself sat in the car like that.'

Rae didn't touch her tea. John was watching her as though she would burst into flames at any moment. 'Alex is dead,' she said, and just like that the atmosphere in the room changed.

John and Connie looked at each other, then John raised his beer to his lips and Connie simply frowned. 'When you say dead ...'

'I mean dead,' Rae said. 'Gone, murdered, buried in the forest.'

Connie raised a brow. 'Did something happen between the two of you?'

A bubble of hysteria threatened to burst from Rae any minute, but she took a deep breath and swallowed it down. 'You're not listening to me,' she said. 'I found her, buried by the oak tree. Her hand was ... it was ...'

Connie laid a hand on her arm. 'Take another breath, Rae. You're amongst friends. Start at the beginning and tell me exactly what happened.'

Rae took several, hoping it would stop her heart pounding right out of her chest – it didn't. She told them about the break-in, and the footprints. About finding the hand half buried in the ground, and that she hadn't heard from Alex for days. John didn't say a word, but his eyes never left her face, not once.

'A hand you say?' Connie said, 'and you're sure it was Alex?'

'Yes,' Rae said. 'She was wearing the ring I gave her for her birthday. The one I bought from you.'

'And it couldn't have been anything else? A dead animal maybe? You're absolutely certain?'

'I know what I saw,' Rae said. She looked from one to the other. 'It was a mistake to come here,' she said, getting to her feet. 'I should've gone straight to the police.'

'Hang on a minute,' Connie said, 'if you're going to the

police, then I'm coming too. Sergeant Hopkins is a friend of mine, and you look like you could do with the support.' She stood and fetched Rae's jacket from the cupboard. 'Give me a moment to use the ladies' room then I'll be right with you. And I'll drive. You don't look in any fit state.'

Rae nodded. Company would be good, even if Connie didn't believe a word she'd said. She waited for Connie to leave the room then turned to John, who so far hadn't said a word. 'You might show a bit more concern,' she said, 'I thought Alex was your friend.'

John narrowed his eyes. 'What were you really doing out in those woods?' he said.

'Is that all you can think about?' Rae said, 'I tell you Alex is dead and all you're concerned about is what I was doing in the woods?'

'Was it you?'

'Was what me?'

'Did you hurt Alex?'

Rae turned and headed for the front door. How dare he ask her that? How fucking *dare* he? She got the door open an inch before it was slammed shut by John. She whirled round to face him, anger bubbling to the surface as hot tears rolled down her face. 'I thought you were a good guy,' she said, 'I told you things I've never told anyone, and you turned your back on me.'

His face was only inches from hers as he held the door closed, and she could feel the heat radiating from his body. 'Why can't you just answer the question?' he said. 'Did you, or did you not, hurt Alex?'

She wanted to hit him, to lash out and hurt him as he had hurt her by leaving when she needed him the most. Instead she sagged against the door, because how could she blame him for thinking such a thing after what she'd told him? 'No,' she said. 'I would never ...'

John closed his eyes and leaned his forehead against Rae's. 'I wish I could believe you,' he said. 'I wish ...'

'Ready then?' Connie appeared behind him and John pulled away, leaving a cold pocket of air where his body had just been.

Rae wiped a hand across her face. 'Ready,' she said, and opened the door.

She stepped out into the rain, not bothering to raise her hood or fasten her jacket. Connie's car was parked next to John's, and she climbed in, not looking to see if John was still there, still watching her with disbelieving eyes. If John didn't believe her, why would anybody else? Connie followed a moment later, silently climbed into the driver's seat and started the car.

They drove through the iron gates and towards the village without a word said between them. The moment Rae told the police about Alex then her time was up. She'd go to prison for sure, maybe even a lab where scientists would prod and poke her for the rest of her miserable life. But it was the right thing to do. There was a killer on the loose, a murderer in her own backyard, and she couldn't keep quiet about that just to save her own neck.

They passed Foxglove Lane, and a short distance further down the hill Connie pulled over to where a hooded figure waited on the roadside. 'Are we're picking someone up?' Rae said. Connie didn't answer, but Rae's door opened and when she turned, she saw Chris standing there, grinning like the Cheshire Cat.

'Hello gorgeous,' he said, and before Rae could react Connie reached over and stabbed a needle in her neck.

29

The first thing Rae noticed as she came around was a sweet, sickly taste at the back of her throat. The second thing she noticed was that she was not alone. The room was in darkness except for a thin sliver of light that escaped through the broken slat of a shutter high up on the wall, and she could hear breathing on the other side of the room – the deep, rhythmic breathing of someone asleep.

She was lay on a cold stone floor, hands tied behind her back, and the air smelled thickly of damp and mould. She pushed up into a seating position then wriggled onto her knees and waited for her eyes to adjust. She could just make out a staircase on the far wall that disappeared into the ceiling, and a large slab table in the centre of the room. Two white objects stood against the wall to her right that she thought might be a fridge with a chest freezer beside it, and next to that was shelving filled with God only knew what. The air in the room couldn't have been more than a couple of degrees above freezing, but someone had removed her wet coat and replaced it with a warm fleece zipped high up to the chin. She pushed up on to her feet, leaned against the wall while she waited for the room to stop spinning, then slowly began inching towards the staircase. She stopped when she heard moaning to her left.

'Dee, is that you?' someone groaned, 'I could do with a little help here if it's not too much trouble.'

Rae froze by the table. She knew that voice.

Suddenly the room was thrown into bright light as a trap door was lifted, and a pair of black boots came into view. Rae took a few steps back, and gasped when she realised who it was. Chris, his face all shiny and new, grinned from beneath a fresh sprouting of dark stubble.

'Well if it isn't our little fire maiden,' he said, 'I trust you slept well?' He was closely followed by a woman in a corseted green dress, who Rae took to be the infamous Dee given her long mane of red hair.

'What in God's fuck am I doing down here?' Rae looked to her left where Darryl was still steadying himself against the table. He didn't even look at Rae. It was as if she wasn't even standing there.

'Change of plan,' Dee said. 'Bit of a hiccup yesterday. We had to bring Rae in sooner than planned and I couldn't risk anyone knowing you were here. You understand?'

Darryl rubbed the back of his neck, hair all dishevelled and expensive designer suit covered with dust. 'What the fuck was in that drink you gave me? I feel like I've been run over by a train. Twice!'

'Nothing permanent,' Dee said. 'You'll feel fine once you've eaten.'

Rae felt like she'd been hit by a train too, but for very different reasons. 'Darryl?' she said, and all three turned to look at her. 'What's going on, Darryl? How do you know these people?'

Darryl looked to Dee, who in turn nodded to Chris. 'We're starting a club,' Chris said, grabbing Rae by the elbow. 'We're thinking of calling it *The Winters Burns Unit*. Has a nice ring to it, don't you think?'

'That's enough,' Dee said. 'Take her upstairs while I talk to Darryl.'

'No,' Rae said as Chris dragged her towards the stairs. 'Darryl, what's going on? Why are you here?'

'Tell her, Darryl.' Chris stopped in front of the man who had once been Rae's fiancé, and who now wouldn't even look her in the eye. 'Put her out of her misery.'

Darryl glared at Chris, then looked at Rae. 'Sorry, Rae,' he said, 'I like you, but this was never more than a job for me.' He nodded to Chris who then gave a tug on Rae's arm.

'Wait, no,' she said, standing her ground. 'What do you mean, it was a job?' Chris pulled harder, dragging her up the stairs. 'Darryl,' she yelled, 'at least tell me what's going on?' She dug her heels in so Chris had to physically pick her up to get her moving.

'You're wasting your time, princess,' he said, 'Darryl doesn't give a shit about you. Never did.'

'You can't keep me like this,' she shouted, 'people will be looking for me.'

'No-one's looking for you,' Chris said. 'You can take my word for that.' He lifted her up by the waist and began carrying her up the stairs, step by step, but she'd be damned if she'd let him take her anywhere. She braced her foot against the wall and pushed.

Chris hit the ground first, head smacking against the concrete with Rae landing heavily on top of him. She managed to wriggle off and get to her feet before Chris had time to recover, but her head was quickly yanked backwards as Darryl grabbed her by the hair.

'This is what happens when you don't keep them on a tight leash,' he said, then pushed Rae forward so she slammed into the wall.

'What are you doing?' Dee said, as he began removing his belt.

'Teaching her a lesson,' Darryl said. 'She needs to know who's boss. And I still owe her for this.' He pulled the neck of his shirt open, revealing a large waxy scar where Rae had burned him.

'Darryl, please don't do this,' Rae said, 'I'm sorry. I should have returned your calls, I—'

'Quiet,' Darryl said, 'you had your chance. Now it's my turn to hear *you* scream.'

Rae turned away just in time as the first lash sliced across her upper arm. She bit down on her lip, refusing to give any of them the satisfaction of hearing her cry.

'If you'd been half this challenging when we were together, things might have been a bit more exciting,' Darryl said.

Rae grit her teeth as the second lash caught her shoulder. 'As I recall, getting excited wasn't the problem,' she said, 'keeping it up was.' An angry growl from Darryl, and the belt came down again, this time across Rae's back.

'That's enough,' Dee said. 'You've made your point.'

'I've made my point when she's begging for mercy,' Darryl said, and swung the belt again, this time catching Rae's legs. She held her breath, ready for the next swing, but this time the belt didn't land.

She heard a gurgle behind her, and turned to see Darryl

clutching his throat, a look of shock frozen on his face. His mouth opened and closed like a fish, eyes wide with disbelief as a curtain of blood spilled through his fingers right before his body hit the ground with a sickening thud that reverberated through Rae's bones. She stared at his inanimate body, too numb to react as Chris climbed to his feet and Dee callously wiped the knife against her skirt.

'Get her upstairs while I clean up this mess,' Dee said. She dragged Darryl's body toward the table and positioned him so his blood spilled into a gutter that ran the length of the cellar. Some of his blood had splattered across the room when he fell, and when Rae saw the crimson splats on her leggings, her chin began to tremble.

'Don't you mourn him,' Dee snapped, 'he was rotten to the core. I did you a favour.'

'You're monsters,' Rae whispered, 'all of you.'

'You should be thanking her,' Chris said. 'He'd have flayed you from the neck down.' The left side of his head was matted with blood, and he held a hypodermic needle in his hand, but Rae didn't have the will or the energy to try and stop him as he unzipped her fleece.

WITH CHRIS and Rae out of the way Dee hurried to the fridge, unlocked it and removed the bottle of spinal fluid she'd been harvesting for the last ten years. It was still a small amount, 90 mls or less, but with Darryl's help there might just be enough. She took a syringe and carefully inserted it into Darryl's spinal canal. It was a tricky procedure at the best of times, and she would've preferred to do this overnight, while Darryl was still unconscious, but Chris had taken to sticking to her side like a limpet and while he knew most of what was going on, she had kept this part a secret.

Chris had agreed to help get rid of Darryl in return for Dee's promise to teach him everything she knew, and that included having Dee all to himself. Pretending everything was normal between them for the sake of keeping up appearances was one of the hardest things she had ever had to do. Harder even than cutting a man's throat in cold blood. Chris' every touch turned her stomach now and if there was anyone else she could rely on not to go snitching to Connie the first chance they got, then she would have gotten rid of him already. But she needed his help – to watch over Rae, to help with Darryl, and to keep Connie in check when the time came to kill Saoirse.

Darryl's spinal fluid was nice and clear as she slowly drained it from his body and injected it into the bottle with the rest. There was a thirty-minute window following death where the fluid could be harvested, after that it was completely useless. Sooner was best, and taken from a live subject better still, but Dee had never allowed herself to do that. All her subjects – Alice, Ivan, Jory, David, Carl and Anthea – had been dead before she even attempted extraction.

On the shelf above the fridge was a large jar, and in it a murky brown liquid. It was a mix of Banisteriopsis caapi vine and Psychotria viridis leaves, brewed and reduced many times over in preparation for the lunar eclipse. Dee had used the brew on numerous occasions for various reasons, but this time it had only one purpose – to aid the transfer of power from Saoirse's body to Dee's. She poured a small amount into the bottle of spinal fluid, gave it a shake then transferred all the liquid into a large syringe. Satisfied that she could do no more, she then wrapped the syringe in a cloth and carried it upstairs just as she heard the front door open and close. In a moment of panic, she threw the wrapped syringe onto her bed, pulled the rug over the cellar door and rushed into the living room just as Connie was making her way through.

She was dressed in a black robe, grey hair pulled tightly back in a bun and had painted the three symbols of Aster on her face with white paint – the Ankh on her forehead, Triquetra on one cheek and the Triple Moon on the other. Dee stifled a smile – it was an interesting visual if nothing else, but if it was protection Connie was after, she would have to do better than that.

'There you are,' Connie said. 'Please tell me everything is ready for tonight. The Order are becoming anxious and I don't want to give them your orange juice too early.'

Dee glanced to the locked door of the spare room and hoped Chris would have the good sense to stay there. 'All set and ready to go,' she said. 'You can tell The Order they have nothing to worry about.' *The Order*, Dee thought, nothing but a bunch of half-breed housewives with nothing better to do. She could almost feel sorry for them knowing what was to come if she didn't know each one of them was ready to support a monster for their own personal gain. They made her sick almost as much as Connie did.

'Good,' Connie said, 'their confidence in you is slipping of late.'

Dee smiled sweetly. 'They're welcome to find another gatekeeper to open the portal. I'm sure there are plenty to choose from.'

Connie sneered but didn't take the bait. 'What about Darryl? Where is he?'

'Never showed,' Dee said, 'I watched two trains come and

go and I've tried calling him several times, but he doesn't answer his phone.'

Connie lifted her chin. 'His loss. I would've thought he'd like nothing better than to watch Raewyn suffer after what she put him through, but no matter. What about the dagger? I trust you have it stored somewhere safe?'

Dee smoothed a hand over the bodice of her dress and smiled. The dagger had mysteriously turned up last night, back in its box and sitting safely on her kitchen table. She had no idea how it had got there, but had silently thanked John nonetheless. 'Of course,' she said, 'why wouldn't it be?'

Connie smiled. 'Drop the pretence, Dee, you never were a very good liar. *I* dropped off the dagger last night while you and lover boy were busy playing hide the sausage. I know you went to see John and I know he turned you away, so let's not pretend this is anything other than what it is.'

'John gave it to you?' Dee said, unable to hide her surprise.

'Of course not. That dribbling fool is wasted as a gate-keeper. I took it from him while he was too drunk to notice, and just as well too. What on earth possessed you to leave something so precious where anyone could find it?'

Dee slipped her hands into the pockets of her dress and clenched her fists tightly. She had hidden the dagger from Louisa in a hurry, not knowing at the time what it would cost, and had been unable to make herself go back to it even when she was able to. 'It was naive of me, I'll concede that much, but it was well protected. Or so I thought.'

'Naive!' Connie said, 'it was downright bloody stupid. If Louisa was here ...'

'But she's not, is she?' Dee said, knowing how much Connie pined for her protégé.

'Mores the pity,' Connie said.

'I couldn't agree more,' Dee said. 'Louisa would have known what John was the minute he stepped foot in Cranston Myre. She always did have a talent for sniffing out fresh meat. I can accept that I missed him, but not you, it seems. How is that Connie?'

Connie didn't break composure, but her mouth twitched ever so slightly. 'Maybe your radar is slipping?' she said, 'just like your loyalty.'

'Perhaps,' Dee said. 'Though my loyalty has, and always will be, to our people.'

Connie waved her hand dismissively. 'Doesn't matter anyway,' she said, 'he's been taken care of.'

'What does that mean?' Dee said, then narrowed her eyes. 'What have you done, Connie?'

'Tied up a loose end,' she said. 'John was far too taken with Raewyn. I had to make sure he wouldn't do anything stupid.'

Dee's stomach dropped. John was angry, unsure of who he was, but him being here had to mean something. It *had* to. Once again she had underestimated Connie's capacity for self-preservation. 'And if John had been willing to open the portal for you, what then?' she said. 'Did you plan to kill me, or hope that Saoirse would do it for you?'

Connie lifted her chin slightly. 'I guess we'll never know. But as it turns out, you're our best hope of seeing this through, much as it pains me to admit it.'

At least she was honest, the conniving old buzzard. 'Your vote of confidence is overwhelming,' Dee said, 'it almost warms my heart.'

'Can you blame me?' Connie said. 'Louisa died because of

you. Things could have been very different if you'd only done as you were asked.'

'You don't need to keep reminding me,' Dee said. 'I'm very aware of my past failings.'

'Let's hope so, because if you back out this time, I don't know what—'

'No-one's backing out of anything,' Dee said. 'I said I'll be there, and I will.'

'Make sure you are,' Connie said, 'because if Saoirse sets you alight this time, no-one is going to put you out.'

30

Once Connie had gone Dee rushed into her bedroom, took out the lockbox and placed it on the bed. There was a half dose of elixir left since treating Chris, and a new, stronger batch distilling in the cellar, but she was saving that for tonight, just in case things didn't go according to plan. She jabbed the needle into her thigh, put the cloth covered syringe with the spinal fluid into the lockbox, replaced the box beneath the floorboard, returned the key and left the house.

She arrived at John's cottage twenty minutes later to find the door unlocked and John slumped in a corner of the kitchen. 'Damn you, Connie,' she muttered, and rushed over to check for a pulse. He had one, but only just. A quick sniff of the glass that had fallen from his hand revealed a spiced-fruity scent just notable beneath the stronger smell of whiskey. 'Oleander,' she said, 'I might have known.' She threw the glass in the bin, switched on the kettle, and took out a small plastic tub and a large muslin pouch from her bag. The tub contained violet root and the pouch, poppy seeds. While the kettle was boiling she crushed the root then tipped it into a pan along with the poppy seeds, then poured the boiling water over the top and left it to steep. She checked John's pulse again. Anyone else would have been dead by now, herself included, but by some miracle John was holding on, albeit by a very small thread. She took her phone from her pocket, made a quick call, then turned back to the steeping violet.

Five minutes later the door was thrown open and Emma appeared in the doorway, cheeks flushed and eyes bright with worry. 'My God, what have you done?' she said, rushing to John's side.

'Don't move him,' Dee said. 'He's been poisoned. I can help him, but I need him on his stomach.'

'You.' Emma angrily pointed the finger at Dee. 'I never should have trusted you. What have you given him?' She was wearing faded jeans with a pastel blue shirt, the most casual Dee had ever seen her look, but had forgotten to wear the silk scarf around her neck. The marks Dee had noticed yesterday were evident beneath the collar of her shirt, but they weren't scratch marks as Dee had first suspected. They were bite marks, and by the angry black welts that circled each one, badly infected.

Now that Dee knew what John was, she knew the tonic she had given Emma would not work on him, and even if it did, she could no more allow Emma to whisk him away than she could save Emma from what was happening to her. Because Dee had seen marks just like the ones on Emma's neck before. Seen the infection take hold and knew how this would end. Emma had been bitten by a Grymlock, a dark creature that roamed the space between worlds. Neither alive nor dead it was the remnant of an essence turned bad. A messenger of the dead with an appetite for blood.

'It wasn't me that poisoned him,' Dee said, 'but you're right, someone did do this to him. He's lucky to be alive but we need to act fast if we're going to save him.'

Emma looked down at John's prostate body. 'Tell me what to do,' she said. 'I'll do anything you say, just make sure he lives.'

Dee had no doubt that she would and shoved a tub of foul-smelling grease into her hand. 'Lift his shirt and rub that into his lower back,' she said. It contained stomach fat amongst other things and would act as a lubricant for the energy that Dee was about to channel – another harvest from friends long dead.

Emma lifted the tub to her nose then held it away with a look of disgust. 'What is it?' she asked.

'You don't want to know,' Dee said. She pulled a piece of hessian cloth tight over a jug, tied it with string and poured the violet root water through it. She would have liked to steep the root for another half hour but was conscious that John may not have that long. She placed the jug of sieved water on the floor then knelt beside John, took a dollop of grease and rubbed it into her hands. 'You do the same,' she said to Emma, then took out another item from her bag. It was a piece of the black tourmaline from her lockbox, bound with leather string and made into a long necklace. The tourmaline had once belonged to her mother, and in all her years of prac-tising magic and medicine, Dee had never once felt the need to use it. Now she handed it to Emma and ordered her to place it around her neck. 'For protection,' she said.

Emma did as she was asked, and sat on one side of John, cross legged, as Dee did the same on the other side. Alone,

Dee was not strong enough to expel the poison from John's body, but by the power of two it might just be possible.

'Now what?' Emma said, 'do we chant or something?'

'Take my hand,' Dee said, 'and place your other hand on John, just here.' She pressed Emma's palm into the small of John's back, just above the sacrum, and placed her own hand just below so they made a loop, a circuit that would hopefully flush out his system. 'I'll do the work,' she said, 'all I need you to do is remain focused, and whatever you do, *do not* take your hand from John, or let go of mine until I say so, understood?'

Emma nodded, willing to do anything to save John's life, as Dee had hoped she would. 'What am I focusing on?' she said, 'are you sure this will work?'

Dee wasn't. She'd never tried this before, but the only alternative was to let John die. She checked John's pulse one more time, then closed her eyes and began. 'I want you to imagine a river,' she said, 'it's flowing through you, from my hand to yours, and from your hand to John, pouring into him as though he is an empty pool in need of filling. Do you feel it?'

There was silence for a moment then Emma gasped as the transference began. Dee could feel it too. It was strong, pulling on the elixir in her body and the power that flowed beneath them. 'That's good,' she said, 'but now I need you to concentrate harder. I want you to pull that river from me and send it crashing into John like a class five rapid, filling him up like a dam. Can you do that?' Straight away she felt a tug on her energy and smiled. Emma was already better than Dee could have hoped. 'That's it,' she said, 'you're doing great. Now it's my turn. You might notice a pull in the other direction, a second river flowing alongside the first, out of John and through to me. I want you to ignore that river. Pretend it isn't there. Can you do that for me?' A slight movement as Emma nodded.

It's working, thought Dee. *It's actually working!* The poison was bypassing Emma and entering Dee even as her own energy was sucked out from under her. A circuit of good and bad, negative energy vs. positive energy, replenishing John as fast as the poison was drained from his body. Dee felt the pull like a hose sucking water from a tap, felt the poison fill her veins like tar. John moaned quietly, then louder as his sacrum was blasted from the elixir in Dee's veins.

'We're hurting him,' Emma said, and Dee felt her grip loosen.

'No,' she said, firmly, 'stick with me, Emma. It's working. If we break the loop now it could kill him.' Emma's hand began to glow where it pressed firmly against John's sacrum, just as the flesh on Dee's hand began to pucker and blacken. The pain was excruciating but through the veil of agony she saw John begin to move. She turned to Emma and nodded. 'OK,' she said, 'you can start to slow it down now. Make the river smaller, more like a stream and then down to a trickle. That's it, you're doing great Emma. Now when I tell you to, let go of both me and John at exactly the same time. Ready? OK ... NOW.'

The roaring in Dee's head subsided the moment Emma broke the connection, and she grabbed the drained violet root and poppy seed, lifted it to her face and drank greedily from the jug. Seconds later she was leaning out the back door, violently retching into the bushes.

'That's the most disgusting thing I've ever seen,' Emma said, coming up behind Dee and screwing her face up at the black mess on the ground. John was propped up against the kitchen wall, head flopped forward like a ragdoll, but considerably better than he had been five minutes ago.

'*That* is what we just pulled out of him,' Dee said, wiping her mouth on the back of her sleeve. 'You should be proud of yourself. You did amazingly well.'

Emma said nothing, only looked back at John, still barely conscious, but alive at least. 'Will he be OK?'

'He'll be fine,' Dee said. 'Just give him time to come round then ply him with hot, sweet tea. He's far stronger than he looks.' She smiled, and for once, Emma smiled back.

'He's one of them, isn't he?' she said, 'one of you?'

Dee looked down at her hand. The pain was gone but the flesh would take time to heel, if indeed it ever would. 'Yes,' she said, 'I believe he is.'

Emma sighed, ushered Dee into the front room, and pulled the door to. 'I know we've never exactly been friends', she said.

Understatement of the year, thought Dee.

'But ...' she grasped for the right words, failed and looked down at her feet where painted toes stuck out from a pair of flip flops – this was not the Emma that Dee knew. 'I finally finished all of Evie's diaries,' she said, looking up, 'and I know who you really are, so please don't lie to me. I also know Evie was pregnant right before she died and that she feared for the baby's life. I want to know what happened to her child.'

Dee blinked, for once lost for words. This was a moment she'd envisaged many times over but never imagined it would actually happen. 'I saved her,' she said at last. 'Evie begged me to, but I would have done it anyway.'

Emma nodded as though she already knew the answer, and moved to stand by the window, looking out into the empty courtyard. 'Am I Evie's daughter?'

Dee took a deep breath and let it out slowly. 'Yes,' she said, 'but you were the second to be born. Raewyn was the first. She's your twin.' Emma didn't turn, didn't shout or scream, didn't give any indication whatsoever that discovering Rae was her sister fazed her in any way. 'It was a difficult pregnancy,' Dee added, 'and if you've read Evie's diaries then you'll know how she struggled to conceive and carry to full term. I tried to help her, but in the end, it was my sister, Louisa, who helped Evie.'

'Why?' Emma said, 'they hated each other. Evie even blamed herself for Louisa's miscarriage. Why would Louisa help her?'

The hard look in Emma's eyes was something Dee had become accustomed to, but it in no way made what was to come next any easier. 'Louisa wanted Evie's first born,' she said, cringing even as the words left her mouth.

'And Evie agreed?'

Dee nodded but was unable to meet Emma's eyes, still ashamed to this day of what she and Evie had agreed to do. 'You have to understand that Evie was desperate for a child,' she said. 'She believed she was cursed, that the miscarriages were her fault because she didn't want to share Richard with anyone. That Louisa miscarried because in a moment of madness Evie wished it so. Because Evie was one of us, same as John, same as you and your sister.'

'Don't call her that.' Emma turned back to the window.

'I tried to explain that the miscarriages had nothing to do with being Draiocht,' Dee continued, 'it was just ... one of those things, but ...' she sighed and closed her eyes, remembering that awful night when she had allowed Louisa to lay her hands on Evie's stomach, and to make Richard believe that Evie was in fact Louisa as he took her to his bed. It was sick and depraved and yet Evie had done it regardless, and Dee had not tried to stop her. 'Evie would've done anything to give Richard a child,' she said, 'that's all.'

'So, you manipulated her?'

'No,' Dee said, 'never. Evie was my friend. I loved her. I would have done anything to help her.'

'Including letting your sister near her, even though you knew what she was. Hah! Some friend.'

'Maybe,' Dee said, 'but Evie would have gone ahead with or without me. At least if I was there, by her side, I could—'

'What? Hand her baby over to your psychotic sister?'

Dee flinched at the ugly truth of what she'd done, but Emma's disgust was the least she deserved.

Emma turned back to the window. 'Why didn't you do it?' she asked, after a moment's silence. 'Why didn't you hand her over in the end?'

Dee thought she detected a note of regret in Emma's voice and thought how Evie would turn in her grave if she knew how one sister hated the other so much. 'Because it was the wrong thing to do,' she said, 'and because Evie begged me not to. Instead I hid you both until I could place you with suitable homes.'

'And your sister? She can't have been happy with your betrayal.'

'She wasn't.' Dee remembered the look on Louisa's face right before her life was extinguished, as though she had known that Dee would let her down. 'But she didn't get a chance to say so. She was killed because of what I had done.'

Emma nodded. 'When I did that thing with you,' she said, 'to save John, I ... I felt things, saw ... things.'

Dee smiled. 'You have the gift of sight. A rarity, even amongst the highest functioning Draiocht.'

'Draiocht,' Emma said, as though tasting the word for the first time. 'It means witchcraft does it not?'

'Amongst other things,' Dee said.

Emma nodded. 'I don't much care for the name. It feels too ... elegant for what you do.'

'Then what would you have us call ourselves?'

Emma shrugged. 'Witch sounds about right to me.' She looked at Dee, goading her, Dee thought. 'I never had this gift before,' Emma said, 'why now?'

'It manifests at different ages for different reasons,' Dee said, 'for some, never at all. I suspect yours was awakened when you helped me save John.'

'So, you knew?' Emma said.

'Not exactly,' Dee said. 'I knew you were Draiocht because I knew you were Evie's daughter, and that was all I needed. The rest is as much a surprise to me as it is to you.'

'Oh, I highly doubt that,' Emma scoffed. She turned back to the window, looking at nothing but perhaps seeing everything thought Dee. 'He's conflicted,' she said, 'he knows what he is, and he knows *who* he is, but he can't accept it, because of ...' Her voice broke and Dee very much wanted to go to her, to lay a reassuring hand on her shoulder as her mother would have done. She took a cautious step closer.

'You mean because of Raewyn?' she said, 'what else did you see? Is John a danger to her?'

'Their lives are linked,' Emma said, 'that's all I know.'

'That's all you know, or all you're willing to say?'

'Am I dying?' Emma said suddenly.

Dee felt herself pale as Emma turned toward her, eyes flat as though she'd done nothing more than enquire about the weather. 'I believe you've been bitten by a Grymlock,' Dee said, 'a creature that is neither alive nor dead. The black welts on your neck suggest its saliva is already deep into your bloodstream.'

Emma touched her chest where the black welts had already spread, and a flash of regret crossed over her pale eyes. 'And the cure?'

Dee shook her head.

Emma closed her eyes and breathed deeply through her nose. She smiled thinly, 'I always knew I would die young,' she said, 'but of every scenario I dreamed up I never envisaged this. How long do I have?'

'A week,' Dee said, 'maybe less.'

Emma blanched, and her eyes flickered to the door as there was a shuffle in the next room. 'It's funny,' she said, buttoning up her collar, 'I always thought I'd be terrified when the time came, but now it's here, I feel only ...'

'Numb?' Dee offered.

'Relieved,' Emma said. 'How do I look?'

'Like a woman about to go to war,' Dee said, and caught Emma's arm as she sidled past. 'I don't know what you saw when you touched John,' she said, 'but try to remember that none of this is Raewyn's fault. She's your sister, and as much a victim as you are.'

Emma looked at Dee with those steely blue eyes of hers and smiled tightly. 'I think you and I have very different ideas of what the word "victim" means,' she said. She pulled her arm free, handed Dee the tourmaline necklace, and hurried into the kitchen.

31

E mma waited until she heard Dee drive away, then double checked her shirt was buttoned to the top and turned to John.

John was everything she'd ever wanted, and yet she felt more detached from him now than she ever had. The bottle of tonic still sat on her bedside table where she'd left it. She'd wanted to use it, had even gone so far as to pour some into a bottle of wine, but she had gotten halfway to his cottage and turned back. Being handed the means to make him hers after the months of wanting was like winning first prize, but no matter how many times she tried to convince herself that she was doing the right thing, it still bore the hollow taste of a lie. John wasn't hers, never had been really, and though it had taken today to finally realise it, she still wasn't prepared to let him go just yet.

He staggered to his feet and with Emma's aide made it to the table where he sat down heavily on the chair. 'You need to take it easy,' Emma said, 'Dee said you'll be fine, but it may take a moment.'

'Dee was here?' he said, blinking as though the light was too bright, 'what did she want?'

'Tea first,' Emma said, 'doctor's orders.' She left him sat at the table – head in hands and eyes closed – while she boiled the kettle. It had been a long time since Emma had felt this relaxed in his company. Always trying to say the right thing, do the right thing or catch his attention. Every movement, every breath, every word geared towards making John see her the way he once had, or the way she once *thought* he had. But now, after what she'd just done, after connecting with him on such an intimate level and knowing what she did, well ... she always thought John was a complicated man, but she now knew that complicated didn't even begin to cover it. She put a tea bag in his cup, four spoons of sugar (Dee had said sweet, but how sweet was too sweet?) and filled the cup with hot water.

'Drink up,' she said, placing it on the table in front of him, 'it'll make you feel better.' John did as he was told, but Emma knew him well enough to know that his thoughts had turned inward. 'How much do you remember?' she said, when he'd finished the whole mug.

John blew out a deep breath and ran a hand through his hair. 'Not much,' he said, but Emma could tell he was lying.

'You were poisoned' she said, 'I got the impression Dee knew how, but didn't want to say.' She waited, but he offered no word of explanation. 'I think it was Connie,' she said, 'I always had a feeling about that woman, and I saw her car here last night.' It had been part of the reason Emma had turned back, bottle of drugged wine in hand, though she preferred to think it was a call of conscience. 'Dee found you this morning and asked for my help. Do you know why Connie wanted to hurt you?'

John fell back in his chair with a sigh. 'I've no idea, Em, honestly. Everything's so fucked up right now. Dee shouldn't have involved you.'

'Well it's a good thing she did,' Emma said, 'someone has to have your back.' John smiled tightly but his mind was somewhere else. Emma leaned across the table and took his hand in hers. 'I know my behaviour has been somewhat ... questionable of late,' she said.

'You don't have to do this, Em,' he said.

'Yes, I do,' she said, 'because I may never get another chance, not like this. I understand why you can't love me, and before you say anything, it's OK, really, but what we had when were together was special, for me anyway—'

'Emma—'

'No. Let me finish, please, this is important.' She sighed and closed her eyes, trying to get the words right in her head. 'I love you, always have, always will, but we both know that where you're going, I can't follow. Call it female intuition,' she said, seeing the look of confusion on his face, 'or ... divine enlightenment, but we both know I'm right. That's why I'm releasing you, John Baxter. Go and do whatever it is you need to do. I won't stand in your way any longer, I promise, and I don't want you to worry about me either, because believe it or not I have plans of my own.'

John looked surprised, and she hated to admit it, but also a little relieved. Then he leaned forward and kissed her on the mouth, and it was so breathtakingly unexpected that Emma forgot herself for a moment and allowed herself to think this was the start of something new. But then she remembered the conflict she had felt inside him, conflict that would tear him apart if she let it. 'I have to go,' she said, standing up. 'Georgina needs me in the kitchen.'

John stood with her, cheeks a much healthier shade than the washed-out grey they had been only moments before. 'I'm sorry if I hurt you, Em,' he said. 'That was never my intention.'

Emma swallowed. 'You were never anything but honest,' she said. 'If I was hurt then it was my own doing. It's taken me a while to realise it, but I got there in the end.'

He pulled her in for a hug and Emma thought her heart might break in two. 'You're a special woman, Emmaline Ashley—'

'*Standford* Ashley,' she corrected, breathing in his scent for one very last time.

'—you just need to believe it, and when the right guy comes along everything will fall into place.'

The right guy already did, she thought. 'I have to go,' she said, 'before I make a fool of myself and start crying.'

'You are many things, Em,' John said, 'but a fool isn't one of them. Just remember that.'

Emma kissed him on the cheek then quickly walked out the door while she still could.

Outside she leaned against the wall, taking a moment to catch her breath as tears flowed freely down her cheeks. She knew it was the right thing to do, a quick clean break before he realised something was amiss. So why then did it hurt so damn much? She brushed a hand across her cheeks and looked up toward the tower, Evie's tower, her *mother's* tower. Then without looking back, she headed for the west wing door and the stairs that would take her to the attic.

32

Dee hurried back home to where Chris had been standing guard over Rae all morning. She was perturbed about her conversation with Emma. That Emma was gifted was of no concern, but her jealousy of Rae's connection with John could be. Or it might prove to be of no consequence at all. She was still unsure where John fit into all this, but given the lunar eclipse was only hours away, she had to tell herself not to dwell on things beyond her control. As long as she kept her head about her and stuck to the plan, then hopefully, by tomorrow, Earth would be a safer place for all.

Dee was under no allusions that what she was about to tell Rae would seem far-fetched at best, but she couldn't risk taking her into the forest without her knowing what was at stake. She only hoped she'd be willing to listen, which didn't seem likely after what had happened with Darryl that morning.

Darryl had arrived the day before as planned, full of his own self-importance and ready to ruin everything that Dee had spent years preparing for. He wanted to kill Rae and have done with it. Bottle her blood for Saoirse's release and take his chances when Saoirse discovered her sister was dead. He was a hot bed of bruised male ego, incapable of seeing the bigger picture, and Dee had known right away that he had to go. He was her first cold blooded kill, and if tonight went to plan, he wouldn't be her last.

But none of that would matter much to Rae when Dee walked in that room. She had watched Dee murder her ex-fiancé, and knew Dee and Chris were in this together – a murderer and a rapist. Not the best foundation for a conversation about trust, was it?

She opened the door and nodded to Chris that he could leave. 'How's she been?' she whispered, as he stepped from the room.

'Quiet,' he said, closing the door behind him, 'hasn't said a word since she came around, other than to ask to use the bathroom.'

'And?'

He shrugged. 'I let her use it.'

'No funny business? You weren't tempted to take revenge for your face?'

Chris smiled, and the faint, waxy scar that remained on his left cheek tugged his eye at an odd angle making him look less than sincere. 'I never touched her, Dee,' he said, 'what would be the point given what's in store for her tonight.'

'And she didn't try to escape?' It had taken some convincing to get Chris to stay in the room with Rae, and some faith on Dee's part. Rae didn't know what she was yet, didn't know how to control her gift otherwise the handcuffs would've been next to useless, but she could tell Chris had still been nervous about babysitting her once the sedative wore off, which was only a good thing, because it would make him think twice before doing anything stupid.

He shook his head. 'Did her business then got back on the bed like a good girl.'

Dee nodded thoughtfully. Acquiescence was one thing, but if there was no fire left in Rae's belly then there was little hope of her getting through tonight. 'Has she eaten?'

'Not a thing. Drank a bottle of Coke though.'

'OK,' Dee said, 'you can go. But don't go far. I'll need you to take her to the clearing later.'

Rae was lay on the bed when Dee walked in, hands cuffed to the frame, but at least they were no longer behind her back. 'Do you know why you're here?' Dee said. Rae gave her a dirty look but didn't reply. 'You're here because of the birth-mark on your belly,' Dee said, 'and because of what it means.'

Still nothing, not even a twitch.

'You must have wondered how you can burn people, Rae. There aren't many people who can do that. Hardly any, actually.'

Still nothing.

Dee sighed. 'OK. First of all, you're not a witch, so don't let anyone tell you otherwise. Secondly, you're not a bad person, either. When you burned Darryl and Chris, it was because you were angry, right? Because they had done something to you that made your blood boil over and the next thing you knew you were frying them up like KFC?'

A slight flicker of movement. Could've been a muscle spasm though.

'It happens to everyone when their gift first surfaces,' Dee said. 'Unless you have someone to teach you how to control it, the gift will react to strong emotions. In your case, anger. You need to be able to focus that anger in order to use your gift at will, otherwise any little thing could set you off. Grace was a wonderful human being, but a teacher she was not.'

Rae narrowed her eyes. *If looks could kill!* thought Dee. She pulled up a chair and sat by the bed. 'We're opposites, you and me,' she said, 'I was born with very little by way of a gift. I've had to work my arse off to get to where I am today. But you, you were *born* great. It's in your blood. You're the prophesised child. The "chosen one" if you like. Destined for greatness or destined for tragedy, it's up to you. You're in control. You're Draiocht Rae. Do you know what that means?'

'Go fuck yourself.'

Dee laughed. 'Well at least you're speaking to me now.' She got up, grabbed a potted plant from by the window and dragged it over to the chair. 'Look, I'm sorry about Darryl, but I did what I had to do to save you, and I would do it again in a heartbeat. But me running around killing useless pricks like that isn't going to save you tonight. *You* have to save you tonight, otherwise we may as well all just open up our veins right now and have done with it.'

This time it was Rae that laughed. 'You're using me to save your own skin, is that it?'

'No,' Dee said, 'that's not it. That's not even close to it. Did you know that the night you were born I held you in my arms? Swaddled you in my shawl and nursed you to sleep? Then I carried you across the fields to a trusted friend just so that I could save your life. This is what I got for it.' She lifted her skirt to show Rae the scar that ran the length of her thigh, the part that she had never tattooed over. 'The woman that did this to me, now wants you. She's called Saoirse and she's like us, she's Draiocht, and damn powerful too. The night you were born I was meant to take you to her, to use your blood to release her from a place called Gestryll. But I couldn't do it.

Couldn't hurt an innocent child any more than I could free a tyrannical monster. So, I saved you instead, and Saoirse killed my sister for it, almost killed me. Now she's angry, angry with the human race, angry with the Draiocht race, but most of all she's angry with you.'

Rae blinked, still with that same *fuck you* look on her face, but Dee wasn't giving up just yet. 'Draiocht don't originate from here,' she continued. 'It's not even our real name, but we've been called it for so long now it's kind of stuck. We're human in the biological sense – we're carbon based, breathe oxygen, need food and water to survive – but our ancestors were not born on Earth. They were born in another world, a place called Aster that has existed alongside Earth for millions of years. But there's one big difference between Asterians and Earthlings. The people of Aster can connect with nature, with the planet and every living thing around them. They can manipulate energy,' she tapped the side of her head, 'it's all up here, in the part of the brain that's dormant in humans but very much awake in Draiocht.' She sighed seeing the lack of interest in Rae's face. 'Maybe it would be better if I showed you.'

She took out the small knife she always carried around in her pocket and made a small cut on her hand. 'When you burned Chris and Darryl, you did it by transferring energy from your body into theirs,' she said. 'Almost all Draiocht can do it, but only a handful can do it well, and almost none can do what you did.' She grabbed the potted plant by the stem and held her hand out so Rae could see the cut at the base of her thumb. 'Every living thing has energy,' she said. 'Plants, for instance, generate energy from sunlight, it's called—'

'Photosynthesis,' Rae said.

Dee smiled. *At last.* 'That's right,' she said, 'people

consume food, which generates chemical energy, and that chemical energy is then transformed into kinetic energy which in turn powers our muscles. At any given time, the human body holds enough energy to power a light bulb. A typical Draiocht can hold ten times that much, and someone like you, considerably more than that. Now watch.' She squeezed the stem of the plant and concentrated on the flow of energy, much like she had with John, only this time she wasn't sucking out poison. As the plant's energy was drained and directed to Dee's hand, her skin began to tingle and knit together. Dee had done this same demonstration a hundred times before, and seen it administered to countless other people, but to Rae it was new, and it showed on her face.

'How did you do that?' Rae still looked at Dee as though she was the Devil incarnate, but it was something at least.

'I took the plant's energy and transferred it to my hand,' Dee said. 'Healing minor wounds is about my limit though. What you did was significantly harder, and impossible for the likes of me, even here on Earth where the source of energy is much more potent than that on Aster. Here, it comes from ley lines, on Aster it's referred to as the flux and is more precious than any gemstone. Because of this, Draiocht have been coming to Earth for thousands of years using portals that are dotted all around the globe. One such portal exists in Dolen Forest. I believe you've already visited it on a number of occasions?' Realisation dawned on Rae's face then, and Dee knew she was finally getting through.

'The portals provide a direct link between here and Aster,' she said, 'but can only be opened *from* Aster, unless you're born of a certain bloodline, in which case you can pretty much open it any time you want with the right equipment. We call these people gatekeepers, and you're looking at one of them right now. But no-one dares to open the portals anymore for fear of retaliation. For years Draiocht lived amongst humans in peace, observing their ways, learning the many languages and dialects, seeking only knowledge in return for their skills as healers. It was a means of under-standing the human race in the hope that, one day, we could live openly and peacefully as one. But times change. *People* change, and when the witch trials were at their peak in the seventeenth century the Draiocht way of life became too conspicuous. They were hunted down for nothing more than lancing boils and healing sores. So, the decision was made to leave, to return to Aster and close the portals forever. It was either that or go to war. But the natural elements of Earth are far richer than those of Aster, and some weren't willing to give that up so easily. Fighting broke out between clans and new leaders emerged, leaders who saw an opportunity to rule. One of those leaders was Saoirse. Saoirse was strong and fearless and could manipulate the energy of an entire tree with just the tip of her pinky. But even she was no match for the great armies of Aster. When word got back what was happening, they came through the portal and apprehended Saoirse and her men. Her generals were executed, and Saoirse was sentenced to death by banishment. Her body was burned, but her soul was sent to spend all eternity trapped in the nothingness between this world and the next. That place is Gestryll, and it's where Saoirse still waits for the only thing that can release her from a life of hell. Her sister's blood.'

Rae blinked and looked away.

'If I'm right,' Dee said, 'then I think you may already know who her sister was. I've seen you at the tree, Rae. I know you've touched it, felt its power.'

Rae stared at the wall as though looking through it to

another time, another place. 'Augustine,' she whispered, and the air around them seemed to come to life.

So it's true, thought Dee. Even right up until this moment Dee had still held on to the smallest scrap of doubt. That the birthmark meant nothing, the burnings accidental, and even the pendant around Rae's neck was a fake, nothing more than a cheap crystal bought from a market stall. 'You're the first to speak her name in a very long time,' Dee said. 'Few even dare.'

Rae turned to Dee, her face a mixture of anger and fear. 'I'm done listening to your hocus pocus bullshit,' she said. 'Either let me go or kill me, but spare me the family history.'

'You can't run away from this,' Dee said. 'Believe me, I've tried. There are too many who would see Saoirse return, too many who would give anything to taste even a drop of what you have, humans included. And that's what Saoirse promises. Power. And she may not have an army yet, but she soon will. Just because she's trapped in Gestryll doesn't mean she can't get to you, or me, or anyone else for that matter. That's why we have to stop her, and I can't do it alone. I need you, and what's inside you if the human race has any chance of survival.'

'Fuck the human race,' Rae said. 'What have they ever done for me?'

'Don't you say that,' Dee said. 'Don't you ever say that. Your mother would be turning in her grave to hear you talk like that after what she went through.'

Rae looked away. 'Who was she?' she said, after a moment's silence.

Dee took a calming breath and straightened her skirt over her thighs. 'Her name was Evelyn Stanford-Ashley, and your father was Richard Ashley.'

Rae laughed. 'And I suppose your sicko boyfriend out there is my brother.'

'No?' Dee said. 'But Emma *is* your sister.'

Rae swallowed as the colour left her cheeks. 'You're lying.'

'What could I possibly hope to gain by lying about your parents?' Dee said. 'Emma is your twin. You're the oldest by thirteen minutes. Look, we could do this all day, but it's not going to change a damn thing. Tonight is a lunar eclipse, a special one, the fourth of a tetrad which means the portal to Gestryll will be weak, and the only time we can free Saoirse.'

'And why would you want to do that?' Rae said. 'If she's so all powerful and evil, why not leave her there to rot?'

'Because she will never stop,' Dee said. 'There will be other eclipses, other opportunities and other gatekeepers will come along who don't give a shit about you, or what Saoirse will do when she gets here. But I do, and I know how to stop her. All I need is a small amount of blood, and—'

Rae began to laugh. Not just a snigger, but big, hysterical roars of laughter that verged on psychotic. 'You really are crazy if you think I'm going to help you with anything,' she said. 'I'd rather get naked with your creep of a boyfriend than give you even a drop of my blood. Alien worlds and magical warriors! Hah! You're sick, and deluded, and a murdering FUCKING MONSTER!' She wrenched against her handcuffs just as Chris came running into the room.

The back of his hand would have collided with Rae's face had Dee not stopped him, but it only made Rae laugh louder. 'Is that the best you can do?' she roared, 'you pathetic piece of shit.'

Dee ushered Chris back out of the room before he did something to Rae that he'd regret, then she dragged the dead plant back to the window and stood looking down at Evie's first born, the child she had nursed and the woman she had thought would come to her aid. 'I had hoped it wouldn't be like this,' she said, 'I had hoped you would understand the importance of what I'm doing.'

'Then release me,' Rae said. 'Let me go and we'll talk some more.'

'The time for talk is over,' Dee said, 'whether you like it or not, you *are* going to help me tonight. I'll do everything I can to keep you safe, for Evie's sake as much as anything, but if I were you, I'd get some rest, you're going to need it.' She walked out of the room and locked the door behind her. 'Stand guard,' she said to Chris, 'and if you hear so much as a whisper you come get me. Looks like we're back to Plan A.' Chris smiled and nodded, and Dee couldn't help but think he was pleased with the outcome.

33

E mma unlocked the attic door and swung it open. The air was cold, more so than usual, but her heart was racing so fast she barely noticed. In no mood for tricks or shadows, she immediately switched on the attic light and walked straight to the west wall where the old tapestry hung. When she first discovered Richard's portrait hidden behind the hastily bricked up wall, she had been reluctant to delve further inside the hole with Alex present. It felt wrong, like robbing a grave, but where Emma had been respectful, Alex had had no such compunctions. She would have torn the place apart looking for family heirlooms had Emma not put a stop to the excavation. So she had told Alex there was nothing more to see and had begun locking the attic from that day forward.

But that hadn't been entirely true.

The feeling that someone else had been in the attic that day, other than Alex and herself, and been strong enough to make Emma cover the hole up with the intention of having it re-bricked as soon as possible. But the temptation to see what was in the small bundle she had spotted in the bottom right-hand corner had proved too strong to resist. She had returned several nights later, drunk on Dutch courage, and discovered Evie's diaries wrapped in a plastic bag and sealed with duct tape. She also discovered a bloody sheet but had not had the courage to touch it – until now.

That same certainty that she was not alone now accompanied Emma as she removed the tapestry and shone the torchlight of her phone into the black chasm. The bloody sheet was still there, and before she could change her mind she reached in and dragged it out. The blood belonged to Evie, to Emma, and to Raewyn. It was the blood from their birth, from Evie's determination to bring two children into the world no matter what the cost, and as Emma unravelled it an earring fell out onto the dusty wooden floor.

Emma bent down and picked it up. It belonged to Evie, a gift from Richard on their wedding day – a silver drop with a small diamond at the end. Emma hadn't read the last of Evie's diaries because Evie hadn't written them. Everything that happened beyond Louisa losing her baby, Emma had learned from Dee. And now she could feel Evie, too.

This new gift she had, this new ... ability, felt like rushing headlong into a room full of people all waiting to tell their story. It was confusing, overwhelming, but most of all just downright unpleasant. Seeing inside someone's head, knowing their thoughts, feeling their feelings, was like being stuck on a merry go round after a belly full of ice-cream, only you couldn't get off. You were stuck there, watching this person's life flash before your eyes like a movie reel on fast forward. And that's what it was like for Emma now, everything that had happened the night Emma was born, written in the stains on the sheet.

Emma ran a hand over the faded blood stains and reeled from the raw emotions that poured from the cotton fabric. She saw Louisa laying her hands on Evie's petrified body, while Daegan – so different to the Dee Emma knew today – held her down. She felt Evie's struggle to overcome her hatred of Louisa in order to give Richard the family he so craved, felt her agony as Louisa's energy worked its magic inside Evie's womb, then felt her joy when her belly began to swell. She felt Evie's anxiety lessen day by day as the babies grew strong insider her, but at the same time the knowledge that she had sworn to give up her first born weighed heavy on her mind. Then Emma saw Richard, his face twisted with disgust when Louisa released him from her spell, and he realised what Evie had done. He thought the babies were an abomination, conceived through an act of evil, and when Evie refused to abort them, he threatened to do the job himself. And Evie had killed him for it. Stabbed him in the heart, and then in her madness attacked his portrait so she would never have to see his face again. But Evie's suffering had not ended there.

Daegan had taken the knife from Evie's hand and confined her to her room for her own safety, until the night of the red moon when her contractions began. Evie, consumed with guilt and dying from a broken heart, fretted for the safety of her children and begged Daegan to save them. The birth was difficult, the babies breached, and when Raewyn was finally delivered, kicking and screaming with an angry red birthmark above her navel, Evie had pleaded with Daegan to hide her away. The fear that Evie had felt, the heart wrenching pain of knowing she could not save her child, sucked the air out of the room. But Daegan had agreed. Then the second child was born, healthy and ruddy and full of life, and both women had wept.

Emma clutched the sheet to her chest. Seeing her own birth through the eyes of Evie was a strange sensation, and brought home the fact that Emma would never know the joys of childbirth for herself. Then Daegan had swaddled both children and left the room, leaving Evie to drown in despair.

Then Evie was up, running through the corridors of Carrion Hall, clutching the bloody sheet in her hand. A fire raged behind her, roaring and hissing as it climbed the walls, smoke stinging Evie's eyes as she ran to the door at the bottom of the attic stairs. Then she was at the wall, mortar still fresh from Daegan's recent reconstruction. Daegan had been the one to remove the bricks and hide Richard's painting inside the cavity, just as she had been the one to drag Richard's body from the Hall and bury him in the garden. But Evie could not live with what she had done, nor could she let the truth die with her. So she dug out the mortar with the key for the attic, removed three of Daegan's bricks and shoved the bloody sheet inside together with her bundled diaries from the tower. She replaced the bricks as best she could then lay on the wooden floor, curled like a foetus, and waited for death to come. But the fire didn't reach her, nor was it the smoke that got her in the end. Instead the fire raged beneath like a roaring dragon but remained on the first two floors, and though smoke swirled about the attic like angry ghosts, it kept to the walls giving Evie her space. And as she lay there in the dark, wondering what would become of her babies and watching the stars through the window that was just too high to comfortably look out of, she suddenly knew a different kind of death was coming for her.

She got to her feet, stood on her tiptoes, and reached for the window just as a murder of crows blasted through the glass. They swarmed around her body, pecking and squawking, scratching and flapping, drawing blood and picking at flesh. Their wings beat around her head like thunder, claws catching in her hair, beaks jabbing at her eyes, until Evie threw up her arms and begged for mercy. But the crows were not merciful, the crows were not crows at all but the wrath of someone who had been wronged, and as Evie's legs finally gave way and she fell to the ground, a blur of black feathers fell with her. The crows feasted on Evie's flesh until her screams were silenced and her blood ran cold, and then Emma sank to the floor and wept.

She was still reeling from Evie's last moments when a figure appeared in the doorway. 'Alex,' she said, brushing a hand across her face, 'how long have you been standing there?'

'Long enough,' Alex said, 'I've been looking for you all morning.'

Emma climbed to her feet. 'I thought you were in London. Has your friend recovered already?'

Alex had a strange look on her face. She seemed ... older, somehow. 'I lied,' she said, 'there never was a friend. What's that your holding there, Cuz?'

Emma glanced down at the bloody sheet and felt a cold sensation creep up her back. 'Nothing,' she said, 'just a dust sheet.'

'You always cry over a dust sheet?'

Emma caught a glimpse of the gun in Alex's hand as she

stepped into the room. 'What do you want, Alex?' she said, 'you know I don't like anyone up here.'

'I thought we could make an exception,' Alex said, 'given what a special night it is.'

Emma took a step back towards the hole in the wall, felt a cold breeze on the back of her neck. 'What special night would that be?' she said, 'is it someone's birthday?'

Alex smiled. 'I suppose you could say that, yes. Want to tell me why you were crying?'

'I wasn't crying,' Emma said, 'I had something in my eye.'

Alex smiled, sat down on an upturned crate, and brought the gun to rest on her knee, loosely pointed at Emma. 'How about now?' she said, 'feel like telling the truth now, or should we just keep going in circles? Here, tell you what ...' She pulled a ring from her finger and tossed it to Emma. It clattered on the floor by her feet. 'Go ahead,' Alex said, 'pick it up. Tell me what you see.'

Emma dropped the sheet, picked up the ring and flinched from the images it showed her. 'You're being ridiculous,' she said, 'I'm in no mood for silly games—'

'This is no game,' Alex said, 'you can either tell me what you see, or I can make sure your last few days are spent writhing in agony. Choice is yours, *Cuz*.'

Emma took a deep breath and closed her eyes. She saw a child being born in the front room of The Briar. Furniture was sparse but the fire burned brightly while a storm raged outside. A woman was there helping with the birth, much younger than she was now but Emma would recognise the cold, flat eyes of Connie anywhere. She pulled the child free from its mother, then Emma saw the mother and gasped. She opened her eyes to find Alex watching her carefully. 'Louisa never miscarried at all, did she?' Emma said. 'You're her daughter.'

Alex slowly applauded. 'I'm impressed,' she said, 'I've never met anyone with the sight before. What else do you see?'

Emma clutched the ring tighter, felt the hairs on her neck stand on end when it showed her all that Alex was, and what would become of her if she were to succeed tonight. Then she saw Chris, his face ravaged with hate. 'Does Chris know about me?' she said. She couldn't bear to think that her baby brother was a part of all this madness.

'Yes, and no,' Alex said, 'he knows what you are, he doesn't know what you can do. And if I were you, I wouldn't tell him. I think he's been emasculated enough living in your shadow, don't you?'

'But he's helping you?' Emma said, 'he knows what's going on?'

Alex nodded. 'There's not much your brother won't do to get what he wants.'

'Then let me help, too,' Emma said. 'I know why you came up here, Alex, but as you can see, I'm already dying, and we both know I'm a better match for Saoirse than that waif of a girl you're planning to use. Use me instead. If only to see the look on Raewyn's face. Please,' she said, when Alex didn't answer. 'I can't bear the thought of that woman with John. Give me the chance to do something about it before I die.' She watched with bated breath as Alex mulled it over, knowing full well that she believed John already dead.

'I suppose you could be useful,' Alex said. 'But how do I know I can trust you?'

Emma took a step forward, handed the ring back to Alex. 'Because I won't let anything happen to my brother, and because Dee doesn't know about you yet, but when she does, she's going to try and stop you. She still thinks she can save Raewyn.'

Alex laughed. 'That's hardly breaking news. Anything else?'

Emma thought hard. She couldn't tell Alex about John or about Dee's serum without putting them both in jeopardy, but she had to give her something. 'Dee killed someone,' she said, 'one of your lot. A guy named Darryl. She cut his throat.'

Alex did look surprised at that. 'How very bold of her,' she said, 'and you know this how?'

'I saw her this morning,' Emma said. 'She sold me a tonic, something I could use on John.' She glanced at her feet, pretending to be embarrassed. 'When I took it from Dee, I touched her hand, and ... saw things, horrible things. That's when I came up here, held Evie's sheet, and ... well, as you saw, it was all a bit too much.' She looked away, praying that Alex didn't see right through her.

Alex didn't seem entirely convinced, but the idea of using one sister against the other, when this whole night was about reuniting two sisters of old, obviously appealed to her because she put the gun away and nodded. 'Alright,' she said, 'you can help. But do anything stupid and it won't end well for you or for John.'

It wasn't going to end well for Emma either way you looked at it, but she refrained from pointing that out to Alex. 'Duly noted,' she said, 'but there's one more thing.'

'I hardly think you're in a position to bargain.'

'Maybe not,' Emma said, 'but I would still ask this one thing of you.'

Alex narrowed her eyes. 'Go on.'

'I want to look them in the eye,' she said. 'Raewyn and

Dee, so they know, so they both know when I give my body over to Saoirse, that I do it willingly.'

Alex's mouth curved up in a smile. 'You're a sick bitch, Emmaline Ashley,' she said. 'But I like it. Your wish is granted.'

'It's *Stanford*-Ashley,' Emma said. 'And don't you forget it.

34

'So, what are you going to do now, kill me too?' Rae said, as Chris drove through the forest. He'd shaken her awake as soon as it turned dark, but in truth she'd only been pretending to be asleep. She had lain awake all afternoon, thinking about what Dee had said and trying to work up enough emotion to burn the damn handcuffs off, but it seemed being kidnapped, told you were the reincarnation of someone from another world and threatened with sacrifice wasn't a big enough motivator.

The road that Chris navigated through the forest was barely wide enough for the car to fit through, and dangerously overgrown. Tree roots sprouted up everywhere and Chris seemed to be making a point of driving over them just to piss Rae off. She was cuffed to the small handle above the door on the back seat, feet bound by rope, and every time Chris ran over a tree root the cuffs would tug painfully on her already bruised and bloody wrists. Dee had personally tied her up, assuring Chris that as long as he behaved himself, she could not escape. He was to take Rae to the oak tree and wait for Dee to arrive, along with another bunch of freaks she referred to as The Order. Then she had torn the pendant from around Rae's neck and slammed the door shut. Rae was still seething over that, but it seemed even the bitch taking her necklace was not enough to get her damn hands to work.

Chris hit another bump in the road and Rae was thrown into the door, banging her shoulder painfully against the glass. 'Who taught you to drive?' she said, 'you almost broke my arm that time.'

Chris didn't say anything but swerved again at the last minute sending Rae slamming into the door once more.

'You're sick, you know that?' Rae gripped the handle to relieve some of the pressure on her wrists as the car bumped again, and she felt it give, just a little. 'How many kittens did you drown before your mum realised you were a twisted fuck?' Chris banked left throwing Rae away from the door this time, and she felt the handle give a little more. She planted her feet and pulled. 'Maybe Emma got all the attention when you were kids, is that it? Or maybe you were a fat kid? A fat kid with a small dick that grew into a fucktard with an even smaller dick?' She braced, ready for the car to jerk sideways, but Chris only looked in the rear-view mirror and grinned.

'You can keep goading me all you want, Winters, but when we get to where we're going there'll be enough time before Dee arrives for a little fun. And believe me, I can think of lots of fun things to do with you that won't even leave a mark.'

'Fuck you.' Rae lifted her knees, and with her bound feet kicked Chris through the back of his seat.

Chris laughed and put his foot down, deliberately hitting every root and pothole so Rae was jostled back and forth until blood slid down her arms. But that's exactly what she wanted. With the handle about ready to break off, she braced her feet against the door and pulled just as Chris cottoned on to what she was doing and slammed on the brakes. Rae was hurled forward, but it was too late. The handle broke off and Rae used the momentum to throw her arms over Chris' chair and pull the chain of the cuffs tight against his throat. She heaved backwards, using her feet against his chair for extra leverage, but it seemed Chris was not as dumb as she thought and produced a large hunting knife from the back of his jeans. The jagged blade sliced across Rae's arm and she yelled out, loosening her grip, but that was all Chris needed to wriggle free. He was out of the car and opening Rae's door before she had time to think and hauled her out by the feet. She hit the ground hard, banged her head on a rock, and thought she must have lost consciousness for a second, because the next thing she knew she was lay in the beam of the car's headlights, face pressed into the dirt with Chris sat astride her legs.

'Thought you were smart, eh?' he said, lifting the fleece jacket up around her shoulders, 'we'll see how smart you are when I carve my name into your back.' He pressed the cold steel of his knife against Rae's lower back, and she froze.

'Chris,' she said, 'I'm sorry. I'll behave, I swear.'

'Too late, princess,' he said, 'now hold still while I give you something to remember me by.'

Rae screamed at the first bite of the blade, and again as it sliced through her skin to form the letter C. A warm trickle of blood slid down to her belly and the musty taste of wet earth filled her mouth as Chris pushed her face further into the ground. The pain was excruciating, like nothing she'd ever felt before, but it served a purpose at least.

As the beginning of an H was cut into her skin, Rae felt the familiar glow at the base of her spine. It hummed like the oak tree, inching up her back one vertebra at a time until it burst into her chest and flooded her limbs. She reached behind her head and grabbed Chris' arm where he held her face in the dirt, then she squeezed as hard as she could, crushing his wrist between her hands. A high-pitched scream pierced the air as Chris tried to wrench his arm free, but Rae wasn't letting go. She squeezed harder, and harder, until his flesh melted like an ice-cream left in the sun, until his screams were deafening in her ears, and when she reached bone, she gave a quick twist, and snapped his hand right off.

Chris' lesson in calligraphy was abruptly forgotten as Rae released him and he rolled onto his back, arm held in the air, eyes wide with shock, as though unable to believe what he was seeing. Rae quickly sat up, grabbed the knife and cut the rope around her ankles. Then she glanced at the dismembered hand, lying on the ground like a discarded stage prop, rolled onto her knees, and puked.

'You,' Chris stammered, 'you ... you took my hand.'

His face was deathly pale, skin slick with a sheen of sweat that did nothing to help Rae's roiling stomach. 'Serves you right, you sadistic prick,' she said. But seeing the cauterized stump only made her realise just how out of control she really was. Chris lunged at her then and grabbed the knife from where she'd dropped it beside the pile of vomit. He swiped at her leg, missed, and swiped again as Rae scrambled to her feet, but she didn't hang around for his next attempt. She ran, fast as she could, deep into the forest and as far away from Chris as she could get.

Twilight filled the forest with mellowing shades of purple as Rae stumbled in the direction she thought would take her home, to The Briar, where her car was, and where she could call for help. But night was closing in like a pack of hungry wolves and she found herself running blindly through the trees, not caring which direction she was going in, only that it was taking her somewhere. She stumbled and fell several times, glanced over her shoulder every so often expecting to see a pair of headlights blazing a trail behind her, but despite being weary from having discharged so much energy into Chris, and still bound by handcuffs, she ran on, heedless of branches that seemed to deliberately reach out and snag her hair, or roots that sprouted up from nowhere in a desperate bid to hinder her getaway.

Darkness descended on the forest like a great black void, and shadows closed in on every side, as the trees whispered to each other on a non-existent breeze. But Rae pushed on, using the full moon as her guide, until she finally spotted a light through the trees up ahead. It was just a glimmer, there one minute and gone the next, but it gave her the strength of will to keep moving as a grey mist crept slowly along the ground like eels sliding over a rock.

The forest was eerily still as Rae cautiously approached The Briar. The air thick and heavy with warning as she stepped from the trees and heard music drifting from the open door. Light spilled out onto the blue picket fence and the driveway beyond, where her car sat right where she'd left it. But so was another – a white pick-up truck that caused her heart to flutter even as the hairs on the back of her neck urged caution. She approached slowly, body crouched low, ears sharp to any sign of movement, and quietly rummaged for her keys, before remembering she was no longer wearing her own jacket. She ground her teeth with frustration and crept towards the back of her car to get a better look inside the cottage. Whoever was inside was keeping themselves well hidden. She could see the kitchen and the hallway, but no sign of anyone inside, no smoke pouring from the chimney, no oversized dog eating cake on her rug. She began edging backwards, eyes fixed on the little blue door, when something solid was pressed to the back of her head.

'Well aren't you just a slippery little snake,' Connie said. Rae froze as Connie inched around to face her, with the gun pointed firmly at Rae's face. 'I should have known that syco-phant was incapable of keeping you under control. Stand up, hands on your head and move towards the cottage.'

Rae did as she was told, even though her guts told her she wouldn't like what she found once she stepped through that door. Inside, her suitcase still stood beside the kitchen cupboard, and the TV was on, playing one of the many singing competitions that Grace had always favoured. Rae felt a pang of longing as she remembered snuggling up beside Grace, box of Quality Street passed between them, and would have given anything to go back in time and never step foot in the village of Cranston Myre. 'I take it you never made it to the police then?' she said, as Connie shut the door.

'What do you think?' Connie said. 'Sit over there.' She nodded towards the table where a black cloak, much like the one Connie was wearing, was slung over a chair. On the table was a wooden bowl with a gooey pink substance inside. Rae pulled out a chair so her back was towards the kitchen, giving her a view of the door should the opportunity arise to use it. Connie sat opposite, gun trained on Rae's face and a hard look in her grey eyes.

'What's with the cloak and paint?' Rae said, 'Halloween isn't for another month yet.'

'Very funny,' Connie said, 'if I were you, I'd keep that

smart mouth of yours shut. Those nifty little hands may be fireproof, but they aren't bullet proof.' She sneered in a way that left little doubt she meant what she said, and Rae wondered what had happened to the kindly woman she'd met in the shop. She hadn't particularly warmed to that Connie either, but at least she had a sense of humour.

'Do you even know what you're mixed up in?' Rae said. 'Dee cut someone's throat right in front of me. The woman is a murderer. Chris would have killed me too if I hadn't escaped. Are you sure you want to be a part of that, Connie? Put the gun away, we'll call the police and I swear to you they will never know—'

'I'm afraid I can't let you do that.'

Rae turned and shook her head when she saw Alex, who looked remarkably healthy for someone who was supposed to be dead. 'You too?' she said, 'why am I not surprised? Is there anyone in this village that *isn't* a murdering, twisted fuck?'

'Watch it,' Connie said.

'No, you watch it,' Rae spat, 'you can't just hold me here. Do you really think no-one is out looking for me? You're both going to spend the rest of your miserable lives locked behind bars for this.'

'No-one is looking for you,' Connie said. 'I personally made sure of that.'

'And what is that supposed to mean?' Rae's heart was beating so loud she was certain the others could hear it.

'That's enough.' Alex gave Connie a warning glance. 'You forget that John was my friend too.'

Rae felt the blood leave her face. 'What have you done, Connie?'

'I took care of an unfortunate situation,' Connie said, 'and if you don't want to be next, I'd shut your mouth and do as you're told.'

'Enough,' yelled Alex. 'Connie, I'll thank you to control your temper, and Rae, if you don't want to be dragged out of here with a bullet in each leg, then I suggest you do the same.'

Rae glared at Connie. 'If you've hurt him ...'

'You'll do what?' Connie said, 'burn me? Go right ahead and try.'

Rae clenched her fists. She would if she could get the bastard things to work! 'So, who did I find in the forest then?' she said to Alex, 'clearly it wasn't you.'

Alex pulled up a chair and sat between Rae and Connie. 'Michelle,' she said. 'She got too close, started asking questions. It was insensitive of me to give her the ring so soon after you gifted it, so for that I apologise.'

'Insensitive?' Rae looked at her incredulously. 'The girl is dead!'

'Not ideal, I'll admit,' Alex said, 'but I did what I had to under the circumstances.'

'And what circumstances are those, Alex? Kidnap and murder? What's next? How much further are you willing to go to play out your sick little fantasy?'

'Well when you put it like that, I suppose it does sound rather grim. But you have to see the bigger picture.'

'You can keep your bigger picture and shove it up your arse,' Rae said. 'I want nothing to do with it, or you, or any of your deranged minions, so if you can tell your Alsatian over there to take her gun out of my face, I'll gladly be on my way.'

'I told you we should drug her,' Connie said.

Alex cut her another warning glance. 'No,' she said, 'I

want her awake. I want her to know everything that's happening to her, as it happens.'

'My God,' Rae said, 'you're monsters, both of you.'

'Takes a monster to know a monster,' Alex said. 'Or have you forgotten what you did to Darryl and Chris? Look, this isn't getting us anywhere. I know what you must be thinking, bu—'

'You don't have the first fucking clue what I'm thinking,' Rae said bitterly.

Alex nodded. 'OK, maybe I don't. And if I'm honest, I don't really care, so let's move this along, shall we?' She pushed the bowl of goo towards Rae. 'If you could rub that gel all over your hands, I'd be ever so grateful.'

Rae made no move to do it, but Connie leaned in a little closer with the gun, daring her to say no. 'You're deluded if you think you're going to get away with this,' Rae said, grabbing the bowl.

'Oh, but we already have,' Alex said. 'No-one cares about you, Rae. No-one even knows you're here, remember? Wasn't that what you wanted? Solitude? A peaceful life away from your estranged family? Or haven't you figured it out yet?' She leaned forward, pink hair looking ludicrous now Rae saw her for what she was. 'Every person you ever knew was fake,' she said. 'Your whole life has been about this moment, about preparing you for tonight. I thought you might have worked that part out by now, but apparently not.'

Rae swallowed. 'You're lying, Grace would never—'

'And yet it was Grace who introduced you to Darryl,' Alex said, 'and Grace who gave you that delightful crystal pendant, which, by the way, doesn't really belong to you. You must have wondered why you weren't hurt when your grandfather died? Why Grace kept it quiet? Why she encouraged you to paint when the nightmares became too much. Those were all tools, Rae, ways of keeping you under control, isolating you, keeping you hooked on guilt so you wouldn't do anything stupid. You've be played, right from the day you were born.'

Rae shook her head as tears stung the backs of her eyes. It wasn't true, any of it.

'Your friend,' Alex said, 'Veronica Maine. She wasn't even pregnant. Did you know that? She was re-assigned to Scotland, so she came up with the whole pregnancy thing as a cover story. She only went to Grace's funeral to make damn sure you made the right decision and moved to Cranston Myre. I could go on but there isn't time. So, the gel, if you please.'

Rae looked down at the bowl, barely able to breathe.

'I need you alive Rae,' Alex said, 'but it's completely up to you how much alive.'

Rae lifted the bowl and sniffed – it smelled strongly of mint and burnt rubber with an undertone of damp, rotten earth. Connie was still scowling from behind the safety of the gun and Rae wondered how far she could get before the old witch fired it. She glanced at the door. It was only a few feet away. If she could make it through, lose herself in the forest ...

'Don't even think it,' Connie said, 'I may be old but I'm quick enough to put two in your chest before you've even moved.'

Rae scowled, picked up a blob of goo and began smearing it over her hands. 'What is this stuff anyway?' she said, pinching the fast-drying substance between thumb and forefinger and watching it snap back into place like a second skin.

'Insurance,' Alex said, 'It'll keep those hands of yours from misbehaving if you become ... upset.'

'I'd say I'm a little way past upset,' Rae said.

'Hence the need for the gel and handcuffs!' Alex said. 'Connie, how long do we have?'

'Two hours, tops,' Connie said.

'Alright.' Alex stood up. 'Let's make a move then, shall we? And don't look so glum, Rae, one way or another this will all be over by morning.'

'Sooner the better as far as I'm concerned,' Rae said, 'I'm tired of listening to your whiny fucking voice.'

Alex laughed. 'Then I shall see you soon.' Connie grabbed Rae's arm and dragged her off the seat as Alex collected the cloak from the back of the chair, threw it over her arm and headed towards the front door. She stopped just short of opening it and turned back to Rae. 'A word of caution,' she said, 'I would prefer you to be whole when the ceremony begins, but if you give Connie cause to put you down, she has my full authority to do so. Like I said, alive is preferable, but we can work just as well with almost dead.' Then she walked out the door as Connie pushed Rae down the hall towards the back of the cottage.

35

Dee paced impatiently before the oak tree, checking and re-checking her watch, but still there was no sign of Chris, Raewyn or Connie. The moon was at its highest peak, which meant the eclipse wasn't far off. It also meant the barrier between Earth and Gestryll was already beginning to weaken, and Saoirse, whilst still trapped behind the walls of Gestryll, would soon be able to reach out. She checked her watch again, frowned, and took out her phone.

The Order watched from the far end of the clearing, huddled together in the dark, each of them dressed in white cloaks with their faces ludicrously painted like Connie's. They were drugged, high on Dee's orange juice so that when their moment came, they would not shit their pants and run. But even in their placid state their patience was wearing thin. Shuffling from foot to foot they discreetly observed Dee, whispering to each other beneath their hoods until Dee thought she could bear it no longer. She turned to order quiet as she dialled Chris' number, but instead caught him strolling towards her, *without* Raewyn.

'About time,' she said, 'where is she?'

'I don't have her,' he said, seemingly unconcerned by his apparent failure to do even one thing right.

'What do you mean, you don't have her?' Dee said. 'Where the hell is she?'

'With Connie,' Chris said, 'they're on their way.'

Dee closed her eyes and sighed deeply. Did she even want to know what had transpired to put Rae in the clutches of Connie? 'Please don't tell me this is a fuck up,' she said. 'I gave you one job to do – get Rae to the clearing in one piece.'

Chris held up his arm. 'Don't suppose you can grow another one of these, can you?'

Dee stared at the pink stump where his hand used to be – nicely healed with no sign of infection – not what you'd expect from something that had happened within the last thirty minutes. 'What the hell happened?' she said. He seemed extraordinarily composed for someone who had just lost part of a limb. In fact, if she didn't know better, she'd say Chris was higher than the mumbling Order behind her.

'Rae happened,' he said, 'she went all crazy on me, attacked me from behind. I was lucky to get away with only this.'

Dee shone her torch in his face. 'What have you taken?' she said. His pupils were dilated to the size of two large saucers, then a thought suddenly occurred to her. 'Please tell me you didn't?' She checked her bag, and sure enough, the two syringes that she'd filled with the fresh batch of elixir were missing. Chris must have taken them before he left with Raewyn. 'Both of them?' she said, and clutched her stomach when Chris smiled. *My God,* she thought, *how are you even still alive?* His eyes glistened with the look of a madman and Dee thought perhaps that's exactly what he'd be before the evening was over. She took a deep, calming breath and forced herself to focus. What was done was done, no point crying about it now. The important thing was, they still had Rae, and Dee still had the dagger.

She took two bottles of oil out of her bag, handed one to Chris and kept the other for herself. 'Make yourself useful and dot that all around the clearing,' she said, 'and use it sparingly unless you want to blow us all up.' Then she moved a few feet away from the tree and unscrewed her own bottle of oil. It contained the distilled fatty acids of Mr Mitts' stomach, along with cinnamon, the crushed leaves of a eucalyptus tree, and the ground salt of her tourmaline crystal, and while Chris secured the clearing she knelt and dug a small well into the ground.

Not a breath of wind blew as she gathered leaves and twigs and piled them into the hole, not a whisper from the forest as she poured oil onto the small mound and threw on the lock of hair that she'd cut from Rae as a child. If people knew what had transpired here over the years, if they knew who was buried beneath the gnarled and twisted roots of the old tree, they would burn it to the ground. But for the few who were privy to the old ways of the Draiocht, then it was a place of incredible beauty and unquestionable power.

She released her red hair – once brown and dull as dishwater, now rich as polished garnet – and took the Servian Dagger from its holster at her hip. The knife felt reassuringly heavy, the blade sharp as it sliced through a chunk of her hair. She threw the red locks on top of the pyre, made a small cut across her wrist and let the blood run free until the hair was sufficiently covered. Then she slid the knife back into place, right beside her pocket where Rae's necklace sat safe and sound and wrapped a bandage around her wrist.

Chris had finished dripping oil around the perimeter and returned to her looking sour and twitchy. A sure sign the drug he'd injected was wreaking havoc in his veins. She checked the moon – already a shadow was creeping across the surface – struck a match and threw it on to the pyre. Fire took hold immediately, burning blue as Lapis Lazuli, and fragrant smoke drifted into the air reminding Dee of the last time she'd attempted to do this. Only that time she hadn't gotten much further before Saoirse unleashed her hell. She sat back on her heels and nervously checked her watch one more time. If Connie didn't hurry, then they were all doomed for sure.

36

T he night had turned bitterly cold as Rae navigated the narrow path that led to the oak tree, closely followed by Connie. She tried time and time again to ignite her internal fire, and even got so far as a gentle flutter deep inside her belly, but that was it, nothing spectacular, and certainly nothing that would aid her escape from beneath Connie's watchful eye. She began dragging her feet to slow their progress and delay the inevitable, but mostly just because she wanted to piss Connie off.

'Pick up the pace before I lose patience and put a bullet in your arm,' Connie said, poking the gun in Rae's back.

'You're awfully brave with that gun in your hand,' Rae said over her shoulder.

'And you're awfully gobby for someone at the other end of it.'

Rae smirked, though she felt anything but cheerful. 'This Saoirse must be really something if you're willing to go to prison for her,' she said. 'It's not too late to turn back. I have money if that's what you want.'

'Money is the last thing I need,' Connie grunted, 'and you'll have no need of it either where you're going.'

Rae stopped in her tracks and turned around. 'If you're so sure I'm going to die, then why not just shoot me now and have done with it?'

'Don't tempt me,' Connie said, 'now pick up your feet and move it.'

THE SOUND of chanting drifted on the air as Rae drew closer to the clearing. Her stomach clenched tightly when she spotted Dee crouched by a blue fire with her deluded followers at her back. Until now Rae had tried to convince herself this was all just some elaborate hoax, that Dee had slipped her some trippy drug and she had only imagined the fight with Chris, and Darryl's death, and the stinging cuts on her back that hurt less and less as the minutes ticked by. But now, as she approached the clearing and the chanting choir grew quiet, a veil of disquiet settled over her shoulders.

Connie gave her a hard shove from behind and Rae stumbled forward, falling hard onto her cuffed hands and aggravating the wounds there. 'Back to chanting,' Connie yelled, 'all of you.' She clicked her fingers, and the white clad followers resumed their hushed, monotonous droning. Rae recognised a few of them – a young girl from the bakery, the waitress from Sadie-Lou's cafe, Damien who had drank more booze than he served, and Henry, John's very own assistant. She thought of John and what Connie had said, and an icy shiver ran down her back. Then suddenly a strong pair of hands lifted her to her feet, and when she saw who it was, she quietly corrected herself. Not a *pair* of hands after all then.

'Fancy seeing you here,' Chris said, brandishing his

stump as though it was something to be proud of. Rae thought she might be sick again.

'Jesus, what happened to you?' Connie said, then looked at Rae and shook her head. 'Never mind. How long has she been like that?' She was referring to Dee, who was leaning over the blue fire, weaving her hands in and out of the flame.

'Few minutes,' Chris said.

'And the Eye?'

Chris glanced at Rae. 'The necklace is in her pocket.'

Rae opened her mouth to ask what her necklace had to do with anything, but Connie made a grunting sound at the back of her throat, prodded her forward and began marching her towards the tree. Dee only glanced at Rae as she walked past, but there was something in her eyes that worried Rae more than the gun pointed at her head.

The woody scent of sandalwood drifted up from a sea of candles that had been laid out around the base of the oak tree like some kind of altar, and Rae felt the tree's pull even before Connie pushed her towards it. It called to her like a name whispered on a breeze, and she rubbed the handcuffs over her wrists to aggravate them further. 'What now?' she said, stopping at the foot of the tree and feeling her skin tighten when she spotted the manacles tied to either side of it, 'should I chant too, or is that only reserved for your loyal supporters?'

Connie ignored her and turned to Chris. 'Tie her up,' she said, and threw him a key.

Chris stepped forward, a glint in his eye, key swinging from his finger.

'You sure you want to do this?' Rae said as he grabbed the cuffs. 'How many more times do you think you can heal before I finish you off for good?'

Chris stopped and looked to Connie.

'Oh, for crying out loud,' Connie said, 'she's messing with you. Another word from you Raewyn, and I'll blow those fingers off!'

Scowling, Chris shoved Rae hard against the tree whilst Connie kept the gun trained on her. He removed the hand-cuffs and replaced them with the manacles, locking them tightly so the cold metal pinched her skin. 'Not so smart now, are you, Winters?' he said, pocketing the key before running his fingers playfully up the inside of her leg.

It took every ounce of willpower for Rae not to cringe. 'You don't really buy in to this bullshit, do you?' she said. 'A magical race of people? Blood moons and sacrifice? Come on Chris, I thought you were smarter than that?'

'Nice try, Winters,' he said, 'but we'll see who has the last laugh when that moon turns red. If you're lucky, once this is over, maybe we could hook up again. Perhaps next time you won't be so frigid.' He laughed and jumped out of the way as Rae tried to kick him in the balls.

'That's enough,' Connie said, 'you've had your fun, now go check the perimeter while I talk to Dee.'

Rae tested her restraints as soon as Connie turned her back, but it was clear she was going nowhere fast. She fell back against the tree, at a loss for what to do next. She could scream and yell, kick up a fuss, but being this deep into the forest so late at night she doubted anyone would hear, let alone come to her aid. Behind her the tree felt alive, humming with energy that reverberated through her bones, but tonight it was different, fringed with a sense of wrongness that set her teeth on edge and sent goose bumps running down her arms. She looked across the clearing to where Chris meandered through the congregation, weaving in and out like a bored child, and wondered if Dee was behind the dark magic that had healed him.

Dee was talking with Connie, both of them glancing over at Rae every now and then before looking to the sky as though waiting for some divine intervention. But as much as Rae still tried to tell herself this was all just some sick fantasy, even she couldn't deny that the air was different tonight, charged as though on the precipice of a lightning storm. Then she felt a rumble underfoot. A shifting of sorts as though a chasm had opened up somewhere beneath, and by the look on Connie and Dee's face, they felt it too. In fact, the only person who didn't stop what they were doing and look around was Chris, who seemed to be in a whole different world of his own.

Dee picked up what looked like a branch with a rag wrapped around the end of it, dipped it into the blue flame and handed it to Connie. Connie then walked to the edge of the clearing, touched the torch to the ground and stepped back as a wall of blue fire shot up around them. It travelled the circumference of the clearing, jumping from spot to spot like falling dominoes until they were all completely enclosed and cut off from the rest of the forest. Then Dee turned to Rae, took what looked like a dagger from the belt at her waist, and began moving towards her.

THE ECLIPSE HAD BEGUN. The portal was weakening, the veil between worlds thinning, and soon Saoirse would be free. Dee glanced over her shoulder to where Connie was anointing the members of The Order with ash from the sacrificial flame – a black dot on each of their foreheads to mark them like targets at a gun range. Each one of them willing to give their lives for a cause they would not benefit from. Each one believing themselves to be martyrs because that's what Connie had told them. Fools, all of them, but Dee would sacrifice them a hundred times over if it meant she got her chance with Saoirse.

Raewyn watched with hostile eyes as Dee approached. No point trying to reason with her now. A fire had been lit beneath her the night Chris tried to take what wasn't his, and no amount of talking was going to put it out. Which was a good thing. She'd need all the fire she could muster once Saoirse arrived. But while Saoirse was an open book, Augustine was anything but, and Dee knew that once Rae realised her full potential there was no telling what she could do.

'You're wasting your time,' Dee said, as Rae pulled anxiously at her chains, 'I fixed them there myself.'

'Then maybe I'll just have to un-fix them,' Rae said, and tugged again, grunting when the chains didn't move.

'I'm not your enemy, Rae,' Dee said. 'Believe it or not I want to help you.' Rae gave her a cold look, hoiked up and spat in her face. 'You know,' Dee said, wiping her cheek with a length of skirt, 'you're more like Evie than I care to admit. She had fire in her too, though I'll admit, you're a little less subtle with yours.'

'Remove these chains and I'll be a subtle as you like,' Rae said.

Dee smiled. 'You can remove them yourself later, but for now the chains stay.' She took hold of Rae's jacket – a fleece that once belonged to Ivan – and pulled the zipper all the way down revealing a white vest beneath. 'I made a promise to your mother to keep you safe,' she said, lifting the vest to just below Rae's breasts, so the birthmark was exposed, angry and red, just as it had been the night she was born. 'So, listen up because we won't get another chance to speak. I need your blood for Saoirse's release, but I'll take no more than is required – a small cut, nothing more. Then whilst the others are fixated on Saoirse's rebirth, I'll dissolve the coating on your hands. I have my own agenda with Saoirse and can't risk sneaking the key from Chris to open your manacles, so you'll have to figure that out yourself.'

'And how am I supposed to do that?' hissed Rae, 'just will them to open?'

'You're stronger than you think,' Dee said, 'I saw what you did to Chris. You have a gift, use it.' She checked no-one was looking then showed Rae the last of her DC powder in the pouch fastened to her belt. 'It will burn through the resin on your hands, but I will not use it until I'm sure Saoirse is safely through the portal. It will hurt, but only for a moment. Do not bring attention to your hands until you are ready to use them.' She looked up to where an orange glow tinged the outer edges of the moon. 'Remember,' she said, 'once I dissolve the resin, you're on your own.'

'And what if I can't break the chains,' Rae said, 'what happens then?'

'Then you die,' Dee said. She nodded to Connie, who nodded back in return and moved to the right of the clearing, as far away as she could get without stepping over the blue fire. Chris joined her, dark circles under his eyes and a grim look on his face. How much longer he would last was anyone's guess.

Dee removed the bandage from around her wrist and held the Servian Dagger to the wound. The blade glowed softly by the light of the candles and hummed with power as her blood touched its edges. The last time she had stood here she had been with Louisa, pleading for mercy as Saoirse lashed out from behind her walls of confinement. The horror of seeing Louisa drained of life was still so raw that even now it put fear in Dee's heart, but she would not let it deter her from what had to be done. Connie was no doubt remembering too. She had been like a mother to Louisa, taking her under her wing, encouraging her to push herself to the point of no return. Connie hated Dee almost as much as Dee hated Connie, but it was Connie who had nursed Dee back to health after Saoirse had burned her with her lightning.

Connie was watching Dee now like a hawk. If not for Connie, Rae would not be here. If not for Connie, neither would Dee. Once Dee had recovered from Saoirse's attack she had retrieved Rae from the family who were hiding her, and run away as far north as she could get, sheltering in an old abandoned house where she took care of Rae as best she could. But it wasn't enough, *Dee* wasn't enough, and on Rae's fifth birthday Connie had finally found them.

Dee had become a bitter old woman by then, though she was barely 19 years old – drained like a battery run dry, and full of what ifs and maybes. What if she'd done things differently? Delivered Rae like she was supposed to, then maybe Louisa would still be alive, and Dee would not have lost her youth to an infant whose psychic energy was off the charts. What if she'd trusted in Louisa, believed in her sister when she swore that she would be a kind and merciful leader, because Louisa had every intention of destroying Saoirse in the same way Dee was going to do tonight. But Dee knew that Louisa would not be a kind and merciful leader, because Louisa was not a kind and merciful sister. She was controlling and deceitful, manipulative and cruel. She would take Saoirse's power and inflict a worse fate on the human race than simply destroying them. She would make them her slaves, just as she had enslaved Richard and every other man that came within spitting distance. So no, Dee had done the right thing in removing an innocent child from the situation, and even now, knowing what she did about Rae, knowing the darkness that dwelled inside her, Dee still believed that something good could come out of the terrible things she'd done. And she knew, without a shadow of a doubt, that sending Rae to Grace the night before Connie showed up on her doorstep was the best thing she could have done.

Grace may have been closely watched by The Order whilst Rae was in her custody, but no-one would have dared touch her, because whilst Grace had chosen not to partake in the ways of the Draiocht, she was still a descendant of one of the most prominent families in Aster, and more gifted than most Draiocht left on Earth. Grace was the perfect mother to raise Rae, to temper her energy until Rae was wise enough to use it, and to guide her through the nightmares that Dee had been too inexperienced to handle. But even so, this day was always going to come – it had to, if Saoirse was ever to be stopped – and Dee knew that Connie would have pulled out all the stops to have Rae taken away the moment another eclipse was upon them, no matter what her age. So Dee had made a promise. That as long as Rae was left alone to grow into a woman, given a chance at something resembling a life before having to confront Saoirse, then Grace would send her back to them when she felt the time was right, when Rae was strong enough to fight for herself. And Dee would open the portal, just as she was supposed to do the night Rae was born. It wasn't ideal, but it was the only chance Rae had of survival, and the only way Dee could free Saoirse with a clear conscience.

RAE HELD her breath as Dee lifted the dagger to a moon that was slowly turning into a glowing orb of red, whilst below, amongst the roots of the tree, she could sense the years of pent up energy just waiting to be free. 'You don't have to do this,' she said, 'there must be another way.' But Dee didn't answer, only stared as her lips moved silently along with the congregation's chanting. A gentle wind caused the candles to flicker and the shadows to dance, and Dee's hair was lifted around her head reminding Rae of the painting she found in the attic, of the pretty redhead with the startling eyes. But Dee wasn't her. As much as Rae hated Dee for what she'd done, she saw none of the malice that had emanated from that painting.

Just then something shifted beneath Rae's feet, as though Earth's tectonic plates had moved a millimetre or two, and a rumble of thunder sounded overhead. Dee turned her face to the sky, eyes rolling back on themselves as she raised the dagger high above her head, tip pointed to the moon, ominous against a starless sky as dark clouds rolled in. Rae thought she recognised the dagger, but then the air seemed to come alive, crackling with life, and all thoughts of visions were lost as a bolt of lightning cracked open the sky. It lit up the clearing like a stadium, silencing the congregation as they looked up and gasped. The birthmark above Rae's navel began to burn, glowing in the dim light like a branding iron while Rae squirmed against her restraints, breath coming fast and shallow. Chris paced up and down, hands in pockets, whilst Connie, dark eyes closely watching Rae, glanced nervously at Dee as another crack of thunder rumbled overhead. The only person who didn't seem anxious was Dee, as she started chanting louder, shouting to the sky as though someone up there could hear her. The words were unintelligible, a language Rae did not understand, and as the chanting became more urgent, another bolt of lightning lit up the sky and shot down to the dagger. Dee turned those milky white eyes to Rae, then a second later slashed through the air with the dagger, sending a bolt of lightning into the tree like a whip from the gods.

Rae thought her time was up, but the tree did not explode or burst into flames at her back. It only shuddered slightly as a thin vein of blue light lit up the roots from inside. Everyone, Chris included, held their breath, and turned to Dee.

Dee's eyes returned to their usual viridian green, and though the others were too far away to see it, Rae caught the look of relief on her face. 'The portal is open,' she said, 'bring Alicia to me.'

The young girl who Rae recognised from the bakery stepped forward, flanked on either side by two comrades in white, and began walking the short distance across the clearing towards the small blue bonfire. Dee never took her eyes from Rae except to glance at the birthmark that was now itching like crazy, and Rae opened her mouth to say something, to beg Dee not go any further, when another crack rang out through the clearing and Dee's eyes grew wide with shock. A second later Chris was by her side, lifting her into his arms before placing her gently on the ground to Rae's left, with her back leaning against one of the enormous limbs of the tree.

Confusion ensued then amongst the congregation, their anger it seemed, directed solely at Connie, who stood just beyond the sea of candles, smoking gun still in hand.

'I'm sorry,' Chris said, brushing the hair from Dee's pasty

face, 'I never meant for you to get hurt.' He turned angrily to Connie. 'What the fuck have you done, old woman? This wasn't part of the deal.'

'She's alive, isn't she?' Connie said, 'look at her, she's already beginning to heal.'

Rae looked down at the patch of red where the bullet had torn a hole right through Dee's abdomen, and saw that Connie was right. The bleeding was already beginning to slow, but Dee looked as far from a picture of health as it was possible to get.

'Don't trust her,' Dee said, as Chris slipped the dagger from her belt. 'She'll kill you the moment Saoirse is free.'

Chris reached into Dee's pocket and removed Rae's necklace. 'This better be worth it,' he said, throwing the dagger, and the necklace, at Connie's feet.

Connie bent to pick up her treasures and smiled smugly at Chris. 'I just did you a favour,' she said. 'Whatever poison is in your veins may be powerful stuff, but everything has a price, Christopher. Once it wears off, and it will wear off, then you'll see exactly what I mean. Take a good look at Dee. She's so full of that shit it's already healing a bullet wound, but look at the toll its taking. If she doesn't inject again soon, she'll be nothing but a withered old woman by morning. Is that what you want? To rely on magic tricks for the rest of your life. Saoirse is the real deal. Her power is the real deal.'

Chris looked back at Dee, and for a moment, just one split second, Rae thought she saw genuine tenderness in his eyes, but just as quickly it was gone.

'She's lying,' Dee said, grabbing for his ankle as he stood up. 'Saoirse will destroy us all.' Chris looked hesitantly to Connie, but even Rae could see Dee's red hair was already fading to grey.

'Make a choice, Christopher,' Connie said. 'Are you with me, or not?'

Chris shrugged, tore his ankle from Dee's grasp, and turned to Rae with a smirk on his wretched face. 'See you soon Winters,' he said, then moved off to stand beside Connie.

'You still need me,' Dee said. 'No-one else can set her free.'

Connie sneered. 'That's what you think.' She pocketed the crystal and turned to the congregation. 'Back to your stations,' she yelled, 'this isn't over yet. You,' she said, pointing to Alicia, 'come with me.' Alicia obediently fell into line beside Connie and accompanied her to the wall of fire where the path that led to The Briar ended. Connie whispered something into Alicia's ear, and even from where Rae stood, she could see the look of shock that crossed the young girl's face. She looked back to the congregation, but Connie didn't wait for a reply. She put a bullet between the girl's eyes and had Chris throw Alicia into the wall of fire, dousing the flames and opening up a gap big enough for a person to fit through.

Dee groaned loudly as Alex stepped over the body, pink hair covered by the hood of her cloak, and Rae's stomach dropped when she saw who followed closely behind.

Emma looked worse than Dee. One side of her face was almost completely covered by a criss-cross of raised black lines, and she walked with the gait of a woman in her senior years. Even her eyes had lost some of their acerbity as she glanced at Rae, but it seemed no-one was more surprised to see her than Chris. He grabbed Emma's arm and pulled her aside as Alex strode confidently towards Dee.

'Well, well, well,' she said, 'how the mighty have fallen.'

Dee clutched her stomach and wheezed as she spoke. 'You're the secret Connie was hiding,' she said. 'All this time, and you were right under my nose.'

'We seldom see what's right in front of us,' Alex said, kneeling in front of Dee, 'but if it's any consolation, I played my part well. Mother would be proud.'

'I should have guessed,' Dee said. 'Louisa never told the truth about anything.'

'I guess it runs in the family,' Alex said, 'you don't mind if I take over from here, do you?'

'Be my guest,' Dee said, 'the serum is in my bag over there.'

Alex reached into the pocket of her cloak and pulled out a small glass bottle. 'Oh, don't worry about that,' she said, 'I have one of my own, courtesy of mother. You didn't think she'd made only one serum, did you? You see, mother never trusted you, not really, so she made a second and hid it where she knew you'd never look. Behind your self-portrait, the one that shows the real you, before you altered your looks.'

Rae had never seen anyone's face turn as pale as Dee's did right then. 'Alex, listen,' she said. She reached out but fell back as pain gripped her. 'Louisa was wrong,' she said, breathlessly. 'The transference will kill you.'

Alex smiled as she got to her feet. 'Now, now, Aunty Dee,' she said, 'jealousy doesn't become you. I think we both know that mother was never wrong about anything.'

'She was about this,' Dee said. 'Don't do it, Alex, I beg you.'

'Too late.' Alex tipped the contents of the bottle down her throat. She waited a moment, and when nothing happened, shrugged and turned to Connie. 'Right then,' she said, cheerfully. 'Shall we get started?'

37

Nothing could have prepared Emma for the sight in front of her. Dee, shot in the stomach and aging rapidly before her eyes. Raewyn, shackled to the tree like Jesus on the cross, and Chris, her own brother, caught up in this unholy mess with a wild look in his eye and missing a hand. If someone had sprung from the bushes crying *April fool* she'd have had a better time believing that than what was going on here.

Chris was not himself, but now that this ... *gift* had been awakened inside Emma, she could see the reason why. Flitting in and out of emotions like a car changing lanes, he was incapable of seeing the precarious situation he was in. Whatever he'd taken was working its way through his system, breaking him down bit by bit, and while he was reasonably stable at the moment, Emma knew that it wouldn't last long. She saw other things too when she touched his skin. Things he had done to Raewyn. Things he would do again given half the chance.

It broke Emma's heart to see what he'd become, and she

scolded herself for not having been a better sister. Maybe if she had, he'd be asleep in some harlot's bed instead of being here, waiting to die like the rest of them. But hindsight didn't change a thing, and while she knew Chris wasn't happy about what she was doing, neither did he try to stop her when Alex beckoned her over.

'Everything alright?' Alex said, as Emma approached. Chris hung back, legs straddled over a branch of the tree.

'Everything is fine,' Emma said, 'let's just get this over and done with.' She looked down at Dee, hair slowly greying, face withdrawn, and wondered what was going on behind those aging eyes. Then she looked to Raewyn, her twin sister, and the reason they were all congregated here tonight, and Emma found she felt nothing at all.

Connie handed a dagger over to Alex, who then ordered Emma to kneel.

Take heart, said a voice inside her, *your brother is lost but there is hope for your sister yet.*

Emma lightly touched the pocket of her jeans where a small piece of the bloody sheet, torn in haste, was hidden, and saw that Dee caught the movement, raising an eyebrow slightly. Emma dared not risk a nod, but hoped that her eyes said what her lips could not, that Evie was there with them, ready to give the last remaining piece of herself to save someone who probably didn't deserve it.

EMMA'S EYES remained cold as she watched Rae from her knees. Dee had said they were sisters, twin sisters, but Rae didn't see the resemblance. 'More blood on your hands, Alex?' she said, bitterly. 'When will it end?'

'When I have what I want,' Alex said, 'and what everyone else in this clearing wants. What you'd want too if you had any sense.' She tore Emma's shirt open revealing the black mess that was all that was left of Emma's chest. Even Alex gasped when she saw it and covered her nose against the smell. 'Jesus,' she said, 'no wonder you want to do this.'

Emma didn't say anything, but Rae saw the twitch at the corner of her eye. Chris stepped forward then, knelt in front of Emma and gave her something to drink. 'For the pain,' he said, 'I don't want you to feel any pain when the time comes.'

'She's already in pain, you moron,' Rae said, 'look at her, she's a fucking mess, and she's going to die if you don't do something to stop this.'

Chris was on his feet in a flash. His fist slammed into Rae's cheek before anyone could stop him. 'You shut your fucking mouth,' he said. 'I should have killed you when I had the chance.' His face was hot with anger, the olive eyes that Rae had liked so much, now dark and fuelled with hate.

Blood welled up inside her mouth and she spat it in his face, smiling when he raised his fist again. 'Do it,' she said, 'I dare you.'

'Enough,' yelled Alex, 'we don't have time for this. Chris, get back to your branch unless you plan on swapping places with your sister.'

Rae grinned. 'Be a good boy now,' she said, 'do as teacher says.'

Chris scowled. 'You'll keep,' he said, and backed away.

Rae felt a hand on her leg and glanced down. Dee, looking even worse than she had five minutes ago, looked up at Rae with warning in her eyes. *Be careful of him*, they said, *he's unpredictable*. But Rae shook her head. Chris was as predictable as they got.

'It's time,' Alex said, 'everyone in position.' She nodded to the congregation who all dropped to their knees and began chanting once again, that strange language murmured from beneath their hoods as they joined hands and began to sway. Alex walked over to the tiny blue bonfire and dipped the blade of the dagger in its flame.

'This is it,' whispered Dee, 'be ready.'

Rae flexed her hands and felt the pink resin hold tight against them. How was Dee supposed to dissolve the resin now? She looked up at the moon, now in full eclipse, and struggled fruitlessly against the manacles as Alex turned the dagger towards her, glowing blue from the fire that clung to it.

'By bone and blood and fire and flesh,' Alex said, 'by the gods of old and the serpents of new. Accept this woman's eternal fire and release the blood of her blood. Give life to Saoirse, White Warrior of Aster, Queen of the Rebels and saviour of all, and take this willing soul in her stead.' She stepped up to Rae and held the tip of the dagger over her birthmark.

Rae's pulse hammered in her veins, arms straining against her restraints as she looked to Dee for help. But Dee was incapable of helping anyone, even if she'd wanted to. Alex slowly pushed the tip of the blade into Rae's stomach, and Rae screamed as fire burned in her belly. But the pain was to be short lived as Alex slowly pulled the knife out again. She grinned as Rae's blood slid down to fill the grooves where ancient symbols had been carved into the knife, and her eyes glistened with excitement as she turned to Emma.

'Ready?'

Emma nodded, but Rae could see that she clutched something tight in the palm of her hand.

'By the blade of Servia,' Alex began, 'I give to you – Saoirse of Aster – life eternal by the blood of your blood.' She turned the tip of the dagger to rest above Emma's heart, then pushed it all the way in.

EVIE DID NOT ANSWER AT FIRST, THEN ...

If I leave you now, Emma, you will die.

But Emma didn't care. She felt no pain as the dagger pierced her heart, only pressure then release as her life slowly ebbed away. Evie had joined her back in the attic when Emma removed the bloody sheet. The sheet was Evie's anchor to this world, a souvenir from her pain and suffering and a way to remain at Carrion Hall until the day came when she could put right one of her many wrongs. Emma had always known her fate was to die young, and while that wasn't OK, she now accepted it, knowing that in some small way her death would pave the way for John to live a full and happy life. But his path was still fraught with danger – she knew that too.

She lifted her eyes to Dee and smiled. Before her soul was replaced by something foul and evil, Emma would do this one last thing. Not for Evie, or Chris, or the sister she never knew she had, but for John, the only man she had ever loved. So as her life slowly slipped away, and her head fell to her chest, Emma opened her hand and let the small bundle of cotton fall softly to the ground. She felt Evie leave her then, and something sinister take her place, like a warm coat sliding from her shoulders as a dark storm crept slowly in. She took one last defiant breath as herself, remembering John, his arms around her waist, soft lips on her mouth, and as the world faded to black one last time, she finally let him go.

———

EMMA DID NOT FALL DOWN. Instead she remained on her knees, rigid and unmoving as everyone held their breath, waiting for something to happen.

For long, painful moments nothing did happen. Connie backed away to join Chris, but Alex remained rooted to the spot. Then a gust of wind blew through the clearing to snuff out the candles, so the only light now came from the wall of fire, and the tiny bonfire that still burned hot and strong. An eerie glow was cast over them all as the congregation began their chanting once again, and crows, lots of them, swooped into the clearing, filling the air with their chatter before coming to land on the tree. A hundred black eyes turned to Emma as Alex laughed and threw her hands up to the sky, revelling in the madness she had brought down upon them. Rae felt another tug on her ankle and looked down to see Dee hold a finger to her lips. Then a moment later she saw a blur as someone skirted around the back of the tree.

Emma still hadn't moved, but as the crows settled a mist rose from the ground, seeping from the roots of the tree and pooling around Emma's kneeling form.

'This is it,' Alex said, turning to Rae. 'She's here. Can you feel her?'

'I don't feel anything,' Rae said, 'maybe you have indigestion?'

'Liar,' Alex said, grinning like they were still friends. 'I see it in your face. You're just as intrigued as I am.'

'Nauseated more like,' Rae said, as a crow pecked at her

hand. She shooed it off with a flick of her wrist, but the movement disturbed the rest of them and as one they alighted from the tree. A great black mass of flapping wings and squawking beaks swooped low, before merging with the inky backdrop of the forest, and disappearing into the night.

Rae watched them go, and out of the corner of her eye caught movement to her right. She turned in time to see a figure leap from a low-slung branch and land bodily on top of Chris. Connie yelled out and jumped out of the way, and Rae's heart almost burst at the sight of John, pummelling Chris's face with his fist. But his rescue was short lived as Connie raised her gun and aimed it at his back. Rae shouted to John to look out, but John was fast on his feet and before Connie could pull the trigger, he leapt off Chris and threw himself into her. The gun flew from Connie's hand and landed somewhere near the wall of fire, and while she scrabbled around in the dirt looking for it, Chris had recovered enough to land a blow of his own in John's face.

'For goodness sake,' Alex yelled at the congregation, 'somebody do something.'

But the congregation didn't move.

'You're wasting your time,' Dee said, 'they're like lambs waiting to be slaughtered. Why don't *you* do something, *niece*?' Alex didn't turn around, but her shoulder's stiffened, and Dee laughed. 'I wonder what your little lambs would say if they knew their new leader was a hollow?'

Alex didn't answer, because just then Chris and John crashed headlong into the candles. Rae's heart was in her mouth as the candles suddenly sprang back to life, and Emma, who up until now had been rigid as a statue, began to stir. Chris's shirt caught on fire, but he ripped it from his body and ducked just as John threw another punch. He brought his stump up into John's stomach, then his knee into his face sending John sprawling as the grey mist swirled in and out of the candles like a bed of snakes. John tried to get up, but Chris was fast and had him a headlock before he could move, squeezing his neck until John's face turned red, then purple, then blue.

Rae looked on helplessly as Connie returned, brandishing the gun before her. She pointed it at John, face livid, and would have shot him if a branch hadn't shot out from the tree, its tip sharpened to a spear, and impaled Connie right where she stood. The look of surprise on Connie's face might have been funny had the whole thing not been so horrific, and even Alex jumped back in surprise. But it was enough of a distraction for John to twist out of his headlock, grab the knife from the back of Chris' jeans, and bury it deep in his chest.

Rae held her breath as Chris, veins straining blue against his skin, pulled the knife from his chest and grinned. Then the gun went off again, and Chris fell backwards into the candles.

Alex pointed the gun at John. 'Don't make me regret saving your life,' she said. 'Over there, beside Dee. And don't try anything stupid or Rae will be the one to suffer.'

John looked at Rae. 'Are you OK?' he said, 'have they hurt you?'

'Nothing that won't heal,' she said, 'but John ... Emma.'

They both looked to Emma who was showing signs of coming around, but Alex stepped between them blocking Rae's view.

'Emma was already dying,' she said, 'she chose to come here.'

'Like hell she did,' Rae said, 'no one chooses to have a knife stuck through their heart.'

'Give me the gun, Alex,' John said, 'it's over. No-one else needs to get hurt.'

Alex moved further around so that Rae was caught between them. 'Come one step closer, and I'll blow both her knee caps off before you even blink.'

'She's bluffing,' Rae said. 'She doesn't have the balls to do it herself.'

John looked uncertainly between the two of them. 'Sorry, Rae,' he said, 'I can't risk it.' He moved to stand by Dee, and Rae rattled her chains in frustration.

'It didn't have to be this way,' Alex said, 'I had hoped we could be partners, it's the whole reason I had Connie give you the dagger.'

'*You* dissolved the resin,' Dee scoffed. 'I find that hard to believe.'

'There's more than one way to skin a cat, *Auntie*,' Alex said. 'I may be a hollow, but I still have my ways.'

'Something's happening,' Rae said, and all of them turned towards Emma.

A vine crept out of the mist and slowly coiled around Emma's body, while at the same time many more appeared by the feet of the congregation, spiralling around each of them in turn. They fell silent, their faces a mask of confusion as the temperature dropped several degrees. Rae's breath came in white plumes of smoke as she shivered against the cold. 'What's happening?' she said. But no-one answered as everyone seemed to be holding their breath, watching as the vines stopped moving and the clearing fell silent.

Rae looked to Dee and saw written on her face everything that Rae had feared since all of this began. That this was no fantasy, no elaborate hoax, or early Halloween prank. It was real, and something terrible was about to happen. Then suddenly the vines lit up, sparking to life like strands of lightning, and the congregation began to scream.

Their cries for help were deafening as one by one their bodies were drained, sucked dry like shrivelled prunes, until they were nothing more than empty husks. And no-one moved to help them, not even John, whose eyes never left Emma's face. Even Alex flinched from the wails of terror that rang out through the clearing, as white cloaks drifted to the ground like sheets in the wind, and when every one of the congregation was dead, and blissful silence was restored, the lightning ended, and Emma opened her eyes.

Dread pooled in Rae's veins as Emma's black eyes took in each one of them in turn, drinking them in before slowly gliding back to settle on Rae. The welts had gone from her face, the black mess cleared up on her chest, but her skin had the pallid look of someone in the late stages of cancer. She smirked as she gripped the hilt of the dagger, slowly pulled the knife from her chest, and pointed it at Alex. 'You,' she said, 'you're the one that freed me?' Her voice was husky, honeyed with an accent that Rae didn't recognise but still managed to stir the hairs on her neck.

Alex lowered her eyes. 'I'm Alexandra,' she said, 'daughter of Louisa, and these are—'

'I know who they are.' Emma slowly got to her feet, walked towards John, each footstep carefully placed, and smiled as those black, unblinking eyes raked over his body, from his head right down to his toes. 'Azrael,' she said, 'how nice of you to join us.'

Knowing they were at the point of no return, Dee had slipped the pouch of DC powder into John's hand, believing him to be their best chance of getting out of there alive. But that was before Saoirse called him Azrael. Dee knew her Asterian history well, and knew Azrael to have been a great General, leading huge armies into war at the command of his king. She also knew who his king was and felt her blood run cold by even thinking his name.

Saoirse trailed a long fingernail down his cheek. 'It's good to see you, old friend,' she said, 'though I would have preferred a more worthwhile body to greet you with.' His jaw stiffened, but John never said a word. 'Perhaps I should have taken one more like my sister's,' Saoirse said. 'It seems even in this life she is favoured by beauty. Would you not agree?' John still didn't answer, but veins bulged in the side of his neck as Saoirse left him to stand in front of Rae. She pressed a taloned finger against the knife wound in Rae's stomach, and laughed when Rae rattled her chains. 'You,' she said, turning to Dee, 'you're the one who chained her?'

'It was him.' Alex pointed to Chris' body, splayed out amongst the candles like a dead starfish. 'But he's dead.'

'So he is,' Saoirse said, 'who killed him?'

'I did,' Alex said, 'he was going to kill John ... I mean ... Azrael. I thought perhaps you would want him alive.' She glanced at the dagger in Saoirse's hand, and Saoirse raised an eyebrow in return.

'If you want my dagger, Alexandra, daughter of Louisa, then come take it from me.' She held the dagger out flat in the palm of her hand, head slightly cocked to one side, and waited.

Dee shook her head as Alex looked to her for help. Saoirse wasn't stupid. She knew what they'd try to do, and knew it wouldn't work, not without the Eye of Eilidh, which as far as Saoirse was concerned, had been destroyed the same night Saoirse had been banished to Gestryll. Dee purposely didn't look towards Connie's impaled body and prayed that Alex would have the good sense to do the same. If Saoirse knew the stone still existed, then this scenario would play out very differently indeed.

'I want only to serve you' Alex lowered her eyes. 'It was Daegan who thought to kill you.'

Dee narrowed her eyes at Alex as Saoirse turned her attention to John. 'Kill her,' she said, flicking her hand dismissively at Dee. John and Dee both looked at each other in surprise.

'Kill her yourself,' John said, 'I'm not here to do your bidding.'

'Oh?' Saoirse turned to face him. 'Then what *are* you here for?'

'He's here for Augustine,' piped up Alex, and Dee could have wilfully throttled her right there and then.

Saoirse glanced at Rae, then back at John and laughed. 'Well this is just priceless,' she said, 'my little sister and the great Azrael. Whatever would your boss say?'

'Why don't you ask him yourself,' John said, 'I expect you'll be seeing him soon enough.' He took a bold step forward and Dee felt the blood freeze in her veins as the smile fell from Saoirse's face.

'You speak too freely, Azrael,' she said. 'Perhaps it's time you remember who I am.'

'And perhaps it's time you remember your place,' John said. He lifted his chin to Rae and a dark look came over his face. 'I wonder, would you be so brave if your sister were free?' He took another step forward, and Dee held her breath. 'Or are you still the coward I remember you to be?'

Saoirse's lip curled upwards as lightning sparked from the tips of her fingers. 'The years have made you reckless, Azrael. You still mock me, even now?'

'It's not mockery to say the truth,' John said, fists clenched at his sides, body taught as though ready to spring at a moment's notice.

Dee didn't know what was going on, but suspected John had just handed himself a death sentence as the air became charged between them. But then Saoirse threw back her head and laughed.

'So be it,' she said, 'but first, a little insurance.' She lay a hand on a branch of the tree and instantly another spear shot out, this time impaling John through the shoulder and lifting him into the air. Rae cried out, but Saoirse only laughed. 'Don't worry, little sister,' she said, 'your champion will live, and when I'm done with you, I'll make him my *personal* attendant. You,' she said, pointing to Alex, 'keep a close eye on Daegan while my sister and I have a little fun.'

She stepped up to Rae and placed a hand on one of the manacles, dissolving it as easily as sugar in water. 'I'm not your sister,' Rae said. Her eyes were wide, her terror palpable as Saoirse hesitated before the second manacle. 'I'm not Augustine.' Rae said, 'they have it wrong. I'm not her.'

Saoirse smiled and lightly touched Rae's birthmark where the knife wound was already beginning to heal. 'This little mark above your navel says otherwise,' she said. 'I knew you were weak, little sister, but I had expected more from you than this.' She tucked the dagger in the back of her jeans, placed a hand on the final manacle, and smiled. 'Ready?'

The moment Rae was free she lunged at Saoirse and

grabbed her by the throat, but Dee knew she could do little with the resin still coating her hands. 'We have to help her,' Dee said, struggling to her feet as Saoirse grabbed Rae's throat in return, lifted her in the air and pinned her against the tree. Alex didn't even bother with the gun, foolishly believing that Dee was too weak to fight. 'And what would you have me do?' she said, 'I'm only a hollow, remember?'

'You can help by doing nothing,' Dee said. She sidled over to where John dangled in the air close to unconsciousness and tugged on the bottom of his jeans. 'John,' she hissed, 'the pouch I gave you. I need it back.' John stirred. His face was an unhealthy shade of grey, and Dee thought if he was ever going to demonstrate his great General skills, then now would be a good time to do it. But he only reached into the pocket of his jeans, slowly and painfully, and dropped the leather pouch into Dee's waiting hand before his head slumped forward onto his chest. Saoirse had flung Rae to the ground and was laughing as Rae struggled to her feet. 'Here,' shouted Dee, throwing the pouch to her, 'for your hands. Remember what I said, you have a gift, *use it*.'

Rae caught the pouch, sprinkled the red powder over her hands and cried out when it burned through the resin. On anyone else it would've burned them like acid, but not Rae. Saoirse realised what was going on and a branch lashed out, knocking Rae into the air. She was thrown across the clearing and landed heavily on the other side, but Dee did not have time to concern herself with how she had fared. Besides, she had seen how the wound in her stomach had healed and was confident that broken bones were the least of Rae's worries.

She scrambled over the branch she had been leaning against and scurried around the back of the tree. Connie was still upright, cloak hanging loosely from her limp, dead body.

Dee crept towards her using the mist as concealment where possible, but Saoirse was too sure of herself to even glance in Dee's direction. The crystal was ice cold as Dee pulled it from Connie's pocket, and dark as charcoal without Rae to warm it, but she knew that once it was paired with the Servian Dagger the crystal would come to life. She risked a glance at the far side of the clearing – Rae was back on her feet and had picked up a log which she hurled at Saoirse – then crept back around the tree to Alex and John. She waited there a moment, catching her breath as another log flew across the clearing, missing Saoirse by miles. *What are you doing?* thought Dee. She was going to have to do a whole lot more than throw logs if she was going to stay alive. Saoirse threw back her head and roared with laughter as another log missed her, this time by mere inches.

'Come now, little sister,' Saoirse said, 'you can do better than that.' A branch whipped out and took Rae's feet from beneath her and Saoirse laughed even harder. She was toying with Rae, testing her limits before she ended this game once and for all, which meant Dee was running out of time.

Rae got to her feet and removed the fleece jacket. She was angry now, and that was good. Anger would serve her well. She reached behind her and stuck a hand in the blue fire, causing Dee and Alex to gasp as one. The wall was there for security, to keep people out, but more importantly, to trap people in, and as long as the moon was in eclipse the fire would continue to burn. No-one could walk through that blue flame unless they wanted their skin flayed from their bones, and yet here was Rae, holding a ball of the brightly coloured fire in her hand as though it was nothing more than a plaything. She hurled it across the clearing, and Saoirse, equally surprised, staggered backwards to get out of the way.

She caught her foot on something sticking out of the ground, something that looked remarkably like part of a hand, and stumbled before falling on her arse. Dee froze, as did Alex, because both of them saw the Servian Dagger fall free of Saoirse's jeans.

The laughter had gone from Saoirse's voice as she rose to her feet. 'Finally,' she said, dusting herself off, 'now perhaps this will be a fight worth having.' She touched a root of the tree then threw her hands forward, and lots of tiny spear-like twigs flew at Rae. Rae managed to dodge most of them by throwing herself to the ground, but some found their target and caught her in the thigh and waist. She lay there motionless and Dee thought for one horrible moment that all was lost, but then she got up, pulled the twigs out and glared at Saoirse with fire in her eyes. At last the fight was on.

Dee struggled back to her feet. The bullet hole had closed up but still caused considerable pain, and though she had retrieved the crystal without difficulty, it had all but used up what little strength she had. Fortunately, she now had a second supply to draw upon.

When Emma had knelt before the tree, Dee had seen Evie's light in her eyes even before she spotted the bloody cloth in Emma's hand. And when Emma had dropped the cloth on the floor, Dee had known what to do. As Saoirse moved closer to Rae, Dee saw her opportunity and crept over to where Emma had knelt, found the cloth, and instantly felt Evie's light warm her body like a shining star. It gave her strength where she would otherwise have had none, and as Rae threw more balls of fire at Saoirse, Dee made a run for her bag that still lay beside the small blue bonfire. Inside it was her syringe, filled with the serum she had painstakingly prepared over the years, with one small addition. Oleander –

a much more potent dose than the one Connie gave to John, and enough to kill Dee outright before she, or anyone else, could make use of Saoirse's power. Alex may have drunk Louisa's serum already, but Dee could no more allow her to absorb Saoirse's power than she could allow Saoirse to live. She would retrieve the Servian Dagger and inject herself with the poisoned serum right before she killed Saoirse, thus ending both their lives. But no sooner had Dee shoved the syringe down the bodice of her dress next to the Eye of Eilidh, than she saw Alex dart across the clearing and take the dagger for herself.

Alex ducked as a fireball flew past her and crouched in the mist while Dee ground her teeth, wondering what to do. She had just about made up her mind to tackle Alex when a voice spoke inside her head. *No,* it said, *free John.*

Dee looked at John, hanging limply in the air, and blew out a frustrated sigh. It was difficult for Dee to understand how saving John was more important than getting the dagger from Alex, but Evie was insistent, and one thing Dee's mother had always said was that the spirits were never wrong.

She edged back round to John, keeping low so as to avoid being in Saoirse's line of sight, and made it back before Alex had even moved. 'Now what?' she said, 'how do I get him down?' She could take some energy from the branch that held him, but even if she was at full strength it still wouldn't be enough. Or she could shimmy up the branch, and somehow try to push him off the end, but she barely had strength enough to walk, let alone climb a damn tree. Whatever Evie had in mind she was keeping it to herself because the voice in Dee's head fell silent. Then Dee felt herself grow cold, and a moment later a light came on behind John's eyes.

He grabbed the branch where it stuck out from his

shoulder and began pulling himself along. The end couldn't have been more than thirty or so inches from where the branch jutted out of his arm but watching him drag himself along like that made Dee want to vomit. He grunted and groaned, and sweat poured from his twisted face, but the closer he got to the tip, the more the branch began to bend, until finally it gave way and snapped. John fell directly onto his injured shoulder and let out a scream Dee hoped never to hear again, but the fall had knocked the rest of the branch out, and while he still had a gaping hole in his shoulder, it was rapidly closing up, courtesy of Evie. Dee bent down to help him up, and as she did so felt a warm breeze brush past her face as her friend left his body. *Goodbye Evie*, she thought, *and thank you, from the bottom of my heart.*

RAE FOCUSED EVERYTHING SHE HAD, every ounce of anger and hate that she felt for the creature in front of her and pushed it all into a compact ball that she suppressed at the base of her spine.

'You forget your place, sister' Saoirse said, circling Rae like a wild predator, 'perhaps it's time you remember.' A vine whipped out from nowhere, caught Rae by the wrist and hurled her across the clearing as though she were nothing more than a rag doll. She hit the tree hard, then rolled out of the way just as a branch came crashing down by her head. She was scratched, cut, bruised, bleeding from countless places, but nothing was broken so far as she could tell, and Saoirse was running out of tricks.

'I told you, I'm not your sister.' Rae grabbed a candle and used its flame to launch another fireball. She had barely raised her hand to throw another before a branch hit her from behind and knocked her clear across the clearing to land in the pile of empty bones that once belonged to Dee's congregation. They disintegrated on impact, and clouds of powdered bone puffed up into Rae's face. She coughed and spluttered, eyes watering from the acrid smell that filled her nostrils and didn't see the spike that came hurtling towards her until it was too late. It crashed into her thigh, tearing through muscle and bone, and sending searing pain to shoot all the way down to her foot. She could hear Saoirse's laughter, like a cackling old witch, and pushed the fresh wave of anger deep into the ball that pressed urgently against her spine.

'This is why I love you, sister,' Saoirse said, 'you offer endless hours of amusement with your grit and determination. But I'm growing tired of these games. Submit to me now and I will let you live, otherwise let us bring an end to this.'

Rae couldn't have agreed more, but she could see what Saoirse could not, that Alex was rising from the misty ground with the dagger in her hand. Alex suddenly hurled herself at Saoirse and buried the dagger deep in the small of her back, catching Saoirse off guard while she was still gloating over Rae. Rae stiffened as she waited, breath held tight in her chest as Saoirse's black eyes blinked once, then twice before her head swivelled round at an impossible angle to look at Alex. Alex had shed her cloak and the pink shock of hair stood on end as she pulled the dagger out and began slowly backing away, and whilst Saoirse was fixated on Alex, Rae seized her advantage and pushed down on that ball of hate. She forced it back like a coiled spring until she was ready to release it, and when Saoirse finally turned her entire body round to face Alex, she let it go.

A shockwave of heat burst from Rae like an explosion, throwing both Saoirse and Alex into the tree. Saoirse took the brunt of it, hitting the tree with such force no human could survive it. But Saoirse was far from human, and while her hair was singed from her head and blackened flesh hung from her body like a raggedy suit, she was back on her feet in seconds. Alex did not fare so well, and lay unconscious on the ground, her body a blistered and bloody mess.

'Now you go too far,' Saoirse said, advancing towards Rae with fury in her eyes. But she only managed a few steps before John appeared swinging the baseball bat that Rae had abandoned the day Alex found her at the clearing. Unfortunately for John, Saoirse was one step ahead. She caught the bat mid-swing and with her other hand raised a vine from nowhere, wrapped it around John's throat and had him dragged off back to where Dee stood, hunched over like a 70 year old woman. Rae tried to raise another fireball, but it seemed the effort of expelling so much energy had left her weak and useless.

'You never learn, do you sister,' Saoirse said, coming to stand before her. Half her face had melted away and Rae could see the sinews in her neck moving where they connected muscle to bone.

'I told you, I'm not your sister,' Rae said, edging backwards as Saoirse moved with her.

Saoirse attempted a grin, but the movement made her already grotesque face look even more horrific. 'Maybe you're not after all,' she said, 'if you were truly my sister, you would have known better than to play your best hand so early in the game.'

Rae felt a rumble beneath her feet and looked down as vines, littered with razor sharp thorns, shot up from the ground. They rose around them both like curlicue spears, twisting and weaving in and out of each other as they stretched above their heads, forming a dome like structure, a barricade of thorns that cut them off from the others. Panic seized Rae, but she was weak from her recent blast of energy and could do little more than watch as she and Saoirse were trapped.

'Now then,' Saoirse said, stepping up to Rae, her fetid breath poisoning the air around them, 'let's see who you really are beneath this pathetic, human skin.'

DEE WATCHED on helplessly as Saoirse raised a wall around herself and Rae. She was cutting them off, isolating Rae before John could try to save her again. But why? Why not just kill John? Why not just kill all of them for that matter? It didn't make much sense to Dee unless there was something else Saoirse was after. She could have flattened any one of them any time she wanted. But she hadn't, and that worried Dee more than the vine wrapped around John's throat.

She tried again to cut it free as John's face took on a worrying blue hue, but every time she touched it the vine squeezed a little tighter. 'I don't know what else to do,' she said, helplessly. She'd tried transference of energy, but Saoirse's power was just too strong. John was pointing frantically at the tree where Alex's body lay at an awkward angle. Did he mean for Dee to use the Servian Dagger to cut him free? She had been using the hunting knife that John had stabbed Chris with, but maybe he thought the dagger would fare better? 'It won't make any difference,' she said. 'I can't cut the vine.' John gesticulated frantically towards the tree, then again pointed at his neck. Dee struggled to her feet and walked over, averting her eyes from Alex's mangled body that for some reason filled her with a fresh wave of guilt (Louisa's daughter! If only she'd known). Then she saw it. The leather pouch that had contained her DC powder lay on the ground where Rae had dropped it. 'There's not much left,' she said, hurriedly returning to John, 'you might want to grab hold of something, this is going to hurt.' John eyes grew wide as Dee sprinkled the remains of the powder over the vine, and some unavoidably touched his skin. His neck blistered and peeled, but there was nothing to be done about that if he wanted to live. The vine hissed and gurgled, but after only a moment's resistance finally released John from its clutches before crumbling to dust. John fell forward, coughing and spluttering as he sucked in great lungs full of air. 'What ... was in ... that powder?' he said.

'Doesn't matter,' Dee said. She pressed the hunting knife into his hand. 'We have to hurry. The eclipse will be over soon, and we have to stop Saoirse before she's at full strength. You try to break down the barrier while I find the dagger.'

John's throat was an ugly shade of purple, but he nodded and climbed to his feet. He was hardly in any condition to fight a four hundred year old warrior with untold strength, but then neither was Dee.

'What happens when I break it down?' he said.

'You just worry about that wall,' Dee said, 'and leave the rest to me.'

RAE HEARD a snigger to her left ... then to her right, and spun round when she was prodded in the back. She lashed out when a shadow moved in front of her and turned again when she felt hot breath on the back of her neck.

'You reek of fear.' Saoirse's disembodied voice came from somewhere to Rae's right, but when she turned there was no one there. 'What could Azrael possibly want with someone like you?' Rae turned to her left, then felt hot breath on the back of her neck.

'Quit fucking around,' she snapped, 'or are you too scared to show yourself now we're alone?' She sounded brave, confident even, but she didn't feel either of those things as Saoirse grew suddenly quiet. A trickle of sweat slid between Rae's shoulder blades, then a second later the thorny barrier parted a little, letting in some much-needed light and fresh air. Saoirse stood in front of her, black orbs glistening by the light of the blue fire that still raged outside. 'What do you want?' Rae said, 'if you wanted to kill me you would've done it already.'

'I want what I was promised,' Saoirse said. A cruel smile played across the torn flesh that was all that was left of her lips, right before a hand shot forward and grabbed Rae by the jaw. Fingers dug painfully into her cheek, squeezing and forcing Rae's mouth wide as black smoke slipped from Saoirse's open mouth. It drifted toward Rae, touching and feeling its way into her mouth like a living, conscious thing, sliding over her tongue, down her throat and into her lungs. It filled her belly and crept beneath her skin, crawled over her brain like a thousand tiny insects, probing, seeking ... *searching*. Rae tried to fight back, tried to prize those rigid fingers from her face, but it was like trying to bend an iron bar and Saoirse just kept on filling her up with poison. Every crevice and corner filled, every thought and feeling stripped bare, and Rae was too exhausted to stop it.

Her terror became a tangible thing. It charged the air around them, froze the blood in her veins and sounded in the frantic beat of her heart. The smoke *was* Saoirse, her energy, her spirit, her *animus*. It clung to Rae's throat, coating the walls of her oesophagus, crawling, seeking, probing – filling every part of Rae until it *was* her. She felt Saoirse's malice as if it were her own, the hunger and craving for power, the suffering she would inflict on those who stood in her way, the horrors she would bring down on the people of Earth if Rae didn't stop her. But Rae couldn't move, couldn't breathe without choking. So she closed her eyes instead, and retreated to the part of her brain where the smoke couldn't reach her, to the tree house at the bottom of the garden that Granddad had built, filled with soft toys and cushions and swaths of fake fur. She crawled in amongst those cushions, pulled over the furs and surrounded herself with the safety of her childhood retreat. She lay there with a teddy bear clutched to her chest – a blue one with one ear missing, and a pink ribbon around its neck. It smelled of a time before Grace, of cigarette smoke and strawberries, and incense and rain. It reminded her of a cold brick room, with ballerinas on the walls and a pink cotton duvet, and a man with a cloak and a wide brimmed hat.

She curled into a ball and felt reassuring lips brush her cheek, a whisper in her ear that all would be well, the weight of her necklace around her neck and the warmth of the crystal against her chest. But then the image began to change. Smoke drifted up through the floorboards of the tree house, seeping through the walls and pouring from the roof. The furs turned black with mould, the cushions like slabs of rock, and even the blue teddy she clutched to her chest crumbled like an aged old piece of fruit. *Fight* a voice said beside her, and she turned to see Grace standing there, white hair soft against the black of the decaying room, her smile warm and her eyes gentle. Rae reached towards her, but then she was gone and in her place was another woman, a woman who looked just like Rae with a tattoo on her face and blood on her hands. She was afraid. Fear emanated from her in waves, but so did courage and strength. She looked Rae dead in the eye, hazel eyes just like her own. *Fight* they said, just like Grace, and Rae felt heavy with shame because she knew she had nothing left to fight with. Then the woman held a hand to her stomach and her eyes pleaded with Rae as she began to fade. 'Don't go,' Rae said, reaching out towards her, but then she was back in the thorny barricade, and Saoirse was looking at her with a knowing smile on her wretched face.

Saoirse's essence began to retreat then, sucked out of Rae like air through a vacuum. Rae could almost feel her gloating as she withdrew, so sure of herself now that she'd gotten what she wanted that she didn't notice John hacking through the thorns behind her. But Rae did, and the sight of his face, his desperation to reach her, was enough to put a spark back in her belly.

The moment Saoirse released Rae's jaw, Rae reached up and grabbed Saoirse by the throat. She didn't have much left to fight with, but she only hoped it would be enough. She wrapped both hands around Saoirse's throat, just like she had with Chris's wrist, and focussed everything on that one spot. Surprise registered on Saoirse's face a second before she grabbed Rae's throat in return, and they glared at each other, monster to monster, until Saoirse's face twisted into a snarl of immeasurable rage.

JOHN WAS ALMOST through the barrier when it suddenly started to collapse, and Dee re-doubled her efforts into finding the Servian Dagger. Alex had dropped it when Rae's blast had sent her flying into the tree, but so far, no amount of searching had turned it up. And now they were out of time. She looked up just as the moon was slipping its shadow and knew all hope was lost. Rae was likely dead, any minute now Saoirse would be at full strength, and Dee and John, as good as dead. But then just as the barrier finally gave way Dee turned to see Alex leap across the clearing, Servian Dagger in her hand, and by some sick twist of fate, the Eye of Eilidh was pressed into its hilt. She slammed into John and knocked him sideways, and before John even knew what was happening, Alex plunged the dagger into the small of Saoirse's back, into her sacrum where the core of her power lay.

Dee was on her feet in a flash, pulled the syringe from the bodice of her dress and threw herself at Alex. The needle pierced Alex's flesh a split second before she withdrew the dagger, and both Alex and Dee were thrown clear of the barrier to land heavily in the clutches of the tree.

38

'I was beginning to think you'd never wake up.'

Rae shaded her eyes against the autumn glare as heavyset curtains were thrown wide. She blinked several times and winced at the bone deep ache in her limbs as she pushed herself up into a seating position. She was in a room she didn't recognise, with a woman she didn't know, and had a tube sticking out of her arm that fed into a bag of clear liquid hanging from a hook at the side of her bed. 'How long have I been out?' she said. Her throat felt raw, tongue swollen, head crammed with cotton wool. She pushed back the covers and tried to swing her legs out of bed, but a wave of dizziness hit her, and a pair of gentle hands eased her back against the pillow.

'Take it easy,' the stranger said, 'you need to stay in bed for a while longer. Doctor's orders.'

Rae gripped the covers as another wave of dizziness washed over her. 'You're a doctor?' she said, resting her head against the pillow. God, she felt awful, as though someone had removed all her organs, smashed them with a hammer and shoved them roughly back in.

'Not quite,' the woman said. She sat on the edge of the bed and handed Rae a glass of water. 'Your head will probably feel muggy for a while yet, and I expect it'll be another day or two before you're back on your feet, but it seems the worst is over.'

Rae gulped the water down. She hadn't realised how thirsty she was until the cold liquid slid down her burning throat. 'Have I been sick?' she said. She certainly felt sick, sicker than she'd ever felt in her life. She rubbed her temples as though doing so would shift the fog that had settled there.

The woman looked at her with gentle eyes, honey-blonde eyebrows arched in that *don't you remember?* kind of way. 'Not sick,' she said, 'you were suffering from severe exhaustion. If not for John insisting you stay here, I would've—'

'John? Is he here?' Rae's heart leaped at the sound of his name, but if he was here then why wasn't he by her bedside? She remembered him in the forest, hacking at the thorns, but couldn't recall what happened after that.

'Rae, how much do you remember from the night you were brought here?'

Blue fire, manacles, a curved dagger ... 'where am I?' Rae said, 'is this a hospital?'

'Not exactly,' the woman said. She took the empty glass off Rae and placed it on the bedside table – a white one, plain, sterile, just like the room. She had a nice smell to her, Rae thought, lavender and rosehip, and gentle grey eyes that regarded Rae with sympathy and suspicion in equal measures. 'You're in a clinic,' she said, 'a veterinary clinic at a farm on the outskirts of Harleybrock. I'm Ursula, and this is my place. John brought you here in the middle of the night three days ago. You were unconscious, unresponsive, dehydrated. You understand that taking care of people is not my field of expertise, but John ...' She smiled, and a wisp of a smile touched her lips. 'Well, he insisted you couldn't go anywhere else, practically begged me to take care of you. Are you sure you don't remember anything at all about what happened to you?'

Rae blinked. Ursula's face was familiar. She imagined her hair in a ponytail. 'Where's John now?'

'Your guess is as good as mine,' Ursula said. 'He stayed through the night but was gone before I could question him the next morning. I was hoping you might be able to provide answers?'

Rae closed her eyes, thought back to the forest ... Dee had been there, and Alex, and ... oh God, poor Emma.

'Rae, are you OK?' Ursula had hold of Rae's wrist, checking her pulse, concern etched on her kindly face. 'Your heart is racing and you're white as a sheet. Maybe you should rest a while longer?'

'No,' Rae said, 'I'm good, really. John didn't say anything at all before he left?'

Ursula gave Rae a dubious look before shaking her head. 'I've pushed you far enough for one morning.' She stood and straightened her skirt over slim hips. 'Maybe we can see how you are later.'

Rae grabbed her wrist before she could go. 'Please,' she said, 'I need to know what happened. It's important.'

Ursula glanced at the open door where Rae could hear a television in the background. She sighed and removed an envelope from her pocket. 'A suitcase turned up for you a couple of days go,' she said, 'this was taped to the front of it. I wasn't going to give it to you until you were stronger, but—'

'Thank you,' Rae said, taking the envelope from her. Her name was written on the front, her full name, Raewyn Elizabeth Winters. Grace was the only one who ever called her that.

'Think you could manage to eat something?' Ursula said, 'some eggs maybe?'

Rae nodded, still staring at the envelope.

'Right then, eggs and coffee it is. I'll be right outside, so yell out if you need anything, but whatever you do, do not attempt to get out of that bed, promise?'

Rae smiled tightly. She didn't think she could even if she wanted to.

She tore the envelope open the moment Ursula left the room and felt her heart sink when she realised the note was not from John at all, but from Dee.

My dearest Raewyn,

I wish I had more time so that we could talk and put any animosity between us to rest, but it is only by a twist of fate that I have made it this far, and I fear that by the time you recover, I will be gone.

I want you to know that your mother (your biological mother, Evie) loved you very much, and I have no doubt in my heart that had he been given the chance, your father would have loved you too. Both died because of circumstances beyond their control but they would be so proud to see the strong, capable woman you have become. The same can be said of your sister, Emma. One of my greatest regrets is that the two of you could not have met under better circumstances, because despite appearances I believe Emma was a good and caring woman. She proved that much by allowing Saoirse to take her body, because in doing so she not only saved John's life, but yours too. I don't say this to lay guilt at your door, but in the days to come I would ask that you remember the sacri-

fice she made, because if I'm right, then your troubles are far from over, and I could not rest easy if I thought that Emma surrendered the final days of her life for nothing.

Which brings me round to the reason for this letter.

I told you I was present the night you were born, but I did not tell you how I cared for you for many years after that. I was only a child myself back then, and you were a force to behold even then. I tried to love you, I did love you in my own way, but I was ill equipped to cope with someone as gifted as you, nor did I have the strength or wisdom to guide you. But Grace did. That's why I sent you to her, where you would be protected and nurtured until you had the strength to protect yourself. Do not feel ill of Grace for sending you back to Cranston Myre. She knew as well as I that your destiny could not be fulfilled until you had faced Saoirse. Your path was set the night you were conceived, and if there had been any other way then believe me, Grace and I would have destroyed Saoirse years ago.

As it stands, I do not believe your troubles have ended. Indeed, I suspect they have only just begun, and what I am about to tell you I say with a heavy heart, because despite what you may think of me, I wish only for your happiness.

I was known as Daegan back when you were born, and it was my sister, Louisa who helped your mother conceive, then later conspired to have you taken from her. I do not deny the part I played in that night – had I been wiser or stronger perhaps things could have turned out differently for all – but I believe that what began twenty-five years ago is far from over. Alex was Louisa's daughter, a daughter she kept secret for reasons I could not fathom, but if there is one thing I know about my sister, it is that she never did anything without good reason. So, I asked myself, what could Louisa possibly have gained all those years ago by pretending her own child was stillborn? And now I believe I have the answer.

There was something troubling me about Louisa's reaction the night I showed up in the forest without you, something that has niggled at the back of my mind every day since. I betrayed Louisa by not taking you to her, sealed her fate in that one small act of defiance, but her face had not been one of anger, only confirmation, as though she had known all along that I could not go through with it. So why then, did she entrust me with something of such importance? She could have sent Connie, who would have been only too happy to snatch a babe from the arms of its mother. But she didn't, she sent me, and I believe she did that precisely because she wanted me to fail.

You will recall the moments before Saoirse took Emma's body that she drained the life from each member of The Order. She did not need to be free of Gestryll to do that, only for the veil between worlds to be weakened by the eclipse, and I believe she did the same thing the night Louisa died. Louisa's physical body turned to dust that night, and I was severely burned, enough to not pay any attention to what Connie was doing, which is why I believe that Louisa's essence was somehow preserved. There is a creature in Asterian history known as a Grymlock. A creature that is neither alive nor dead and feeds on misery, fear and despair. It can manifest as many things, a wolf for instance, or birds – more specifically, crows. When Saoirse drained Louisa that night I believe, somehow, Connie saved her essence, though it would take a Draiocht far more powerful than Connie to achieve such a thing. But I have seen the Grymlock for myself, felt its presence on more than one occasion, and had the unfortunate luck to stumble upon several of the carcasses left behind from one of its feeding frenzies. A Grymlock is an unpleasant creature, but to return to the realm of the living, to become mortal once again, is more unpleasant still. But Louisa was as cunning as she was beautiful.

My mother had a book that neither I nor Louisa were ever

allowed to touch. It was a book of the dead, tales of sacrifice, necromancy, alchemy, blood magic etc. But Louisa and I defied her and read much of it before we were caught and severely punished. Louisa was fascinated with it, and I recall her particularly liking the section about the legend of the Grymlock.

It is a gruesome and terrible path to follow in order to return from the dead, as you witnessed by Saoirse's re-birth, but for a Grymlock it is more heinous than you can imagine. You would need to feed from four members of a particular bloodline, a powerful bloodline such as the one you and Emma belong to. Evie was consumed the night she died, by crows if the rumours are to be believed. Emma was bitten on the neck by something in the forest and later showed all the signs of Grymlock poisoning, and if I'm correct (and I pray to all that is good in this world that I am not), then I believe that you too may have come across such a creature since returning to Cranston Myre. But that is not the worst of it. The Grymlock would still need the blood of a fourth. I did not tell this even to Evie, but I believe she and Richard were distant relations. The Ashleys have lived at Carrion Hall for centuries, but a long time ago some of the younger children were sent away, for reasons I will not go into now. I believe Evie's great-grandmother was one of those children.

We already know that you and Emma are born of Richard's bloodline, but if I'm right, then Evie was too. And of course, the fourth, would be Alex.

John carried you from the forest and took you to safety after Saoirse died, then he came back for me, and later on, for Alex. But if Alex had not been dead when he left, she most assuredly was when he returned. I will not go into details for the sake my own stomach as well as yours, but needless to say, the Grymlock had its final feed.

So now you see why I fear for your safety. What reasons

Louisa would have for going through such a terrible ordeal, I cannot imagine, only that I am as certain as I can be that I am right. It is because of this I have written an address on the back of this letter. It is an island off the coast of Scotland where my mother grew up, Grace too. If you seek answers, then that is where you will find them, but I urge you to go there with caution in your heart. You may not like what you find. You are also now the sole heir to Carrion Hall, though you will find no papers to prove this, no record of your birth and nothing to tie you to the Ashley family. However, my solicitor holds a document signed by me and by Emma. It is a record of sale, a rather hurried and basic document, but legal, nonetheless. It records the sale of Carrion Hall to an undisclosed purchaser. That purchaser is you, Rae. Contact my solicitor (his details are also on the back of this letter) and he'll know what to do. Do what you will with this information but know there is much more to Carrion Hall than just bricks and mortar!

And now I must bid you farewell. You are special Raewyn. I knew that the moment I laid eyes on you and didn't need a birth-mark to tell me so. It was an honour taking care of you. I only wish I could have served you better.

Forgive me.

Daegan xxx

P.S. Do not go looking for John (his words, not mine). I guess you're not the only one who needs to figure out who you were, before you can become who you are supposed to be.

Rae dropped the letter into her lap, swallowed, then re-read it twice before turning it over. The solicitor's name was there on the back, along with an address in London. There was also an address in Scotland, on the island of Jura. No word from John, and no mention of what happened to her pendant either.

She reached up to her chest where the crystal always sat and felt empty at not finding it there. Years of not knowing who she was or where she came from, and now that she knew she almost wished she could turn back the clock and return to a life of ignorant bliss. She folded the letter, placed it back in the envelope and slipped it beneath her pillow. A phone rang somewhere in the house and she heard Ursula's heels clip clopping on the tiles as she ran to answer it. Maybe it was John, checking to see if Rae was OK, if she was even alive, or maybe it was just someone calling their local vet. Either way it didn't matter. Rae didn't need anyone anymore, her experience in the forest had taught her that much at least.

EPILOGUE

Georgina loaded the tray with freshly baked bread, honey, jam, butter, bacon, eggs, a hefty portion of black pudding, and a fresh pot of tea, tucked the morning newspaper under her arm and headed towards the west wing hallway. When she reached the library she turned left, entered the guest wing and tapped lightly on the large double doors to the master bedroom. A voice called out for her to enter. She inserted her key and opened the door.

'About time.' Louisa was off the bed in a flash and grabbed the tray from Georgina, stuffing black pudding into her mouth as she headed back towards the bed.

Georgina re-locked the door, dropped the newspaper on the bed and began fussing around the room, picking up broken crockery, dumping shredded clothes into a pile ready for burning, and returning books back to their place on the shelf. Four nights had passed since Georgina and her father had carried Louisa from the forest up to Carrion Hall, and while Louisa was now considerably stronger it would be a few more nights before she could be trusted to leave this room.

'I thought you were bringing ice-cream,' Louisa said through a mouthful of bread.

'I'll bring it with lunch,' Georgina said, dropping another shredded t-shirt onto the pile. 'Must you really tear the clothes from your body. Can't you just remove them like a normal person?'

'Normal people don't feel like they're about to combust. And besides, I didn't like that one anyway.'

Georgina tutted and turned her eye to the bathroom. Water was everywhere, as it had been yesterday, and the day before that. She looked at Louisa who just shrugged and opened the newspaper. 'Honestly,' muttered Georgina, 'it's like taking care of a two-year-old.'

'I heard that,' Louisa said.

Georgina picked up the towels and began wiping down the walls. Seeing Louisa break through the wolf's skin like a filly bursting from its mother had been enough to put Georgina off eating for life. But not Louisa it seemed. She glanced round the door to see Louisa had finished the entire tray of food and was flicking through the paper. She'd come a long way since the night of the eclipse, when she had been bloodier than a new-born babe and just as helpless. But with Georgina's cooking, and the right amount of rest, she'd soon be fighting fit.

As though reading Georgina's thoughts, Louisa appeared in the doorway, arms folded, red hair trailing over her bare shoulders. 'Any news on her whereabouts yet?'

Georgina took some clean towels from the linen basket and hung them on the rail. 'Not yet,' she said, 'would it make any difference if there was?'

'Not yet,' mimicked Louisa. She flashed a smile at Georgina, green eyes twinkling with mischief. 'You know, if I wanted to, I could take that key from you right now and let myself out.'

'I'm well aware,' Georgina said, 'but we both know that you won't.' She squeezed past Louisa, gathered the tray from the bed and headed towards the door.

'She'll go to Scotland,' Louisa said, throwing herself back on the bed. 'That's what I would do, so you can bet your arse that Daegan told her to.'

'*If* she's even alive,' Georgina said.

'Oh, she's alive,' Louisa said, 'but what I'm more interested in, is where that man of hers has disappeared to. Surely you must know something. I know you were sweet on him, *Georgie*.'

Georgina felt herself blush and scowled at Louisa. It was true, she had taken a liking to John, but not for the reasons Louisa was thinking. 'If I knew where either of them was, I would tell you,' she said. 'I serve you, do I not?'

Louisa rolled onto her back and propped her long legs up against the wall. 'That you do, Georgie old girl, that you do. And don't you forget it.'

The End

ACKNOWLEDGMENTS

Thank you to my husband, for never doubting me and for turning a blind eye while I stared out the window dreaming up fantasy men.

Thank you to my mum, for being a passionate supporter from beginning to end.

Thank you also to my amazing children. To Charlie, for the endless kisses and cuddles that kept me going, and Joe, for your unwavering thoughts on corny tag-lines and long-winded blurbs.

And last but not least, special thanks to Brian Hendry, Judy Beale, and Kelly McClurg, for your invaluable time and effort in reading *Augustine*. Your input was appreciated more than you can know.

Thank you all.

ABOUT THE AUTHOR

Emerson Laine was born and raised in Salford, England, but now lives in New Zealand with her husband and two children. She loves writing, autumn walks, reading by the fire, and watching anything with a great hook and a twist she never saw coming. She also has an unhealthy obsession with notebooks and bookcases!

Augustine is Emerson's debut novel, and the first in The Knights of Aster series. Book Two of The Knights of Aster is currently in progress, and if you would like up-to-date information regarding its release, you can find Emerson on Facebook @EmersonLaineBooks.